A piece of crystal about the size of her thumbnail lay on the floor.

Kayl leaned closer, staring at it. Three sides were perfectly flat. The fourth side was slightly curved and had an irregular rim, as though the crystal had been chipped . . .

She looked up. Glyndon was staring at the bit of crystal and his face was gray. For a moment she thought he was 'seeing' things again. "Glyndon?" she said softly. "Do you know what that is?"

"I—no, it can't be—I don't—"

"Glyndon! What's the matter with you? What can't it be?"

"It can't be from the Twisted Tower," Glyndon whispered, his eyes still fixed on the piece of crystal. "It can't be!"

Ace Fantasy Books by Patricia C. Wrede

PATRICIA C. WREDE

CAUGHT IN CRYSTAL

ACE FANTASY BOOKS
NEW YORK

This book is an Ace Fantasy original edition,
and has never been previously published.

CAUGHT IN CRYSTAL

An Ace Fantasy Book/published by arrangement with
the author

PRINTING HISTORY
Ace Fantasy edition / March 1987

ISBN: 0-441-76006-6

Ace Fantasy Books are published by The Berkley Publishing Group,
200 Madison Avenue, New York, New York 10016.

PRINTED IN THE UNITED STATES OF AMERICA

For my parents,
especially my mother,
who taught me to love books.

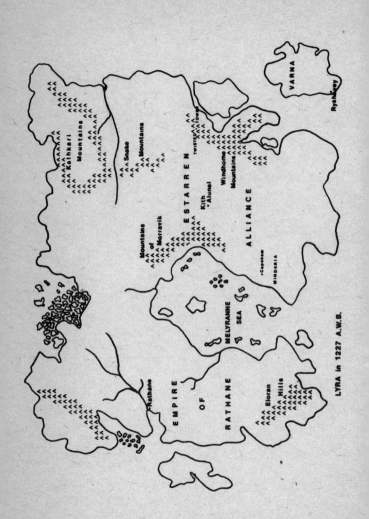

LYRA in 1227 A.W.S.

PROLOGUE

After the Wars of Binding ended, the Four Races of Lyra—the catlike, furred Wyrds, the shimmering, sea-dwelling Neira, the proud, pale Shee and the quarrelsome, energetic humans—went their separate ways. For a long time, they were concerned primarily with survival, for the War had permanently altered the face of Lyra. The center of the main continent sank, creating an inland sea; the coastline moved miles inland in other areas; mountains rose and fell; the island of the Kulseth seafarers sank, taking with it one of the Talismans of Noron'ri and leaving an entire nation homeless.

The climate, too, had altered. Ice crept down from the north, threatening to destroy what little the wars with the Shadow-born had left untouched. Only the sorcery of the wizards of the isle of Varna kept the cold confined to the northern lands.

Slowly, civilizations began to emerge from the rubble. Rathane expanded south in search of more temperate weather, sowing the seeds of an empire that eventually encompassed most of the lands west of the new inland sea. The eastern countries recovered more slowly. It was not until 577 A.W.B. (After the Wars of Binding) that Kith Alunel signed the first of the trading treaties which eventually grew into the Estarren Alliance.

The people left homeless by the sinking of the central part of the continent were less fortunate. A few found homes on

1

the islands of the newly created Melyranne Sea, while others merged with the peoples already living on either side. Most, however, remained in the north. As the climate cooled and the land became less hospitable, these folk took up a nomadic life. They called themselves the Thar, and they supplemented their hunting with occasional raids on the northernmost towns and villages of the more settled lands.

All four races mingled at least occasionally throughout the sprawling trading empire, and relations among them were generally cordial.

By 950 A.W.B. the northern ice was beginning its retreat, and the Varnan wizards could spare the time to look at the societies developing around them. They suffered a rude shock. The Estarren Alliance, with Kith Alunel at its center, had grown to dominate the East.

The Varnans saw the Estarren Alliance as a threat to their own position. In 1003 A.W.B. they invaded the mainland on the flimsiest of pretexts, intending to teach the upstarts their place. But the Varnans were badly outnumbered, despite their magic, and the war dragged on for over twenty years before finally spluttering out.

The Wizard's War, as the Varnan-Alliance conflict came to be called, reawakened the mainlanders to the possibilities inherent in the magic they had lost during the years of struggle for survival. Wizardry became an obsession, particularly in the southeastern lands which had borne the brunt of the Varnan invasion. As the interest in magic intensified, the nonhuman races became more and more unpopular. They were looked upon with suspicion because they had not employed their presumed magical arts in the War. Relations between humans and the other races deteriorated, culminating in the murder of hundreds of Shee, Neira, and Wyrds at Darkwater in 1183 A.W.B.

The Estarren Alliance began to disintegrate. One after another, outlying countries and principalities recalled their representatives from the Senate in Kith Alunel. The few Wyrds and Shee remaining in such places either quietly left or were systematically persecuted in hopes of learning their supposed secrets. By the time of the Half-Day War between Varna and the Neira in 1517 A.W.B., the Estarren Alliance had collapsed completely into independent, squabbling countries.

Virtually all of the nonhumans had left the southern lands or gone into permanent hiding.

The sinking of Varna by the Neira as the culmination of the Half-Day War added a new and unwelcome set of refugees to the population of the mainland. The Varnans had been feared and resented ever since the Wizard's War, and their casual assumption of superiority had done nothing to improve their popularity in the years since. No village, city or country was willing to welcome them, and the refugees were forced steadily northward. In 1533 A.W.B. they reached the mouth of the River Selyr and settled there, the first human inhabitants of the lands which eventually became Alkyra.

> — *From the introduction to* A History of Alkyra, *by Flindaran Kensal Sterren, Journeyman Historian of the Ciaron Minstrel's Guildhall. Presented to Alethia Tel'anh Atuval in 3030 A.W.B. on the thirtieth anniversary of her coronation as Queen of Alkyra.*

PART I
Hearth and Sword

CHAPTER

ONE

The travel-chariot was black and so were the horses that drew it. It came down the road silently, like a moving shadow or the fingers of death. Kayl pushed her brown hair out of her face with the back of one hand and made herself continue sweeping the stone step. Some Prefect with a macabre sense of humor, no doubt, or perhaps a wealthy merchant. Horses were rare in Mindaria; only a noble or an exceptionally wealthy tradesman would hire . . . Kayl's thoughts froze as she realized that the travel-chariot was turning onto the hard-packed area that served as a courtyard for the inn.

The rasping of the cicadas was suddenly loud in her ears. She forced herself to breathe. "It's a customer," she said under her breath. "Just a customer."

The customer's chariot halted just in front of her in a cloud of dust. Kayl knew immediately that this was no aristocrat's whim; she could feel power emanating from the chariot, pulling at the old bond— She cut the thought off as she realized where it might take her, and waited.

The driver jumped down from his seat and pulled back the curtains that hid the interior of the chariot. With a rustle of movement, a tall woman emerged. Her robes were black, her hair was black, and her eyes were the color of midnight. On her right hand she wore a ruby ring the color of blood, on her left an emerald green as poison, and in the hollow of her throat, suspended from a chain as thin as a spider's web, hung

7

a tiny silver skull with diamond eyes.

"You have a room," the visitor said, and her voice was dark music.

Kayl moistened lips that had gone suddenly dry, but her voice was steady. "Five pence the night, lady. Seven if you want an evening meal." Then she remembered the driver. "That's each."

The woman raised a perfect eyebrow. "The last three inn-keepers charged nothing at all."

"They don't have Prefect Islorran's tax to pay, lady."

"You mistake my meaning." The woman studied Kayl for a moment more, and slowly her lips widened into a smile. "I shall take a room. One week, at the price you named. After that, we shall see." Without waiting for Kayl's response, she turned and gave an order to her driver. He nodded and sprang back up to his seat; a moment later, the travel-chariot drove back the way it had come.

The woman turned and held out a hand. Automatically, Kayl extended her own, and seven thin copper coins dropped into it, one after the other. Kayl stared at them, then slowly closed her fingers around them. "This way, lady," she said, and went into the inn. She did not have to turn her head to see whether her unwelcome guest was following. Though she heard no sound but her own footsteps, she could feel the woman's presence like the heat of a fire on her back.

Inside, Kayl's rope sandals made a hissing noise against the stone floor as she circled the hearth in the center of the room. She crossed between the tables to the foot of the stairs. As she started up, she heard the woman's musical voice once again. "And do you wish no name to put on your board?"

Kayl turned and met the woman's gaze. "Whatever name you wish to give, lady," she said with a touch of sarcasm.

"I am Rialynn, called Corrana of the Sussewild." A smile flickered over her face and was gone. "Corrana will do, I think, for your guest record."

Shaken, Kayl nodded and turned away. The woman had given her true name; Kayl had felt the pull of it, and she was certain. Corrana—or Rialynn—was a sorceress. And she had studied magic with the Silver Sisters, though she did not seem to be one of them. No other wizards placed such dangerous power in their names. But why would such a one trust a mere innkeeper? Especially if she knew that Kayl . . .

"This is your room, lady," Kayl said, deliberately flinging open the first door in an attempt to interrupt her train of thought. "You've paid for an evening meal; it's served at the seventh hour, downstairs in the main room."

The woman called Corrana smiled and moved inside. "I will be there," she said, and closed the door behind her.

Kayl stood staring stupidly at the wooden planks, then turned and started down the stairs. The routine tasks of running the inn would be a comforting distraction from fruitless wondering about her enigmatic customer. She hoped.

The door banged below. A boy's voice, breathless with running, called, "Mother? Mother!"

Kayl's ears caught the undercurrent of fear being sternly suppressed by eight-year-old pride. Habit and instinct combined to set her personal worries aside at once. "I'm here, Mark," she said, taking the last few steps two at a time. "What is it?"

Mark stood by the outer door, holding a bronze-bladed dagger in his right hand. His thin chest heaved in panting breaths, and his blue-gray eyes darted around the serving room. Kayl's gaze followed his, but she saw no signs of danger. Mark straightened from his fighter's crouch when he saw Kayl, but his eyes remained wary. "Mother! You're all right?"

"Of course I'm all right," Kayl said. "Why shouldn't I be? And how many times have I told you not to come banging through the door like that? You'll scare away what few guests we have."

The familiar scolding was even more reassuring than Kayl's presence. The last traces of tension left Mark's shoulders, and he shoved the dagger into a sheath at his belt. "I was in a hurry," he said defensively.

"And why was that?"

"Tully said he saw the death-coach drive right up to the inn! I thought—" Mark stopped and eyed his mother warily.

"You thought it was coming for your aged mother and you came running home to defend me, hmmm?"

Mark looked down, and nodded. "I guess it wasn't very smart," he offered.

Kayl snorted. "Not at all. Brave, perhaps a little, but not smart."

"Really?" Mark's head came up. "You really think it was a brave thing to do?"

"Were you scared?"

"No!" Mark said indignantly. Kayl looked at him, and his eyes dropped. "Well, maybe a little."

"If you were afraid and you came in anyway, you did a brave thing," Kayl said. "That's what being brave means."

Mark considered. "But you said it was a stupid thing to do."

"Being brave doesn't automatically make you smart," Kayl said. "They're two different things."

"You mean I have to be *both*? At the *same time*? That's not fair!"

Kayl laughed and rumpled Mark's blond hair affectionately. "Lots of things aren't fair. Enough talking; we've a new guest and there's work to do."

"A new guest?"

"Tully saw her arriving."

"In the black coach?" Mark cast a dubious look at the stairs, as if he expected a Wyrm to appear around the corner at any minute.

"It was just a travel-chariot. Now, you go and—"

"Where is she?"

"Mark! Don't interrupt. She's in the room at the head of the stairs, and you're going to take up water right away."

"Do I have to?"

"Yes, you have to. Go on!"

Mark left, looking much put-upon. Kayl watched him until the rear door of the inn closed behind him—with a bang—and shook her head. Mark would never make an innkeeper. He might become a good fighting man, if he could only control his impulsiveness long enough to survive the learning. And if Kayl could find a way of training him. Dara, on the other hand . . .

"Mother?"

Kayl turned. Dara was peering around the edge of the front door, her brown eyes wide. "What's the matter with you?" Kayl said crossly.

Dara flushed and stepped inside. She tossed a long strand of dark, fine hair defiantly over one shoulder and said, "I saw a black chariot stop here, and, well . . ."

"Not you, too." Kayl rolled her eyes. "It was just a guest."

"Oh." Dara studied Kayl. "You're sure?"

"Of course I'm sure," Kayl said with what she hoped was

sufficient firmness to discourage further questions. Dara was four years older than Mark, and far more perceptive.

"Huh." Dara scowled. "I thought that it might at least be somebody special."

"Special in what way?"

"Oh, you know. One of Father's friends, from before."

"I hardly think any of your father's friends would come looking for him five years after his death," Kayl said sharply. Dara was closer to the truth than she could suspect, though it was not her father's past that was the problem.

"Well, who is it then? Driving around in something like that and scaring everybody."

"She calls herself Corrana, she's paid for an evening meal, and you're going to run over to the market and get what we need to feed her decently. That's all you need to know right now."

Dara groaned. "Errands? But, Mother, I went last time. Can't Mark—"

"Mark's drawing water for the new guest. Do you want to trade chores with him?"

"No."

"All right, then. Get greens and a little meat, if you can find any that's not too dear. And we'll want more bread; stop at Brazda's on the way back and see if she has extra today." Kayl handed Dara three of the copper pennies Corrana had given her. "Oh, and while you're out, try to let a few people know that I haven't been killed or cursed or carried off. One customer won't even begin to pay Islorran's tax, especially if she drives everyone else away."

Dara's eyes narrowed in sudden thought. "That's right, people will be worried. I'd better go right away." She shoved the coins into her pocket and darted for the door.

"Dara!" Kayl waited until Dara turned to face her. "You are not to go telling stories to Jirod to lure him out here to-night. Do you understand?"

"I wasn't going to do anything like that!" Dara said. Her tone was unconvicing, and her eyes slid away from Kayl's face.

"No?"

"Well, all right, but what difference would it make? He's bound to hear about it sooner or later."

"At least if someone else tells him, I won't have your

matchmaking to contend with."

Dara flushed. "Mother!"

"If you want to be successful at that sort of thing, you need to learn a little subtlety," Kayl went on relentlessly. "Did you really think I hadn't noticed?"

"You never said anything."

"I'd hoped you would think better of it. And I'm saying something now."

"Well, you *ought* to get married again," Dara said defensively.

"If I ever decide to remarry, I'll choose my own partner, thank you."

"Jirod's nice."

"Yes, he is. And he's a good friend. But I've no interest in him as a husband, and I'd rather not have to tell him so to his face just because my daughter thinks we'd make a good match."

"But there isn't anyone else in Copeham!"

"Then I won't marry. It's my affair, after all."

Dara's eyes fell. "I suppose so."

"Now, promise me you'll stop this nonsense with Jirod once and for all."

"Well . . ." Dara sneaked a glance upward. "Oh, all right. I promise."

"Off with you, then."

Dara nodded, looking considerably subdued, and left. Kayl sighed as the door closed behind her daughter, feeling the familiar guilt rising inside her. Not having a father was hard for the children. Perhaps she should remarry, for their sakes. Jirod was a kind man, and he had made no secret of his admiration for Kayl. He was quiet and steady, too; he would be good for Mark. Yet, much as she liked the thoughtful farmer, she never seemed able to bring herself to encourage him. Or any of the other eligible and semi-eligible men of Copeham Village, for that matter.

She chalked Corrana's name on the slate by the stairs, then picked up the broom she had left by the door and went out to finish her sweeping. Perhaps the real problem was that she'd never met anyone else like Kevran. She smiled sadly, remembering the laughter in his face and the warmth of his touch. Five years had done much to dull the pain of his loss, but his memory was still clear in her mind. The time they'd had together had been worth the price they'd paid, and neither of them had regretted it.

But she'd never found another man worth giving up . . . what she had given up for Kevran. And she could never be content with less, even now. Kayl scowled and gave the step one final brush with the broom, then went back inside. She hadn't thought even obliquely of the days before her marriage in years. It was the fault of that woman, Rialynn, Corrana, whatever she called herself. She had no right to come here, stirring up things Kayl had no wish to remember.

Kayl paused, turning that thought over in her mind. No wish to remember? They had been good times, despite their bitter ending, and Kevran had shared some of them with her. Why was she so afraid of them now? Absently, she set the broom in its corner. Mark had already brought the water in; she could tell by the irregular trail of drops he had left in his wake. She would have to remind him again to be more careful.

She went into the kitchen to prepare for Dara's return. The distorted image of herself in the bottom of a dented brass pot was oddly disturbing today, though she had seen it every afternoon for . . . how long had she had that pot? Kayl shook herself. She was trying to avoid thinking, she realized, and doing a pretty poor job of it. All right then, face the question and answer it. Why *was* she so disturbed by Corrana's appearance?

The answer came almost as soon as the question had been phrased. She was afraid of the disruption the woman's arrival might bring to her orderly way of life. Kayl stared at the kitchen wall for a long moment, appalled. When had she begun to cling to the somewhat dubious security of life as an innkeeper in a small Mindaran village? She had wanted more, Kevran had wanted more, once. And how had she not noticed what was happening to her?

Her mind ran quickly through her years here, pointing out the little changes in attitude that had summed to such a terribly unwelcome total. The difficulty of being accepted by the villagers when they first arrived; the comfort of having a place that was *theirs*; working side by side with the villagers the time the river had threatened to flood; Dara's birth, and the nameless child who had died, and Mark; Kevran's death of the summer sickness; the struggle to be both mother and father to two small children; the growing acceptance by the village in the wake of Kevran's death; the wanderers who didn't pay their bills or tried to intimidate her into lowering her prices; the rising taxes Islorran demanded. So many things, and so small.

And there was nothing she could do about it now. She was what she was; the years had shaped her as surely as a smith shaped steel.

The rear door banged. Kayl snatched up a cleaver and an onion, and began to chop. Mark knew that her eyes always watered when she chopped onions; even if he noticed, he would not ask his mother why she was crying over the kitchen pots.

CHAPTER

TWO

The evening meal was normally the busiest time of day at Kayl's inn, and this evening was even busier than usual. Far from frightening Kayl's customers away, Corrana's dramatic arrival was a magnet. Nearly everyone in Copeham had found some excuse to stop in, and, once in, they stayed.

Just as the sun was setting, Corrana descended the stairs at last. She had changed her loose black robe for a clinging one of deep forest green. Her dark hair hung loose around her shoulders, hiding whatever clasp held the sweep of the robe's neckline. She had put off her rings, and Kayl saw no sign of the silver skull necklace. She seemed to float down the stairs, oblivious to the sudden silence below.

Kayl greeted her appearance with a relieved sigh. Perhaps now some of the merely curious would leave, and she would have a chance to relax a little. She moved forward, no faster or slower than she would have gone to greet any other guest. "My lady," she said, inclining her head slightly.

Corrana's lips curved. "Greetings, innkeeper." There was the briefest hesitation between the two words, just long enough for Kayl to take note of it. Her eyes were fixed on Kayl, as if no one else in the room was of any importance. Kayl nodded again, with as much respect as she could muster, and turned to lead the way between the tables.

The villagers drew back almost imperceptibly as the two women came among them. Kayl caught the eyes of Holum, the metal worker, and quirked a corner of her mouth at him. Holum's eyes narrowed; then, reluctantly, he smiled back and hoisted his beer mug. The movement, small as it was, broke the atmosphere of tension. A murmur went through the crowd, and then the hum of conversation rose once more. Kayl felt some of the tightness leave the muscles in her shoulders and back.

She reached the head of one of the long tables and arranged a place for Corrana, close enough to the window to have the benefit of the night breeze. The woman seated herself gracefully as though unaware of the fascinated eyes of the villagers. Kayl signaled Mark. "A bowl of the stew," she told him.

"You're sure you want her to have that?" Mark said.

"Why not?"

"It has too many onions in it."

"You think stew has too many onions in it if I wave one at the pot while it's cooking," Kayl said without irritation. "Go along and get it."

Mark shrugged and left, threading his way rapidly among the benches and tables. Kayl turned back to find Corrana watching her with speculative and slightly disapproving eyes. "You are remarkably easy with your staff," she said, glancing at Mark's retreating back.

"That," Kayl said coldly, "is my son, Mark."

A look of surprise came into Corrana's eyes. She made a little motion with her left hand, the first completely unnecessary gesture Kayl had seen her make. The movement made something glint beneath the heavy black tresses that lay across her left shoulder. "Your son."

"My youngest," Kayl said. She did not know why this woman was discomfited by the thought, but, after the way Corrana had disrupted her peace of mind, Kayl took a malicious satisfaction in seeing her even momentarily at a loss.

"You have others?"

"A daughter. They're a great help to me."

Mark chose that moment to return with the stew. Corrana pulled away from the table as he leaned over to set the bowl before her. Her hair fell aside momentarily, revealing the silver clasp that held her robe at the left shoulder.

It was a heavy, sculpted piece in the shape of an eight-pointed star. The metal had been polished until it seemed to shine with its own light, and in the exact center was a milky white stone. Kayl stiffened in shock. With the last of her presence of mind, she turned away before Corrana or Mark noticed her expression.

Corrana *was* a sorceress of the Sisterhood! Kayl stared blindly out the window at the night, her mind churning. Was it coincidence or deliberate planning that brought Corrana to Copeham? Coincidence, surely; if the Sisterhood had wanted Kayl back, they would not have waited fifteen years to send someone looking for her. Kayl took a deep breath and let it out slowly, counting, then turned away from the window. She made certain that Corrana was satisfied with the meal, noting as she did that the badge of the Sisterhood was once more invisible beneath the sorceress's hair. Then she went back to her other customers.

As she worked, Kayl watched Corrana surreptitiously. Unanswered questions chased themselves through her mind. Why had Corrana hidden the fact that she was one of the Silver Sisters? And why reveal it now, to Kayl? Corrana must have wanted her to see the clasp, or she would not have worn it at all. Kayl handed a fresh mug to Zia, the seamstress, and gave her a mechanical smile, then glanced at the sorceress again. One week, she thought. She'll be gone in a week. A week isn't long.

Corrana did not appear to notice Kayl's scrutiny. She ate slowly, then rose and ascended the stairs once more. The buzz of conversation grew louder as soon as she was gone. Everyone had some speculation as to who she was, where she had come from, and why she might have chosen to spend a week in Copeham.

Kayl did not participate in the discussion, though she was occasionally tempted. She sifted with care the scraps that came her way, trying to piece together a picture of village opinion. No one else had noticed the badge of the Sisterhood, that much was clear. Her eyes narrowed. Corrana had deliberately allowed Kayl, and only Kayl, to see the clasp she wore. Then Kayl shook her head. She was getting as full of fancies as Mark and Dara.

"Kayl."

The deep voice behind her made her jump. She turned. Jirod was seated in the corner behind her, a little apart from the rest of the crowd. He was watching her with warm concern. "Good evening, Jirod," Kayl said. "Need a refill?"

"No," the man replied, and Kayl realized belatedly that his beer had barely been touched. "I wanted to talk to you."

Kayl hesitated. She glanced quickly around the room; no arms were raised in summons, and Dara was poised by the counter, ready to answer the next beckoning hand. Hoping her daughter hadn't noticed whom she was talking to, Kayl said, "I think I can take a short break."

"I was afraid you were going to say you were too busy," Jirod said as she took an empty place across from him.

"I am, which means I can use the rest. Mark and Dara can handle things for a little while."

"You work too hard."

"Who doesn't? What did you want to talk to me about?"

Jirod looked down. "I just wanted to make sure you were all right."

"All right?" Kayl said, puzzled.

"Your new guest looks as if she could be a problem."

Kayl stared at him as comprehension dawned. "Has Dara been talking to you?" she demanded.

"I don't need a twelve-year-old to point out what's under my eyes!"

"That's not what I meant. Oh, never mind. I'm fine, Jirod, and Corrana's no more a problem than any other noble with more money than sense. In fact, she's easier to deal with than most of them; she's quiet and doesn't expect flame-jugglers and musicians in a town this size."

"She's a witch, Kayl."

"Maybe. But what if she is? She pays good coppers for her board, the same as any other customer."

Jirod looked at her with a somber expression. "Kayl, you've been jumpy all evening. And I saw your face when Mark served her. You were frightened for him. You can't make me believe that you'd react that way without a reason."

"I'm fine, Jirod," Kayl repeated, her lips tightening. "Just fine."

"All right, then. You know where to find me if that changes."

Kayl nodded as politely as she could, and rose. There was no point in continuing the conversation. She'd only end up snapping at him for trying to be helpful. "Thank you, Jirod," she said with as much warmth as she could muster. "But it's time I was getting back to work."

As she left the table, she saw Dara glance worriedly in her direction. There were customers at three different tables calling for beer, so it was some time before she had a chance to speak to her daughter. Finally they were both behind the counter at the same time.

"I didn't say anything to him, Mother," Dara said in an urgent whisper. "Honest I didn't."

"I know that," Kayl said.

"Oh." The word held a wealth of relief. "When you got up frowning like that, I was afraid you thought I had."

"I wasn't annoyed with you, Dara."

"Jirod said something wrong?"

"That's between him and me. The last table on the right wants more stew; see if there's any left."

Dara rolled her eyes and left. The evening dragged on interminably. Slowly, the villagers trickled out. Jirod stayed. Kayl avoided his corner, letting Dara and Mark handle the customers on that side of the room, but she was aware of his eyes on her as she worked.

His presence annoyed her; the man acted as though she was a helpless featherhead who needed taking care of. She knew she was being unfair, but it was a relief to be angry at someone. When he left at last, she was washing mugs in a bucket behind the counter. She did not look up from her work until the door had closed behind him.

Finally the last of the villagers departed and the few guests climbed the stairs to their rooms. "Whew!" Mark said, surveying the inevitable litter of dirty plates, crumbs, spilled beer, and half-empty mugs. "What a night!"

Dara flopped down on one of the benches. "Oh, my feet hurt!"

"I'm not surprised," Kayl said. "There were more people in here than we had the night the Prefect's son came through." She fished the last of the coins she'd collected out of the leather pouch sewn inside her belt and added them to the main collection in the heavy wooden box where she kept the night's receipts. She relocked the box and set it on the counter where she wouldn't forget to take it with her when she left the serving room.

"How did we do?" Dara said anxiously.

"I haven't counted up the total yet, but I think we did very well indeed," Kayl replied.

"I bet it'll be just as bad tomorrow," Mark said gloomily.

"You don't have anything to complain about," Dara retorted. "You sat in the kitchen most of the night while I was running around the tables."

"It's hot in there!" Mark said. "Hot and sticky. And I ran tables, too. Didn't I, Mother?"

"You both did a wonderful job tonight, and I'm proud of you," Kayl said. "I'll finish up down here; you go off to bed. If tomorrow night is anything like this one, you'll need a good night's sleep."

The two children did not wait for a second invitation. They left at once, as though afraid Kayl might change her mind and call them back to sweep floors and clean dishes. Kayl watched them go, then set about clearing up the mess. She let the lamps burn low while she worked. When she finished at last, she put out all but one lamp and sat down by the window. She stared at the thick darkness outside, while the shadows deepened around her. Once she glanced over at the smooth, gray stones of the seldom-used hearth. She half rose, then shook her head and sank back into her seat, and for a long time she did not move. Finally, she rose and started toward the money-box. Halfway across the room, a tingling ran down her spine, the half-forgotten but unmistakable feeling of magic.

Kayl whirled. The room was empty, but the tingling grew stronger. She forced herself to stand motionless, trying to feel the direction from which the sensation was coming. Her head turned. Upstairs. She hesitated, then retrieved the money-box and started forward. She hesitated again beside the lamp, then went on without it.

She moved slowly but surely; she knew every inch of this inn, even in the dark. The tingling grew stronger as she climbed the stairs. Her lips tightened. Demons fly away with Corrana! She had to be behind this; there was no one else in Copeham who knew more than the most basic spells.

Kayl reached the top of the stairs and stopped short. Pale lights flickered across the door of Corrana's room, like the cold shine of light on the scales of invisible snakes. They were so faint that if she had been carrying a lamp, she would have missed them. The pattern was a warding; Kayl had seen enough of them to recognize it at once, though she herself was no magician. She stared at it, feeling angry and a little frightened. She had a momentary urge to pound on the door, but she suppressed it. Annoying a sorceress, even a minor one, was seldom a good idea, and she had the uncomfortable feeling that Corrana was rather more than minor.

After another moment's consideration, Kayl turned and went back the way she had come. The warding spell was doing no harm, and it was unlikely that anyone else would notice it. She was climbing into bed, having hidden the money-box in the safety hole beneath it, when the thought struck her. What was Corrana doing that she felt a need to guard her door with spells in a town as small and quiet as Copeham?

CHAPTER

THREE

Kayl was awakened next morning by the sound of Mark and Dara squabbling outside her door. She frowned, as much at her own tardiness as at the noise of the quarrel. Normally she was awake well before either of the children. She pulled her under-tunic on hastily and went out to see what the problem was this time.

"There!" Dara said as Kayl approached. "I *told* you she'd wake up if you kept shouting."

"I wasn't shouting!" Mark shouted. "You were the one who—"

"Quiet," Kayl said sternly. "How many times have I told you to be careful in the morning? You'll wake the guests."

"That's what I told him, and he—"

"But Mother, she won't let—"

"I said, quiet." Kayl waited a moment, then continued. "Now, *one at a time* please. What's this all about?"

"He wouldn't stop—"

"She thinks I—"

"Stop! Dara, suppose you explain your side of it first."

"We woke up early, so we decided to surprise you and do the morning chores before you got up," Dara said. "Only Mark wanted to start with taking wash water up to that weird lady who came yesterday."

"She's not weird!" Mark interrupted. "She's a sorceress."

"How do *you* know she's a sorceress?" Dara said scornfully.

"Everybody said so!"

Kayl intervened before the battle could resume. "So Mark wanted to carry water up to Corrana's room. What then?"

"She wouldn't let me!" Mark burst out.

"It's too early," Dara said. "And you can't go waking up guests just because you're curious about them."

"I wasn't going to wake her up," Mark said in tones of wounded innocence. "And I wasn't curious. I just wanted to make sure we did everything right. She's important."

"If she's so important, I should be the one to take the water up," Dara retorted. "You always spill."

"I do not!"

"That's enough," Kayl said. She looked from Mark to Dara and sighed. It was just like them to plan a pleasant surprise for her and then end up arguing about which of them should do what. And she didn't care for Mark's apparent interest in Corrana. She'd have to tread carefully, though; if she simply forbade him to hang about the woman, he would immediately begin thinking up ways to do so anyway. She looked back at Mark. "I'm afraid Dara's right, Mark; it *is* too early to be carting things up to the rooms. I'm glad you're worried about giving good service, but I don't think waking up a guest is the way to impress her."

"I wasn't going to—"

"If she's a light sleeper, you may have done so already," Kayl said.

Mark frowned rebelliously, but he could hardly deny it after the furious argument had wakened Kayl. "Well, maybe."

"I think you should draw a jug or two and heat it up over the kitchen fire. Then it'll be ready as soon as Corrana wakes."

"Can't I—"

"No."

Mark glared at her, trying to decide what his chances were of winning a continued argument. The verdict was apparently not favorable. He turned the corners of his mouth down in a ferocious pout and started for the back door, stomping his feet as hard as he dared.

"Mark!"

"What?" His tone was half-sullen, half-belligerent.

"You will not continue pounding through this inn like an overweight otterlan. Understand?"

"I can do what I want to!"

"And I can find some other way for you to work off your temper. Splitting firewood, for instance."

Muttering angrily, Mark turned away. "What was that?" Kayl said.

"I said, all right!"

"And don't bang the door!" Kayl called after him. She listened until he was outside, then looked at Dara.

"I *tried* to tell him," Dara said defensively before Kayl could say anything. "I really did! But he won't listen to me. He *never* listens to me."

"Maybe you should try being a little less dictatorial."

"But, Mother—"

"Mark doesn't like being told he's wrong, particularly by his sister. Try to be a little tactful."

"With *Mark*? But he's, he's . . ."

"He's younger than you are, and more impulsive. I don't expect him to worry about waking the guests up before he starts a shouting match; I do expect it of you."

"I'm sorry, Mother," Dara said, flushing.

"You're old enough to stop and think before you get into things like this."

Dara looked after Mark, her face thoughtful. "It's hard to stop and think when Mark's yelling at me."

Kayl could not help smiling. "I know, dear. But try, please."

"All right," Dara said doubtfully. Kayl gave her a hug and sent her off to start making breakfast. Then she went back into her room to finish getting up. She hoped fervently that the rest of the day was not going to be as difficult as its beginning.

It was worse. Dara burned the porridge and tried to cover the taste with honey and too many herbs; the result was all but inedible. Mark filled his jug to the brim, so that water sloshed over the top as he staggered back to the inn with it. The overflow made the back steps and parts of the hall treacherously slippery. He ended by dropping the jug as he was trying to fill

the kettle. Since he had not bothered to move the kettle away
from the brick stove, this drowned the fire and set the kitchen
awash in ashy gray water.

The mishap was the excuse that began another fight between
Dara and Mark. Kayl squelched the argument firmly, then
set them to cleaning up the mess. In the process, Dara discovered that the jug had cracked down one side when Mark
had dropped it. This came close to starting another fight; Kayl
ended it by scolding both children. She then packed Mark and
the jug off to see if Bryn, the village's general handywoman,
could mend the crack.

As he was leaving, Dara came in from the serving room and
announced that the leg on one of the benches was broken and
it was a miracle the thing hadn't collapsed under a customer
the previous night. Kayl sighed, called Mark back, and told
him to ask Bryn to stop by later and look at the bench if she
could. Mark considered visiting Bryn a treat; he went off in
high spirits, swinging the water jug so wildly that Kayl wondered whether it would survive the trip.

Kayl emerged from the kitchen to discover two of her guests
standing at the foot of the stairs, impatiently awaiting their
morning wash-water. She soothed their irritation as best she
could, but she had the dismal feeling that the two customers
would make it a point to avoid breaking their future journeys
at Copeham.

Just as she finished with the customers, the first of a string
of curious villagers stopped by. The visit was ostensibly to see
if Kayl needed an egg or two, but the man's eyes kept straying
toward the staircase that led to the guestrooms. Kayl got rid of
him as politely as she could, and retired to the rear of the inn.

She was barely in time to catch one of the unhappy early
risers attempting to slink out the back with all his baggage and
an unpaid bill. An acrimonious discussion ensued, during
which Kayl was able to release a good deal of her pent-up
frustration. There was very little else she could do; Copeham
did not have the facilities to deal with reluctant patrons, and
Prefect Islorran had long ago made it clear that he had no interest in such petty grievances.

The man left at last, having paid barely half of what he
owed, just as Mark arrived with the news that the water jug
was beyond help and they would have to buy a new one. His
contrition was almost as difficult to deal with as his earlier fit

of sulks had been. Kayl took advantage of it to send him off to
the market for a new water jug and a basket of vegetables. The
errands would keep Dara from starting another argument with
him for a while, and with luck, they would also keep Mark out
of Corrana's way for most of the day.

Finally, Kayl found a moment to sit down in the empty serving room and try to relax. She was just beginning to recover
from the hectic events of the morning, when a cool voice from
behind her said, "Good morning, innkeeper."

Kayl jerked, then turned her head. Corrana was standing at
the foot of the stairs, regarding her with a mildly questioning
expression. She was wearing her black costume once more,
and her hair was braided into a crown about her head. There
was no sign of the badge of the Sisterhood. She made a dramatic and somewhat ominous figure, but Kayl was too tired to
be intimidated. Her only thought was that Corrana looked out
of place in a village inn.

"Forgive me, lady," Kayl said. "I'm afraid you startled
me. Is there something I can get for you?"

"I thank you, but no, there is not. I have come, instead, to
give you something."

"Oh?"

Corrana smiled. "Your fee for this night's lodging." She
moved over to Kayl's side and set seven coppers on the table.

Kayl looked at them. "Tonight's fee."

"Is there some problem? It is as we agreed."

"There is no problem. I was . . . surprised, that is all. Most
visitors prefer to pay at the end of their stay." Kayl thought of
the man who had tried to leave, and added under her breath,
"If they pay at all."

Corrana laughed. She lowered herself gracefully to the
bench on the other side of the table and said, "It seems you
speak from experience."

"More so than I'd like," Kayl admitted.

"You need have no worries in my regard. I shall keep my
part of our agreement."

"I meant no criticism, lady; far from it. I appreciate your
promptness."

Corrana nodded but did not speak. She sat all but motionless, watching Kayl from under half-lowered eyelids. One
long, slender finger traced absentminded circles on the top of
the table.

Kayl found herself becoming irritated. This woman wanted to play games; let her take a dose of her own brew. "Why are you in Copeham?" she asked abruptly.

Corrana's eyes flickered. "I enjoy travel, and I have already seen the villages near my home."

"One village is very like another."

"Perhaps. But the people who live in them are not."

"True." Kayl suppressed a twinge of uneasiness. She was beginning to regret ever starting this conversation. She was groping for a graceful way of ending it, a task made more difficult by the slightly predatory quality of Corrana's smile, when the front door opened and Dara stuck her head in.

"Mother? Oh, excuse me; I didn't mean to interrupt. But that man of Prefect Islorran's is here, and I think you'd better come talk to him."

"In a moment, Dara. You will excuse me, lady, I'm sure." Kayl stood, nodded politely, and picked up the seven coppers still stacked on the tabletop.

"Of course," Corrana said. "Perhaps we can continue our conversation some other time." Her eyes flicked to the door, and then away. She rose and glided unhurriedly to the stairs.

Kayl breathed a small sigh of relief and turned her mind to her newest problem. The tax collector wasn't due for another week, so Islorran must want something special. She sighed again, and went outside.

Islorran's messenger was a short, fat man with bright eyes half buried in his puffy face. Kayl had dealt with him several times in the month he had spent as Islorran's secretary; his officious air never failed to set her teeth on edge. She could only hope his tenure as Prefect Islorran's secretary would be even briefer than that of his predecessor, who had been summarily dismissed after barely two months of service.

"Sorry to have kept you waiting, Utrilo," Kayl said as politely as she could. She came up behind Dara as she spoke and gave the girl a tiny sideways shove with her hand. Dara bobbed a curtsey and faded out of sight around the corner of the inn as Kayl went on. "I was with a customer."

"Quite so, quite so. And that, of course, is precisely what I have come about," Utrilo said, puffing out his chest. "Pre-cise-ly."

"Be good enough to explain."

"So I shall, so I shall. Though you may not find the explanation good." He snickered at his own wit, then coughed, but his sharp eyes never left Kayl. "Ahem. Word has reached the Prefect Islorran that there is someone staying here, someone very interesting indeed."

Kayl was torn between anger and a strong desire to laugh at the man's posturings. "I do not pry into the business of my guests," she said after a moment. "If there is someone among them whom the Prefect might wish to see, I am not aware of it."

"Ah, but there are some persons of interest who are easily identified."

"I don't think I understand you," said Kayl, who was all too afraid she did.

"I will be quite plain," Utrilo said ponderously. "The Prefect Islorran has heard that there is a great worker of magic staying here, at your inn. Perhaps," he paused as though for dramatic emphasis, "perhaps even a Shee."

Anger was quickly overcoming Kayl's sense of humor. "No Shee have come through Copeham in more than five years, as the Prefect knows quite well," she snapped.

"Yes, yes, of course. But simply because something has not happened, does not mean it cannot happen." He regarded her with a complacent smile, but his eyes were cold and hard. "And there are laws about such travelers, you know."

"I know the Prefect's laws," Kayl said even more waspishly than before. "And you may be sure that if a Shee had come to my inn I would have reported it as the Prefect requires. Along with my opinion of such foolish laws as that one." From the corner of one eye, she saw a movement at one of the upper windows of the inn. Corrana, perhaps? Well, let her listen if she chose. Inquisitive woman.

"I am sure Prefect Islorran will be delighted to hear that, Mistress Kayl. Simply delighted." Utrilo's smile widened into a toothy shark's grin. "But are you quite certain you have seen no Shee? You realize that failure to notify the Prefect could result in the confiscation of your property."

"I am well aware of that, Utrilo," Kayl said between her teeth. Islorran and his previous secretaries had never taken much interest in Copeham's inn, except to make sure the taxes were paid promptly. Utrilo, however, was another matter. In the few weeks that he had been in Copeham, there had hardly been two days running in which he had not found some excuse to visit the inn and criticize its management or make increasingly open threats regarding fines, penalties, and confiscation. Kayl had concluded that he was trying to demonstrate his competence and dedication to Islorran. She wished very strongly that he would find some other way of doing so.

Utrilo's smile did not waiver. "And you still maintain that no Shee arrived here yesterday?"

"I have never seen a Shee with black hair or black eyes, and the only person who arrived yesterday has both."

"There are dyes . . . ," Utrilo said with less confidence.

"A Shee, dye his hair to avoid notice by humans? Don't be ridiculous. No Shee would bother."

"As you clearly know so well, Mistress Kayl."

"As anyone who's ever met a Shee knows, including the Prefect. They've never thought much of humans, and I doubt that all these regulations have improved their opinions any. Not that I blame them."

"That is precisely the point," Utrilo said pompously. "Prefect Islorran knows how unwise it is to allow a few people to flaunt their disregard for the law."

"How nice for the Prefect," said a new voice from behind Utrilo. "Presumably that is why his son was not even fined when he got drunk last month and broke half the pottery in Pesek's shop."

Utrilo jumped and whirled with a speed that was amazing in one of his bulk. Behind him, showing pointed teeth in a fierce smile, stood Bryn, woodworker, handywoman, and one of the few Wyrds still remaining in Copeham.

CHAPTER
FOUR

Utrilo recovered himself quickly and his eyes contracted to slits. "Ah, Mistress Bryn," he said with a false heartiness. "What an unexpected surprise! Oh, but a pleasant one, I do assure you." For a moment Kayl was afraid he was going to reach out and pat Bryn's head as though she were a child or the cat she resembled.

"I'm glad you find it so," Bryn said. "Good afternoon, Kayl. Mark said you had a job for me?"

"One of the benches inside has a cracked leg. It's hanging on by a splinter; I'm lucky no one heavy sat on it last night." Kayl glanced at Utrilo.

"Yes, I heard you had quite a crowd," Bryn said. "It's just inside?"

"Leaning up against the wall on the right," Kayl said. "I didn't want to chance someone sitting on it."

"Good. It shouldn't take long," Bryn said, and started for the door.

"Just a moment, Mistress Wyrd," Utrilo said.

One of Bryn's large, foxlike ears twitched. Unhurriedly, she turned back to face Utrilo. They made an interesting contrast, the fat, red-faced man in a loose robe of dusty linen and the small, brown-furred Wyrd in her plain leather tunic. Bryn looked less than half Utrilo's size, though she was not too much shorter than he was, but she was clearly unimpressed by

30

Islorran's fat, city-bred secretary. "What is it?" she said in a bored tone.

"Tell me, if you please, why it is you have come to see Mistress Kayl today."

Bryn glanced at Kayl in surprise. Kayl shrugged. "Don't ask me what he's hunting for."

"I came to fix one of the benches," Bryn said, looking back at Utrilo. "If you're that interested, you can watch me work. It'll be a change; usually it's only the children who enjoy watching a carpenter."

"A bench?" Utrilo said in an unpleasantly oily tone. "Not, *not* to visit a new arrival at the inn?"

Bryn studied him. The short fur covering her face made it unreadable. "I think you've been standing too long in the sun," she said at last. "I understand you humans have to be careful about such things. Why should I want to visit one of Kayl's guests?"

"Ah! But if the guest were a Shee?" Utrilo said. "What have you to say to that?"

"I say you haven't just been standing in the sun, you've been chewing efron leaves as well. There haven't been Shee in Copeham in years."

"Prefect Islorran is not unskilled in magic," Utrilo said. Something in his tone made Kayl look at him sharply. "Not at all unskilled. And he detected someone's arrival yesterday, a sorcerer of great power. And—"

"You mean a sorceress of great power," said Corrana from the doorway of the inn.

Kayl turned, and felt the blood drain from her face. Corrana stood regally on the step of the inn, clad in the silver robe of an Elder Sister of the Sisterhood of Stars. The heavy folds hung straight from her shoulders, leaving her arms bare. The cloth rippled over the silver-twined linen belt, hiding all but the dangling ends, and fell in long folds to her ankles. Her black hair was bound back by a net of silver set with diamonds. On her left shoulder the star-shaped badge of the Sisterhood shimmered and gleamed in the sunlight. And the years rolled backward in Kayl's mind.

She was a frightened six-year-old again, one of a handful of

Thar left behind when the raid on the village went so suddenly wrong. Her hands worried at the coarse, prickly rope that bound them while the villagers debated angrily what to do with her. Their accent was barely intelligible to her; the sense of their conversation kept slipping away as she lost her concentration in twisting at the rope.

Suddenly the harsh voices fell silent. Kayl looked up. A woman had come out of one of the houses and started toward the knot of angry people in front of Kayl. She wore a garment of shimmering silver that glittered and gleamed in the sunlight, surrounding her with a corona of light. Kayl gaped at her, full of wonder and fear. Even the Thar had heard of the Silver Sisters, the strange sorceresses who wore the color of magic.

The woman frowned at the villagers and said something too rapidly for Kayl to follow. Then she looked down at Kayl. "I am Dalessi, of the Sisterhood of Stars. Would you come with me, child, and be raised by my sisters and me?"

The threats of the villagers were forgotten. Kayl tried to speak and found she could only nod.

The silver-clothed woman smiled like the mother Kayl had never known, and reached down to untie her hands.

Utrilo cleared his throat uncertainly, and the memory vanished. It left behind a bittersweet tang and a feeling of precariousness. Kayl took a deep breath and forced her mind back to the present. She would have to deal with her private demons later; there was no time now.

"I, um," Utrilo said, and stopped. His eyes were fixed on Corrana. For an instant, Kayl thought she saw hatred in his expression; then his face settled into an almost comical dismay. Kayl could understand his reaction. The Silver Sisters were powerful, as well as respected, even in Mindaria. Utrilo must know that Islorran would have his hands if he antagonized one of the Sisters. He rocked backward slightly, and his sandals made a crunching noise against the ground.

"I do not believe I know you," Corrana said coldly. She turned her head to look at Kayl.

"Forgive me, Your Virtue; my mind was elsewhere," Kayl said. "This is Mistress Bryn saMural, Copeham's carpenter, and this is Utrilo Levoil, one of Prefect Islorran's secretaries."

"Thank you, innkeeper." Corrana turned to Bryn. "May the Tree guard your way, Mistress."

"And may the stars look kindly on your own," Bryn returned.

Corrana inclined her head, then straightened and looked at Utrilo. She studied him with a dispassionate gaze and an expression of mild distaste, as she might have viewed a slug crawling on one of the plants in her garden. "You have some interest in my presence here?"

"Ah, yes, my lady. I mean, no, my lady. That is, Prefect Islorran—"

"The proper form of address for an Elder Sister is 'Your Virtue,' " Corrana said coldly. "Has Mindaria lost all knowledge of manners?"

Kayl saw hatred flash in Utrilo's eyes again; then he was the unctuous servant once more. "No, my—Your Virtue. Would Your Virtue condescend to tell me when you arrived in Copeham?"

"No."

Utrilo blinked. "Your Virtue?"

"I said no. Is your hearing as bad as your manners?"

"But, Your Virtue, Prefect Islorran charged me with the duty of bringing him information about the arrival of the sorcerer—ah, sorceress staying at Mistress Kayl's inn."

"That is your problem, not mine," Corrana said indifferently.

"But Prefect Islorran will—" Utrilo said in a desperate whine.

"I am on the business of the Sisterhood of Stars, and your Prefect has no authority over me. That is all you need to know."

"Of course, Your Virtue." Utrilo's forehead was shiny with perspiration. "But Prefect Islorran is most interested in magic. I am sure he would give you a most gracious welcome, should you wish to visit his villa."

Utrilo rocked forward hopefully as Corrana paused, considering. "Perhaps that can be arranged," she said magnanimously. "I cannot say for certain until my business is concluded."

"If there is any way we can be of service—"

"The affairs of the Sisterhood are no concern of yours," Corrana snapped.

"Yes, Your Virtue. I mean, no, Your Virtue."

"Bear it in mind," Corrana said, and swept back into the inn before Utrilo recovered enough to respond.

Utrilo stared after her. Then he closed his mouth and glared at Kayl, as though attempting to make up for the deference he had shown Corrana. "Wait until Prefect Islorran hears about this!" he hissed. "You'll regret this day's work, innkeeper Kayl!"

Before Kayl could respond, Utrilo whirled and stalked off. Kayl stared after him, wondering at his unsettled behavior. Was it just the effect of Corrana's unexpected appearance? The Silver Sister had humbled Utrilo in front of both Kayl and Bryn; he would find some way of taking it out on them after Corrana left. Kayl shook her head and went inside.

To her surprise, Corrana had not left the serving room. She was sitting on a bench beside the empty hearth, watching Bryn inspect the broken bench-leg. Kayl joined them, nodding a greeting to the Wyrd. Corrana looked up. "Welcome, innkeeper."

"Your Virtue," Kayl responded warily. Corrana did not answer immediately, so Kayl turned to Bryn. "How bad is it?"

"Well, the one leg will have to be replaced, but you knew that already," Bryn said. "The other one is showing the strain, too. It hasn't cracked yet, so I could just brace it, but you'd be better off in the long run if I replaced it as well."

Kayl nodded. She had noticed nothing when she had inspected the damage earlier, but Wyrd senses could learn far more about wood than human eyes. "Replace them both," she told Bryn. The Wyrd twitched an ear in surprise and Kayl gave a twisted smile. "I'd rather have it fixed now, while I can still pay you for it, than wait for it to break after Islorran raises the taxes again."

Bryn nodded understandingly. She sat down on the floor and began pulling tools from her leather pouch. Corrana raised an eyebrow. "May I assume from that that your Prefect's man has left, and not altogether happily?"

"Exactly," Kayl said. "Though it might have been much worse without Your Virtue's assistance. I thank you for your timely help."

"My presence here gave rise to the incident," Corrana said. "The least I could do was aid you."

"Your Virtue is too kind."

"There is no need to use the formal title. I insist on proper address only when it seems . . . necessary."

Kayl thought of Utrilo and smiled in spite of herself. Bryn looked up from her carpentry and said, "If that's your rule, you'll have to resign yourself to being 'Your Virtued' for as long as you're in Mindaria."

"Perhaps you are right," Corrana said. "I must admit that I had not expected such a scene as that. Why is this Prefect Islorran so obsessed with Shee?"

Bryn sniffed. "It's not the Shee he's interested in, it's magic. He'll do anything to get his hands on a little more of it."

"He expects the Shee to give him knowledge for the asking?" Corrana said skeptically. "He could not be such a fool!"

Kayl and Bryn exchanged glances. "I don't think you understand," Kayl said. "Since Mindaria left the Estarren Alliance, the nonhuman races have not been kindly looked on. Islorran doesn't have to ask politely."

Corrana's lips tightened. "I see. I had not thought the taint would have reached here so soon."

"It's been eight or ten years since Mindaria recalled its representative to the Senate, and things weren't exactly good then," Bryn said.

"And since?"

"It's gotten worse." Bryn shrugged. "Travel restrictions, taxes, all sorts of things. That's why there are so few of us left in Mindaria."

"What?" Corrana looked startled and dismayed.

"They've gone elsewhere," Kayl said in a matter-of-fact tone. "No Shee has passed through Copeham for at least five years, and this used to be a regular stop for them. It's not as bad for Wyrds; the King of Mindaria values their woodworking too highly to allow more than minor harassments."

"You mean, it wasn't as bad," Bryn corrected. "Islorran's father, the old Prefect, was a decent man, for a human. Islorran's another matter."

"So it has reached even here," Corrana said softly. She looked at Bryn. "Why do you stay?"

Bryn gave her a long, unblinking stare. "I don't plan to," she said, and turned back to the bench-leg.

"What do you mean?" Kayl said.

"I mean that Alden, Xaya and I will be leaving Copeham within a month," Bryn said. "For good."

"Why now?"

"Because I can see what's coming, and so can every other Shee and Wyrd and Neira with eyes. Ever since Darkwater, none of us have had any illusions about what this sort of thing leads to."

Kayl shuddered. The memory of the Darkwater Massacre was over forty years old, but its horror still lingered. Nearly a thousand Wyrds, Shee and Neira had been killed by Prince Fazendin, tortured to death in a desperate attempt to extract magical secrets they did not possess. The Estarren Alliance, led by Kith Alunel, had retaliated, razing Fazendin's home, sowing his fields with salt, and leaving the Prince himself stretched on his own rack for the crows to feast on. "Even Islorran wouldn't condone a slaughter!" Kayl objected.

"He won't get the chance," Bryn replied, calmly measuring the disassembled bench-legs and marking the results down on a small wax tablet. "By the time he thinks of it, we'll all be gone. I'd have left long ago, but Xaya wasn't old enough to travel."

"Where will you go?" Corrana asked. "Bridden?"

"No, not Bridden, or even Kith Alunel. Not that Kith Alunel isn't well disposed toward Wyrds now, but who can say how long that will last? North of the Thar lands, maybe. I hear the ice is moving back."

"Is there anything you'll need?" Kayl said.

"Prompt payment on this job," Bryn said, flashing pointed teeth in a grin. "The rest we'll manage ourselves. We've been preparing for a long time."

Kayl nodded. "Good luck to you, then, whenever you go." There was nothing else to say. She would miss the furry little Wyrd, and Copeham would miss her fine touch with carpentry, but she could not deny the wisdom in Bryn's choice. Mindaria was going the way of most of the non-Alliance countries, and nonhumans were better off elsewhere. Kayl felt a sudden, fierce anger; these were her friends being driven from their homes!

The anger faded into grim frustration. There was nothing she could do about it, nothing at all. Islorran was not the only nobleman more interested in sorcery than in justice; half the

Mindaran court was greedy for knowledge of magic. Remembrance of the punishment inflicted on Prince Fazendin might keep them from overt measures, so long as the Estarran Alliance remained strong. It would not keep them from whatever threats they thought they could get away with. And the more Shee and Wyrds withdrew from Mindaria, the worse the situation grew for those who remained behind.

Kayl felt like smashing something, preferably Islorran's head. Even that would do no good; Islorran's son was as bad or worse than his father. With difficulty, Kayl reined in her anger and frustration and bent to help Bryn pick up her tools.

CHAPTER

FIVE

Bryn left with her measurements and the pieces of the bench, promising to return and finish the repairs before evening. Kayl was grateful; if the crowd was as large as it had been the previous night, she would need every bench and chair in the inn. Kayl shut the door behind the Wyrd and turned to find Corrana still watching from her seat beside the hearth. "Is there anything I can do for you, Your Virtue?"

"We must talk," Corrana said. She was frowning into the distance as she spoke.

What now, Kayl wondered. She crossed back to the hearth-side and seated herself. "I am at your service."

"I hope so," Corrana murmured. Her eyes came back to Kayl's face. "I shall not be staying the full week, as we arranged."

"It is kind of you to tell me, but—"

"Word that an Elder Sister is in Copeham will spread, and I wish to be gone before the Magicseekers hear of my presence." Corrana paused. "I fear they will do so soon."

Kayl nodded. The members of the Circle of Silence, more commonly known as the Magicseekers, were known to be devious and unscrupulous; some even thought that they had been the true instigators of the Darkwater Massacre. The Sisterhood of Stars opposed them openly, and had been instrumental in forcing them out of Kith Alunel entirely some twenty years ago. The Magicseekers could do little to harm the

Sisterhood itself, but they could make things extremely unpleasant for any individual Sister who happened to fall into their hands. Suddenly Kayl understood the presence of the warding spell she had found guarding Corrana's door the night before.

"What does this have to do with me and my inn?" Kayl asked uneasily.

"Have I said it has to do with you?"

"People normally don't bother to tell innkeepers the reasons for their comings and goings," Kayl pointed out. "So I ask again—what has this to do with me? And no more games, lady."

Corrana's head dipped in assent. "Very well. I apologize. I had hoped to give you more time, but your Prefect's man forced my hand."

"Did he?" Kayl said skeptically. "Your help was welcome, but hardly necessary. I have managed Utrilo before."

"Not under such circumstances as these. And I had reasons of my own for wishing you to remain."

"What do you mean?" Kayl demanded.

"I think you must already know," Corrana said. "I seek a woman, born among the Thar and raised from early childhood by the Sisterhood. She left our order some fifteen years ago, after a disagreement with the Elder Mothers. We have need of her knowledge and her skill. Her name was Kayl Larrinar, and I think you are she."

Kayl closed her eyes briefly, then opened them again. "I am."

Corrana let out her breath in a long, quiet sigh of relief. "We have need of you, Sister."

"Why?" Kayl was startled by the cold hardness of her own voice.

"I think you can guess."

"No games, lady!" Kayl slammed a hand down on the tabletop with enough force to numb her fingers. "What do you want of me?"

"Your help. The Elder Mothers think someone is tampering with the Twisted Tower."

Kayl's face stiffened. "Impossible!"

"So the Elder Mothers thought. But there is a shadow on the stars, and they believe the Tower is its origin."

"And you want me to help you find out who is doing things,

what they're doing, and how to stop them, because I was one of the ones who went to the Tower in the first place."

"I think that is a fair summary, though it is not as I would have put it."

The calm in Corrana's voice angered Kayl, and she said sharply, "You're forgetting something, Corrana. I'm not one of the Sisters anymore. I'm not even a warrior anymore. I'm an innkeeper and a mother with two children to raise."

"And if you refuse me, and our efforts fail, what then? Whatever is happening at the Tower, it can be nothing good."

"It's no concern of mine."

"Is it not? The rot that is creeping through the lands of the Alliance is spreading. Will you go to your grave knowing that you could have tried to stop it, and did not?" Corrana's voice tolled like a death knell, and her eyes were darker than a moonless sky at midnight. "Is that the example you would give your children? Is that the world you would bequeath them?"

Kayl stiffened. "The decision isn't that straightforward."

"We are asking for very little."

"You're asking for my life! It would take months for me to get to the Windhome Mountains and back. By then there'd be nothing here to return to. Utrilo Levoil would be knocking at the door with a writ of confiscation before I was gone two days. And what would happen to Mark and Dara then?"

"The protection of the Sisterhood—"

"Outside the borders of the Estarren Alliance? You're leaving four days sooner than you'd planned because you aren't sure you can protect yourself from the Magicseekers. I'd trust the Sisterhood to take care of two children, but how are you going to protect a whole inn?"

"We'll build you a new one, if we must. We *need* you, Kayl."

"The Sisterhood has plenty of swordswomen," Kayl pointed out. She was sure that Corrana had not yet told her everything, though she could not have given the reasons behind her certainty.

"But none better suited to the task." Corrana shook her head. "I feared that you would react unfavorably if I put my question too soon. I had intended to go more slowly, but that choice is no longer mine. I must leave tomorrow. Until then, think on what I have said. Your decision—"

"Mother!" Mark's shout came clearly through the unshuttered window. "I got the things you wanted. Did Bryn come yet?" The door opened and he came plunging into the room, covered with dust and laden with packages. "She said she'd be—" He stopped short as he caught sight of Corrana in her silver robes, and his eyes widened.

"In a minute, Mark," Kayl said. She looked at Corrana. "Is there anything else, Your Virtue?" she said politely. "I have work to do."

"Go, then." Corrana rose, her face expressionless. Her eyes raked Kayl up and down. "But I shall ask for your answer tomorrow."

Mark looked uncertainly from Corrana's back to Kayl's set face as Corrana swept out of the serving room. "Is she really a star-sister?" he said tentatively.

"Yes."

"Why didn't she tell us that when she got here?" he said in an injured tone.

"Possibly because she didn't want to be pestered by small boys with more curiosity than sense."

"I wouldn't!" Mark said indignantly. He looked speculatively up the stairs. "What did she mean, about your answer?" he asked after a moment.

Kayl hesitated. "It's a bit complicated," she said at last. "I'll explain it to you and Dara later."

Mark stared, and his expression held a ghost of the one he had worn when he came charging into the inn just after Corrana's dramatic arrival. "Something's wrong, isn't it?" he blurted. "And it's *her* fault."

"Not exactly," Kayl said. She felt a wave of fierce protectiveness; whatever else might happen, she would *not* let it harm the children. She looked at Mark's face and sought refuge in a half-truth that would be reassuring because of its familiarity. "Utrilo Levoil was here a little while ago."

"Oh, him," Mark said. His worried expression changed to one of revulsion. "Why does he have to bother us so much?"

"It's his job, dear," Kayl said. "And it's all right for you to use that tone when you speak of him to me, but if I catch you doing it anywhere else you'll get a month of heavy chores."

"I wouldn't do that," Mark said, and grinned suddenly. "Well, not much, anyway."

Kayl shook her head, smiling in spite of herself. "Go wash

the dust off those vegetables. And next time you go to market, try not to bring half the road back along with the vegetables.''

Mark nodded and vanished into the kitchen. Kayl stared after him for a moment, smiling. Then her eyes turned to the stairs, as if irresistibly drawn, and her smile faded. She sank down heavily on the nearest bench and leaned her head into her hands.

They had come for her, after all this time. They had come for her, and they wanted her to go back. Kayl swallowed. The choice she had dreaded, avoided, walled out of her life, was being forced on her, and she was not ready to face it.

How could she leave everything she had worked so hard to build, the accomplishments that had cost so much? How could she stay knowing that the things she thought she had lost forever were still awaiting her return? How could she go back, after such a bitter, painful parting? How could she refuse to go, when old friendships and old loyalties called to her so strongly?

She raised her head. The familiar room had gone suddenly strange and distant, and she shivered. Then, slowly, she rose. It was not much longer before her dinner customers would begin arriving, and there was still a great deal to do. Once again, she shoved her present worries to the back of her mind and mechanically set about readying the inn for business.

Late in the afternoon, it began to rain. The weather did nothing to keep the people of Copeham away from the inn. On the contrary, tenant farmers and laborers who would otherwise have been at work in their fields or Islorran's appeared to join in the throng. Kayl kindled a small fire in the serving room, though normally the hearth was used only in winter, and hung her customers' cloaks around it to dry.

Bryn arrived with the bench-legs just ahead of the rush. She finished the repair work quickly and stayed for a mug of beer. If she noticed Kayl's irritability, she did not show it. But then, Bryn always had known when to be tactful.

Kayl found herself wishing for a similar inscrutability. Though she did her best to appear untroubled, she was well aware that she was not entirely successful. Her customers might laugh and tease as usual, but Mark and Dara tiptoed around her as though she were made of glass. With the clear perception of children, they knew that something had disturbed her deeply. Jirod, too, watched her more closely than she liked.

Their scrutiny only added to her irritation, and again she was almost glad when Corrana made her appearance in the serving room. The sorceress had apparently decided to abandon pretense. She wore the full dress robes of the Sisterhood, the same ones she had worn for her confrontation with Utrilo that afternoon. There was a murmur of respectful admiration from the diners, and a place appeared almost magically at the end of one of the tables. Corrana bowed, a glint of amusement in her eyes, and made her way to it.

Kayl sent Dara with Corrana's meal; she was not going to serve Corrana herself if she could help it. Corrana glanced once in Kayl's direction when Dara set the stew in front of her. Kayl took a deep breath and returned to her duties. She was busy with three beer mugs when Dara touched her shoulder. "Somebody new just came in," she said when Kayl turned.

Kayl glanced toward the door. A tall man in a wet, travel-worn cloak and hat stood quietly just inside. The shadow of the dripping hat brim hid his face, but he was no man of Copeham. Kayl frowned slightly; he seemed familiar nonetheless. She handed Dara the mugs and went to greet him.

"Gracious welcome to you, sir," she said as she came up to him. "How may I serve you?"

"I'm looking for the innkeeper," the man said in a pleasant baritone that still held traces of a Varnan accent. He removed his hat as he spoke, shaking it carefully to avoid spattering any of the nearby diners. His hair was brown, cut neatly just below the ears, and he wore no beard. His smile was tired, and the planes of his face were sharper than they should have been.

Kayl's eyes narrowed, then widened as a fifteen-year-old memory surfaced in her mind, and with a shock she knew him. Before she could speak, his hazel-green eyes met hers with a look that held both recognition and warning. "I'm the innkeeper," Kayl said, swallowing the warmer welcome she had intended. Glyndon shal Morag had been Kevran's friend, and her own. If he wanted to pretend to be a stranger, she would trust him—at least long enough to hear his explanation. "Are you looking for a room?"

"I am, if you have one."

"I do. Five pence the night, seven if you want an evening meal."

"Done. I'd be grateful if you would show me the room now; I'll be down for the meal as soon as I'm dry enough not to dissolve your benches."

"Very good. This way." Kayl signaled Mark and Dara to cover the serving room, then led the new guest up the stairs. As soon as they were out of sight and hearing of the room, Kayl turned. "It's good to see you again, Glyndon. What brings you to Copeham? And why the playacting?"

"I thought the playacting might be necessary. As to why I'm here . . ." His eyes dropped. "I . . . saw something that disturbed me."

Kayl reached out in sympathy, then let her hand drop before the gesture was complete. "The visions didn't leave you, then."

"No." His tone was restrained, but his eyes seemed suddenly haunted.

"No one could . . . do anything?"

Glyndon's lips twisted. "My Varnan compatriots weren't anxious to assist a second-rate wizard. Particularly a renegade second-rate wizard. And off Varna . . ." He shrugged. "It's been two hundred years since the Wizard's War, and you still can't find anyone who'll trust a Varnan, much less help one. I tried, of course."

"I'm sorry."

The bitter, haunted look gave way to a gleam of wry amusement. "No sorrier than I, believe me." He hesitated. "Where's Kevran? Away?"

Kayl found to her surprise that the old wound could still be painfully fresh. "Kevran died five years ago, Glyndon. I would have sent word, if I'd thought it would reach you."

Glyndon's shoulders sagged in a curious mixture of relief and hurt and shame. "I see." There was a moment's silence. "I'm sorry. If I'd known, I'd have come sooner."

"I know." Kayl paused. "I don't suppose you'd care to explain a little more just why you're here?"

"Tomorrow, if you'll indulge me. I'm tired, and I don't think it's quite that urgent."

Kayl looked at him, considering. Something in his tone rang

false, but it was plain that he did not wish to begin a discussion now, and she had customers waiting below. "All right. I can see you're in need of rest. But if you don't have a good explanation ready for me tomorrow morning, you'll wish you'd gone on to the inn in Cedarwell, even if their beds have fleas."

"I won't disappoint you," Glyndon promised solemnly.

"You'd better not," Kayl said, grinning. "Will this room do?"

Glyndon did not so much as glance inside. "Yes."

"Then I'll leave you to your drying off."

"Could you bring that meal you mentioned up here?" Glyndon said with a touch of diffidence.

Kayl looked up in surprise that swiftly changed to understanding. "So you saw Corrana."

"If she's the vision in Sisterhood silver, yes. I'd rather not cross swords with one of them."

"I understand." The Sisterhood had a long-standing antipathy toward Varnans, dating back to its misty beginnings in the confusion following the Wars of Binding. "I'll send Mark up with something in a few minutes."

"Mark . . . the boy downstairs? Your son?"

"Yes, and the girl is my daughter, Dara." Kayl did not even try to keep the pride out of her voice.

Glyndon shook his head. "Somehow, I find it hard to imagine you with children, though I've known of them for years."

"Kevran sent you word?" Kayl said, surprised. "I didn't think he knew where to find you, either!"

"I didn't hear of them from Kevran," Glyndon said shortly, and belatedly Kayl remembered his unwanted visions.

"I'm sorry, Glyndon. I wasn't thinking."

He waved her apology away. "I should know better than to be so touchy. I've had long enough to grow accustomed to it." But his smile was forced.

"I hope you're accustomed to children," Kayl said, deliberately turning the conversation. "They'll be after you constantly as soon as they find out you knew Kevran."

"Kayl—" Glyndon hesitated. "Do a favor for me."

"Of course. What?"

"Don't tell Mark or Dara who I am, or even that we know each other, until we've had a chance to talk."

"If you insist," Kayl said. His request surprised and worried her; it was unlike him, and it made his presence seem as ominous as Corrana's.

"I . . . don't want anything to slip out in front of that starsister you have downstairs."

Kayl snorted to hide her concern. "You never could lie to me, Glyndon, and there's no need to. I won't say anything to them until we've talked. But that explanation of yours had better be very, very good."

Glyndon smiled. "Thank you."

"You're welcome." She turned to go.

"Kayl."

She gave an inquiring look back over her shoulder. Glyndon stood framed in the doorway, watching her.

"It's good to see you again," he said, and smiled. "You haven't changed at all."

Kayl made her lips return his smile, and left.

CHAPTER

SIX

Kayl returned to the serving room and resumed her work as calmly as she could manage. She could feel Corrana's eyes on her, and Jirod's, and her children's, but she had no reassurance for any of them. She could only hope that they would think her distraction a continuation of her earlier moodiness, and not connect it with Glyndon's arrival.

Fortunately, the serving room was busier than ever. Corrana tried several times to attract Kayl's attention, which annoyed Kayl. Couldn't the woman see that Kayl had no time now for involved conversations and cryptic hints? Kayl turned away and pretended not to see.

A few minutes later, she felt a touch at her elbow. She turned and found Corrana watching her with unfathomable black eyes. "I would speak with you," the sorceress said.

"Very well, Your Virtue." Kayl handed the bowl of stew she was carrying to a young farm laborer, collected his coppers, and turned. "What is it?"

"Your new customer, the man who entered a few minutes ago. Who is he?"

Kayl shrugged, hiding a sudden rush of fear for Glyndon. "He hasn't given me a name for the guest-board yet."

"I heard him say he would come back for his meal, but he has not appeared."

"He changed his mind after he had to shove his way

through this crowd, and decided to eat in his room."

Corrana's brows arched. "He is so wellborn? He did not look it."

Kayl shrugged again. "He pays well, whatever his birth. And he seems an unlikely person to attract your attention, lady."

"Perhaps." Corrana seemed to be speaking more to herself than to Kayl. "Yes, you may be right. I will not keep you longer."

Kayl nodded and returned to her work. A few minutes later, she saw Corrana making her way up the stairs. She tensed slightly, wondering whether the woman would knock on doors until she found Glyndon's room, and what would happen if she did.

No disturbance occurred, and gradually Kayl relaxed. The rest of the evening passed in a dull blur of faces and mugs and the damp, smokey smell of the cloaks hanging around the fire. Corrana's appearance in the robes of the Sisterhood had given the villagers something new to speculate on, and they stayed even later than they had the previous evening.

Finally the last of the customers left. Kayl sent Mark and Dara off to bed at once; she had no intention of suffering through another day like this, and if they didn't get enough sleep they'd be arguing again as soon as they awoke. Then she collapsed onto a bench with a huff of relief.

"Kayl."

She jerked at the sound of the quiet voice, and almost slid off the bench. Turning, she peered into the shadowed corners of the serving room. "Who's there?" she said sharply.

"Me." Jirod's form appeared beside the black hole that was the doorway to the kitchen. "I'm sorry I startled you."

"What are you still doing here?" Kayl said, only a little less sharply than before.

"I wanted to talk to you."

"You might have asked earlier."

Jirod returned her gaze steadily. "If I had, you'd have said you were too busy or too tired. Wouldn't you?"

"Probably," Kayl said, and sighed.

"She wouldn't have been lying, either," said a voice from one of the shadowed corners. Kayl turned, startled, to see Bryn strolling toward her.

"What is this, a plot?" Kayl said, half seriously.

Jirod gave Bryn an annoyed look and turned to Kayl. "May I sit down?" he said, ignoring the Wyrd woman.

Kayl nodded. Jirod came around the tables and folded himself onto the other end of the bench. Bryn took the seat across from Kayl without asking, and Jirod gave her another look. "Well?" Kayl said. "What is it?"

Jirod glanced at Bryn and hesitated, then said carefully, "I heard Utrilo was here again this afternoon."

"He was here, all right," Bryn said before Kayl could reply. "Throwing his weight around as usual—all of it. What's that got to do with anything?"

"I was worried about Kayl," Jirod said with a cold dignity that betrayed his embarrassment at having to say it aloud, in front of Bryn.

"I appreciate it, Jirod, but you can see there's nothing to worry about," Kayl said. Silently, she blessed Bryn for distracting Jirod long enough for Kayl to see the situation in perspective. Otherwise, she would have snapped his head off.

"I—" Jirod stopped short, and glanced at Bryn yet again. "I'll come see you tomorrow, Kayl, if that's all right?"

"You're always welcome, Jirod," Kayl said sincerely.

Jirod nodded farewell, a little stiffly, Kayl thought, and left. As the inn's door closed behind him, Bryn shook her head. "I don't think he likes me," she said mournfully.

Kayl laughed. "Do you blame him? You upset all his plans for a quiet tryst."

"I'll call him back, if you like," Bryn offered, showing her pointed teeth in a wicked grin.

"I don't think he'd come."

"You're very patient with him," Bryn said. "Or is it just my viewpoint that makes him seem overprotective?"

"No, he's just as bad as you think he is," Kayl said, and sighed. "I'm glad you were here; I'd have lost my temper otherwise, and Jirod didn't do anything to deserve that."

"Long day?"

"Dara and Mark have been running me ragged, Utrilo Levoil was looking for an excuse to fine the inn, and people keep asking questions about Corrana that I don't have answers for. What do you think?"

Bryn nodded sympathetically. "I think you should get some

sleep. I'll see you tomorrow, or the day after."

Kayl nodded. She sat and watched the Wyrd leave. She didn't feel tired, but she needed to be alone, to think. Too many pieces of her past had come hurtling back into her life too quickly. Corrana's appearance had dealt a major blow to a mental wall already eroded by time and the monotony of life in Copeham; Glyndon's arrival had smashed it into jagged fragments. Kayl stared into the dying fire and let the memories wash over her.

The initiation court was dark and silent. The pool at its center reflected the pale starlight of a moonless night. Kayl stood beside the glimmering water, shivering slightly with anticipation. This night would determine the course of her future training, and her place among the Sisterhood.

In the covered walkway that ran around the edges of the court, the Elder Mothers were gathering. Kayl could hear the faint rustling of the shapeless black cloaks they wore over their silver robes. The first voice sent a shock of surprise down her spine, though she had thought she was expecting it. "Who are you, that waits in the Court of Stars?"

"I am Kayl Larrinar, Your Serenity," Kayl said, and her adolescent voice cracked slightly.

"What do you ask of us?" came another voice, disembodied by darkness.

"I ask a place among the Sisterhood of Stars."

"Then demonstrate for us your knowledge. Who are the men of the raven?"

"The Shanhar, who came out of Kith Alunel and who live now in the Mountains of Morravik by the Melyranne Sea." Kayl was relieved that the first question had been an easy one.

"Describe the olskla plant, and explain its uses."

"It is a small plant, dark green, with—with white flowers. A tincture made from the root brings down fevers, if the roots are harvested before the plant flowers."

"Olskla flowers are gold in color, and you neglected to mention that the plant blooms but once in every hundred years."

Kay felt herself flushing in the darkness. "Yes, Your Serenity." And the testing went on.

The questions came more and more rapidly, jumping from history to healing to cookery to sword-skill to magic, without apparent pattern or reason. Kayl answered as well as she could, hoping that her weakness in esoteric lore would be more than covered by her undeniable mastery of more practical knowledge.

The examination ended at last. A rustle ran around the edges of the court, and a voice from in front of her said, "You have satisfied the assembled Elders of the Sisterhood. Look up, and take whatever the stars bestow."

Wondering, Kayl tilted her head back. At first she saw only the stars; then, high above her head, a patch of sky began to glow silver. As it grew brighter, shapes flickered within the light—the silver eight-pointed star of the sorceress, the branching tree of the healer, the bright, slender blade of the warrior, and the broken chain of the demon-friend. The glow sank toward her. Kayl held her breath, willing the sword to be the final shape.

The light grew brighter still, and then something swished to earth in front of her with a blinding flash of brilliance. Kayl had to close her eyes. When she opened them, a silver sword stood in front of her, driven point-first into the paving stones of the court. She reached out and took the hilt in her hand.

The sword vanished, and she was holding only a milky stone. As she stared at it, the covered walkway shimmered into view as the Elder Mothers discarded their black cloaks and lit their tiny oil lamps. Kayl felt a stir of triumph. She had done it!

Mother Dalessi was the first at Kayl's side. "Welcome, daughter," she said, and kissed Kayl's cheek. "You are truly one of us now."

"Harder! Swing that sword as if you meant it!" the drill-master shouted at the hot, sweaty group of sixteen-year-olds. "Come on, you usless children, work!"

"Bitch," muttered the girl next to Kayl as they lunged and drew back. "She enjoys this."

"Ritha ri Luethold! Extra work on the exercise tonight, two candlemarks' time. Cut left! and right! and left!"

Kayl swung the weighted sword with grim intensity, trying

to achieve the same accuracy, power, and elegance as the instructor. There was a rhythm in the strokes, and if she could just feel it clearly enough . . . The pattern started to come together, and she was so intent on it that she missed the instructor's command to turn and was nearly brained by her neighbor's next stroke. Embarrassed, she accepted the instructor's caustic reprimand without comment and resumed her place in the line.

When the lesson ended, the drillmaster called her over while the rest of the advanced class went grumbling off to the baths.

"Just what were you trying during the exercises, Larrinar?" the woman demanded.

Awkwardly, Kayl tried to explain. To her surprise, the drill master listened patiently until she finished, then said, "Why?"

Kayl took a deep breath. "Because I want to be the best."

"Do you." The instructor studied her with interest. "Well, we'll see. In the meantime, you can join the ri Luethold girl tonight for the extra work. And you'll do the same every night until you stop making mistakes in the exercise pattern. You may go."

Kayl went. "But I will be the best," she whispered to herself as she hurried after her classmates.

"Me, too," said a voice behind her.

Kayl stopped and turned, raising her sword automatically. She found herself facing a tiny, black-haired imp of a girl. Kayl recognized her in a vague sort of way; she was in a different section of Kayl's own age group. "Sorry," Kayl said, lowering her sword.

The girl grinned. "S'all right; I duck quick. What're you going to be best at?"

"I'm a sword-wearer; what do you think?" Kayl replied with a touch of annoyance. She hadn't meant to be overheard, and she was afraid she was going to be laughed at.

"There's lots of possibilities," the black-haired girl said seriously. "There's swordplay, and knife work, and barehand, and throwing, and archery, and that's not even all the fighting skills. So—which one are you going to be best at?"

"All of them," Kayl said sharply, hoping that when she had her answer the girl would go away. "Fighting and tactics and—"

The girl interrupted with a crow of delight. "I knew it! I knew you were the right one! Come on, come on, you have to meet Varevice."

She grabbed Kayl's arm and succeeded in pulling her several steps before Kayl found the presence of mind to dig in her heels. "Wait a minute! Who are you? And what do you think you're doing?"

"Didn't I tell you? I'm Barthelmy. Varevice and I are putting a Star Cluster together."

"Aren't you in the same group as I am? It'll be two years yet before we're allowed to make up our Stars!"

"There's nothing that says we can't practice now. Besides, you have to start early if you want to be the best," Barthelmy said sagely. "And we're going to be the best."

"And you want me to join? What makes you think I'm the best at anything?"

"You're not, yet. None of us are. But we're going to be."

"How can you tell?" Kayl asked, intrigued.

"Well, first you pick out the people who are good. That part's pretty easy. Then you pick out the ones who work, even though they're already good. And *then* you look for someone who really *wants* to be the best."

"Oh? And what do you want to be best at?"

Barthelmy tossed her head, sending witchlocks of black hair flying in all directions. "I'm a demon-friend," she said defiantly. "And someday I'm going to go to Varna and make them let every one of their *sklathran'sy* go free."

Kayl laughed in spite of herself. "All by yourself?"

"Of course not. I'm not *stupid*!" Barthelmy said. "That's why I need to be part of the best Star in the whole Sisterhood." She looked at Kayl anxiously. "Well? Will you at least come meet Varevice?"

Kayl hesitated, then nodded. She felt warmed by Barthelmy's interest, and it couldn't hurt to go along with her now. It would be two years before any of them were assigned to permanent Stars.

"Good!" Barthelmy said. She linked elbows with Kayl and did a little skip-kick as they started walking. "Now all we have to do is find the best healer, and we have our Star!"

●　　●　　●

Kayl sat beside the narrow window, grinning broadly and swirling the wine in her cup as she watched the others. All four of their tiny lamps were burning scented oil tonight in celebration.

"We did it!" Barthelmy crowed, raising her cup high.

"You've said that at least eight times since Mother Anaya told us we could be a Star," Varevice pointed out, but she raised her own cup to join the salute.

"Well, I haven't tired of hearing it yet," Kayl said, joining them. "Come on, Evla, you too!"

Evla rose. Her slanted green eyes narrowed in amusement as she raised her cup. "How could I not? Someone must uphold the quality of our Star Cluster, and I would not leave that task to you humans!"

Kayl laughed with the others. Evla had faultlessly imitated the aloof and occasionally superior tone adopted by many Shee when speaking with the human inhabitants of Lyra.

"To the best Star in the Sisterhood!" Barthelmy said, and drained her cup.

"To the success of two years of hard work," Varevice said with satisfaction as she followed suit.

"To the friendship that brought us together, and the work that will keep us so," Evla said softly, and sipped at her wine.

"To all of us," Kayl said. She looked at their familiar faces and felt a lump rise in her throat. "To all of you. My family." She held her cup aloft a moment more, then drained it dry.

"You've made quite a name for yourselves in the last three years," Mother Anaya said. "Congratulations."

"Thank you, Your Wisdom," Evla said for all of them.

"Normally we wouldn't ask you to go out again so soon, but this is . . . rather special." She paused. "You do have a choice."

"Special in what way?" Kayl asked. She was their strategist and warrior, as Evla was healer and Varevice sorceress.

Mother Anaya's mouth wrinkled in distaste. "For one thing, there will be several Varnans traveling with you."

"Varnans!" Barthelmy said angrily. "But—"

"I know, child, but there's no help for it," Mother Anaya said. She sighed and sat back. "There's something odd going on in the Windhome Mountains. Varna still lays claim to parts of that area; if we send a Star to investigate without their permission, we run the risk of starting a second Wizard's War.''

''What sort of goings-on require the attention of a Star so urgently?'' Varevice asked quietly.

''Magic. Something old, powerful, and very well hidden. The Elder Mothers discovered it by accident; some kind of echo effect in one of their spells.''

Varevice looked intrigued, but she had sense enough not to ask for the details and the theory of the spell immediately. Mother Anaya glanced at her sharply, then went on, ''If it's as powerful as the Elder Mothers think, I don't have to tell you what will happen if the Circle of Silence hears of it. And it wouldn't matter to them if they started another war.''

''We understand,'' Varevice said. Kayl nodded her agreement. Barthelmy scowled angrily.

Evla put a restraining hand on Barthelmy's arm. ''You know it is important,'' the healer said gently.

''Yes, but cooperating with Varnans?''

''The alternative would be worse.''

''Well . . . all right. I'll go.''

''Then you're all agreed.'' Mother Anaya looked pleased. ''I'll let Mother Dalessi know. You'll have a few days' rest before the Varnan group arrives; make the most of it.''

''How many of them will there be?'' Kayl asked.

''Three wizards, and five slaves.'' Mother Anaya's mouth wrinkled again, as if she found the word distasteful.

Barthelmy started to object again, but Kayl frowned her into silence. ''And their names?''

''They didn't give us the names of the slaves. The wizards will be Beshara al Allard, Glyndon shal Morag, and Kevran ker Rondal.''

The fire was almost out. Stiffly, Kayl rose and knelt on the stones of the inn's hearth. Her fingers traced the familiar shapes, feeling for the hidden latch. When she found it, she hesitated. Then she scowled at her own indecision and pressed the catch.

For a moment she was afraid that the mechanism had rusted or jammed during the years it had gone unused. Then, without

so much as a click, the stone in front of her dropped three
fingers' breadths into the floor and slid to one side. Kayl
leaned forward and picked up the heavy, cloth-wrapped bundle in the cavity beneath it.

The hidden cache extended under the other hearthstones,
and the bundle was a tight fit. Kayl had lost the knack of
removing it quickly; she had to work it carefully back and
forth until she found the angle that allowed her to lift it free.
She set it gently on the hearth in front of her, and hesitated
once more. Then she reached out and turned back the thick
folds of oilcloth.

The dying fire gleamed golden from the hilt of a sheathed
sword and sent back shining splinters from a rod of dark,
oiled wood. The rod was a slender, unmarked cylinder; Kevran had never been one for decorations. The sword was a
wicked-looking rapier with a hilt made of silvery metal. The
hilt was inlaid with an eight-pointed star, with a milky stone at
its center.

Kayl reached out and took the hilt of the rapier in her hand.
It felt cool and familiar, and at the same time a little strange,
like a half-forgotten dream. She drew the blade and stood,
hefting it. Then she swung it in a hard, flat arc.

The air sang softly as the sword cut through it, then was
silent. Slowly, Kayl lowered the sword. She could feel the
unaccustomed weight pulling at her muscles. Too much of
that and she'd be sore tomorrow. The hilt pressed against her
hand in all the wrong places; her calluses came from brooms
and buckets now, not weapons.

It was foolish to think she might go back. Swordplay was a
game for younger women. Kayl was thirty-six; even if she had
kept in training, she would be starting to lose her edge. Experience could compensate for slowing reflexes and muscles
that tired more easily, but her experience was nearly fifteen
years in the past.

And even if she could harden her muscles and hone her
reflexes once more, what could she do with Mark and Dara
while she trained—and afterward? The life of a wandering
warrior was hardly suitable for raising children. The Sisterhood would help, if she went back to them, but they would not
be able to do anything about the separations that would be
necessary when she had to go to Toltan or Rathane.

Kayl stared down at the sword. Then, even more slowly than before, she stooped and replaced it in the oilcloth bundle. Carefully, she set the bundle back into its hiding place beneath the hearth. Her fingers touched the latch, and the stone slid smoothly back into place. She stood and banked the fire with mechanical precision, then left the room without finishing the clearing up.

CHAPTER
SEVEN

Kayl woke at dawn next day; her usual habits were reasserting themselves. A steady, drenching rain still fell outside her window. As she dressed in the semidarkness, Kayl thought of the mud and groaned. Mark was sure to drag it all over the inn if she didn't watch him closely.

She finished dressing and went out into the serving room. The unwashed bowls and mugs reproached her with their silent presence. Kayl looked at them with resentment. Even an innkeeper ought to be allowed a few moments of self-indulgence now and then! Two of the mugs clacked together as she scooped them angrily off of one of the tables. Kayl blinked and shook herself. She was behaving as badly as Mark, sulking because the world would not turn to her liking. She set the mugs down more carefully and went on with her work.

The familiar tasks were oddly comforting. Kayl did them like a sleepwalker performing a ritual: light the fire, draw the water, open the shutters, sweep the floor. She did the children's chores as well as her own. Mark and Dara were tired after two busy nights in a row; let them sleep for now.

The children emerged at last, just as two of the inn's guests were leaving. Kayl collected her money and saw the guests off before turning back to Mark and Dara. Dara was frowning after the departing guests and chewing her lower lip. "Something wrong?" Kayl asked.

"Nnnnno. It's just that we've only got one room full now.

And that's not enough; I heard you tell Bryn so once."

"Two rooms," Kayl corrected. "You've forgotten the man who arrived last night." She caught herself just in time to avoid giving Glyndon's name, and wondered again why he had asked for such secrecy.

"Oh." Dara's expression lightened. "That's all right, then. Where's breakfast?"

"Waiting for you in the kitchen. I've done most of your early chores, so you two can go right in and get started."

"Done the chores?" Mark said, staring in bewildered surprise. "But—"

Dara dug her elbow into his ribs. When he turned to glare at her, she gave him a significant look. "Thanks, Mother," she said. "Come on, Mark."

"Thanks," Mark echoed, and followed her.

Kayl watched them go, wondering what they'd been plotting this time. They ought to go to Currin's for lessons today, and for once she wouldn't have to worry about how to pay him. After two busy evenings, she had a pleasant surplus of coins. She frowned, wishing she could afford more than two afternoons of lessons each week. Perhaps if her luck held, and the inn stayed busy until people started heading for the Fall Fairs . . .

She heard a sound on the stair and looked up. It was Corrana, dressed once more in her black traveling robes. Kayl cleared her throat, knowing what was coming. "May I help you, Your Virtue?"

"I have hope of it. I have come for your decision."

"I still don't see why you want me," Kayl temporized.

"Because you have been to the Twisted Tower," Corrana said. "And because you were one of the best."

The unconscious echo of Barthelmy's long-ago dream struck Kayl like a blow. "We failed at the Tower," she said harshly. "And I'm not one of the best anymore, not after fifteen years without even practicing. You'll have to look elsewhere, Your Virtue; I have no reason to go back to the Tower."

Corrana sighed. "Will you at least come with me to Kith Alunel and hear the Elder Mothers' reasons for wanting you to return to the Twisted Tower?"

"Kayl, don't do it."

Kayl turned her head, startled, to find Glyndon shal Morag

standing on the stairs. "Glyndon, what—"

"Don't go back," Glyndon repeated. His face was pale, and he looked unwell. "Anywhere else, but not the Tower."

"A Varnan!" Corrana said with loathing.

"A guest at this inn," Kayl corrected. She was surprised that Corrana had placed Glyndon's accent so quickly, but her main emotion was irritation. She had no wish to be caught in a confrontation between Corrana and Glyndon.

Corrana ignored her words. "So this is why you resist my appeal! I should have guessed. Your husband was also a Varnan, was he not?"

"Get out of here," Kayl said in a voice of deadly calm. "Take your magic and your memories and go. And tell the Elder Mothers not to send anyone else. I'm staying here."

"No!" Glyndon half fell the rest of the way down the stairs. "You musn't stay, either." He staggered to the nearest table, sank onto a bench, and hid his face in his hands.

Corrana's expression changed to surprise, then wariness. When Glyndon did not move or look up, she leaned forward. "Don't touch him!" Kayl said sharply as the sorceress reached for Glyndon.

"I mean no harm," Corrana said coldly. "I only wish to know if he is unwell, as he seems."

"He is," Kayl said grimly. "Don't touch him! You'll only make it worse."

Corrana's eyes narrowed, but she let her hand drop. "You seem to know much of this 'guest.' "

Kayl rose without replying and fetched a mug of wine. She set it on the table a handspan from Glyndon's elbow and watched the Varnan carefully until he gave a deep, shuddering sigh. Then she said, "Glyndon. Drink."

Glyndon lowered his hands and reached for the mug. He half drained it in three swallows. When he set it down, he still looked tired and worn, but some of the color had returned to his face. "Thank you," he said.

"I'm more interested in an explanation than in thanks," Kayl said. "Particularly since you chose your time for this so carefully."

"What?" Glyndon looked around. When he saw Corrana his shoulders sagged. "So. That much was real."

"Who are you?" Corrana demanded.

"My name is Glyndon shal Morag."

Corrana nodded. "You were one of the three Varnan wizards who went to the Windhome Mountains with the First Star of Kith Alunel," she stated.

"Yes."

"I see." Corrana glanced at Kayl. "Now I understand more fully your willingness to take his advice."

"You know nothing of the matter," Kayl said.

"I know enough to apologize to you both for my hasty words." Corrana looked from Kayl to Glyndon and went on with difficulty. "I have no love for Varnans, but I should not have spoken as I did. I am sorry."

Glyndon nodded tiredly. "After fifteen years away from Varna, I've heard far worse than anything you said. For myself, consider it forgotten."

Corrana dipped her head in acknowledgement, but her eyes stayed fixed on Kay. "And you, sister?"

"I accept your apology as well," Kayl said in a tight voice. "But if you are wise, you will not speak of my husband in that tone again." Corrana nodded without speaking, and Kayl went on: "Now, I wish to speak with Glyndon. Alone."

"No," Corrana said calmly. "Not if it has bearing on my errand here."

"You presume a good deal, Your Virtue."

"I think not. Your friend overheard enough of our conversation to interrupt with some precision. I think that in simple justice I should hear his reasons."

Kayl heard the determination in Corrana's voice. She pressed her lips together, knowing that she could not keep the sorceress from staying. Glyndon might try, but that would precipitate just the confrontation Kayl had hoped to avoid. "This is a personal matter," she said at last.

Corrana raised an eyebrow. "Is it?" she said, looking pointedly at Glyndon.

Glyndon shook his head. "No. Still, I think Kayl's right. You presume a good deal."

"How nice that you agree," Corrana said politely. She settled herself more comfortably on the bench and raised one hand to toy with the tiny silver skull at her throat.

The corner of Glyndon's mouth quirked and he turned to Kayl with a look of mischievous amusement. Kayl knew that look well. The last time she'd seen it was just before the incident with the Bridden army officer, the mug of ale, and the dead mouse. Before Glyndon could say anything, Kayl said, "That's enough, both of you."

The two magicians looked at her in surprise and Kayl went on: "I listen to enough of Mark and Dara's squabbling; I don't want to listen to you as well. If you won't talk like reasonable people, I have work to do."

There was a moment's silence. Kayl started to rise. Glyndon and Corrana looked at each other, and Glyndon sighed. "All right, Kayl."

Kayl turned to Corrana. The sorceress gave a small, humorless smile. "I will respect the peace of your inn. But I will not leave until I hear what this Varnan has to tell you."

"I see. I'm afraid we'll have to wait until tomorrow to talk, Glyndon."

"No! We may not have that much time."

"You weren't in such a hurry last night."

"That was last night."

Kayl sighed. "Then will it cause any harm to either of us if Corrana listens? Not that I like the idea much, but we don't seem to have a choice."

Glyndon's eyes went blank; then he shook himself. "No," he said reluctantly. "It will cause no harm."

Kayl let herself back down onto the bench. "Then explain."

"I was 'seeing' things."

Corrana looked at Glyndon, startled. Kayl made an exasperated noise. "I could tell that much, even if I haven't watched you go through it in years. What were you seeing?"

"The Tower," Glyndon said. He looked at her with sudden grim intensity. "You mustn't go back there, Kayl. The thing inside will escape."

A shadowy memory surfaced in Kayl's mind, of standing in a high-ceilinged room, slashing uselessly at a dripping, pulsing curtain of dull blackness that ate away her sword as it oozed closer. She blinked and concentrated, trying to make the memory clearer. The picture slid away and was replaced by a more vivid recollection, of herself and Kevran dragging Glyndon down the last few stairs and through the crooked arch of the tower door, just ahead of a voracious black wave that splattered on the ancient protective spells guarding the door. Kayl felt gooseflesh rise along her back. "You're sure it will get out?"

Glyndon hesitated, then slowly shook his head. "Not certain. Almost certain."

"What is this indecision?" Corrana demanded. "A born Seer sees truly or not at all."

"But I was not born a Seer," Glyndon said. "I see many visions. Some I know are true, others false, but most of what I 'see' is simply . . . possible."

"I have never heard of such a gift," Corrana said doubtfully.

Glyndon's smile was bitter. "More of a nightmare than a gift, I think."

Corrana waved away his objection. "It is the uncertainty you claim that interests me, not the name you give this sight of yours."

"The uncertainty is there. Sometimes what I 'see' occurs; sometimes it does not. And sometimes it can be avoided." Glyndon looked at Kayl. "That is why I've not come here for so long, and why I stopped sending you word."

"What do you mean?" Kayl asked.

"I was avoiding one of my visions," Glyndon said, and looked away. Kayl waited for some further explanation, but when Glyndon turned back all he said was, "It is not the first time I have succeeded in doing so. I know from experience that what I 'see' is not always true."

Kayl's eyes narrowed but she stopped herself before she asked more about the nature of the vision he had been avoiding. Instead she said, "Then what did you see that brought you here in spite of it?"

"Yourself, on the steps of that tower we found, with the edge of the black thing drawing nearer. And through the door I could see it outside the tower, spreading like a black storm."

"But it is not certain to happen," Corrana said quickly. "You yourself said as much."

Kayl gave the sorceress a cold look. "No one who has seen that black thing would take a chance of letting it escape. Particularly since three Varnan wizards and the best Star in the Sisterhood couldn't figure out what kept it in there in the first place."

Corrana looked suddenly thoughtful. Kayl waited a moment, then turned back to Glyndon and said, "And you don't want me to stay here, either? Why?"

Glyndon hesitated, then said bluntly, "Because if you stay, you'll be killed. Unpleasantly."

Kayl swallowed. Glyndon's voice was a flat statement of fact; the only way of avoiding this vision would be to leave Copeham. "And the children?" she said at last.

Glyndon closed his eyes. "Also will die."

His voice shook slightly, and Kayl wondered how bad the vision had been. She decided not to ask. "Who?" she said instead.

"No one I've ever seen outside a vision. There were at least seven of them, and they all had eagles on their helmets."

Corrana's eyes went wide. "Magicseekers!"

Kayl shook her head. "It doesn't make sense, Glyndon! What would the Magicseekers want with an innkeeper?"

"With an ordinary innkeeper, perhaps nothing," Corrana said before Glyndon could reply. "But you are a former member of the Sisterhood of Stars who has been visited privately by an Elder Sister. I fear it is I who have brought the Circle of Silence down upon you."

Glyndon shifted uncomfortably, but neither he nor Kayl replied. At last Kayl said, "You're sure this vision can be avoided, Glyndon?"

"I'm sure. I've been avoiding visions of the eagle-helms for years."

Kayl stared, momentarily jerked out of her own concerns. "The Magicseekers are looking for you?"

Glyndon shrugged. "I've never gotten close enough to one of them to ask."

"Even if they do not know of your part in seeking the Twisted Tower fifteen years ago, the Magicseekers would look for you," Corrana said dispassionately. "Their hatred of Varnans is greater even than their hatred of the Sisterhood."

"Then we seem to have an enemy in common."

"And the only way to avoid a slaughter is for me to leave Copeham?" Kayl asked again. Glyndon nodded, and she sighed. "If it was anyone but you, Glyndon . . . How much time do I have to set things in order?"

"I don't know," Glyndon said. "Not very much. A few days, at most. Maybe not even that."

Kayl felt numb. "Why didn't you tell me all this last night?"

"I didn't know it was so close. I thought I had at least a

couple of weeks to convince you, perhaps as long as a month. It wasn't until just now that I could tell that it's so close. You have to get out of here quickly, Kayl!"

Irritation prickled the hairs along Kayl's neck. Corrana's oblique approach had been bad enough; discovering that Glyndon, too, had intended to take his time about delivering his warning was even more annoying. "You might have said something anyway," Kayl said, her voice cool.

"I'm sorry!" Glyndon ran his left hand distractedly through his hair. "But you will go, won't you?"

The rear door of the inn banged. "Mother!" Mark's excited voice penetrated the walls of the inn with ease. "Mother, wait till you hear!"

Kayl looked at Glyndon. "I won't take chances with the children's safety," she said. She could hear the muffled sound of Dara's scolding in the kitchen, and then Mark came boiling through the door into the front room, with Dara close on his heels.

CHAPTER

EIGHT

Mark's hair dripped rainwater and his clothes were soaked, but he was still calling in excitement as he came into the front room. "Mother! You'll never—oh, excuse me." Mark added the apology automatically when he saw that Kayl was not alone. Then his eyes widened as he took in Corrana's black robes and Glyndon slouching over the end of the table. He looked questioningly at Kayl.

"Bar the front door, Mark," Kayl said wearily. "Then go put on something dry. And don't dawdle; I have to talk to you and Dara." She noted that her earlier fears had been justified; Mark had indeed tracked mud across the floor. She did not bother to mention it. Other things were more important now.

"Bar the door? In the middle of the *day*?" Mark looked at his mother in disbelief.

"That's what I told you."

Mark blinked, then moved slowly toward the door. He paused with his hand on the latch. "But what if the soldiers come? They won't want to stay at an inn if the door's barred when they get there."

"Soldiers?" Kayl said sharply. "What soldiers?"

"I was just going to tell you!" Mark said. "Tully saw them marching up the road from Cedarwell, six of them. He says they're from Kith Alunel, because they're wearing scaled lorica, but even Prefect Islorran's men wear that kind of armor, so it doesn't mean anything, does it? And Kith Alunel soldiers don't have wings on their helmets. So they can't—"

"Wings? Mark, did you see these men yourself?"

"No, Tully told me. I came home right away to tell you, so we could get ready for them," Mark said. "They'll be here in a little while."

"Not even a day," Glyndon murmured. His face was drawn and haggard. "I didn't even have a full day."

"These soldiers may not be the Magicseekers you saw," Kayl said, but even to herself her tone was unconvincing.

"Will you wager your life on that, innkeeper?" Corrana said. "And the lives of your children?"

"Magicseekers!" Mark said with relish. "Tully saw Magic-seekers?"

"Yes, and we have to be away from here before they arrive," Kayl said firmly. Corrana was right; this was no time to sit debating the proper course of action.

Mark stared at her, then turned and set the bar in place across the door. When he looked back at Kayl, his eyes were frightened. "Mother—"

"I'll have to explain later, Mark; there isn't time now." Kayl turned her head. "Glyndon, if there's anything in your room you need, go get it. Quickly. Dara, I want those baskets Bryn made for us last summer. You and Mark put your good clothes in the bottom, and the blanket off your bed. Then bring them to the kitchen."

Dara swallowed hard and nodded. Kayl headed for the back of the inn. When she reached her bedroom, she scooped the money box out of its hiding place and quickly transferred its contents to her pockets. Thank the stars she'd been too busy to spend much, these past few days! Kayl left the empty box lying in the middle of the floor and turned to the chest that held her clothes. It took only seconds to find what she wanted. Then she went on to the kitchen with hurried steps.

Dara arrived with the baskets at the same time as Kayl. Kayl ignored her daughter's worried questions and set to work filling the baskets. A cheese, a loaf of bread, the bag of meal, a couple of empty wineskins to fill with water later. "Get your cloak," Kayl told Dara at last. "And tell Mark to get his. We're leaving right now."

Dara nodded. Kayl went back into the front room. Corrana and Glyndon were standing beside the door; Glyndon had retrieved his staff, and Corrana had covered her dramatic black robes with a shapeless brown cloak. Kayl hesitated, then knelt by the hearthstone. If the Magicseekers searched the inn thoroughly, they would surely discover the cache. She could not leave Kevran's rod for them to find, nor her own sword. Her sword . . .

The stone slid away. Kayl heard Corrana's hiss of surprise, but she did not look up. Gently, she withdrew the bundle of oiled cloth and touched the hidden latch to close the hole. She rose and turned to find that Mark and Dara had joined the group. "Let's go."

"Where?" Mark demanded. "What is that thing? And who's he?" He jerked his head in Glyndon's direction.

Kayl paused. "We'll go to Jirod's, I think," she said, ignoring the rest of Mark's questions. "They won't know to look for us there unless someone from the village tells them, and I don't think anyone will. Come along. And cover your head; I don't want you catching a cold on top of everything else."

Mark sighed and draped a fold of his cloak over his head. Kayl nodded and picked up the largest of the baskets. Covering her own head against the rain, she led the group out the rear door of the inn and along the narrow alley behind it. As they reached the street, another problem occurred to her, and she stopped. "Dara."

"Mother?"

"I want you to go to Bryn's and warn her that at least six Magicseekers have just arrived in Copeham. Tell her we'll be at Jirod's for at least a few hours, and if she and Alden want some company for their trip north, they should look for us there. Try not to be noticed, and don't tell anyone else where we've gone. Then come straight to Jirod's. Have you got all that?"

Dara nodded. "Yes, Mother." She looked worried, and more than a little frightened. Kayl wanted desperately to be able to give reassuring answers to all the unasked questions she could see in her daughter's expression, but there was no time. They had stood too long on the street already.

"It'll be all right, dear," Kayl said. "Go on!" She tried to smile as she took Dara's basket.

The expression on Dara's face did not lighten. As she turned and started off, Mark said, "I'll go if Dara doesn't want to."

"No," Kayl said sharply, still looking after Dara. "Now, come on." Then she turned, and saw relief and hurt mingled on Mark's face. "If Jirod is out when we get there, I'll want you to take him a message," she said more gently.

"Oh," Mark said, and his hurt look lessened. He started to say something else, then glanced sideways at Corrana and Glyndon and changed it to a mumbled, "All right."

"If you are quite finished, should we not be going?" Corrana broke in with ill-concealed irritation.

Kayl nodded and they set off once more. She led her companions by a circuitous route, avoiding the open square at the center of town. She took the narrow, little-used streets behind the butcher's and the tanner's; unpleasant odors were certainly preferable to being seen and remembered by villagers who might give later searchers a hint of Kayl's whereabouts. Fortunately, the rain had kept most people inside. The few villagers they saw showed no interest in the little group.

They reached Jirod's small house safely. As Kayl had half expected, the farmer was not at home, but the cottage door was not barred. Feeling obscurely guilty, Kayl pushed the door open and they went inside. Then, swallowing her misgivings, she sent Mark to find Jirod and warn him of his unexpected and potentially dangerous visitors.

"Try Holum's shop first," she said, trying to think of the possible errands that might take a farmer out on a rainy day. "Jirod may have gone to get some tools repaired. Then try the wheelwright, and the potter, and—"

"I'll find him, Mother," Mark said impatiently.

"Remember, Mark," she said sternly as he put his hand to the door. "You're not to tell anyone where we are, not even Tully."

"Yes, Mother," Mark said.

"And keep your head covered!" Kayl said as he pushed the door open and went out into the rain.

Mark did not reply, and Kayl stood staring at the rough wood of the door. Dara was a sensible child. Even without explanations, she'd run her errand carefully. And Mark was reliable enough. He'd hunt until he found Jirod; once he delivered his message, Jirod would make sure he came back safely. Unless someone had already told the Magicseekers about Kayl's children.

The sound of a throat being cleared behind her brought Kayl back to herself with a jerk. She turned and found Glyndon and Corrana both watching her. "Well?" she said.

"I had not thought that you would send your children into danger," Corrana said. Her eyes held a speculative gleam.

"They won't be in danger until someone tells the Magicseekers who they are," Kayl said, fighting down her own fears. "And there was no other reasonable choice."

"You could have taken the message yourself," Corrana pointed out. "And I am quite capable of following directions. Also, your Wyrd friend and I have met."

"Yes," Kayl said tiredly. "But we don't know whether the Magicseekers are looking for you or for Glyndon. Or me. I doubt that they're aware I have children, so they won't be looking for Mark or Dara. Assuming, of course, that the men Tully saw are, in fact, Magicseekers."

"Who else could they be?" Glyndon said.

"I don't know. Mercenaries, perhaps, or some new idea of King Valda. You realize that if they aren't Magicseekers I'm going to miss out on at least thirty coppers for their lodging tonight? Not to mention the wine they'd have drunk."

"You'd have had to leave soon anyway," Glyndon said uncertainly. "That, or—" He broke off and his eyes dropped.

"If the men your son's friend saw are not members of the Circle of Silence, I will make good your loss, innkeeper," Corrana said smoothly.

Kayl stared at her for a moment, feeling her anger rise. The woman's satisfaction was evident, and it took only a moment's thought to guess the reason. Magicseekers or not, the soldiers' arrival had persuaded Kayl to leave the inn at last, however reluctantly. "Thank you, Your Virtue," Kayl said coldly. "But that will not be necessary."

Corrana inclined her head. "As you wish."

Kayl nodded without speaking. There was a moment's silence, then Glyndon said, "Kayl, do you suppose your friend would object if we sat down?"

"Of course not," Kayl said. As Glyndon seated himself on the bench in the corner, Kayl realized that she was still holding both Dara's basket and her own, as well as the oilcloth bundle from the secret hiding place beneath the inn's hearth. She crossed to the table and set her burdens down beside the basket Mark had left there. Then she unloaded the baskets and began repacking their contents into three compact bundles.

She worked steadily, and at first she was grateful that neither Glyndon nor Corrana tried to talk to her. Then her fears for Mark and Dara resurfaced, and Kayl began to wish for something to distract her. She finished the second bundle and paused, her hands hovering over the oilcloth. If the soldiers *were* Magicseekers . . .

With sudden decision, she picked up her basket and the oilcloth bundle and rose. "I'll be back in a few minutes," she said, and was through the kitchen door before either Glyndon or Corrana could reply.

As the door closed behind her, she set the basket on the floor and began rummaging through it. The package she wanted was in the bottom, one of the first things she had seized during the hasty flight from the inn. She opened it quickly, half afraid that if she hesitated she would change her mind.

The soft leather over-tunic and leggings were still supple. Kayl stripped off her loose outer garments and pulled the leathers on quickly. They had an awkward, half strange, half familiar feel, like meeting a childhood friend after years of separation and discovering little in common save the past. Lacing the top of the leggings was difficult; three pregnancies and fourteen years of sampling the inn's stew as it cooked had added more to her hips than she would have believed.

In the end, she left the lacing loose, thanking the stars that the over-tunic was long and full. The belt that went with the tunic had vanished, worn out or lost years before. Kayl had to make do with the doubled cord she wore every day. Then she knelt and gently laid back the folds of the oilcloth bundle.

The star-gem in the hilt of the sword winked at her as she picked the weapon up. The scabbard had never been intended to hang from a belt of cord; it took awhile to fasten it so that the sword's hilt was properly positioned. Kayl wanted to test the ease of the weapon's draw, but Jirod's kitchen was too small for her to get a true feel for it. She settled for grabbing the hilt and half drawing the weapon several times. It seemed good enough, but she made a mental note to test it more fully later, somewhere where there was more room.

As Kayl folded her usual clothes and packed them in the basket, doubt struck her. She must look like a fool in these leathers, a middle-aged woman trying to recapture something of her lost youth. Yes, she could move more freely without the folds of her linen robe hampering her legs, but what did it matter? She could not successfully fight six or seven Magicseekers after so many years without practice; even at the height of her abilities, she would have been lucky to avoid death or capture. And if they fled Copeham altogether, her normal clothes would attract far less attention than these.

Yet the weight of the sword against her hip was comforting, and the leather warrior's garb gave her confidence. "Trust your instincts, Kayl Larrinar," Kayl muttered, and bent to pick up the oilcloth and Kevran's rod.

The dark wood of the rod shone even in the dim light from the kitchen window. Kayl was suddenly reluctant to muffle it in the folds of oilcloth once more. Perhaps Glyndon would want to see it. After all, it had been the focus of Kevran's magic, and it was the only thing of Kevran's she had left. She lifted the rod, and memory struck her like a blow.

"This is *not* going to work," Barthelmy said decidedly.

"It's too soon to say that," Kayl replied. "We've only been on the road two days."

"Which is at least a day and a half too long. We should have turned back as soon as that officious blonde started trying to take over."

"Varevice and I have settled that." For the time being, at least; Kayl wasn't sure how long their agreement with Beshara al Allard would last if they ran into real trouble.

"Those slaves give me chills," Barthelmy muttered. "And I don't like Varnans."

"If Evla can put up with them, surely you can."

"Evla's a Shee."

"That's what I mean."

"Excuse me, but is there some problem I can help with?" a quiet voice broke in from behind Kayl.

Kayl turned to find Kevran ker Rondal, whom she privately considered the most sensible of the three Varnan wizards, studying her. "No," she said.

"Yes," Barthelmy said irritably. "You can go away!"

The Varna's lips quirked. "I take it you are not fond of Varnans."

"I don't like any slave-keepers!"

"Barthelmy!" Kayl was appalled by her companion's lack of manners, but fortunately Kevran did not take offense.

"Not all Varnans keep slaves, or even approve of the practice," he said seriously. "Zylar'ri—"

"I'm sick of hearing about Zylar'ri!" Barthelmy said. "Every time someone wants to prove that Varnans aren't all bad, they drag out Zylar'ri and hold him up as an example. Well, I don't think one decent person in twelve hundred years is a particularly good record!"

"Barthelmy." Kayl pitched her voice to the note of command her Star had learned to obey unhesitatingly. "Weren't you going to speak to Evla?"

Barthelmy gave her an angry look, but she left. Kayl turned to Kevran. "I apologize for my friend's rudeness. I hope you won't hold it against her."

"I was hoping she'd be more comfortable with me," Kevran said, staring after Barthelmy. He glanced at Kayl and added apologetically, "Since I don't look much like most people's idea of a Varnan wizard."

Kayl blinked, and realized it was true. Kevran was half a head shorter than she was, with fine, dark hair that was constantly falling in his eyes. He was young, too; he couldn't be more than seven or eight years older than Kayl, at most. He looked more like a miller or a tailor than a wizard. "Barthelmy's a little oversensitive on the subject of Varnans," Kayl told him.

"She's your demon-friend, isn't she?" Kevran asked. Kayl nodded, and Kevran said thoughtfully, "And Beshara insisted on bringing Odevan. No wonder your friend is upset. It must be hard for her to see the way Beshara treats him."

"If the Sisterhood had known one of the slaves you wanted to bring was a demon, we'd have insisted that you send someone else," Kayl said, allowing some of her own anger to show.

"I wasn't going to say what she thought," Kevran said abruptly. His right hand was absentmindedly fingering a slender rod of dark wood that hung from his belt.

"What?"

"I wasn't going to hold up Zylar'ri as a Varnan you mainlanders would approve of."

"What *were* you going to say, then?"

"I was going to point out that he couldn't have started his campaign to free the demons if there hadn't been a lot of people on Varna who agreed with him." Kevran gave her a sidelong look. "There still are, you know. Varnans who agree with Zylar'ri, I mean. You might mention that to your friend;

it may make her feel a little more comfortable about this trip.''

Before Kayl could answer, the Varnan walked off. Kayl stared after him. She found herself wishing fervently that Kevran ker Rondal had been put in charge of the Varnan half of the group, and not Beshara al Allard. She suspected that it would have made the trip a great deal easier on everyone.

Kevran's rod slid from Kayl's fingers. She drew a deep breath, shaken by the vividness of the memory, and by its unexpectedness. She hadn't realized how strong a reminder of Kevran the rod would be. Or was it a side effect of Varnan magic? She wondered suddenly whether Varnans had some special way of disposing of the things they used in their spells. Kevran had not had time to tell her, and there had been no one else to ask, until now. She would have to talk to Glyndon later, when Corrana was not around.

Kayl wrapped the rod in her robes and stuffed it under one arm. Then, swinging the oilcloth in her other hand, she went back into the front room of Jirod's house.

CHAPTER

NINE

Glyndon's only comment when Kayl reappeared wearing leathers and the sword of the Sisterhood was, "So *that's* what you had in that oilcloth!" Corrana said nothing, but her smile was smug. Kayl was glad she did not have to make conversation with the woman; she would have found it all but impossible to remain polite.

She returned to her original task, making up the last of the food and clothing into a bundle for herself. Just as she was finishing there was a tentative knock at the door. Kayl rose and swung around to face it.

The door opened and Dara peered around the edge. "Mother?"

"Come inside, Dara, quickly!" The last thing they needed now was for someone to notice the unusual number of visitors Jirod was having.

Dara stepped inside and pushed the door shut behind her. "I saw Bryn, and she—" Dara stopped short, staring at Kayl. Her brown eyes widened even more as they fell on the sword of the Sisterhood hanging from Kayl's belt. "Mother, what—"

"In a minute, Dara," Kayl said hastily. "What did Bryn say?"

Dara swallowed. "She—she said she'd be here after dark. And that she appreciated your trust. Mother, what is going on?" The last words were almost a wail.

Kayl put a comforting arm around her daughter's shoulders. "Come sit down and I'll explain everything. Or at least, as much of it as I know." She glanced at Glyndon as she spoke.

"It's all right now," the wizard said. "You've heard what I had to tell you."

"All of it?" Kayl asked sharply, prompted by something in Glyndon's tone of voice.

"All that matters," the wizard replied wearily.

"Mother!" Dara begged. "You said you'd explain."

"Yes, of course," Kayl said. She hesitated, searching for the right words and the right place to begin. "A long time ago, I was a member of the Sisterhood of Stars."

"You were?" Dara said incredulously. "Then . . . that's *your* sword?"

"Yes. I was a warrior. My Star and I did a lot of different things for the Sisterhood; I'll tell you about them some other time, perhaps. That was how I met your father."

"And you fell in love, and left the Sisterhood for him!" Dara said excitedly.

"No," Kayl said firmly. "Or rather, not quite. I had other reasons for leaving."

"Oh," Dara said, sounding disappointed. She paused, considering, then nodded at Corrana. "Is that why she came? Because you used to be a Sister?"

"Yes, child," Corrana said. "That is why I came."

Dara jumped at the sound of Corrana's voice. Kayl gave her a reassuring hug and went on, "And Glyndon is a kind of Seer. He came to warn us about the Magicseekers' coming."

"Why?" Dara asked. She looked warily in Glyndon's direction.

"I was a friend of your father's," Glyndon said simply.

"You knew Father?" Dara burst out. She looked indignantly at Kayl. "You didn't tell us!"

"I asked your mother not to say anything to you until I could talk to her," Glyndon said.

Dara flushed. "But—"

A loud thump just outside the door interrupted Dara in midsentence. The door swung open, letting in the sound of Mark's indignant voice, "—not making it up!"

"I didn't say you were," Jirod said. "We'll sort it out inside." He came into the room as he spoke and stopped abruptly when he saw Corrana. His eyes darted over the rest of the room's occupants, moving past Kayl without recognition. Then his look returned to her, and his eyes widened in disbelief and slowly deepening bewilderment. Kayl straightened and returned his gaze.

Mark pushed his way past Jorod and kicked the door shut behind him. "I *told* you," he said with some satisfaction.

"Mark!" Kayl said automatically. "Where are your manners?"

"Well, I *did* tell— Mother! Where'd you get the leathers? And the sword? Can I see it?"

"Later, Mark. Apologize to Jirod, then sit down somewhere."

Mark mumbled something that would pass for "I'm sorry" and crossed the room to where Kayl was standing. Dara, Glyndon and Corrana occupied all of the chairs, so he settled himself on the floor beside Kayl, where he could study her sword.

Kayl looked back at Jirod. He was still staring at her; he did not appear to have noticed Mark's movement at all. "Hello, Jirod," Kayl said, trying not to show the uncertainty she felt. "I'm afraid we've more or less taken over your house; I'm sorry."

"Kayl, what is all this?" Jirod said at last. "Mark said something about you hiding from Magicseekers, but I don't see why. And the way you're dressed, and . . . I don't understand."

"It's a long story, Jirod," Kayl said. She leaned back against the table, stretching her legs. "But before I start, let me introduce you to my companions. This is the Elder Sister Corrana of the Sussewild, from the Sisterhood of Stars. And this is Glyndon shal Morag, an old friend of Kevran's and mine."

Jirod made a small, hostile bow in Corrana's direction and nodded with noncommittal suspicion to Glyndon. "Friends of Kayl's are welcome in my house," he said, putting a shade too much emphasis on the first word.

"Our thanks for your hospitality," Glyndon said.

Jirod's eyes narrowed, as though he suspected Glyndon of mocking him. Hastily, Kayl said, "Have you got any more chairs, Jirod? I'll explain as soon as everyone's comfortable."

"There is no need to wait," Glyndon said, rising. "Our host

may have my chair. I've sat still long enough."

Jirod hesitated. Glyndon smiled and stepped away from the chair; Corrana, seated against the opposite wall, shifted slightly so that the Varnan remained in her direct line of vision. Jirod glanced at Kayl, then sat down, still watching Glyndon with a trace of suspicion.

"Thank you, Glyndon," Kayl said.

"The pleasure is mine," Glyndon said.

Jirod's eyes widened suddenly, and he half rose from the chair. "You're a Varnan!"

"You're quick," Glyndon said. "I can usually spend at least a day in a town this small before that particular suspicion occurs to somebody. If I make a point of talking very little, that is."

"A Varnan!" Mark said eagerly. "Are you a wizard Varnan?"

"After a fashion," Glyndon said.

"And Mother says he knew Father!" Dara told Mark in a piercing whisper.

Jirod stared at Glyndon, ignoring the children; Kayl could not decide whether his expression was one of apprehension or of anger. "What are you doing in Copeham?" he demanded.

"Glyndon came to warn me about the Magicseekers," Kayl said.

"Warn you? But the Magicseekers don't have any interest in—" Jirod hesitated, eyeing Kayl's clothing and the sword she carried; then he finished weakly, "—people like us."

Kayl sighed. "Jirod, fifteen years ago I was a member of the Sisterhood of Stars. The Circle of Silence has plenty of reason to be interested in me, if only for what I carry." She tapped the glowing stone in the hilt of her sword, ignoring Mark's muffled exclamation.

There was a moment's silence. Kayl could almost see the pieces falling together in Jirod's mind. "Why shouldn't they be looking for *her*?" he said, not quite glaring at Corrana.

"It is possible," Corrana said calmly before Kayl could reply. "But many things are possible."

"And I will not take risks with the children's safety," Kayl said. "It'll be easy enough to go back to the inn, if I'm wrong and the Magicseekers are just passing through." Her words mocked her with double meanings even as she spoke. Easy to go back? She doubted it.

"But they didn't stop," Jirod said with relief.

Kayl's eyes narrowed. "You saw them?" she said sharply.

"We both saw them," Mark burst out eagerly. "Six of them! They went right past Holum's just when we were going in. I got to see them even closer than Tully."

Kayl turned questioningly to Jirod. "They were Magic-seekers then?"

"Yes," Jirod said, looking at her uncertainly. "I thought you knew that."

"And they went on through? You're certain?"

"I wasn't about to stand out in the rain watching them!" Jirod said with some annoyance. "But when Mark here dragged me out of the smithy, they were heading over the hill."

"How many of them did you say there were?" Glyndon said. His voice sounded strained.

"Six," Jirod replied, sounding even more annoyed than before.

"No," Glyndon said. "That's wrong. There are—there are seven." He swayed on his feet, and Kayl saw that he had turned white. "Seven eagle-helmeted soldiers, bringing fire and blood . . ."

"Dara, get up," Kayl said. "Don't touch him, Jirod, it only makes things worse." She shoved Dara's empty chair at Glyndon, and the Varnan collapsed into it, shaking violently.

"What is it?" Jirod said. "It's like the falling sickness Ban's girl has, but he's not—"

"He is a Seer, of sorts," Corrana said, and Jirod jumped. The sorceress smiled very slightly and went on. "I begin to agree with his opinions of it; it seems an uncomfortable talent."

"Jirod, have you got any wine?" Kayl snapped. "No? Water, then, please. As quickly as you can."

Jirod brought the water just as Glyndon gave the shuddering sigh that signaled the vision's end. Kayl handed Glyndon the mug and watched narrowly while he drank.

"Thank you," Glyndon said as he lowered the mug. "And my apologies, that you should have to deal with this twice. I am usually more careful."

"Careful?" Kayl said. "You have some control of the visions?"

"No, but I can control where I am when they take me."

Glyndon's tone was bleak. "Until recently."

"And do your visions usually come so close together?"

"Again, not until recently. But they've always been capricious. I'd go months without 'seeing' anything, then have three of these fits within a week."

"But not two in one day," Kayl said.

"No."

"Then what you 'see' is presumably of some importance," Corrana said cooly. "Tell us."

Kayl shot her a look of dislike. Glyndon shook his head. "The same as before. Seven eagle-helmed soldiers smashing things at the inn, and Kayl . . . We haven't escaped it yet."

"Seven Magicseekers," Corrana said. "Yet those who came today were but six."

"Islorran!" Kayl said. "His villa is farther down that road, away from town. There must be another one staying with him."

"I don't think Prefect Islorran would help the Magic-seekers," Jirod said.

"Why not?" Kayl said. "Mindaria isn't part of the Estarren Alliance anymore; the Circle of Silence has come and gone as they pleased for the last five or ten years."

"Your Prefect would not be the first to bargain with them for support," said Corrana.

"And it would explain why Utrilo Levoil was poking around my inn so determinedly two days ago."

"What?" Glyndon said. "You didn't tell me anything about that."

Quickly, Kayl summarized Utrilo's visit to the inn. "He isn't usually so persistent, but if Islorran has a Magicseeker visiting him, Utrilo would be under a lot more pressure."

Jirod was staring at Kayl, and she realized suddenly that she had begun to pace. She stopped short, feeling foolish. Jirod's gaze did not waver. "Kayl," he said, "can I talk with you privately?"

Kayl blinked, surprised by the suddenness of the request. "Yes, if it won't take too long. I don't think we have much time."

"I suspect you are right," Corrana said. "Perhaps you should stay, and hold your conversation here."

"No, lady," Kayl said. "Not this time." She held the sorceress's eyes until Corrana gave a little nod; then she looked at Jirod. "The kitchen?"

Jirod nodded abstractedly and rose. Kayl followed. He did not speak until the kitchen door was firmly shut behind them; then he said, "Kayl, you don't have to do this."

"What do you mean? Jirod, I won't let the children be—"

"I don't mean that! Of course you'd never let them be hurt, and I can see why you think they might be if you stayed. But you don't have to go away with these wizards!"

Kayl took a deep breath and let it out again slowly. "I don't see any reasonable alternatives," she said carefully.

"You could stay here, in my house," Jirod said. "For as long as you like."

Kayl could think of half a dozen insoluble problems with doing any such thing, but she was touched by the offer nonetheless. "And bring the Magicseekers down on you, too? I couldn't do that."

"But you'll leave Copeham for a stranger's story."

"Glyndon is an old friend, Jirod. I trust him, and Corrana as well. At least, to a point."

"They're wizards, Kayl," Jirod said earnestly. "You can't believe them."

"Oh?"

"Wizards and witches are nothing but trouble for everyone. Look at the mess the Wizard's War left, and the trouble the Magicseekers have caused. You don't belong with them."

"My husband was a Varnan wizard," Kayl said in a tone that was as expressionless as she could make it.

Jirod stared at her. Then his face reddened and he looked away.

When she was sure he was not going to respond, Kayl said, "Is there anything else?"

"I seem to keep saying the wrong thing," Jirod said quietly. "I'm sorry."

Kayl sighed, her anger evaporating. "I think I understand. Still, I have to leave Copeham. For my own sake, as well as the children's."

"But you belong here," Jirod said.

Kayl looked at him. She could feel the weight of the sword of the Sisterhood hanging at her side, and smell the faint, musty odor of the leathers she wore. She thought of the inn and her children; of the growing hunger for magic and the rising tide of resentment facing Bryn and other nonhumans outside the Estarren Alliance; of her husband Kevran and of Jirod's mistrust of magic; of all the ghosts that had begun stirring in her memories since Corrana's arrival at the inn.

"No," Kayl said slowly, after a long pause. "I don't belong here."

Jirod's face went very still. "You mean that," he said.

"Yes," Kayl said gently. "I do." She waited a moment; when Jirod did not reply, she walked past him to the door, and back into the other room.

CHAPTER

TEN

The first thing Kayl heard when she entered the front room was Dara's voice saying, "What was he like?"

Glyndon glanced up from whatever he had been discussing with the children, and saw Kayl. "I'll tell you later," he said.

Dara followed his glance and said, "All right. Mother, I'm hungry."

Kayl did a mental change in step and said, "There are vegetables and some cold stew in the basket. We should all have something; it may be awhile before we can stop again." She heard Jirod come into the room behind her, but she did not turn. Instead, she went to the table and began helping Dara get out the food.

"What are we going to do now?" Mark asked.

"We'll be leaving Copeham as soon as we've eaten," Kayl said briskly.

"I thought you didn't want to be seen!" Jirod objected. "Shouldn't you wait until dark?"

Kayl turned. "If one of the Magicseekers is staying with Prefect Islorran, he probably knows everything Utrilo does about Copeham. Which means he'll know who my friends are, and where I'd be likely to hide. When they get to the inn and find no one, they'll know where to start looking. I'd counted on them having to hunt a little."

"It's still raining!"

"Then there will be fewer people around to see which way

we go. I'm sorry, Jirod, but we have to leave. Quickly.''

"Perhaps you should join us," Corrana said. "The Magicseekers will not be pleasant company, when they arrive."

"No," Jirod said. "That is, I'd rather not, my lady. Begging your pardon."

"You're sure, Jirod?" Kayl asked. Corrana was right; there was no telling what the Magicseekers might do if they thought Jirod could tell them where their prey had gone.

"I'm sure." His eyes met hers. "Copeham is my home. I belong here."

"I understand," Kayl said. She sighed. "If the Magicseekers leave anything worth having when they're done at the inn, it's yours."

"I'll take care of things for you," Jirod said. "Until you get back."

The stubborn set of his chin told Kayl there was no use in trying to convince him that she might not be coming back. "Thank you," she said. Another thought struck her, and she added, "If you see Bryn, tell her we couldn't wait."

"I'll tell her," Jirod promised. He paused. "Where will you be going?"

"East," Kayl said without hesitation.

"East? But I thought—" Jirod broke off and glanced at Corrana.

"I think my husband's family will be just as capable of protecting the children as the Sisterhood would be," Kayl said firmly. "And without asking a price in return."

"Varna is a long way. Are you sure—"

"I'm sure."

"Varna?" Mark said eagerly. "We're going to Varna?"

"Finish your stew, and we'll see," Kayl said.

"I *am* finished," Mark said.

Dara was frowning in puzzlement. "Mother, what you just said—does that mean Father was a *Varnan*?"

"It does," Kayl said. "I'll explain later." She was accumulating a considerable list of things to explain later, she thought uncomfortably, but there was no help for it.

"Yes, I think it's time we left," Glyndon said before Mark could voice any of the questions he was obviously bursting to ask.

Kayl nodded. Grumbling, Mark and Dara put the containers of stew back in the basket. Kayl checked to make sure that Mark had repacked his jar of stew properly. Reassured that the jar was not likely to tip over during the journey and soak everything in the basket, she bundled the children into their cloaks and handed them their bundles. She picked up her own package and adjusted the folds of her cloak to hide as much as possible of the sword she wore.

"Is everyone ready?" she said at last. "Then let's go."

Corrana rose and led the way. Mark and Dara followed. Glyndon rose, but hesitated, looking from Jirod to Kayl and back. Then he scowled and swept out of the house.

Kayl looked at Jirod. "Good-bye, my friend," she said.

"Good-bye, Kayl."

The quiet words seemed to hang in the air until the door of Jirod's house closed behind her, cutting them off with a ruthless and unanswerable finality.

They walked eastward for most of the afternoon. Their progress was poorer than Kayl had hoped, for the steady rain had turned the road to a heavy mud that slid underfoot and clung like leaden weights to boots and sandals. Their cloaks quickly became sodden burdens, and the muddy hems slapped against their calves, cold and unpleasant. Kayl's only consolation was the hope that the rain would delay the heavily armed and armored Magicseekers even more.

A few miles past the last of the cultivated land that surrounded Copeham, Kayl called a halt. Mark and Dara searched in vain for a dry rock to sit on. Finally they gave up and stood huddled together under their cloaks, a picture of misery.

"I'm cold," Mark grumbled. "And this stupid cloak drips down my neck."

"It would help if you wrapped it properly," Kayl said as she adjusted the haphazard folds around Mark's head. "There. Try to keep it that way for a while."

"Why can't one of them do something about all this rain?" Mark said, nodding toward Glyndon and Corrana. "And the mud and the cold?"

"Such as?"

"They're wizards, aren't they? Can't they make it stop? Or at least keep us dry?"

"No," Kayl said severely. "Magic isn't used so casually."

"Why not?" Mark demanded.

"A good question," Glyndon said. "And one that doesn't have a simple answer, I'm afraid. Partly, it's a respect for the power we use. You *could* chop onions with a sword, but it's usually easier to use a kitchen knife. Does that explain it?"

Mark nodded and scowled. "What's the good of traveling with a wizard if you can't even be comfortable?"

"Very little," Glyndon said apologetically. He turned to Kayl and asked, "How much farther is it to the next town?"

"We aren't going there," Kayl said, scanning the rocky wastes on either side of the road. "We're turning north."

"You mean we aren't going to Varna?" Mark said. "But I wanted to see all the wizards!"

"They don't look any different from other people," Kayl said. "And we aren't making this trip to satisfy your curiosity."

Warned by Kayl's tone, Mark fell silent. Dara hunched her shoulders. "Well, where *are* we going, then?" she demanded crossly.

Kayl looked across at Corrana. "Kith Alunel, I think," she said.

The sorceress gave a satisfied smile. "I am glad you have seen the wisdom of such a course of action," she said, half lowering her eyelids.

Kayl returned the smile grimly. "I have some property to return to the Sisterhood of Stars," she said, and shifted her cloak to allow Corrana a brief glimpse of the hilt of her sword.

Momentarily, Corrana's face showed consternation; then her expression smoothed into its usual unreadable mask. "As you will have it. You may yet change your mind when you have spoken with the Elder Mothers."

"Perhaps," Kayl said noncommittally. She had no intention of returning to the Twisted Tower in the Windhome Mountains, whatever the Elder Mothers might say. Still, it couldn't hurt to listen to them, and they might have some other task she could do. After all, she would have to find some way of supporting herself and her children. The little hoard of money in her belt-pouch would not last long. She looked at Glyndon. "Will you come with us, or have you other plans?"

Glyndon shrugged. "I have no plans," he said shortly. "Kith Alunel is as good a destination for me as any."

Annoyed and a little hurt by Glyndon's abrupt manner, Kayl jerked her head toward the wet, rocky ground north of the road. "Start walking, then."

Glyndon blinked at her, then suddenly grinned. "At your command," he said, bowing, then lifted his staff and strode off. Kayl shook her head and followed.

They camped that night on the rocky waste. They were still too close to Copeham and the possibility of pursuit to risk a fire, so they constructed a makeshift tent from their wet, mud-splattered cloaks and huddled inside it. They spent a damp, muddy, miserable night. No one got very much sleep.

The second day of the journey was worse. Kayl was stiff from sleeping on the ground, and her muscles were sore from the unaccustomed walking. She forced herself to go through some of the stretching exercises her drillmasters had taught her so long before, and was appalled by how difficult they seemed. The children were tired, cross and hungry; cold stew did not noticeably improve their tempers. Dara sneezed twice while she was eating, and Kayl began worrying that the girl was catching a cold.

Glyndon looked positively haggard. Kayl suspected he had had another of his visions during the night, but he did not volunteer any information and she was unwilling to pry. Corrana was the only member of the group who bore any resemblance to her usual self. Even with her cloak muddied to the knees and her hair in snarls, she had an air of calm power that must command respect anywhere.

At least the rain had stopped. By midmorning, the summer sun had come out, and the little group could shed their cloaks. Walking became easier as the ground dried off, though the children continued to complain. Despite the better footing, the group still did not move as quickly as Kayl had hoped. She developed a habit of scanning the southern horizon whenever they paused to rest, but she saw no sign of pursuit.

They saw no one the day after, either, and Kayl began to relax. They stopped early that evening, and Glyndon set snares to supplement their dwindling supply of food. His efforts garnered a partridge and a brace of rabbits, and they dined royally around a small fire.

On their fourth day of walking, they reached the North

Road, and two days after that they came to the town of
Yanderwood. They slept warm and dry at an inn whose sign
bore a wolf's head. Next day, Corrana hired an ox-drawn
wagon, and they continued their journey in considerably more
comfort. Within a week, they were out of Mindaria altogether.

Kayl continued to do her sword drills every morning, no
matter how stiff and sore she felt. Gradually her muscles
hardened and her skill began to return. Both Mark and Dara
showed considerable interest in the process, and after some
thought Kayl instituted a daily lesson in swordcraft and
fighting skills.

Corrana remained a source of uneasiness. The woman's attitude did not change; if anything, she grew more aloof and
more cryptic as the journey continued. She took to studying
Kayl and her children with an unfathomable expression that
made Kayl increasingly irritable.

Glyndon, too, was a source of concern. His visions continued to come close together, sometimes with daily fre-
quency, though as they left Copeham farther behind, the more
nightmarish sights seemed to grow fewer. Even the pleasant visions took their toll, however. Once Kayl found him staring at
the horizon, his expression bleak.

"Another bad one?" she asked.

"No," he said, and his mouth twisted. "To the contrary.
The problem is, it wasn't true."

"Not true?"

"I can tell, sometimes, whether a vision is true or not,"
Glyndon said without looking at her. His hand clenched.
"This one wasn't."

"I see." Kayl was silent for a moment. "Glyndon, you told
me you'd managed to avoid some of the unpleasant visions.
Have you ever tried to make some of the better ones actually
happen?"

"What?" Glyndon's head jerked around to face her.

"Have you ever tried to make one of the good visions happen?" Kayl repeated.

"No," Glyndon said slowly. "No, I haven't." He sounded
as if he was not sure whether to be afraid or pleased. "I
wouldn't know where to start."

"Think about it," Kayl said, and left him.

But though Glyndon seemed more cheerful after that conversation, the visions continued without respite. He grew thinner and more worn-looking as the journey progressed. By the time they were halfway to Kith Alunel, it was clear to Kayl that if something were not done to slow or stop the visions, Glyndon would waste away completely. She even went so far as to question Corrana privately, but the sorceress could only suggest a consultation with the Elder Mothers of the Sisterhood. Glyndon's visions were totally outside her experience.

As they drew nearer to Kith Alunel, their progress became more rapid. As soon as they were within the borders of the Estarren Alliance, Corrana began wearing her silver robes openly. The roads improved steadily as well, from the muddy tracks around Copeham to rutted gravel to the wide, paved roadways that were the pride of the Alliance.

Six months after leaving Copeham, they entered Kith Alunel.

INTERLUDE:

Kith Alunel

Kith Alunel is possibly the oldest city of Lyra. It is known to have been founded prior to the Wars of Binding; more than that is impossible to establish with any accuracy. Local tradition has it that the city was settled some four hundred years prior to the beginning of the war, and specifically some thirty years prior to the settling of Rathane. It is impossible to tell whether there is any truth to this tradition; besides, the people of Kith Alunel claim to have done or invented practically everything earlier than Rathane. All that is certain is that Kith Alunel and Rathane are the only existing human cities which date from a time prior to the Wars of Binding.

The so-called Dark Times, followed by the Wars of Binding, are the main reason for the dearth of information regarding times prior to the wars. The Shadow-born, who ruled much of Lyra during the Dark Times, made a concerted effort to destroy both knowledge and magical ability. Kith Alunel was a major target of this effort.

Fortunately, the inhabitants of Kith Alunel and its environs exhibited considerable creativity in hiding and preserving their heritage. Books and other documents were buried beneath the cornerstones of new buildings, walled into specially-constructed niches, even sealed with pitch and hidden in barrels of wine. The ninth Baroness Kyel-Semrud, to preserve the Kyel-Semrud's ancestral home of Castle Ravensrest, is supposed to have built an exact duplicate of the castle, complete with copies of family heirlooms, and somehow tricked the Shadow-born into destroying the duplicate instead of their intended target. Though this seems unlikely, Castle Ravensrest is undeniably ancient and extraordinarily well preserved.

Not all the ruses were as successful as the Baroness's legendary trick. Some caches of books and magical equipment were discovered and destroyed; some were so well hidden that they were forgotten and lost. Enough survived, however, to make Kith Alunel a major source of knowledge and culture following the end of the Wars of Binding, and this undoubtedly contributed to the city's preeminence in the centuries that followed.

Many of the cities and countries along the eastern shore of the Melyranne Sea owe their existence, directly or indirectly, to Kith Alunel. The cities of Toltan and Morsedd were colonies of Kith Alunel, begun in 109 A.W.B. and 274 A.W.B. respectively. Mindaria was settled by dissidents in 248. Later, Kith Alunel was the prime mover in persuading the Senate of the Estarren Alliance to rename the Seaguard Mountains as the Mountains of Morravik and cede them to the Shanhar (an elite military band whose name was later corrupted into "Cilhar").

Possibly the most notable achievement of Kith Alunel was the Estarren Alliance, the loose federation of nation-states and independent cities which dominated the lands east of the Melyranne Sea for nearly eight hundred years. Though the Alliance was conceived to facilitate trade, it grew into a power capable of everything from building roads to fighting the wizards of Varna to a standstill. Even the bickering which followed the Wizard's War of 1003-1026 A.W.B. did not result in open ruptures within the Alliance for nearly two centuries, and the core of the Alliance remained a power to reckon with well into the 1300s.

With the break-up of the Estarren Alliance, Kith Alunel's ascendancy began to fade. The center of political power passed on, first to Imach Thyssel, later to Ciaron. Curiously, this change in their supposed position has never appeared to bother the citizens of Kith Alunel in the slightest, and the city shows no sign of losing its vitality. To the contrary, innovations of all kinds continue to have their origins in Kith Alunel.

—Kith Alunel: Legend and Reality *by Najid Sar, Archivist of the Temple of the Third Moon, 2942 A.W.B. (From the library of Duke Dindran of Minathlan.)*

PART II
Sisterhood of Stars

CHAPTER

ELEVEN

Kith Alunel appeared to have changed very little in the years since Kayl had last been there. The street inside the city gates was wide, and lined with buildings made of sun-baked brick. Brightly painted signs hung above the shop doors, depicting the merchandise for sale within.

The weather was mild for early winter, and despite the frosting of yesterday's snow on the roofs the street was crowded. Many of the shops had their shutters open. Tantalizing aromas drifted out of the many little hot-pastry places, tempting tired and hungry travelers to purchase fresh meat-pies and hot, spiced wine. Scattered among the food vendors were potters and glassmakers, leatherworkers and basket weavers, smiths and herbalists, jewelers and winesellers, all with exotic wares to beguile and bewilder the newly arrived.

Kayl breathed in the familiar aroma and smiled. The first time she had come to Kith Alunel, she'd spent every quarter-copper Mother Dalessi had given her within three blocks of the city gates. If she hadn't had the hall of the Sisterhood to go to, she'd have spent the night sleeping on the street.

She was not wearing the sword of the Sisterhood now, and she had made a wool traveling garment to wear instead of her leathers. This garment tied around each of her legs. Sword and leathers formed the bulk of the bundle she had tied to her back; the baskets had fallen apart long ago.

"Mother! Look at that!" Mark said, pointing at a shop

with a tray of weapons on display.

"Weapon shops aren't unusual in Kith Alunel, dear," Kayl said. "If you're interested, we can look at some of them tomorrow."

"Almost nothing is unusual in Kith Alunel," Glyndon put in. "If you want to buy something, go down to the gates. If you don't see it, wait awhile; someone will turn up with it before the day is over."

"Well, I want to buy dinner," Dara muttered, pulling her cloak more tightly around her. "That smell makes me hungry."

"Me, too," Mark said more loudly. "Mother, can we get something to eat?" He looked longingly at a small hot-pastry shop.

Kayl did a quick mental calculation. There was very little of her carefully hoarded money left; still, the children deserved some sort of treat to celebrate their arrival. "I think we can manage it, Mark. Where do you want to stop?"

"That one," Dara said, pointing.

"I would prefer that we continue on to the Star Hall," Corrana's cool voice broke in. "There will be time for this later."

"Mother, you promised!" Mark said.

"Hush, Mark," Kayl said, and turned to face Corrana. "I told the children they could have a treat, and I am going to give it to them," Kayl said simply. "Coming?"

Corrana looked at her for a moment, then nodded. Kayl led the way into the pastry shop. She was more than usually thoughtful as she watched Mark and Dara make their choices. Corrana had been relatively quiet during the early weeks of their journey, but the nearer they had come to Kith Alunel, the more she had behaved as though she was in charge of the little party. Kayl did not want to encourage the Sisterhood of Stars to adopt a similar attitude. While Corrana was watching the children with ill-concealed disapproval, Kayl slipped around to Glyndon's side and said softly, "Glyndon, do you have any money?"

"Quite a bit, actually," he replied, though he looked a little surprised that she would ask. "I was lucky in that last dice game."

"Would you slip away and get rooms for us at one of the inns before we get to the Star Hall?"

Glyndon raised an eyebrow. "Before you've even had a chance to talk to them?"

"I want to keep my choices open," Kayl said. "Will you do it?"

"Of course." He swept her a bow. "Until later."

He turned and was gone, leaving Kayl glaring after him in irritation. "Slip away," she'd said, not make a production of his exit!

"And where is your Varnan friend off to?" Corrana said from behind her.

Kayl shrugged. "He has business of his own in Kith Alunel. He'll catch up with us later."

"If he must." Corrana's voice held the slight edge that it always did when she spoke of Glyndon. "Shall we continue on our way?"

"Not until Mark has finished his meat-pie. Unless, of course, you want to make apologies to all the people he'll bump into while he tries to walk and look and eat, all at the same time."

Corrana lifted one eybrow and smiled slightly. "I withdraw my suggestion," the sorceress said. "Purely out of sympathy for your son's prospective victims, you understand."

Kayl grinned and bit into her meat-pie. Six months on the road seemed to have given Corrana a somewhat better understanding of both Mark and Dara; Kayl could only wish the woman had achieved as much sympathy for Glyndon, or for Kayl herself.

They finished their meal and went back out into the crowd. Mark and Dara stared wide-eyed at everything and everyone they passed, from bell-covered jugglers to armor-clad guards and wool-wrapped merchants. As a result their progress was slow. Several times they saw litters pass along the center of the street, draped with fine woolens and silks and borne on the shoulders of muscular men and women with expressionless faces. When the first of the litters went by, Dara studied the bearers, then asked, "Mother, are they slaves? I thought Kith Alunel didn't let people have slaves!"

"No, they're not slaves," Kayl told her. "They're paid for their work. Paid very well, as I remember, which is why only the wealthy or nobility ride in litters."

"Why do they look so . . . so . . ."

"So grim? It's part of their training. It's considered improper for a litter-bearer to express an opinion of his employer's actions while he's carrying, and even a smile is deemed an expression of opinion."

Mark looked after the retreating litter and wrinkled his nose. "That's weird," he said emphatically.

Kayl laughed. "The people who do it don't think so."

"Well, but—" Mark broke off, staring at something behind Kayl, and his eyes widened.

Kayl turned. A tall, platinum-haired Shee was passing a few paces away, his green eyes narrowed into slanting slits in contemplation of whatever business drew him on.

"A Shee!" Mark breathed.

"Where?" Dara craned her neck in an effort to catch a glimpse for herself. "Why didn't you say something sooner?"

"I said as soon as I saw him!" Mark said defensively.

"You did not!"

"That's enough," Kayl said. "There's no reason for you to start quarreling over the first Shee you see. There are plenty of Shee in Kith Alunel; it's not like Mindaria."

Dara brightened and began scanning the crowd, looking for another of the nonhumans. Not to be outdone, Mark joined her. Their efforts were quickly rewarded, this time with the sight of a Shee woman bargaining in the door of an herbalist's shop. Mark and Dara were immensely pleased with themselves, but the incident left Kayl wondering uneasily just why it was that they had seen only two Shee since entering the city. Surely there should be more, or was her memory playing tricks on her?

Kayl began her own surreptitious study of the crowd. What she saw did nothing to soothe her; she counted only four Shee in two blocks. Wyrds were more numerous, but there had been a Wyrd settlement near Kith Alunel for centuries. She saw no Neira at all.

At the top of a hill the street widened into a square. The middle of the square was occupied by a wide, shallow pool, now thinly crusted with ice and a dusting of snow. On Kayl's right was the colonnaded front of a theater, with a granite dome, probably a school, beside it. To the left, sixteen shallow steps, flanked by carved pillars, led up to the triple-arch doorway of a huge building. Above the door, three warriors in bas-relief held off seven nightmarish-looking creatures, while behind them a man and woman with their arms full of scrolls escaped.

"What's that?" Mark asked, awed.

"The Queen's Library," Kayl said. "The carving over the door is from the story of Deardan and her brothers—Deardan and Tylmar saving the Scrolls of Knowledge from the Shadow-born. Queen Irhallen the Fourth built it about three hundred years after the Wars of Binding."

"That whole building is full of *books*?" Mark said incredulously.

"That's right," Kayl said, laughing. "They have scrolls and books about everything, from dancing to Shanhar hand-fighting."

Mark's ears perked up. "They have books about Shanhar in there?" He looked speculatively at the library. "Maybe I should look inside."

"I'll take you there sometime," Kayl promised.

"Mother, what's that?" Dara asked, pointing at the theater on the other side of the square. Kayl took a deep breath, hoping the children wouldn't ask more than she knew how to answer, and launched into another explanation.

Eventually, they turned off of the main street. The soaring arches and pillars of the library and theater gave way to sturdy, practical buildings of mortared fieldstone. Behind them, in the shadow of the city wall, Kayl could see the roofs of the flimsy, four-story tenements that housed the less well off. She frowned; there seemed to be more of them than she remembered. Then Mark distracted her with a question, and she forgot her misgivings for the time being.

They continued on toward the center of the city. Soon houses of carved granite blocks began appearing, some with decorations of mosaic tile around their doors. Beyond lay the pillared homes of even wealthier merchants and the marble halls of the nobility, encircling the great palace of Kith Alunel at the heart of the city.

They turned again, long before they neared the haunts of the rich, and suddenly they were standing in front of the Star Hall of Kith Alunel. Kayl stopped and looked at it, swallowing hard.

It was a low, sprawling building. A wide path of pale gray flagstone led from the street through a tiny garden to a porch, roofed in white marble supported by columns of the same material. The floor of the porch was made of mosaic tiles in shades of gray; beyond was the arched opening that led to the outer courtyard of the Star Hall. From where she stood, Kayl could see the tops of the side domes that would flank the long central hall; they, too, were of white marble. The Star Hall shone in the winter sunlight, like a pearl among the gray-brown rock of the surrounding buildings.

"Is this where we're going?" Dara asked a little doubtfully as Corrana started up the path toward the doorway.

"Yes," Kayl said, surprised. "Something wrong?"

"No, not exactly," Dara said. "It's just so *grand*, and we're all . . ." Her voice trailed off and she waved vaguely at her dusty, travel-stained clothes.

"Don't worry," Kayl reassured her. "The Sisters are used to receiving guests in even worse shape than we are."

Dara nodded, but she still looked unhappy. "Go on," Mark said, giving her a poke. "I don't want to stand here all day. It's getting cold."

"You stop that!" Dara said furiously. "You never think of anybody but yourself! You—"

"Dara! Mark! Both of you, stop it right now," Kayl said firmly.

"But I didn't do anything!" Mark said in an injured tone.

"I don't care," Kayl said. "I don't want to hear a word out of either of you until we're inside and I'm done talking to the Sisters. Understand?"

"But—"

"Not a word!" Kayl said. "Now come on." She took their hands in hers and went into the Star Hall.

Two Sisters in medium-gray robes were waiting in the outer courtyard; Corrana had summoned them while Kayl was dealing with Mark and Dara outside. They led Kayl and her children through the front atrium and around the outside of the great hall. Kayl felt as though she were seeing double. She knew the way as well as she knew her kitchen at the inn in Copeham, yet it was somehow strange as well. The hall was narrower than she remembered, and she had forgotten the odd rose tiles that ringed the pool in the atrium. The lighting was too dim, and there were too many doors. Then, suddenly, there was a niche in the wall that fit her memory perfectly, and even that felt strange. Kayl suppressed a shiver of uneasiness and hurried after the Sisters.

The Sisters led them to a small chamber ringed with wooden benches. One wall was covered with a mosaic depicting a stylized eight-pointed star in shades of blue; the other walls were the same polished white marble as the rest of the building. On the opposite side of the chamber were two wooden doors.

"Baths have been prepared for you in the next rooms," one of the Sisters said, indicating doors in the opposite wall of the chamber. "We will bring clean clothing for you while you refresh yourselves."

Dara shot Kayl a reproachful look, but was wise enough not to say anything. Kayl thanked the two Sisters and saw them out, then sent Mark and Dara to bathe. As they left the room, she unwrapped her cloak and sank down onto one of the benches. Absently, she undid the cords holding her bundle, and sighed in relief as the weight left her shoulders. She set it on the bench beside her and stared at it.

Coming back wasn't supposed to feel like this, she thought, but she didn't know what she had expected it to feel like. She didn't even know, really, why she had come. She had insisted, when Corrana pressed her, that she only wanted to return the sword of the Sisterhood to the Elder Mothers. But could she give it up? It had been a part of her for so long; even, she now admitted, when she had hidden it beneath the floor of the inn and denied its presence. And if she hadn't given up the sword on that last, horrible day when she thought she hated the Sisterhood and everyone in it, how could she imagine that she would return it now?

Kayl sighed and leaned back, remembering.

Starlight glimmered on the mirror-smooth surface of the pool in the center of the Court of Stars. Kayl stood alone at one corner of the pool, staring straight ahead of her, trying not to think of the erstwhile companions of her Star Cluster. On the other side of the courtyard, the most senior of the Elder Mothers of the Sisterhood were gathered, their silver robes a dim reflection of the shimmering starlight.

"And is that all of your story?" a voice said from the midst of the silver mass.

"The return trip was uneventful, Your Serenity," Kayl said. Her voice rasped in a throat worn raw with weeping.

"Then we thank you for your service." The voice paused. "You have our sympathy as well, for your fallen companions."

There was a murmur of agreement from the collected Mothers, and for a moment Kayl was comforted. Then another voice said, "It is hard to speak of this now, and harder for you to hear, yet it must be done. Your choices now are two: find among the unfledged and uncommitted students of our order new companion Sisters to form a new Star Cluster, or take your place among the Sisters who serve the Star Halls and go afield no more."

"I—" Kayl stopped, not knowing what she was expected to say. She didn't like either of the choices, but she couldn't say that. Not to the Elder Mothers. She rubbed at her eyes, wishing she weren't so tired. Maybe when she was rested this would all make more sense.

"You need not make this decision now," one of the Elder Mothers said kindly. "Wait awhile, until the Varnans have been punished and the first of your grief has passed."

Kayl stiffened, her weariness forgotten. "What do you mean about punishing the Varnans?"

"Surely it is obvious that the Varnans are to blame for this catastrophe." The voice was kind, almost soothing. It raised prickles along the back of Kayl's neck.

"That's not what I said at all!" Kayl objected. "They didn't do any better than we did—Beshara al Allard *died* and Glyndon . . . Those visions of his have crippled him as much as losing an arm would have! You can't blame them!"

"That is not your decision to make." Kayl could hear the steel underlying the gentle tone.

"But I am the one who took the Star into the Tower, Your Serenity," Kayl insisted. "And no one knew about that thing inside. No one!"

"So you have said, and we have heard you." The voice was dry and noncommittal.

"You're implying that the Varnans deliberately led us into a trap!"

"It is a possibility that must be considered."

"But it isn't true! Your Serenities," Kayl added belatedly.

"We must be the judges of that. Your duties in this matter are finished," the Elder Mother said firmly. "And you are tired. Leave us to deal with the Varnans."

The voice seemed to echo in Kayl's mind, knocking loose bits of knowledge she had overlooked or ignored. The bits fell together into a horrifying pattern. Kayl shook her head, trying not to believe the words she heard herself saying. "You *planned* this. Right from the beginning, you *planned* to blame the Varnans if anything went wrong!"

"And if we did?" The Elder Mother's voice was cold. "What is your concern for Varnans?"

"Glyndon and Kevran are my friends," Kayl said, feeling anger rising inside her. "And even if they weren't, what you're saying about them isn't true. I won't be a party to it!"

"You question our judgment?"

"Yes!" Kayl shouted. "You can't do this!"

"We can. It is in the best interest of the Sisterhood."

"Then the Sisterhood is a lie. You're no better than the Circle of Silence, or the Varnans themselves!"

There was a stunned silence. Then, "Leave us," said a cold voice. "You are overwrought."

"I know what I'm saying," Kayl said, her anger turning suddenly cold. "I've worked for you, bled for you, and nearly been killed doing your precious business, but I won't lie for you. If this is what the Sisterhood really is, I'm leaving."

She waited, but no one spoke. Briefly, she was tempted to make some grand gesture, to break her sword over her knee; then she turned on her heel and left. Her boots rang faintly on the tiled courtyard. As she reached the door, she heard a faint, frozen whisper: "Go, then." Her steps did not falter, and she left the court without looking back.

Kayl sniffed, and wiped away a tear with the back of her hand. She had left the Star Hall next morning, after spending half the night writing everyone she knew, inside or outside the Sisterhood, telling them the truth. And, for whatever reason, the Sisterhood had *not* laid the blame for the disastrous ending of the trip on the shoulders of the Varnans. Kayl had remained in Kith Alunel long enough to make sure of that, then left the city with Glyndon and Kevran. She had been hurt, confused, and bitter; she had given up the work she loved and the only family she could remember. But she had not given up the sword of the Sisterhood. How could she pretend that she would do so now?

With a sigh, Kayl leaned back against the cool marble wall, staring at the mosaic opposite her. It made no impression on her; her eyes saw instead the faces of her friends. Barthelmy, her black witchlocks flying, grinning impishly. Evla, her slanted green eyes cool and serene and her silver-white hair braided close to her head. Varevice, a lock of brown hair escaping her cap, her brows furrowed in concentration. Mother Dalessi, her gray hair in a loose braid over one shoulder, her face creased with smile lines. Kevran, his dark hair falling into his gray eyes, his smile warm and friendly. Beshara al Allard, every blond hair perfectly in place, one eyebrow raised in cold appraisal. Odevan, gray-skinned and hairless, unmistakably a demon.

Perhaps this was the real reason she had come back to Kith Alunel and the Sisterhood, Kayl thought. To lay to rest the ghosts in her memories.

Kayl heard a thump behind one of the doors to the bathing rooms. She turned her back on it, hastily wiping her cheeks. A moment later, Mark came bursting into the outer chamber, wrapped in one of the drying cloths "Because they said they were going to bring us clean clothes, didn't they," and Kayl went in to take her own bath.

CHAPTER
TWELVE

Kayl bathed quickly, reveling in the feel of hot water and soap but unwilling to linger too long. When she emerged, she found Mark and Dara dressed and waiting for her. The Sisters had brought them soft, shapeless charcoal gray robes that fell to just above their knees and belted at the waist. Mark looked uncomfortable and out of place; somehow he had managed to belt the robe so that the left side hung significantly lower than the right. Dara, on the other hand, looked entirely at home. Kayl frowned slightly, wondering why that thought made her uneasy. Then she saw the pile of pale gray cloth beside her bundle.

"That's what they left for me?" she said, startled.

"Well, it's too big for either of us so it must be yours," Dara said. "Why? Is something wrong?"

"No, I was just surprised," Kayl said as she crossed the room and picked up the pile. "Only the Elder Mothers wear silver inside the Star Halls; everyone else wears gray. The shade of the robe indicates rank. The nearer the color is to silver, the most important the person wearing it is. I didn't expect them to give me one of the lighter shades, that's all."

"How come we got dark ones then?" Mark asked, sounding injured.

"Dark gray is for visitors and students," Kayl told him. "I was a member of the Sisterhood, but you and Dara aren't."

"What about—"

"Mark, I would appreciate it if you would save the rest of your questions until after I've changed into this," Kayl said gently. "It won't take long."

Mark flushed and nodded. Kayl slipped back into the steamy warmth of the bathing room, carrying the pale gray robe. She stripped hastily, then, with a curious mixture of eagerness and reluctance, she lifted the robe and slid it over her head.

The soft wool grazed the floor when the garment hung loose; belted, the robe was ankle-length. Kayl noted with misgiving that the color was even lighter than she had first thought. She had never gotten past the middle grays while she was at the Star Hall. Why were they giving her a status she had not earned?

Kayl picked up her old clothes and went back out to Mark and Dara. She unstrapped her sword from the back of her bundle and hung it at her waist. The star in the hilt winked up at her as she turned back to her children. "Now, what was it you were going to ask, Mark?"

"What about Father? Would he have had to wear this color?"

Kayl's lips tightened. "Your father was a Varnan," she said as calmly as she could manage. "I doubt that the Sisterhood would have let him in at all. Varnans are not welcome in the Star Halls."

Mark started to say something, then stopped, frowning. Dara looked at Kayl. "Is that why you sent Glyndon away before we got here? I saw you talking in the shop."

"It's part of the reason," Kayl said.

"Mother," Mark said, and stopped.

"I'm listening; what is it?"

Mark hesitated, then said carefully, "Do I have to wear this?"

"I'd prefer you did, for a number of reasons, but I won't make you if you dislike it that much," Kayl replied.

"It's not that. I just don't think I ought to take anything from these people if they felt like that about Father. It doesn't seem right."

"We'll be giving the robes back at the end of the visit, but I understand what you mean," Kayl said, and smiled at his serious expression. Mark had done a lot of growing up on the trip to Kith Alunel. "Go ahead and change, if you feel that way about it."

Mark nodded solemnly and picked up his bundle. Dara looked stricken. "Does that mean I have to change, too?" she asked, fingering the soft folds of her robe wistfully.

"I'm not making Mark wear the robe, and I won't make you wear something else if you don't want to," Kayl said. "It's your decision."

"You're not going to change," Dara said accusingly.

"The Sisterhood already knows exactly how I feel about their attitude toward Varnans."

"Oh." Dara plopped onto the bench, frowning.

Mark came back a few moments later, dressed once more in his traveling clothes. As he handed Kayl the folded gray robe, there was a knock at the outer door of the chamber. "Enter," Kayl called.

The door swung open to reveal Corrana. Her robe was the same shade as Kayl's, and the star of the Sisterhood shimmered on her left shoulder. She looked vaguely disgruntled, as if she did not approve of the task she was set to do. Her eyes swept the little chamber, and she frowned. "I understood there were to be clean robes for all three of you," she said.

"My son chooses not to be indebted to a group which considers his father's people their enemies," Kayl said.

Corrana's eyes narrowed. "And I suppose that if I say he must remain in this room, you will insist on remaining with him. Very well, then; he may do as he wishes. But if trouble comes of it, the fault lies with you."

Kayl made a quarter-bow in acknowledgement. Light flashed from the gem in the hilt of her sword.

Corrana's eyebrows rose. "You choose to wear your sword in the Star Hall?"

"As I wore it when I last was here," Kayl replied.

Corrana made a small, exasperated gesture. "Come, then." She turned and left, and Kayl and her children followed.

She led them down a long, straight corridor of white marble to one of the small rooms that bordered the inner court. She threw open the door and said in a disapproving tone, "They are here, Your Serenity."

Kayl motioned Mark and Dara forward as she went in. Her eyes swept the room, taking in the pale blue hangings on the walls, a bronze gong in one corner, and four chairs, piled high with cushions, grouped beside a closed brass brazier in the center of the room. Then she stopped short. One of the chairs was occupied by a white-robed woman. Her hair was white and the lines on her face had deepened, but otherwise she had not changed. "Mother Dalessi!" Kayl said without thinking. Then she remembered Corrana's salutation and corrected herself. "Elder Mother, I mean; forgive me."

"It is good to see you again, daughter. Come and sit down, and let me know your children."

Kayl drew Mark and Dara forward, noting as she did that Corrana had left them alone with the Elder Mother. "My son, Mark; my daughter, Dara," Kayl said, then turned to the children and went on, "Elder Mother Dalessi was the first Silver Sister I ever saw."

Dara's eyes widened as she bobbed her head in acknowledgement, and she glanced quickly up at her mother. Mark kept his gaze on Elder Mother Dalessi, his expression wary.

"Welcome to you both, Mark Kevranil and Dara Kaylar," Dalessi said.

"My name is Mark Rondalis," Mark said with an uncertain frown.

Dalessi smiled. "So it would be, in Kith Alunel and most other countries of the Estarren Alliance, where a child's name follows his father's family. But there are other ways of naming; among the Thar you would be named for your mother's family, Mark and Dara Larrian. We of the Sisterhood make second names of a parent's name, the father's for a boy, the mother's for a girl. So I called you. If I have erred, forgive me. Names are of great importance, and I would not willingly miscall anyone."

"Oh." Mark looked thoughtful. "I want to think about that for a while."

"Of course. But now, come join me. I have a great deal to say to you all, and little time."

As they took their seats, Kayl glanced toward the closed door. "Corrana—"

"Corrana does not approve of this meeting," Dalessi said with a slow smile. "She would have stayed, had I allowed it. A little denial of her wishes may do her good."

"Is that entirely wise?" Kayl said.

Dalessi's smile faded. "Perhaps not," she said. "Still, it

was necessary. For if she were present, I could not ask you openly: how great has the friendship grown between each of you and her, on your journeying here? Children, you first.''

Mark and Dara looked uncertainly at Kayl. "It's all right," Kayl told them. "Tell her exactly how you really feel."

"I don't like Corrana," Mark said positively. "She's too bossy. And she thinks she knows everything."

"Well, I do," Dara offered. "She's so beautiful and elegant, and she tells me things. Only—"

"Go on, dear," Kayl prompted after a moment. "Only what?"

"Only she doesn't like Glyndon," Dara said. "And she doesn't have any reason. He's nice, even if he is Varnan."

Kayl looked sharply at her daughter; she didn't like the thought of Corrana's attitude toward Varnans rubbing off on Dara.

Before she could speak, Elder Mother Dalessi leaned forward. "Glyndon? Not Glyndon shal Morag?"

Kayl nodded. "He came with us from Copeham. Didn't Corrana tell you?"

"No." The Elder Mother pressed her lips together briefly, and Kayl thought that she would not like to be Corrana when Elder Mother Dalessi next crossed her path. Then Dalessi went on: "And you, Kayl—how do you feel about Elder Sister Corrana of the Sussewild?"

"She has been a good traveling companion, and I wish her no ill," Kayl said slowly, "but I cannot feel at ease with her. She is too much aware of her own ends, and not enough of the desires of others."

"You have found the center of the knot," Dalessi said. "Corrana has her own designs and purposes, always, and it is not wise to trust her overmuch."

"You say that?" Kayl said, startled.

Dalessi nodded. "That one would be a second Varevice Tamela, if she knew how. In truth, she has the skill, but she lacks Tamela's heart.

"How much of what we ask have you been told?" Dalessi asked abruptly. "And how much have you agreed on?"

"Corrana said the Sisterhood wants me to go back to the tower we found in the Windhome Mountains," Kayl said. "She said someone has been tampering with it somehow. I agreed to nothing. If it hadn't been for the Magicseekers, I would never have left Copeham."

"Magicseekers?"

"Six of them!" Mark said with remembered relish. "And I got to see them right up close."

"I think you had better give me the details of the things that have brought you here," Dalessi said.

Kayl did so, beginning with Corrana's arrival at the inn. She let Mark and Dara tell their own portions of the story, and ended with their entry into Kith Alunel.

"And we saw Shee in the market!" Mark said, satisfaction strong in his voice. "Two of them!"

"Mark gets excited because Shee didn't come through Copeham very often," Dara put in with all the worldly-wise superiority of almost-thirteen over just-turned-nine.

"I can understand your interest," Dalessi said gravely. "Perhaps you would both like to meet our senior drillmaster; she is a Shee. I believe she is free now."

"Could we?" Mark said eagerly. Dara struggled for a moment with her dignity, then nodded emphatic agreement.

Dalessi rose and crossed to the bronze gong in the corner. She removed a round-headed stick from a nearby stand and struck the gong with it. As the echoes died away, the door opened. A girl of perhaps eighteen, dressed in dark gray, entered and said, "Yes, Your Serenity?"

"Mark Kevranil and Dara Kaylar would like to meet Eshora," Dalessi said. "Please show them the way."

"Yes, Your Serenity," the girl said.

The children got up to follow her. When Kayl did not join them, Dara looked at her. "Mother, aren't you coming?"

"I'll catch up with you in a little while," Kayl said. "I want to talk to Elder Mother Dalessi."

Dara nodded, and the children left. Kayl waited until the door had closed behind them, then looked at Dalessi. "Well?"

"It is good to see you again, daughter, yet I could wish that the circumstances of your return were otherwise." Dalessi sighed. "What Corrana has told you is true, but there is a great deal you do not know."

"You mean there is more to this summons of Corrana's than someone tampering with the magic of an obscure tower that no one really understands anyway?" Kayl said wryly. "Somehow it's no surprise. What's really going on?"

Dalessi shook her head. "The Sisterhood is changing, and

the Elder Mothers are not in agreement. I may tell you only this: In three days' time, you and Corrana will be called before a meeting of Elder Mothers to settle what is to be done regarding the Tower. There will be those who wish to talk with you before then; learn from them, but say little."

"Wise advice, if I were considering making the trip to the Tower for you," Kayl said, nettled. "But I've already told you the same thing I told Corrana—I'm not going anywhere near the place."

"If that is true," Elder Mother Dalessi said gently, "why are you here?"

"I don't know," Kayl said, half to herself. "I don't know."

"Then you had best find out, and quickly. You cannot choose well if you do not know the wishes of your own heart."

Kayl nodded but did not reply, and after a moment Dalessi turned the conversation to other things. Kayl told her more of the details of her fifteen years since leaving the Sisterhood; Dalessi spoke of women Kayl had grown up with, scattered now to other Star Halls. Finally Kayl sat back. "I'm afraid I should go. Mark and Dara will be wondering what's become of me, and we should find out whether Glyndon has found rooms for us yet."

Dalessi's eyebrows rose. "You will not be staying at the Star Hall? You would be welcome."

Kayl hesitated, tempted. Then she shook her head. "Some would welcome me, perhaps, but not all. And I think the children would be happier elsewhere."

"Perhaps you are wise," Dalessi said after a moment. "I will not press you." She rose and started for the gong, but Kayl waved her back.

"Does the senior drillmaster still room on the east side of the inner court? Then I can find my own way."

"Very well. I have duties to return to. But come again tomorrow, and ask for me." Dalessi embraced Kayl, then let her go to find her children.

CHAPTER

THIRTEEN

Mark and Dara were right where Kayl had expected to find them—in the inner courtyard with Eshora, the Shee drillmaster. What Kayl hadn't expected was the crowd of students grouped around them. Kayl stopped, stricken with sudden nostalgia as she heard the drillmaster's voice: "Cut left! and right! Step into your swing!" She started forward again, and the students fell back before the pale gray of her robe.

In the center of the ring of onlookers, Mark and Dara stood facing Eshora. They each held one of the weighted practice swords, and they were running through one of the standard exercise patterns. Eshora watched the children with cool, bright eyes that noted every hesitation, every misstroke, every flaw. Her own weapon swung smoothly, seemingly without effort, as befitted a senior drillmaster. Dara was frowning in concentration as her practice sword wove through the air; Mark, on the other hand, was clearly enjoying himself.

Kayl stepped forward, to the edge of the invisible circle that separated the onlookers from those who were drilling. Eshora did not appear to see her, but at the end of the next repetition she gave the signal to halt. Mark and Dara lowered their swords, panting. Dara saw Kayl, and a brief smile flashed across her face.

Mark's attention was still on Eshora. "Well?" he said impatiently when she did not speak.

"You need more practice on the fourth figure," Eshora

said. She raised her eyes and glanced dispassionately around the circle of watching students. Her expression did not change, but the onlookers began to melt rapidly away.

"Is that all you're—" Mark stopped suddenly to glare at Dara, who had sidled up to him and poked him in the ribs. Dara jerked her head in Kayl's direction, and Mark turned. "Mother! Did you see us?"

"I saw the last repetition," Kayl said.

"We could do it again," Mark offered eagerly, though he was still breathing hard.

"I think not," Eshora said. "Take your swords back to the arming room. There will be no more practice for you today. At least, not here."

Mark's face fell, but he nodded and sketched a bow. The children trudged off toward a nearby doorway. When they were out of earshot, Kayl asked, "And what *did* you think of their performance?"

"I think your son needs more practice on the fourth figure," Eshora said. She studied Kayl coolly for a moment, then half smiled. "You trained them yourself?"

"As well as I could. Teaching was never my field."

"So I have heard." Eshora's tone was expressionless, but her slanted eyes held green glints of amusement. "Still, you seem to have done as well as anyone could have."

"What do you mean?" Kayl demanded, nettled by the implied criticism of her children.

Eshora shrugged. "The girl has no talent for the sword. She may, if she works hard, achieve a minor competence, but no more. I doubt that the stars will send her the sword when she stands in the Court. She'll have to make do with one of the magic-related specialties, if she can."

"Dara is not of the Sisterhood," Kayl said sharply. "Nor will she be."

"Indeed. Your son, on the other hand, has promise. Were he one of my students, I would have him carefully watched and trained. It's a pity he's not a girl; he could have become a real asset to the Sisterhood. But then, your children are not of the Sisterhood, nor will they be." Eshora's voice was faintly mocking.

The return of the children spared Kayl the necessity of a direct reply. Instead she thanked the drillmaster gravely and shepherded Mark and Dara back through the marble halls to the street. She paid little attention to their chatter; her mind was busy with the implications of the conversation just passed.

Why had she reacted so strongly to Eshora's assumption that Dara would be entering the Sisterhood of Stars? Surely it was reasonable enough, especially when Dara wore the robes of a student and Mark did not. And the life the Star Halls offered was not a bad one. Yet Kayl knew with sudden certainty that it was not a life she wanted for her daughter.

The thought disturbed her. How could she consider returning to the Sisterhood if she would not consider letting Dara join it? And she was considering returning; the pleasant hour spent with Dalessi and the familiar sights and sounds of the routine within the Star Hall had strengthened her longing for the place she had once called home. She shook her head. Dalessi's dark hints were not particularly encouraging, Kayl reminded herself. And there was something else, something Eshora had said . . .

Abruptly it came to her. "She'll have to make do with one of the magic-related specialties," the drillmaster had said, with a tiny edge of contempt in her voice, as if the position of warrior held more honor or status than that of healer or sorceress or demon-friend. And the same assumption had been there when Eshora spoke regretfully of Mark as potentially "a *real* asset to the Sisterhood" because of his talent with weapons. Kayl frowned uneasily. Elder Mother Dalessi had spoken of changes in the Sisterhood, but could something so fundamental have altered so much in so short a time? The members of a Star Cluster were equals, bonded each to each; they had to be!

They had nearly reached the outer courtyard, and Kayl put her troublesome thoughts aside for more immediate worries. She found a Sister in a robe of medium gray and asked for the cloaks and packs they had left in the bathing rooms.

"They have been taken to your quarters, Your Virtue," the woman replied.

"I would like them brought here," Kayl said firmly. "We will not be staying at the Star Hall. And I am not an Elder Sister; you should not call me 'Your Virtue,' " she added as an afterthought.

"But—" The woman hesitated, looking at Kayl's pale gray robe and the star-hilted sword she wore. "Her Virtue, the Elder Sister Corrana, said you would be staying here."

"Corrana should have learned by this time not to make assumptions," Kayl said. "Will you please bring our things, or must we fetch them ourselves?"

"Elder Sister Corrana will not be pleased."

Kayl swallowed a sharp comment to the effect that she had no interest in pleasing Corrana. This Sister had done nothing to deserve the sharp edge of Kayl's temper; besides, the woman was clearly worried that Corrana would blame her for Kayl's defection. "You may tell Corrana that I discussed the matter with Elder Mother Dalessi," Kayl said. "Her Serenity and I agreed that I and my children would not stay at the Star Hall, at least for a time."

The Sister nodded, relief flickering across her face. Corrana would not openly question the will of an Elder Mother. She went briskly down the hall, and soon returned with the cloaks and packs. Kayl thanked her and was about to leave, when it occurred to her to ask whether anyone had left a message while she had been inside the Star Hall. Glyndon would not have tried to enter, but surely he would have sent someone to let her know where he was waiting.

The Sister directed her to a niche in the wall beside the door. On a waist-high shelf lay a bit of parchment, folded, with her name inscribed on the outside. The message within read, "The inn with the red star on the sign, in the street behind the library where the weavers work." There was no signature, but the letters were after the Varnan fashion, with extra flourishes and curlicues wherever there was the slightest excuse for them. Kayl smiled, and led her children out into the street.

It took much longer to reach the inn than it should have, chiefly because Mark and Dara were still full of eager questions about everything they passed. Kayl saw no reason to hurry them. She answered as best she could, enjoying their enthusiasm, and she was surprised and sorry to see the sign of the red star dangling above the street a little way in front of them.

They found Glyndon in the front room of the inn. The place looked neat and prosperous, and Kayl felt a pang of regret for the lost inn in Copeham. She told herself not to be silly. She was still feeling the longing for the Sisterhood that had overcome her in the Star Hall; it was sheerest folly to begin longing for her old inn at the same time. The regret persisted. Kayl shook herself and crossed to Glyndon's table.

Glyndon took them upstairs to their rooms, and there was a brief bustle of activity as the children dug through their packs to make certain various essential treasures had arrived intact. With a sigh of relief, Kayl unwrapped her cloak from her shoulders. Glyndon turned to say something to her, and his face froze.

For a moment, Kayl did not understand his reaction; then she realized that she was still wearing her star-sword and the pale gray robe the Sisters had given her. Glyndon turned away. "I'll meet you downstairs," he said over his shoulder.

"Glyndon, it's not—" Kayl started, but he was already gone. Kayl scowled and shook her head; didn't the man know her well enough to at least *say* something if he was upset? Well, she'd drag it out of him later, and explain what had happened. She turned her attention to cleaning up Mark and Dara in preparation for dinner; it was amazing how much dust and grime they had managed to pick up in the relatively brief time since their baths at the Star Hall. Particularly Mark.

Next, Kayl changed and made Dara do so as well. It would cause a stir for them to appear in the common room in the informal robes of the Sisterhood. Kayl found herself reluctant to leave her sword in the room, but there was nothing else to be done. The rapier would attract as much attention as the Sisters' robe.

At last they descended the stairs. Glyndon was hunched over one of the tables, a heavy bowl sitting almost unnoticed in front of him. Kayl led the children over and sat down. Glyndon raised a hand, signaling, as the children took their places. "I would have had them bring something for you earlier, but I didn't know how long you'd be," he said. "I was afraid it would get cold."

"You'd do as well to get a fresh bowl for yourself," Kayl said. "The fat's already hardening around the edges."

The innkeeper arrived, and Glyndon asked for four bowls of the stew. As the man left, Mark sighed in satisfaction. "The best part of traveling is having other people bring you supper," he said.

"No, it isn't!" Dara contradicted. "It's seeing all kinds of new things and meeting new people and . . . and everything!"

"And what kinds of new things have you been seeing today?" Glyndon asked.

Mark and Dara needed no further encouragement to launch into a highly colored description of their visit to the Star Hall. Kayl let their voices wash over her unheeded as her thoughts returned again to the puzzle of the Sisterhood. Something was very wrong in the Star Halls, but what?

"—and then she said she wouldn't want to call anyone the wrong name, and I said I'd think about it," Mark said. "Mother, why did she think it was so important?"

"Who?"

"That Serenity person we met at the Star Hall, the one in the silver robe."

"You mean Elder Mother Dalessi?" Kayl asked.

Mark nodded. "Why did she think my name was so important?"

"It has to do with the way the Sisterhood of Stars uses magic," Kayl said. "Do you want the whole explanation right now?"

Mark and Dara nodded as one; Dara's eyes were wide.

"All right, then. There are four . . . specialties within the Sisterhood. I was a warrior, a sword-bearer; the other three are sorceress, demon-friend, and healer, and each of those uses magic."

"What's a demon-friend?" Mark asked.

"A friend of the Changed Ones, the *sklathran'sy*," Kayl replied with a smile. "Most people outside the Sisterhood refer to them as demons."

"Why?"

"Because it's easier to say," Dara said.

"Partly," Kayl said. "But you're getting ahead of things. Now, magic works best if it is focused somehow. That's what spells and chants do for magicians; they focus the power on what the magician wants to do. But it also helps if there is a channel for the power to flow through, and that can be almost anything—a ring, a clasp, a circlet, anything."

"Like Glyndon's staff!" Dara said.

Glyndon looked startled, but answered readily enough, "Yes. Most Varnan wizards use a staff or a rod as a channel; I suppose I've never gotten out of the habit."

"What does the Sisterhood use?" Mark asked.

"Names," Kayl said, and smiled at his expression. "It takes a great deal of training, and some very special spells. And even then, if the stars don't aid the effort, it fails. But if the spells succeed, a sorceress's power is tied to her name, forever."

"It sounds dangerous," Dara said with a shiver. "I mean, couldn't someone who knew your name be able to use it somehow?"

"They could, if they knew it," Kayl acknowledged. She was surprised by the sharpness of Dara's insight; the girl had put her finger exactly on the main problem the Sisterhood had faced for so long.

"Then why do they do it?" Dara asked.

"Magic can be used more easily and quickly if it is channeled through a name. It's the closest humans can come to the kind of instinctive power the Shee or the Neira have," Glyndon said. He smiled. "The Sisters claim they have more power as a result; I would not know. There are other advantages, too. No one can steal a name."

"And placing power in a name strengthens the bond of friendship between the Sisterhood and the Changed Ones," Kayl said. "*Sklathran'sy* are even more vulnerable through their names than Sisters."

"Some think that the founders of the Sisterhood learned their magic from demons," Glyndon put in. "It would explain the friendship between the two groups, as well as the reason the Sisterhood uses such a dangerous channel for its magic."

"I still wouldn't do it," Dara said emphatically. "Think of all the people who know your name!"

"The sorceresses don't tie their power to the name they use," Kayl said. "They choose a new one during the ceremony, and it becomes their true name, to which their power is linked. They keep it secret from everyone except, possibly, their closest friends."

"Oh." Dara considered. "I still don't like the idea. It feels funny somehow."

Kayl was surprised by Dara's reaction, but not altogether unpleased. The magical specialties of the Sisterhood would, apparently, have little appeal for her daughter. She turned to Mark. "Do you understand now why the Sisters think names are important?"

Mark nodded. He was very quiet for some time, mulling over what Kayl had said, while Dara told Glyndon the story of their visit with the Shee drillmaster.

"And I don't think I did very well," Dara finished in a discouraged tone.

"Do you want to be a sword-wielder?" Kayl asked.

"Nnnnoo, I don't think so," Dara said.

"Then you needn't worry about it. Eshora told me you were competent; if you don't plan to earn your bread with a sword, you're not likely to need more skill than that."

"I suppose so." Dara did not look convinced.

"What did she say about me?" Mark demanded.

Kayl laughed, remembering. "She said you needed more work on the fourth figure. Remember?"

"Mother! That's not what I meant."

"It's what you said. Eat your stew; then both of you are going to bed. It's been a long day, and I don't want to have to listen to you quarrelling all day tomorrow."

There was an immediate outcry from both the children. The argument lasted through the remainder of the meal; Kayl ended it by summarily ordering them off. They went, still grumbling in low voices, and Kayl rose to follow. As she left, she said to Glyndon, "I'll be back as soon as they're settled. Will you wait for me? I want to talk to you."

"I'll wait."

Kayl looked at him sharply, disturbed by the gloomy tone of his voice, but Glyndon was staring down at the remains of his stew and did not see her. She hesitated, then turned and went after the children. The sooner they were asleep, the sooner she could come back and settle whatever was disturbing Glyndon.

CHAPTER
FOURTEEN

Mark and Dara were still too excited to settle easily into sleep. Kayl was forced to remain upstairs for some time while the two children used as many delaying tactics as their fertile minds could create.

Eventually Kayl got them into bed. She glanced at the door, sighed, and shook her head. She was not about to leave Mark and Dara until she was certain they would not get up and into mischief the moment she was out of the room. That could mean a long wait, the way they were shifting about. The strange noises of the city outside the window wouldn't help any, either. With the patience learned through thirteen years of mothering, Kayl set herself to wait.

Her first act was to adjust the wick of the small oil lamp until it was a mere nubbin, barely enough to see by. Then she began methodically going through the contents of her pack. It was a task she had been avoiding for weeks, and the last of her excuses was gone, now that she had time and room enough for sorting and straightening.

She was surprised at the number of things she had picked up on the journey; no wonder the pack had seemed heavier these last weeks! Slowly, she worked her way through the accumulated layers. As always, some of the "essentials" she had packed in Copeham had sunk to the very bottom and never surfaced again. There was a flint she'd forgotten; they'd used Glyndon's throughout the trip. And a square of wool, and a small bronze knife. And . . .

Abruptly, Kayl sat up very straight as she realized what was in the long, narrow bundle at the very bottom of her pack. It wasn't exactly that she had forgotten Kevran's rod; she had simply set the thought of it aside when she realized that she could not safely discuss it with Glyndon as long as Corrana traveled with them. And after so many months on the road, Kayl had become accustomed to the stiff presence of the rod in the bottom of the pack.

But Corrana was at the Star Hall now. And Glyndon was downstairs. Kayl smiled and drew the bundle out of the pack. As she did, the wrapping slipped and her fingers touched the wood.

Varevice was waiting in the hall just inside the door to the courtyard. Kayl took one look at the tiny crease between her brows and said, "What's wrong?"

"The Varnans have arrived. They're waiting out there." Varevice nodded toward the courtyard.

"And?"

"Barthelmy is going to have real trouble dealing with them."

Kayl raised an eyebrow. When Varevice did not expand on her statement, Kayl went to one of the window-slits and peered out. The three wizards were easy to pick out; they stood in front, and their robes were richly embroidered. The first was a tall, brown-haired man with a kind of angular good looks, the second a dark-haired, ordinary-looking man on the short side of average. The third was a willowy blonde, whose head was tilted at an aristocratic angle that proclaimed her contempt for the Star Hall and everything in it.

Behind the wizards stood their slaves, five men in coarse brown robes, each with several bundles at his feet. No, not five men; the last one was completely hairless, and his skin was the same gray color as Kayl's robe.

"Sweet stars above," Kayl whispered. "They've brought a *sklathran'sy*."

The rod slid from Kayl's fingers, and the memory ended. Kayl sat staring at the gleam of wood that showed through the oiled wrapping. After a while, she realized that her hands were shaking.

Carefully, she set the bundle down on top of the nearest pile. She leaned back, trying to put her thoughts in order. Kevran's rod could not, simply *could* not be the cause of her sudden remembrance. The rod was the channel he had used, nothing more; in and of itself, it was not magical. With Kevran's death, the rod should have become simply a piece of oiled wood.

Should have . . . but this was not the first time her memories had risen at the touch of Kevran's rod. Something similar had happened in Copeham, when she had picked it up in Jirod's kitchen, but she had seen no significance in it then.

Kayl shook her head, denying the connection, but her eyes were drawn again to the sliver of wood that gleamed through the gap in the wrappings. There was one obvious way of finding out whether this was real or a product of her imagination. Slowly, Kayl laid back the cloth that covered the rod. Then she bent forward and picked it up in both hands.

Barthelmy sat hunched under her cloak, staring into the fire. Her black hair was even more wildly disordered than usual, and she kept casting dark looks in the direction of Beshara al Allard and the gray-skinned *sklathran'sy* who was waiting on her. Beshara pretended not to notice, though she seemed to find more tasks than usual for her servant to perform. Kevran and Glyndon sat nearby, playing some sort of game with carved twigs thrown into a circle they had drawn on the ground. Kevran's dark hair was falling into his eyes, as it usually did when he was concentrating on something.

Kayl stood in the flickering shadows just outside the ring of firelight, watching Barthelmy and Beshara. She frowned, wondering whether it would be better to try distracting Barthelmy or to leave her alone. They were only a few days from their goal; surely Barthelmy could keep her feelings under control that long!

"Beshara should not bait Barthelmy so." Evla's voice came out of the darkness behind Kayl, echoing her own thoughts.

Kayl turned. "No, but what can we do about it? I've tried to tell her, but she only smiles and behaves worse than ever."

"I don't think that's the right—" Evla stopped as Beshara rose.

"Is the tent ready, Odevan?" the woman asked lazily.

"Yes, Mistress," the *sklathran'sy* replied. Kayl could see

Barthelmy squirming at his submissive tone.

"Come, then," Beshara said. She started off, then paused beside Barthelmy. She smiled slightly and said, "You seem to have an interest in my demon."

"*Sklathran'sy*," Barthelmy corrected coldly. "And yes, I do."

"I suppose it is only natural; they are a rare and dying race. But do, please, be careful. I have no wish for Odevan to get above himself."

Barthelmy leaped to her feet in indignation, but Beshara had already turned away. Odevan gave Barthelmy a wide grin, showing a great many dark, pointed teeth, then followed his mistress. Barthelmy stared after them, her fists clenched.

Kayl shook off her paralysis and went over. "Barthelmy—"

"What did she mean?" Barthelmy said. "About *sklath-ran'sy* being a dying race?"

"I don't know," Kayl said. "I think she was just trying to irritate you."

Impatiently, Barthelmy shook off Kayl's hand. "No! At least, that's not the only thing she was doing. You!" She gestured at the two Varnan wizards studiously concentrating on their game. "What did Beshara mean?"

"When?" Glyndon said cautiously.

"Just now, when she said *sklathran'sy* were a dying race! You must have heard her."

"I—" Glyndon hesitated and looked at his companion.

"She meant what she said," Kevran said quietly. "They're dying out. In another two hundred years, there won't be any demons left."

"*Sklathran'sy!*" Barthelmy corrected furiously. "And it's not true!"

"I'm afraid it is. A lot of them are sterile, and those that aren't don't breed true. And whenever a . . . *sklathran'sy* breeds with one of the Four Races, the child is Wyrd or Neira or Shee or human, never a demon."

"Breeds with— You're lying! No Varnan would ever . . ."

"Oh, but they do. Quite frequently, I'm told." Kevran's smile was slightly crooked, as though he were laughing at himself.

"Even if they do, the children of such a union couldn't possibly be normal!" Barthelmy's voice was hard.

The twist in Kevran's smile grew stronger. "No? But I'm normal enough, wouldn't you say?"

"You mean *you*—"

"There's demon blood in my family. A couple of generations back, but still recent enough to make the point."

"Oh!" Barthelmy whirled and ran out into the night. Kayl started to follow, but a hand on her arm held her back. She turned and saw Evla.

"Let her be," the Shee healer said. "She needs to think."

"She should have done her thinking a little sooner, and spared us a scene!" Kayl growled, torn between irritation and sympathy.

Evla sighed. "Kayl, it isn't that simple. You know how Barthelmy feels about *sklathran'sy*. And if they are a dying race, what will become of the demon-friends? And what will the Sisterhood do, when one of the points of the Star is no longer needed?"

Kayl stared. She had been so wrapped up in the concerns of their mission that the larger implications had escaped her. Slowly, she nodded.

Evla turned to the two Varnans. "I think you should try to keep out of Barthelmy's way as much as you can. She'll probably blame you for making her believe what Beshara said. It isn't reasonable, but it happens."

"I understand," Kevran said, and Glyndon nodded.

"We'd better go tell Varevice," Evla said, touching Kayl's shoulder. Kayl nodded, and they went in search of her while the Varnan wizards returned to their game.

Kayl heard a soft thunk as Kevran's rod fell out of her hands onto the wrapping. She blinked stupidly at it, then reached out and folded the oiled cloth carefully over and around it. She sat back, feeling numb.

The memories were the rod's doing, somehow; it brought them back as real and vivid as if she were living through them again. Another thought struck her: all of them were memories of that last journey with her Star Cluster. Was that because of her current preoccupation with the Sisterhood, or was it something in the rod itself?

Kayl looked speculatively at the covered rod. If she took it up again, this time concentrating on a different memory . . . She started to reach out, then stopped. What was she thinking of? She knew better than to take chances with unknown spells! Experimentation could wait until she had talked to Glyndon.

She picked up rod and wrappings together and dug among the little piles of belongings until she found a length of yarn. She tied the wrappings tightly around the rod, then put it back in the bottom of her pack. The rest of her belongings went in on top of it. It would be a nuisance to get it out again to show Glyndon, but that was better than having one of the children unwrap it out of curiosity.

Satisfied at last, she rose. Mark and Dara were sleeping soundly; unpacking and the interlude with the rod must have taken more time than she had thought. She picked up the lamp, adjusted the wick so that it burned more brightly, and left the room.

The serving room below was half-full when Kayl came down the stairs. Most of the patrons sat at the tables closest to the fire that burned on the raised hearth in the center of the room. The few hardy souls at the farthest tables kept their cloaks wrapped loosely about them against the drafts that leaked around the edges of the shutters.

Kayl scanned the room again. Finally, she located Glyndon. He was still hunched over the table in the shadows by the far wall, staring at a plate and mug in front of him. Kayl smiled in relief; she had been half-afraid that he had grown tired of waiting and had left in search of companionship.

Glyndon looked up at her as she sat down. He blinked, owl-like; then suddenly he gave her a disconcertingly charming smile. "Did you know that it's easier to be overlooked if you sit in the middle of the wall? People always check the corners when they're looking for suspicious characters, but their eyes slide right by the middle of the wall."

His speech was too precise, too careful. Kayl sighed in exasperation. "Glyndon, you're drunk."

"Not at all," Glyndon replied. "You asked me to wait; I've waited."

"And you just had a mug or two to pass the time."

"Or two, or three," Glyndon agreed. "I had to do something, you know."

"Of course." Kayl shook her head. "Are you sober enough to hold a sensible conversation?"

"Always. For you, I will be sober as the High Mage's Chamberlain and sensible as the Keeper of the Keys to the Queen's Treasury."

"Glyndon!"

He gave an exaggerated sigh. "Oh, very well. But let me

guess—you're going back to those bigoted women in the gray and silver robes, and you're wondering how to break it to me.''

''No,'' Kayl said quietly. ''It's nothing like that.''

Glyndon looked up, his face suddenly serious, searching her expression. ''It's not?'' he said at last.

''I don't know yet what I'm going to do about the Sisterhood,'' Kayl said, holding his eyes with her own. ''But when I do decide, I'll tell you first; I promise. That's not what I wanted to talk to you about.''

''Oh.'' Glyndon looked pensively down at his mug. ''Then I have used up a good deal of winter wine by mistake. Pity.'' He raised his mug again.

Kayl caught at his arm. ''Glyndon! You're drunk enough already.''

''Enough for what?''

''Never mind. I think this had better wait until morning; you're in no state to be discussing Kevran's rod now.''

''Kevran.'' Glyndon took a long drink from his mug. ''Yes, it's always been either Kevran or the Sisterhood, hasn't it? One or the other. I could never . . .''

Kayl waited, but Glyndon did not finish the sentence. ''I think you'd better come upstairs,'' she said at last. ''While you can still walk relatively straight.''

Glyndon muttered something and shoved himself to his feet. He swayed, then started around the end of the table. Kayl rose hastily; Glyndon's coordination had obviously been far more affected by the drink than had his speech. She helped him across the room and up the stairs, holding the tiny oil lamp with one hand and Glyndon with the other.

At the door to his room, they stopped. Glyndon pushed it open, then turned unsteadily and looked at Kayl. ''I'm sorry,'' he said. ''I didn't realize.''

''How far off you were getting? Don't start worrying about that now! Go on in and lie down before you fall down.''

''I—'' Glyndon stared at her a moment, then sagged against the doorjamb. ''Never mind. I'm not quite *that* drunk.'' He lurched upright once more, gave Kayl a smile full of self-mockery, and went in.

Kayl stood and watched as the door closed behind him. Then she shook herself and, in a very disquieted frame of mind, crossed to the room she shared with Mark and Dara.

CHAPTER

FIFTEEN

The following morning Kayl awoke well before the children, and discovered that, once she had dressed, she had nothing to occupy her time until they awoke. The only thing that came to mind was mending the holes Mark had managed to get in his robe, and she had no more thread to do that with. She'd used the last of it in Thurl Wood, two weeks before, and hadn't gotten around to purchasing any more.

Perhaps she should simply buy him a new robe. Mark had grown on the trip from Copeham, and even with leggings below it his robe was beginning to look decidedly short. Kayl sighed. Having nothing to do made her feel cross; she was accustomed to being busy, usually with yet another task in mind to do as soon as she was finished with her present work.

That could be part of her problem, she thought, and grimaced. In Copeham, she had buried herself in the work of running the inn and raising the children, to avoid thinking. Corrana's arrival had shaken her out of that rut, but she realized with chagrin that she had fallen into the same pattern again. The needs of the journey had replaced running the inn: finding food and water and firewood, choosing a place to camp, practicing her swordcraft, teaching Mark and Dara, deciding how far to travel next day and whether to spend some of their dwindling store of cash on an inn.

And she had allowed them to occupy her mind, seldom thinking of the decisions that lay ahead at the end of the journey. Now she was faced with those decisions, and she felt almost as unprepared for them as she had been in Copeham.

Kayl rose and walked softly to the window, careful not to wake Mark or Dara. The wooden shutter and the oiled cloth nailed over the opening kept direct winds more or less at bay, but it was still a cold and drafty place to stand. Kayl peered out the cracks around the edges of the window, trying unsuccessfully to see what sort of day it was outside. Finally she abandoned the attempt and returned to the slightly warmer area beside the door.

What *was* she going to do about the Sisterhood? Part of her wanted desperately to be one of them again, to have Dalessi's warm and friendly wisdom to lean on, to know other women who understood what she meant because they shared the same background and beliefs. To have a family again. Another part of her whispered persuasively of the more tangible benefits the Sisterhood could offer: food, clothes, shelter, an education for her children, work that suited her.

Yet she knew it was not so simple. Even if she could forget everything that had happened in the aftermath of her long-ago trip to the Twisted Tower, there would be Sisters who could not. And Kayl had spent fifteen years outside the Sisterhood, eight of them married to a Varnan wizard; she no longer shared the background of most of the Sisterhood. Nor did she share all their beliefs.

As for her children, Kayl doubted that Mark would ever be happy in the Children's Hall. Dara, on the other hand, would probably adjust fairly well. But Kayl knew from experience what such an upbringing meant. She did not want to become a stranger to her children, separated from them for six months or more every year when she traveled to other cities on the business of the Sisterhood. Nor did she want Dara pressured into joining the Sisterhood.

There was also the matter of the Sisterhood's attitude toward Varnans. Kayl sighed again. If Corrana were typical, the Sisterhood had changed little in that regard, and all for the worse. There seemed to be other changes, too, changes Kayl did not yet completely understand. And there was the mission to the Twisted Tower, and Glyndon's visions, and Kevran's rod. Somehow they were tied together, and Kayl could make no firm decisions about any of them until she understood how and why.

Mark stirred restlessly and sat up. Kayl rose to begin getting her children ready for the new day. She hoped Glyndon would be down in the serving room by the time they arrived. She had a great deal to discuss with him.

Though Kayl and her family lingered over breakfast, Glyndon did not put in an appearance before they finished. He was presumably sleeping late; on reflection, Kayl found this quite reasonable. She was considering the advisability of going upstairs and awakening him, when she became aware of someone standing beside her.

Kayl looked up. A girl of about fifteen stood waiting patiently to be noticed. She was wrapped in a heavy wool cloak; the dark gray robe of a student at the Star Hall showed beneath it. She bobbed her head and said, "Sister Kayl Larrinar? Your Justice?"

"I'm Kayl Larrinar," Kayl said, ignoring the startled looks Mark and Dara gave her. "But I'm no longer of the Sisterhood. Just call me Kayl."

"I bear a message for you from the Star Hall," the girl said, and drew a folded parchment from inside her robe.

Kayl took it, broke the seal, and read it. It was a politely neutral request that she come to the Star Hall as soon as she could; her children would be welcome as well. There was no signature, only the stylized figure of the eight-pointed star of the Sisterhood.

"How did the Sisters know to send you here to look for me?" Kayl asked the girl, frowning. "I didn't tell them where I would be staying."

"This is the third inn I've been to," the girl said. "And I think they sent out other messengers besides me."

"Thank you." Kayl smiled slightly. The Sisters were more anxious to see her than the tone of the note implied, then. Kayl was tempted to refuse the summons, but she had no real reason to do so, and she was curious. She could wait a few more hours to talk to Glyndon.

"Uh, Mistress?" the girl said uncertainly. "Will there be any reply?"

"I'll come," Kayl said. "Mark, Dara, run up and get your cloaks. And bring mine down with you, please."

While the children were gone, Kayl borrowed a charcoal

stick from the innkeeper and wrote a brief note to Glyndon on the back of the one from the Sisterhood. She folded it with care and left it with the innkeeper. At least Glyndon would know where to find her if he needed to.

Mark came clattering down the stairs with Dara close behind. Kayl took her cloak from them and wrapped it around herself, then checked to make sure that both children were warmly wrapped as well. The messenger waited with growing impatience, then led the way.

The day was cold and gray. A low sheet of clouds hung in the sky, threatening more snow. Kayl's breath rose in a white column of mist, only to be snatched away by a brief gust of wind.

"Ugh," Mark said. "I hate winter."

"You didn't say that yesterday," Dara pointed out.

"Yesterday it was sunny and everybody was out doing things."

"It will be warmer by the time we're on our way back," Kayl said. "And if it's nice enough, we'll take the long way around and I'll show you where the nobles live."

"And the Queen's Palace?" Mark said. "With the Shanhar guards, and the messengers waiting on horses all the time?"

Kayl laughed. "If the weather's better."

Mark gave an excited skipping bound and almost bumped into the messenger girl from behind. Kayl called him to order, and they walked a little way in silence.

"Mother," Dara said softly as they rounded a corner, "why did that girl call you 'Your Justice'?"

"Because that's how warrior Sisters are addressed," Kayl said. "Healers are 'Your Mercy,' sorceresses are 'Your Prudence,' and demon-friends are 'Your Compassion.' "

"That's weird," Mark said.

"You never called Corrana any of those things," Dara said.

"Corrana is an Elder Sister; they are all addressed as 'Your Virtue,' no matter what their specialty, just as Mothers are all addressed as 'Your Wisdom' and Elder Mothers as 'Your Serenity.' "

"Like that woman we saw yesterday," Dara said.

"That's right," Kayl said.

"Do we have to remember all that stuff?" Mark asked with trepidation.

"If we're going to have much to do with the Sisterhood,

you'll have to learn," Kayl told him. "You may as well start now."

Mark groaned and gave Dara a disgusted look. "You had to ask, didn't you?"

The remainder of the walk to the Star Hall was consumed by instructing Mark and Dara on the general points of etiquette among the Sisters of the Stars. Mark was determined to remember only the absolute minimum necessary to meet his mother's standards of politeness, but Dara was fascinated by the elaborate shadings of address that were possible. Kayl had to caution her not to attempt to use them herself. It would be all too easy for Dara to accidentally offend someone.

When they reached the Star Hall the messenger left them in the outer courtyard. The wait was brief; Mark's restless prowling had taken him less than halfway around the boundary of the courtyard when a brown-haired young woman with a scar across one cheek arrived. She took charge of Mark and Dara with brisk firmness, and directed Kayl to one of the inner waiting chambers.

"I would rather keep the children with me," Kayl said. "And I'd like to know why I've been called here."

"I believe it has something to do with checking some old records," the woman said. "I don't think these two would find it very interesting, do you?"

"Checking records?" Kayl asked. "Are you sure? The message sounded more urgent than that, and besides, I'm no scholar."

"I'm sure it will all be explained to you. It's the second door from the end, remember; make yourself comfortable while you wait." The woman nodded a farewell at Kayl and guided the children out of the courtyard.

Kayl let them go, though she felt uneasy about the whole situation. She told herself not to be foolish; she was simply overreacting to this highhanded rearranging of her plans for the day. She would have a few things to say to Dalessi or Corrana or whoever had summoned her so peremptorily. Frowning, she went into the main building, through the atrium, and down the hall. She paused before the second door from the end, then entered without knocking.

The room was quite small; the two wooden chairs and brass brazier were almost the limit of the furnishings it could comfortably hold. A wide band of brown and cream tile circled the walls at shoulder height. On the opposite side of the room, a small woman in a light gray robe stood with her back to Kayl, staring out the window into the inner courtyard. Her dark hair was pulled back into a smooth, tight knob at the nape of her neck.

At the sound of the door closing, the woman turned. Her eyes widened and she took a step forward. "Kayl!"

"Barthelmy?" Kayl said incredulously.

"Who else?" Barthelmy hesitated a moment more, then ran across the room and threw her arms around Kayl. "Oh, Kayl, it's so good to see you!"

Kayl returned the hug and felt a knot of tension dissolving in her mind. Tears stung her eyes. She released Barthelmy and stood looking down at her for a moment, then grinned.

"What's funny?" Barthelmy said, sniffling above her own smile.

"Your hair's coming down."

"Blast. I should have known better, but Cera was awfully persuasive." Barthelmy frowned, then reached back and rummaged in her knob of hair with her fingers. A moment later she shook her head, sending the mass of black hair flying in all directions.

"Now I know it's you," Kayl said. Her grin broadened as Barthelmy looked around for a place to put the pins that had held her hair in place. "Leave them on the window," Kayl suggested.

Barthelmy nodded absently and crossed to the window. When she turned back, her face was grave. "Kayl, I—I'm sorry about that last night," she said with difficulty. "I wouldn't really have let them blame Glyndon and Kevran, you know."

"I know. I should have known then."

"Why? You didn't expect the Elder Mothers to plan it, but they did. And the way I was talking, I sounded as if I agreed with them."

"We were both tired and hurt and confused," Kayl said. "Don't blame yourself."

"But I do," Barthelmy said quietly. "If I'd kept my mouth shut, I might have persuaded you to stay here."

"Maybe," Kayl said. She remembered Barthelmy saying in a hard voice, "The Elder Mothers are right! Why *not* blame the Varnans?" Had that really been the final straw, the last betrayal that had made her flee the Sisterhood into fifteen years of exile? Kayl shook her head uncertainly. "I don't know. I think I would have gone anyway. It would have been a little harder to leave, that's all."

Barthelmy did not look convinced, but she did not pursue the subject. She motioned Kayl to one of the chairs and took the other herself, then said, "What did you do? After you wrote all those letters, I mean."

"I left Kith Alunel with Glyndon and Kevran. They were going to go back to Varna to see if there was a way of stopping Glyndon's visions." Kayl smiled reminiscently. "Kevran and I sort of got sidetracked along the way."

"I suppose that's one way of putting it," Barthelmy said with a grin. "But why didn't you ever send word back?"

"After the scene I made when I left? And then marrying a Varnan wizard? It would just have stirred everyone up again."

"It might have been good for them."

"Possibly. But at first I didn't want to take the chance, and later . . . later I had other things to worry about."

Barthelmy nodded sagely. "Two children, Corrana said."

"Two children and an inn. That's enough to keep anyone busy!"

"I wish I could have seen it," Barthelmy said.

"I'm surprised you didn't. Or is there some special reason the Elder Mothers sent Corrana looking for me, instead of sending you?"

"Didn't Corrana tell you?" Barthelmy said, frowning.

"Apparently not. She wasn't exactly forthcoming about anything, frankly."

"Oh. Well, the Elder Mothers wouldn't let me go out to look for you because we were at the Twisted Tower together. They think we know more about it than we told them, and they're sure it has something to do with the problems the Sisterhood has been having with magic. They've been being very careful and secretive with everyone involved. I'm surprised they put us in the same room to wait for the Council meeting."

Kayl stared, then slowly shook her head. "Barthelmy, I didn't get more than a third of that. And what's this about a Council meeting? Mother Dalessi said that wasn't for another two days!"

"Elder Mother Dalessi," Barthelmy corrected. "You've

seen her? That's why they moved the meeting up, then."
Barthelmy nodded in satisfaction. "I was wondering."

Kayl took a deep breath. "Barthelmy, if I don't get an explanation of all this, and get it right now, I'm going to shake
you until your teeth rattle."

Barthelmy grinned, and for a moment looked exactly like
the impish girl Kayl remembered. "All right, then, but it'll
take awhile."

"I've got time," Kayl said, and leaned back in the chair.

"The main problem," Barthelmy began, "is the magic. The
Elder Mothers noticed it first, about twelve years ago, as a
kind of shadow interfering with their far-seeing. No one could
discover a reason for it, no matter how subtle the spells they
used. It was just a puzzle, at first, nothing serious. But it kept
getting worse.

"It started affecting more spells, not just the complicated
ones the Elder Mothers use. It was very slow; it took almost
five years to be a problem with anything really important. The
Elder Mothers discussed it thoroughly—you know how long
that takes—"

Kayl snorted.

"—and eventually they decided to do a joint spell, with all
the Elder Mothers cooperating."

"All of them?" Kayl had never heard of more than sixteen
Elder Mothers working together on a single spell, and that had
been to counter the Varnans' magic during the Wizard's War.

"All of them. They sent messengers all over the Alliance,
even to the tiniest Star Halls." Barthelmy shook her head,
remembering. "I don't think there's been a spell-casting like it
since before the Wars of Binding, but it didn't work. The
shadow or the interference or whatever it is was as bad as ever.
And the thing hit back. Twenty of the Elder Mothers died
before they could break out of the linkage, and all the others
were sick for days."

"Twenty dead!" Kayl swallowed. "Did I know any of
them?"

"Anaya and Saret and Passalessa, I think. The thing killed
mainly the oldest of the Elder Mothers."

Something in Barthelmy's tone made Kayl frown and
ask, "Barthelmy . . . when you say 'the thing,' you don't
mean . . ." Kayl let her voice trail off without finishing the
question.

Barthelmy looked away and swallowed hard. "They brought me to look at some of the bodies, to make sure. They were just like the ones we pulled out of the Twisted Tower."

"That's impossible!"

"I saw them!" Barthelmy snapped. "Don't tell me it's impossible!"

"I'm sorry," Kayl said.

"All right, then. When the rest of the Elder Mothers recovered, they held a meeting and decided to send another expedition to the Tower."

"And Varna cooperated?"

"They didn't have to; the Alliance had settled the dispute by then. The Elder Mothers didn't have to worry about starting a war if there were no Varnans with them. They were very careful about everything else, though. They spent a long time choosing people and training them and so on. And they didn't go inside at all."

"Then what were they supposed to do?"

"Check to make sure the place was still sealed. And it was. They couldn't get even a whisper of a spell past the door, and they couldn't detect the smallest trace of magic leaking out. So they came back. That was about five years ago."

Kayl frowned. "I suppose that's when they came looking for me. But why did it take five years for them to find me? I wasn't trying *that* hard to cover my trail."

"No, they didn't start looking for you until last year. I'll get to that in a minute."

"All right. What's been happening since this expedition?"

"Nothing," Barthelmy said. "That is, the interference with magic has gotten worse, but no faster or slower than before."

"How bad is it now?"

"No one dares to do any but the simplest spells anymore, wardings and short-range seeking spells and so on."

"I can see why Corrana wouldn't want to say anything about that," Kayl said. "I'm surprised Glyndon didn't mention it, though. We traveled together from Copeham," she added in response to Barthelmy's look of surprise. "And if something were interfering with magic, a Varnan wizard certainly ought to know of it."

"There's no problem with most kinds of magic," Barthelmy said. "Only with the magic of the Sisterhood."

"*What?*"

"The shadow falls only on us," Barthelmy repeated.

"And the Elder Mothers have decided it has something to do with the Twisted Tower."

"Not at first. When the expedition five years ago reported that there was no trace of magic coming out of the Twisted Tower, the Elder Mothers decided the problems with their magic must be caused by something else. Or someone else."

"Magicseekers?"

Barthelmy nodded. "The Circle of Silence may not be behind this, but they're certainly doing all they can to take advantage of it."

"That figures."

"Until last year, the Elder Mothers were sure the Circle was causing the problem. Then one of the merchants in the Old Town found a cache of old scrolls sealed up in the wall of a building she was tearing down. There was a complete copy of the Book of the Seven Wizards, and one or two of the others seem to date from before the Times of Darkness. The merchant's daughter is one of us, a sorceress called Halisor, and something of a scholar. So the merchant got her to take a look at the find."

"And?" Kayl prompted.

"And one of the scrolls had a lot of information about the Twisted Tower in it. It's a diary or a memoir of some kind, written by someone whose grandfather had actually been there. That's when the Elder Mothers decided the Tower had something to do with the problems the Sisterhood's been having with magic."

"What did the scroll say about the Tower?"

"I don't know." Barthelmy looked away from Kayl's incredulous stare. "Only the Elder Mothers have read the scroll; it's been kept secret from almost everyone else."

"You must have *some* ideas, especially if this scroll is what started them looking for me again."

Barthelmy shook her head. "They don't trust me."

Kayl blinked. She opened her mouth, then closed it without speaking. Finally she said baldly, "Why not?"

"Partly because I'm the only spell-caster in the Sisterhood who doesn't seem to be affected by the shadow," Barthelmy said, not looking at Kayl.

"Barthelmy . . ." Kayl did not know what to say. No wonder her friend seemed more subdued than Kayl remembered!

There couldn't be a sorceress in the Sisterhood who didn't at least resent Barthelmy's unique power; many must be actively hostile and suspicious. It was a painful position for someone who cared as much about the Sisterhood as Barthelmy did; words seemed an inadequate comfort.

"They also seem to think you and I ought to know some of the things they found in that scroll," Barthelmy went on hurriedly, as if to avoid discussing the implications of her magical ability. Kayl took the hint and nodded; Barthelmy continued with less urgency. "Since we never mentioned them, some of the Elder Mothers don't trust us. Either of us."

"I see," Kayl said grimly. This explained Corrana's secretiveness and Dalessi's cryptic hints. "And when the Elder Mothers found out I'd been talking to Dalessi yesterday—"

"They moved their Council meeting up two days, so you wouldn't have time to do anything if you really were working against the Sisterhood."

"Why didn't they just put both of us under guard the minute I arrived?" Kayl said sarcastically. "It would seem to make as much sense."

Barthelmy shook her head. "They don't *all* think we're against them. Dalessi doesn't, and there are others who believe us."

"And there are some who think we're no better than the Circle of Silence, aren't there?"

Reluctantly, Barthelmy nodded.

"In that case, I don't see any reason for me to stay." Kayl rose as she spoke. She was tired of being lied to and manipulated, and angry as much on Barthelmy's behalf as her own.

"You can't just leave!" Barthelmy cried.

"Why not?"

"Kayl, please! We need you."

"Corrana said something like that, too, but she never really explained. How can the Sisterhood 'need' someone they're half-convinced is an enemy?"

"The Elder Mothers are going to send another expedition to the Tower. They're desperate, Kayl! This time they'll be going inside. They want both of us to go along, if they can be convinced that we aren't enemies of the Sisterhood. We're the only ones who've ever been inside the Twisted Tower; they need our knowledge."

"Why should I try to convince the Elder Mothers of anything?" Kayl said angrily. "I don't want to go anywhere near that tower! It wasn't even my idea to leave Copeham."

"But the Sisterhood needs—"

"I'm not a member of the Sisterhood anymore, Barthelmy. If the Elder Mothers want something from me, they can send someone by the inn with a full explanation. But I don't promise to listen." Kayl pulled the door open with a jerk and went through it, then paused just outside the room. "Good-bye, Barthelmy. I hope we'll see each other again under better circumstances." She swung the door shut on Barthelmy's cry of protest.

CHAPTER

SIXTEEN

Kayl was three strides down the hallway when the door flew open again and Barthelmy came flying out like a small whirlwind. She grabbed Kayl's arm, forcing her to stop, and said, "Kayl, you can't!"

"No? Watch me." Kayl shook herself free and turned away.

"You're doing just what you did the last time, and it's just as big a mistake!" Barthelmy cried in exasperation. "Haven't you learned *anything* in fifteen years?"

Kayl stopped. "What do you mean?"

"You're furious with the whole Sisterhood, so you're storming off without thinking," Barthelmy said bluntly. "Oh, it's a fine show of righteous indignation, but all you'll succeed in doing is to convince the Elder Mothers that you really *are* against them. And once you've done it, you won't back down, and they won't apologize, and you'll never get the misunderstanding straightened out."

"Misunderstanding?" Kayl snorted. "Hardly."

"How do you know, if you don't give anyone a chance to explain?"

"They've had plenty of chances. Particularly Corrana." Kayl made her voice hard, but an inner voice reminded her that Corrana had told Kayl her true name. It was a profound gesture of trust; Corrana, at least, must not believe that Kayl was an enemy.

"Then stay and *tell* them why they're wrong. You won't convince anyone of anything by running off again."

Kayl hesitated. Her anger still simmered strongly, but it was no longer the boiling rage and hurt that had driven her out of the room. And despite herself, Kayl recognized the truth in Barthelmy's words. "Where did you find out so much about me?" she said finally, in a voice that sounded sulky even to her own ears.

"I've had a long time to think about the way you left the Sisterhood," Barthelmy said seriously.

Kayl nodded reluctantly. "I suppose—"

A tall woman with the silver-blond hair and slanted green eyes of a Shee came around the corner behind Barthelmy and stopped short. Kayl broke off in midsentence, and Barthelmy turned. The Shee woman frowned slightly, which was as flustered as Kayl had ever seen a Shee get, and said to Barthelmy, "Your Virtue, I had expected to find you in the first waiting room. Alone."

"Your pardon, Mother Lorea, but I was not told that I was to be isolated," Barthelmy said.

"I mistook the directions I was given," Kayl put in. "Barthelmy came out here to set me straight."

"Indeed." Mother Lorea studied Kayl for a moment. "You must be Kayl Larrinar, formerly a warrior of the Sisterhood."

"I am."

The Shee woman looked from Kayl to Barthelmy and back in cool appraisal. "Come with me, then, both of you."

Barthelmy gave Kayl a sidelong, questioning look. Kayl hesitated, then nodded. Barthelmy was right; she should not make impulsive gestures that it would be impossible to back away from. As she fell into step beside Barthelmy, she berated herself for consistently overreacting to the Sisterhood. She seemed to shift from longing for them to wishing never to see a Silver Sister again. She hadn't felt so off-balance since her training years.

The Shee Mother turned down a narrow hall whose floor was covered in deep blue mosaic. Kayl stared down at the tiles as she walked, forcing her emotions back under control. Pretend this is a meeting with Islorran's caretakers about a new tax, she told herself. It wouldn't be pleasant, and she was certain to disagree with most of what was said, but Kayl had learned over the years that she could find out a good deal about Islorran's true intentions if she listened calmly and patiently and did not commit herself during the meetings.

Kayl smiled suddenly at the image of Islorran's servants in the silver robes of Elder Mothers. She felt better now that she had decided what she was going to do and how. She looked up and found Barthelmy watching her with eyes full of concern.

"I'll be all right," Kayl whispered. Barthelmy's answering nod did not convey much conviction.

They reached one of the doors that led into the Court of Stars. Their guide entered without pausing to knock. Kayl followed the woman in, then stopped in the shadows to scan the courtyard. Her eyes widened in surprise.

The huge courtyard was over half-full. Elder Mothers in silver robes filled the ambulatory on three sides of the Court of Stars and spilled out between the slender columns into the roofless center of the Court. The fog of their breath hung above their heads in the wintry air. They must have come from every Star Hall in the Estarren Alliance, Kayl thought. Her eyes searched them, looking for Dalessi, but she was lost somewhere in the sea of silver.

The Court of Stars seemed strange and unfamiliar, and not simply because of the crowd. After a moment, Kayl decided it was because she had seldom seen it in daylight, and never in winter. She noted with detachment that the reflective pool in the middle of the Court was coated with ice; someone had swept the snow from it and from the flagstones that paved the courtyard.

The Shee woman motioned them forward. A rustle of surprise ran through the silver-robed women as Kayl and Barthelmy came into the open. A querulous voice from somewhere on Kayl's left said, "What is this, Lorea? We summoned only the Elder Sister; that other one was to wait."

"I found them together in the hallway, Your Serenity," said the Shee woman who had brought Kayl and Barthelmy to the Court. "Kayl Larrinar claims she was misdirected, and that Elder Sister Barthelmy was correcting her. Under the circumstances, I thought it better to bring them both to you."

"Quite so," said a thin woman on the other side of the frozen pool. "And what does Elder Sister Barthelmy claim?"

"I was certainly correcting Kayl," Barthelmy, and Kayl caught the faintest quiver of amusement in her voice.

"Is that all? You are such . . . old friends." The woman's

voice was level, but the pause held a wealth of insinuation.

"Indeed we are," Kayl put in smoothly. "And we had quite a lot of catching up to do. But I didn't think anyone else would be particularly interested in the details."

"Perhaps not," the thin woman said. "We, however, are."

"You may be interested, Stennis, but some of us have more serious concerns," another woman said. She looked a few years older than Kayl; a little young for an Elder Mother, but only a little. Her hair was a rich, dark brown. "If they've talked, they've talked; it's too late to do anything about it now. I don't see any reason to waste time hearing about it."

"I hardly think—"

"I'd noticed."

"Stennis! Javieri! Enough." The speaker was a small, bright-eyed woman whose face was a mass of wrinkles beneath snow-white hair. "It is time to proceed."

"Very well, Mika," Stennis said stiffly.

Javieri nodded agreement; as her head came up, she winked at Kayl.

"Then I think you may go, Mother Lorea," Elder Mother Mika said. "Thank you for your service."

Lorea bowed and left. As the door closed behind the Shee woman, Mika swept the assembly with an imperious gaze. "All three of the ones who have yet to speak to us are now present. I propose that we dispense with the separate questioning nonsense; it's a waste of effort and time, and at my age I'm not willing to waste either."

There was a murmur of amusement, but Stennis frowned. "You aren't in charge of this meeting, Mika!" she said.

"Someone ought to be, or we'll never get anything done," Mika retorted. "What say you, Sisters?"

The discussion that followed was relatively brief. Kayl watched it with interest. She could see tempers fraying beneath the veneer of cordiality. The Elder Mothers were accustomed to working in much smaller groups, four or five to a Star Hall, where consensus was easier to reach. Dealing with so many equals had many of them slightly off-balance. They *are* a lot like Islorran's councilors, Kayl thought, and felt a touch of sadness.

In less than half an hour, the assembled Elder Mothers had agreed to let Mika order their meeting. "Good," Mika said briskly when the decision had been reached at last. "Where's the other Sister? Bring her out here and let us begin."

Kayl had time to wonder who the third person could be; then Corrana appeared out of the crowd on Kayl's right. Kayl nodded, half in greeting, half in sudden understanding. Corrana inclined her head to Kayl, then bowed to the Elder Mothers and came to stand beside Barthelmy.

"We will begin with you, Elder Sister Corrana," Mika decreed. "Tell us your part in the search, and what you have learned. You will not be interrupted," she added pointedly as Stennis stirred.

Stennis scowled but did not speak. Kayl saw the corners of Corrana's mouth quirk, and concluded that Corrana did not like Stennis much. Then Corrana bowed again and began.

"I am a sorceress and Elder Sister of the Star Hall of Kith Alunel. Six years ago, the shadow that stands between us and the stars first affected my spells. For three years I continued to work as best I could despite it; then I was forced to turn to scholarship to serve the Sisterhood, for my spells no longer had power. Yet I continued to practice them, hoping that a remedy for the shadow might be found."

Stennis stirred again, her expression a combination of boredom and irritation. Mika gave her a sidelong glance and she subsided.

"Among the scholars was one called Halisor," Corrana went on. "She and I became friends. And when the ancient scrolls were found and brought to her, she asked me to help her unravel their intricacies. So I learned of the contents of the scroll that deals with the Twisted Tower. Because I knew, and because I had not completely abandoned the practice of magic, the Elder Mothers of Kith Alunel chose me as one of those they sent to seek Kayl Larrinar.

"The Elder Mothers advised me to travel alone, and not to wear the robes of the Sisterhood past the borders of the Estarren Alliance. In this way, we sought to mislead the spies of the Circle of Silence. We succeeded only in part; the Circle is more active outside the Alliance than we knew."

A murmur of dismay rose from the listeners. Kayl shifted her weight and wrapped her cloak more tightly around her body. She was glad there was no wind in the courtyard; it was cold enough as it was. She wondered how the Elder Mothers managed.

Corrana waited until the murmur had died away before she

continued. She skipped over much of her search for Kayl and went quickly on to her arrival in Copeham. She covered events from then on in great detail, including descriptions of Kayl's dealings with the villagers, her children, Utrilo Levoil, Bryn saMural, and Jirod. She spent several minutes on Glyndon shal Morag, reporting his visions, warnings, and behavior with scrupulous accuracy and careful neutrality.

Kayl was surprised and disturbed to discover just how much Corrana had noticed. Kayl mulled over the implications while Corrana summarized the escape from Copeham and the trip to Kith Alunel. Then the sorceress finished her tale, and for a moment the Court was silent.

"An interesting narrative," Stennis said coldly. Her narrow eyes shifted to Kayl. "What is your opinion of it, Your Justice?" Her voice held a sarcastic, mocking undercurrent, particularly on the last two words.

Kayl almost smiled. Stennis was very like Islorran's steward, though the steward had been far more blatant in his attempts to bludgeon Kayl into acting rashly. "I have no major disagreement with Elder Sister Corrana's account," Kayl said calmly.

"Is that all you have to say?"

"For now, yes."

Stennis turned away, a baffled expression on her face. Other Elder Mothers began questioning Corrana about various details of her story, chiefly those regarding Glyndon or the Magicseekers. Mika let them go on until they began repeating themselves, then cut the discussion short. "Two questions more, Elder Sister. Did you find it difficult traveling with the Varnan, Glyndon shal Morag?"

"Difficult at times, but hardly impossible," Corrana said carefully. "There is little love between us, yet I think there is some respect."

"And what is your opinion of Kayl Larrinar after your travels in her company?"

"My opinion of her is unchanged," Corrana said in a steady voice, without so much as glancing in Kayl's direction. "She is honest, strong-minded and fair, loyal, somewhat impulsive, and inclined to be hot-tempered."

Kayl felt her face grow hot. Stennis gestured impatiently. "But you do not trust her," she said.

Corrana smiled. "I trust Kayl now as I trusted her when we

met. I have given her my name.''

Astonishment rippled through the Elder Mothers, and
Stennis frowned in chagrin. Elder Mother Mika only smiled
slightly. Still looking at Corrana, she said, ''Thank you, Your
Virtue. You may leave now, if you wish.''

Corrana bowed and stepped back. Mika turned to Kayl.
''Now, Kayl Larrinar, I think we will hear you next. Many
years ago, you gave an account of the journey your Star
Cluster made to the Twisted Tower in the Windhome Mountains. All of us here have, I think, read the record of that account. Indulge us, please, and tell us again what you found
there.''

''As you wish, Your Serenity,'' Kayl said. She paused to
collect her thoughts. ''Exactly where do you want me to
begin?''

''With your arrival at the valley.''

''Very well. We found the valley late in the day. It was a
dry, barren place, very unpleasant looking. The Tower is in
the center of the valley, and it's just as grim looking as the
valley. It's black and bent, and there are grooves here and
there in the walls, running slantwise in a kind of spiral. I think
Varevice Tamela was the first of us to call it the Twisted
Tower, but the rest of us picked the name up quickly. It was so
appropriate.

''We camped on the hills; nobody wanted to go down into
the valley for the night. In the morning, we all went down to
the Tower. We had some trouble getting inside. The wizards
said there was some sort of sealing spell on the door. Varevice
and Evla and the three Varnan wizards all had to work together to get through it, and it took them all morning.''

''Why was that?'' Stennis demanded.

''I assume it was because it was difficult,'' Kayl replied. ''I
really can't say for sure; magic isn't my specialty.''

''Go on,'' Mika said, directing a quelling look at Stennis.

''Beshara insisted on sending her *sklathran'sy* slave, Odevan, inside first, to make sure it was safe,'' Kayl continued.
''He looked around, then came out and told us the Tower
seemed to be deserted, so the rest of us decided to go in
together.

''There was a little room just inside the door of the Tower,
with a stone staircase on the other side. Beshara left all of her
slaves except Odevan in the room, and we started to climb the

stairs. Beshara had Odevan climb first, right in front of her. Varevice and Glyndon came behind Beshara, then Evla and Kevran. Barthelmy and I went last.

"The staircase was a large spiral, so Odevan and Beshara were out of my sight much of the time. We came around a curve and Beshara was opening a door at the top. My memory gets a little confused after that." Kayl paused and took a deep breath, hoping she could keep her voice steady. "There was . . . something on the other side of the door."

"Something?" asked a voice from the crowd of Elder Mothers. "Can you not be more specific."

"It was a dull, dead black," Kayl said. "It must have been huge, because it filled the stairwell when it came after us. It didn't seem to have any particular shape, but it moved as if it were alive."

"Continue."

"The black thing came out in a kind of wave that engulfed the top five or six stairs, and then started oozing toward the rest of us. I remember Odevan shoving Beshara out of its way, and then he was buried up to his waist in it and screaming. Beshara tried to pull him out, but it got her, too. I think Varevice shouted for everyone to get back, but—"

Kayl broke off, shuddering. A kaleidoscope of memories whirled through her mind, distorted fragments set in a background of horror. She took another deep breath, and shook her head to clear it. When she looked up, Elder Mother Mika was looking at her with sympathy.

"It is painful to remember, even after so long," Mika said. "Take what time you need."

"Thank you." Kayl waited for what seemed a long time, until she was sure her voice would not shake, before she went on. "I don't remember the thing getting to Varevice and Evla. Barthelmy and I managed to drag them along with us, but they must have been dead already. We didn't know that then.

"I'm not really sure how we got down the rest of the stairs. The black thing followed us in short rushes—it would take five or six steps in a single gulp, then inch down the next couple, then take another five or six at once. That's the only reason any of us got away. Beshara's slaves saw us coming and ran for the door. There was still some sort of sealing spell on it; all of them died as they went through.

"Kevran and Glyndon were still trying to hold the thing off

on the stairs. Kevran saw what happened to the slaves and yelled something to Glyndon. Then he jumped past Barthelmy and me and pointed his rod at the door. He shouted that it was safe to go through now, and the three of us dragged Varevice and Evla outside. Kevran and I went back for Glyndon.

"We got to him just in time, and we barely made it back out before the black thing hit the door. The spell stopped it, thank the Stars. Evla and Varevice were dead; we buried them on a hill outside the valley before we came back to Kith Alunel. Glyndon had his first vision that night."

Kayl stopped. She had nothing more to say about the ill-fated trip to the Twisted Tower, and she felt too limp to bring the tale to a well-rounded conclusion. Let the Elder Mothers make of it what they would. She saw Stennis frowning at a small scroll, and wondered whether the Elder Mother had even been listening.

The silence in the Court of Stars was brief. "Is this the sum of your tale?" Mika asked.

"The return trip was uneventful, Your Serenity," Kayl replied.

"Then we shall proceed directly to your former companion, the Elder Sister Barthelmy." There was a stir among the Elder Mothers, but Mika raised a hand and quieted it. "I have been given charge over this assembly, and I have reasons for what I do. You may argue with me later. Your story, Elder Sister."

Barthelmy nodded and began. Her story paralleled Kayl's up until Odevan opened the door at the top of the stairs inside the Tower. Her view of the retreat down the stairs had differed considerably from Kayl's, and her memory of it was at least as confused. Several times, Kayl saw Stennis glance down at the scroll she held, her frown growing deeper with each glance.

When Barthelmy finished, there was a buzz of conversation among the Elder Mothers. A sandy-haired woman turned and eyed Barthelmy for a moment, then said to Mika, "Their tale makes no mention of the Crystal."

"The Ri Astar Diary doesn't say which room it was in," said the dark-haired woman who had winked at Kayl earlier. Kayl dug briefly at her memory and uncovered the name Mika had called her—Javieri, that was it. Kayl wondered whether the Elder Mother had named the scroll deliberately, and decided she had. She wanted to grin, but she kept her face expressionless, hoping that the rest of the Elder Mothers would become involved enough in arguing to let slip a few more bits of information.

"Nor does it mention this black thing," another woman pointed out. "I, for one, think we have placed entirely too much emphasis on one obscure phrase in that scroll."

"Obscure phrase?" Javieri raised an eyebrow. " 'What other magic was used in its presence, the Crystal took unto itself, to bind forever.' That seems clear enough."

"As a description of the Crystal, perhaps, but as the key to our difficulties? I am not so certain."

"I agree," the sandy-haired woman said. "And I find it odd that both of these women are confused in their minds about certain parts of their tale."

"Have you a clear memory of any battle of your own?" Dalessi's voice said gently. Kayl turned her head and finally managed to locate Dalessi in the crowd. She almost smiled, but caught herself in time. It would be better not to call attention to herself just now.

"Dalessi has a point," Stennis said smoothly. "Few of us could stand such a test." She paused, and Kayl stiffened slightly. Stennis glanced around to make certain she had everyone's attention, then held up the scroll she had been looking at and went on, "I find it curious, therefore, that the stories we have just been told match word for word the tale these two told on their return from the Tower some fifteen years ago. A prodigious feat of memory, is it not?" She tapped the scroll against her hand for emphasis.

Kayl's eyes widened as the implications of Stennis's statement hit her. If this were true—and she had no reason to think Stennis would lie about something so easy to check—then there was something wrong with her mind or memory. She forced her sudden fear aside and looked at the Elder Mothers, to see how they were reacting.

Heads were turning toward Kayl and Barthelmy, and distrust was clear on many faces. Stennis had timed her revelation well.

Mika looked from Kayl to Barthelmy and back. "Have you any explanation?" she asked.

"No," Kayl said with more calm than she felt. She wished she had time to think, to understand what had happened.

The ghost of a frown flickered across Stennis's thin face. "Do you understand what you are saying?"

"Quite well," Kayl said. "But I can hardly offer an explanation for something I didn't know was happening. Nor do I see any reason why I should try."

"Then you forfeit any claim to our trust or belief," Stennis said grandly. She turned to the other Elder Mothers. "Clearly, we cannot send her—"

"One moment, Stennis," Javieri interrupted. "Aren't you presuming a little, to make such a sweeping statement? I, for one, don't follow your reasoning, such as it is, and I certainly don't agree with it."

"Surely you cannot believe her!"

"If you mean Kayl Larrinar, yes, I do believe her. I doubt that I'm the only one."

"You aren't," Dalessi said from the other side of the frozen pool.

Several other Elder Mothers nodded, and a Shee woman said, "Do you seek to imply that they lie, Stennis? I think they would have found a cleverer way of doing so, had they wished."

"Does it matter?" Stennis countered. "It may be a lie, or it may be enchantment; in either case, we cannot trust their stories." She glanced triumphantly in Kayl's direction.

Kayl let the exclamations die down a little. Then, pitching her voice to carry through the continued muttering, she said, "I don't really care whether you believe me or not."

"Oh?" Stennis said skeptically.

"No." Kayl smiled. "You seem to think I have to convince you of something. Actually, it's the other way around."

Mika raised a hand to still the muttering and said sharply, "What do you mean?"

"I'm not a member of the Sisterhood anymore," Kayl said. "You can't send me back to the Twisted Tower if I don't wish to go, and you can't keep me from going if I decide I want to. Unless, of course, you decide to chain me up in one of the waiting rooms."

"Why are you here, then?" Mika demanded.

"I had to go somewhere, and I thought I'd listen to what you had to say."

"And that is all?" Stennis's voice dripped skepticism.

Kayl reined in on her temper. "And that's all. You sent Corrana looking for me; I didn't come to you. Your interference in my life has cost me my home and my livelihood. I still haven't heard your reasons, and I'm not sure I want to anymore. I've told you what I know about the Tower; it's no concern of mine if you don't believe me."

The buzz of conversation rose around the court as soon as Kayl stopped. Kayl looked around the courtyard, noting reactions. Barthelmy looked surprised, shocked, and pleased, all at once. The corners of Corrana's mouth were quirked upward in satisfaction or amusement; Kayl was not certain which. Stennis looked as if she were barely in control of her fury, while Javieri was nodding thoughtfully. Only the Elder Mother Mika showed no change of expression; she simply stood and looked at Kayl out of bright, unfathomable eyes.

Suddenly Kayl was desperately tired of the games. "I have no need to stay here and listen to veiled insults," she said, bowing. "If you want me again, send a message to the inn where your messenger found me this morning. But if I'm not satisfied as to exactly what you want and why, I won't come back. Good day, Your Serenities." She turned and brushed past Barthelmy and Corrana as she left the Court of Stars.

CHAPTER

SEVENTEEN

Kayl collected Mark and Dara and left the Star Hall. No one objected. The children were subdued at first, but the excitement of seeing Kith Alunel took over all too quickly. Soon they were arguing and running about as much as ever, despite the cold. Remembering her promise, Kayl took a route that led toward the center of the city, where the nobility lived.

She let Mark and Dara chatter at each other while she considered what had happened at the Star Hall. She should have asked for a look at the records Stennis had been waving, she thought. No, that wouldn't have solved anything; she didn't believe Stennis had been lying anyway. Something must have affected her memory, hers and Barthelmy's. And Glyndon's?

Oddly, the thought was comforting. Kayl resolved to discuss it with him as soon as she got back to the inn, and forcibly turned her attention to the other things she had learned. She understood, now, the odd attitude of the Shee drillmaster toward the magicians of the Sisterhood; without magic, what good was a sorceress or demon-friend? Poor Barthelmy . . .

Kayl wrenched her thoughts away from that fruitless and depressing line of thought, and went on. The Ri Astar Diary and the crystal it spoke of sounded fascinating. Kayl wished she had more than the few scraps of information the Elder Mothers had let fall. Still, it was not quite fascinating enough to persuade Kayl to return to the Twisted Tower, even if the Elder Mothers decided to ask her. She understood their desperation—the Sisterhood must be falling apart, if magic was so curtailed! But it was their problem, not Kayl's. She squashed a tendril of guilt at the thought and repeated it firmly. She did not owe the Sisterhood anything. They would have to solve their problems themselves; Kayl had enough of her own.

Two of Kayl's most importunate problems distracted her at that moment by throwing balls of snow at her. Kayl's dodge was too slow, and the snow spattered against her shoulder. She laughed and called Mark and Dara to order. Mark objected, but Kayl was firm; she did not want them catching innocent passers-by with their missiles.

"I have better aim than that!" Mark said indignantly.

"Possibly," Kayl said. "But I still say no. There'll be other times."

"Huh." Mark kicked, sending a fat lump of snow skittering into the street. "You said that last year, and all the snow melted."

"You forget that Kith Alunel is considerably farther north than Copeham," Kayl said. "And winter is just beginning. In another month the Frost Fair will start."

"Frost Fair? What's that?"

"It's a little like the Fall Festivals, only much larger. There are flame-jugglers, ice sculptors, knife-throwers, and all kinds of entertainers. People come from all over; even the King and his court spend a day or two at the Frost Fair. You'll see it, if we're still here in a month."

"Really? Will you take us?"

"I suppose," Kayl said with a mock show of reluctance. "If you and Dara are interested." She glanced back and stopped. "Where's Dara?"

"She was here a minute ago."

Kayl frowned, feeling annoyed and mildly worried. "We'd better go back a little. If she gets lost in Kith Alunel . . ."

"Oh, Mother," Mark said in an even-a-mother-should-know-better tone. "Dara won't get lost. There's hardly any people, and she knows which way we're going."

"Come on, Mark," Kayl said firmly. "And look carefully; I don't want to miss her."

They headed back toward the scene of the aborted snow-fight. Kayl was beginning to feel the first stirrings of real anxiety when she saw Dara on the opposite side of the street, talking to a tall man in a voluminous dark green cloak.

"Dara!" Kayl called. The girl turned and her face lit. Kayl started across the street, pausing to let a litter pass by. When she reached the other side, Dara was alone.

"Oh, Mother, I'm glad you came back!" Dara said before Kayl could say anything. "I was getting worried about finding you again."

"What happened?" Kayl asked.

"That man stopped me. He said he'd seen us come out of the Star Hall, and he kept asking me questions and wouldn't let me leave."

"I see." Kayl looked quickly up and down the street, but there was no sign of the green-cloaked man. "I think we had better head back to the inn now," she said briskly. "It's getting colder, and Glyndon will be wondering where we are."

"I'm not cold, and I want to see the Palace!" Mark objected.

"Tomorrow," Kayl said, and started for the inn. She kept a sharp eye on both children during the remainder of the walk, and tried with what was left of her attention to determine whether anyone was following them. She did not see anyone, but it was a relief when they reached the inn at last.

Kayl shook out her cloak with a sigh of pleasure; it felt good to be somewhere warm. She looked around and saw Glyndon talking to the innkeeper on the other side of the room. He was wearing his cloak, and his staff was leaning up against the counter. He was squinting in the light from the windows, and every time someone slammed the door of the inn he flinched. Kayl grinned knowingly to herself. She sent Mark and Dara to sit at one of the tables, then went over to join the conversation.

"Good day, slug-a-bed," she said as she came up behind Glyndon.

Glyndon jumped, then winced and half raised a hand to his head. He turned, looking sheepish and rather guilty. "Um, good day yourself, Kayl."

Kayl smiled and glanced at the innkeeper. "Could I trouble you for something to eat for those two?" she asked, nodding toward Mark and Dara. "They've been running around like Thar raiders all morning, and they're liable to starve to death if they don't get something soon."

The innkeeper chuckled. "I know what you mean; I've

three of my own that are much the same. I'll take care of it as soon as I've finished adding up his score for this gentleman."

"Adding up . . . You're leaving?" she said to Glyndon in surprise.

Glyndon shifted uncomfortably. "I'd planned to, yes."

"Why?"

"I just thought it would be better if I went somewhere else."

"Better how?"

"Last night . . ."

"So you got drunk. I've seen you drunk before, and last night wasn't one of your worst. You didn't even say anything offensive, that I remember."

Glyndon gave her a long, searching look, then took a deep breath and blew it out. "Never mind. I've decided to stay." He grinned at her suddenly. "Join me for breakfast?"

Kayl sighed in exaggerated exasperation. "For us, it's lunch. Oh, come on; I suppose the sooner you get some food, the sooner you'll get rid of that hangover."

"How do you know I—"

"I told you, I've seen you drunk before," Kayl said meaningfully, and grinned. "Over this way."

They joined Mark and Dara beside the fire. The innkeeper brought them a loaf of dark, crusty bread, a slab of creamy yellow cheese, and four pottery mugs of ale. Kayl cut chunks for everyone. "Did you get my note?" Kayl asked Glyndon as the innkeeper walked away from the table.

Glyndon nodded with some care. "What did the Sisterhood want you for?"

The children looked at Kayl expectantly. Kayl sighed. "They'd called a council of the Elder Mothers, and they wanted me there as head victim. I have a lot to tell you, but not here."

"Mother!" Mark protested. "You can't just send us off somewhere and not tell us anything. It's not fair!"

"Did I say I was going to do that?" Kayl asked.

"Well, no, but—"

"There are some odd things going on, Mark, and some of them are very serious. I don't think a public room is a good place to discuss them. Particularly after what happened on the way here."

"What's that?" Glyndon asked sharply.

Kayl looked around uneasily. The room was nearly empty; the innkeeper and the other two customers were crowded around the counter, arguing amicably about the proper way of making winter wine. Kayl looked back at Glyndon. "A man in a green cloak stopped Dara and asked her a lot of questions about the Star Hall."

"I see." Glyndon looked at Dara. "And what did you tell him?"

"Nothing much," Dara said.

"What does that mean?" Kayl asked.

"Well, he acted as if I were stupid or something. So I pretended I was, and kept repeating things and correcting myself and going on about things like how much I'd rather wear red than gray." She grinned suddenly, and Kayl was reminded vividly of Kevran in one of his mischievous moods. "He didn't like me much. I think he was getting annoyed."

"I bet he was a spy," Mark said.

"It's entirely possible," Glyndon told him.

Mark's eyes widened. He opened his mouth, then shut it again, looking very thoughtful. Kayl closed her eyes briefly; all she needed now was for Mark to go looking for Dara's mystery man. She resolved to have a long talk with him very soon. In the meantime, she had more pressing worries. "Can you describe this man, Dara?"

"He had a mustache, and his hair was dark. He was just a man."

"What kinds of things did he ask about?" Kayl went on.

Dara frowned, concentrating. "What the Star Hall was like, how many Sisters did we see, what did we do, what did people talk about. Things like that."

Kayl and Glyndon exchanged glances. "We'll have to tell the Sisterhood," Kayl said. "You did well, Dara, and I'm proud of you."

"I could've done better," Mark muttered under his breath.

Kayl decided to have her talk with him that evening, sooner if possible. "There seems to be no harm done. Still, I want you two to be careful about discussing the Sisterhood and what goes on in the Star Hall, even between the two of you. I suppose I should have made a point of this before, but it didn't seem particularly necessary."

Mark and Dara nodded in unison. "Good," Kayl said. "Now, if you're all finished eating, I think we should continue this conversation upstairs. You, too, Glyndon.''

The children were subdued as they rose and followed Kayl. Glyndon brought up the rear. Kayl waited until they were all inside her room, then said, "Glyndon, would you mind warding the room?''

Glyndon looked startled, but he nodded. Mark and Dara watched in fascination as the wizard made a series of intricate passes before the window, then repeated them in front of the door. He spoke three unfamiliar words and struck his staff lightly against the floor. The draft from the cracks in the window shutters ceased abruptly.

"All secure," Glyndon said, leaning his staff against the wall.

"Thank you," Kayl replied with a glance at the window.

"My pleasure," Glyndon said, and bowed.

"Sit down and let me tell you what's been happening.''

Glyndon settled himself cross-legged on the floor beside the children and looked at her. Kayl took a deep breath and started. She covered most of the important things she had learned at the Star Hall, stopping occasionally to clarify something for Mark or Dara. She hesitated briefly when she came to Barthelmy's revelation about the waning power of the Sisterhood's magic, then included it in her narrative anyway. The Sisterhood might not trust Glyndon, but Kayl did.

She did not, however, mention whatever had happened to her memory; that would have to wait until she could speak with Glyndon alone. She did not want Mark and Dara fussing over her, or casting worried looks at her back, and they would certainly do both if she let them get the idea that something was wrong with her.

Glyndon stopped her only once. "Are you sure you want these two to have all the details?" he asked, nodding at Mark and Dara.

The children made protesting noises. Kayl raised a hand to stop them and said, "One way or another, this is going to affect Mark and Dara as much as it affects me. I want them to understand what's happening. And they're old enough to be trusted not to let things slip in the wrong places.''

Mark and Dara exchanged glances and sat up straighter, looking solemn. Kayl went back to her narrative. When she reached the Ri Astar Diary and the Elder Mothers' cryptic comments regarding it, Glyndon turned white. She looked at him inquiringly, but he gestured for her to finish. She did so, then said, "Now, Glyndon, why did the Ri Astar Diary hit you so hard?"

"I have to see that scroll, Kayl," Glyndon said. "I *have* to. If it's that old, if it has information about the Tower, I might be able to understand . . ." His voice trailed off and he gestured aimlessly with one hand.

Kayl stared at him, appalled by her own thoughtlessness. She had been so intent on the Sisterhood and its plans that she had forgotten Glydon's visions. "I can try, Glyndon," she said after a moment. "But you know how the Sisterhood feels about Varnans."

"You say they spoke of a crystal?" Glyndon said as though he had not heard. "I have to see that book!"

"Glyndon!" Kayl said sharply.

He blinked, then looked at her. "Sorry," he said apologetically. "It's just that, well, it means a lot to me."

"I can see that. I'll do what I can." Kayl sat up suddenly. "Which reminds me, I have something else I want you to look at. Kevran's rod."

"You have it with you?" Glyndon said, sounding surprised.

"Did you think I'd leave it at the inn for the Magicseekers to find?" Kayl snagged the bundle with the rod in the bottom and dug through it until she found the carefully wrapped package.

"What is it?" Mark demanded, staring at the oilcloth as if he could see through it if he looked hard enough.

"It's the rod your father used to channel his magic," Kayl said. She looked at Glyndon. "Every time I touch it, I . . . remember things. Mainly the trip to the Tower."

"It shouldn't be doing that. You're sure it's the rod itself, not just associations?" Glyndon said. There were harsh edges to his voice, but his tone was gentle.

"I'm sure."

"Can I try it?" Mark asked.

"No." Kayl passed the package to Glyndon, taking care not to dislodge the wrappings.

Glyndon stared at it for a moment. "I suppose I'd better look at it," he said finally, and laid back the folds of oilcloth.

Mark leaned forward eagerly as the dark, shiny wood came

into view. Dara was looking at Kayl with a troubled frown. "Mother, why didn't you ever *tell* us about any of this?" she said.

"There was no reason to," Kayl said.

"There was no reason not to!"

"I thought there was."

"What?"

"I don't think this is the time to go into it. Later—"

"Later, later, you always say you'll explain later and you never do!" Dara said angrily.

"That's enough, Dara," Kayl said quietly. "I said we'd discuss it later, and that's the end of the matter."

Dara sat back on her heels, her expression mutinous. Kayl waited until she was sure her daughter was not going to try to press matters, then turned away, feeling tired and a little guilty.

The rod lay on the bare floorboards. Glyndon knelt beside it, scrutinizing it with his hands clasped behind his back to avoid an accidental touch. He looked up as Kayl's head turned. "Nothing's changed in its appearance, and I can't find any traces of magic lingering on it. Would you mind demonstrating?"

"If you insist," Kayl said. Seeing Glyndon's expression, she added quickly, "It's not that bad, Glyndon. They're only memories. Just tell me when."

Glyndon started to say something, then stopped short and simply gestured Kayl toward the rod. She leaned over and brushed her fingers across it.

The man was tall and lean, with gray eyes and dark hair that was just beginning to show streaks of gray. Kayl watching him closely as he talked, letting her companions ask most of the questions.

"Yes, I know the mountains well," he told Beshara. His voice was smooth as currant wine, and surprisingly deep for such a lean man. "I've lived in them all my life."

Kayl blinked. Was there an undercurrent of anger in his last few words? Her eyes narrowed and she leaned forward as Beshara smiled and said, "Would you feel capable of acting as our guide, then?"

"I'm capable enough," the man said pleasantly, "but I'm

no guide. I can direct you, though, if that's what you need."

"That is what we need. Among other things," Beshara murmured.

"This is ridiculous," Barthelmy snapped. "Ask him what we want to know, or let him go, but in the stars' name stop sidling around the question!"

"Barthelmy." Evla put a soothing hand on her arm.

"She has a point," Kevran said quietly.

Beshara glanced at him and shrugged. "Oh, very well, do as you like."

Kevran turned to the dark-haired man, who had been watching the exchange with interest. "We are, as you may have guessed, searching for something. We know it is somewhere in the Windhome Mountains, and we suspect that it is . . . unusual."

"Not much of a description," the man commented.

"No, but we are hoping you can suggest a place to start looking." Kevran smiled wryly. "The Windhome Mountains are a lot to search, otherwise."

The dark-haired man hesitated. "There's a place I know of," he said, and stopped.

"Tell us. Please," Varevice said.

"It's a valley, a little less than two weeks' ride north and east of here," the man said reluctantly. "There's a tower . . . It's an evil place; no one lives there. Those who know of it avoid it."

Kevran exchanged glances with Beshara and Varevice. "It's somewhere to start, and it's in the right area," he said. He turned back to the dark-haired man. "Can you tell us how to find it? We'll pay well for the information."

The man looked startled, and his eyes darkened. For a moment, Kayl thought he was going to refuse; then he said, "I will tell you how to reach the valley, but I will not take your money for it."

"So?" Beshara raised an eyebrow, then shrugged. "As you wish. Are you lettered? Write out your directions, then, and give them to Kevran there in the morning, and we will thank you for it."

The man nodded and turned away. As he passed Kayl on his way out, she heard him mutter, "For this, there should be no thanks."

• • •

Kayl's fingers bumped against the floor of the room, and she blinked. Mark and Dara were looking at her with wary fascination. "That was weird," Mark said tentatively.

Kayl smiled at him. "You don't know how right you are." She looked at Glyndon. "Did you find out anything?"

"Something happened, but I'm not sure what," Glyndon admitted. "What was it like?"

"Like daydreaming, I suppose," Kayl said. "I remembered the inn where Beshara found the man who told us about the Tower and the valley."

"Mmm." Glyndon looked down at the rod. "I suppose the next step is obvious," he said, half to himself. As he spoke, he reached forward. Kayl's protest was a fraction of a second too late to keep him from touching the rod.

Glyndon went white to the lips. Kayl knocked his hand away from the rod, then caught him as he swayed sideways and almost fell on top of it. He gasped and went limp in her arms. Frightened, she shook him. He did not move at once, and for a moment, she thought he had lost consciousness. Then he shuddered and pushed himself back up to his knees.

Kayl steadied him briefly, then let her hand drop. "See if there's any water left in the wash pitcher, Mark," she said.

"That's not necessary," Glyndon said, raising his head.

Mark looked uncertainly from Glyndon to his mother. Kayl nodded. Glyndon was still white, but she could tell from the set of his shoulders that he was going to be stubborn, and there was no point in getting Mark caught in a tug-of-war.

"Thank you," Glyndon said as Mark settled back. He looked at Kayl and there was a gleam of amusement on his face. "I do believe you are right about this thing," he said, indicating the rod.

"Good of you to admit it," Kayl said, grinning back at him in relief. She wanted to ask what he had seen or remembered, but could not quite bring herself to do so.

"The question now is why." Glyndon stared speculatively at the rod, curiosity chasing the signs of strain from his face. "Kevran said something once, a long time ago. . . . I wonder if he ever did it?"

"Glyndon!" Kayl said in much the same tone she used to Mark and Dara. "Make sense."

"Hmmm? Oh. It's just an idea. Kevran was experimenting for a while with using different woods and herbs and so on as channels. He said once that he was going to have a compartment made in his rod, so he could see what effects he could get by using two different things at once.''

As he spoke, Glyndon picked up the oiled cloth that had wrapped the rod. He covered his hands with it and picked up the rod. For a long moment, he studied it, turning it over and staring down the length of it, then shifting it so the light caught it at different angles. Then he let his breath out in a little exclamation of satisfaction. He slid his hands along the oiled cloth to either end of the rod and gave a sudden, sharp twist.

The center of the rod came apart along a clean line. Kayl leaned forward. The joining had been painstakingly made; when the two halves were fitted together the crack was all but invisible. The left half of the rod ended in a short, grooved protuberance like the tang of a knife, but the right half of the rod had been hollowed out for some way. Kayl could see dried moss filling the cavity.

Glyndon set the solid half of the rod on the floor. "Have you got something I can use to pull this out?" he asked, indicating the moss-packed hole. "Under the circumstances, I'd rather not use my fingers.''

"Here,'' Mark said before Kayl could reply. He pulled his dagger from his belt and offered it hilt-first to Glyndon. "Will this do?''

"Very well, I think,'' Glyndon said, taking the dagger. He picked at the moss with the dagger's point, then turned the rod over and shook it.

A shower of powdery moss fragments fell out of the hole. Glyndon muttered something and hit the rod sharply with the hilt of the dagger. A wad of moss dropped out and something hit the floor with a rattle. Kayl leaned forward. Something gleamed up at her from the center of the dry debris.

It was a piece of crystal about the size of her thumbnail.

CHAPTER

EIGHTEEN

Kayl leaned closer, staring at the crystal. Three sides were perfectly flat and intersected at right angles, forming three straight edges. The fourth side was slightly curved and had an irregular rim, as though the crystal had been chipped . . . or as though it was a chip of something larger.

She looked up. Glyndon was staring at the bit of crystal and his face was gray. For a moment she thought he was '*seeing*' things again, and she went cold. "Glyndon?" she said softly. "Do you know what that is?"

"I—no, it can't be—I don't—"

"Glyndon! What's the matter with you? What can't it be?"

"It can't be from the Twisted Tower," Glyndon whispered, his eyes still fixed on the piece of crystal. "It can't be!"

"Is it magic?" Mark said curiously. "It doesn't look like anything special to me."

"Do you think you can tell whether something is magic just by staring at it?" Dara said scornfully.

"Don't touch it!" Kayl said as Mark leaned forward, frowning.

"I wasn't going to," Mark said in an injured tone. "I was just *looking*."

"Look from a little farther away, then." Kayl turned to Glyndon, who had recovered some of his color. "The same thought occurred to me—that crystal the Elder Mothers were talking about. But Kevran couldn't have found anything in the

Tower without the rest of us knowing."

"I suppose so," Glyndon said without conviction.

Kayl gave him a sharp look. "Do you know something I don't?"

Glyndon's head came up. "Quite a lot," he said with the ghost of a smile. "Unless you've spent a couple of years studying on Varna since the last time we met."

"Glyndon! Be serious. Did Kevran go back to the Tower that first night, when I thought he was helping you?"

"No," Glyndon said flatly. His voice held an undercurrent of relief. "Kevran was with me all night."

"Then there's no way that crystal could be from the Twisted Tower. None." Kayl wondered whether she was trying harder to convince Glyndon or to convince herself. She looked down at the crystal again and said slowly, "I suppose you're sure that this is what was making Kevran's rod do whatever it was doing?"

"Quite sure." Glyndon picked up the two halves of the rod, one in each hand, and joined them together again. "See? There's nothing special about it now."

"It was Father's!" Dara said indignantly.

"Then can I have it?" Mark said almost simultaneously.

"Not now," Kayl said to Mark. She was beginning to wish she had sent the children somewhere else, anywhere else, while she and Glyndon discussed the rod. Not that she had anywhere to send them. She looked down at the crystal and sighed. "I suppose we ought to make sure," she said, half to herself, and reached toward it.

"Kayl!" Glyndon said in alarm. He bent forward hastily, also reaching for the crystal. Simultaneously, their fingers touched it.

The circular room was full of light. Large, arched windows were spaced at regular intervals around the curving walls, providing an uninspiring view of the dead valley below. The side wall where the stairway came up was covered with a tapestry in cream and crimson, and more tapestries hung between the windows. A cream-colored frieze circled the wall just below the high, domed ceiling. The only furnishings were a marble bench on one side and the waist-high pedestal in the center of the room, where the huge crystal cube rested. The place should have seemed pleasant and airy; instead, Kayl felt as if she were standing in a tomb.

The wizards were all clustered around the pedestal, muttering over the crystal. Kevran was taking measurements, while Glyndon hunched over one side, feeling for any irregularities in the surface. Varevice and Beshara seemed to be arguing about something; Evla was staring into the cube as if she were in a trance. Only Barthelmy and Kayl hung back. Barthelmy watched Odevan standing behind his mistress in an attitude of respectful attention. Kayl prowled the perimeter of the room, looking for conventional, nonmagical threats.

"I give up," Kevran said at last. "The thing's a perfect cube, as near as I can tell, and that's *all* I can tell."

"You've done better than I have," Varevice said sourly. "I've done every spell I can think of, and that lump of rock is still just a lump of rock."

"Odevan!" Beshara said peremptorily. "Can you see anything?"

The *sklathran'sy* came forward and pressed his long, spidery fingers against the top of the crystal. "No, Mistress."

"Could it be witch-glass?" Evla asked. "I can't think of anything else that's so dead to magic."

Beshara looked speculatively at the Crystal. "I hadn't thought of that, but you're probably right. It's a pity, in a way; we'll have to destroy it now."

"Destroy it?" Glyndon said, looking up from his crouch beside the cube. "Why?"

"Beshara's right," Varevice said reluctantly. "If it is witch-glass, a lump this size would account for that odd echo in the Elder Mothers' seeing spells."

"Not to mention the blur in the ones the High Mage cast," Beshara put in. "I'm afraid the only way of stopping the interference is to break the cube up into smaller chunks."

"I don't think that's a good idea," Glyndon said. "Especially since we still aren't sure what this really is."

"Have you some alternate suggestion?" Beshara asked sweetly.

"We could try breaking off a small piece to test," Kevran said. "That ought to at least tell us what the cube is made of."

"But that will spoil the cube!" Glyndon objected.

"I don't like the idea either, but I think it's the only way we'll ever find out what we need to know," Varevice said.

"And it's better than just breaking it up."

Evla nodded agreement. Glyndon looked from one to another, then threw up his hands. "All right, then, go ahead. You will anyway. Just don't slip and hit me instead." He crouched and began again his examination of the Crystal's surface, his palms pressed flat against one vertical side of the cube.

"Everyone agrees, then?" Kevran asked, looking at the other magicians. "All right." He drew his dagger and raised it over his head, then brought it down, hilt first, in a hard, sharp blow on one corner of the crystal cube. The Crystal rang with a high, pure note, but did not break. Kevran raised the dagger and brought it down again.

With a loud crack, a small corner of the cube broke off. The ringing of the crystal filled the chamber, still a single high note but without the same purity. Momentarily, it mingled with Glyndon's scream of anguish; then he collapsed forward over the top of the crystal cube, his hands still pressed against its surface.

Evla was on her feet at once, bending over the unconscious Varnan. Kayl started forward to see if she could help.

"Behind you!" Barthelmy's cry of warning snapped Kayl's attention away from Glyndon. She turned, and took an involuntary step backward.

A thick, dull blackness was oozing from the wall behind her. It spread rapidly, forming a dark, wet curtain that shut out the light from the windows, then began creeping forward like a cat stalking. Kayl drew her sword and backed away. The blackness wiggled and moved up another foot. She heard screams and shouting behind her, but she could not take her attention off of the black thing long enough to glance around. Somehow she was certain that if she did, it would engulf her.

The thing moved forward. The light in the room dimmed as it blocked more of the windows. Kayl cut at it with her sword, but the blackness closed behind the blade like molasses flowing together behind a knife. She slashed at it again, and again, and felt the balance of her blade change in her hand. She looked down and saw that the metal was dull and pitted, and the edge of the sword visibly eaten away.

She retreated again and glanced around. Her companions, except for Glyndon, were casting spell after spell at the dripping black curtain, with no apparent effect. The blackness covered half the chamber wall now—including the door to the stairway. They were trapped.

A long tendril whipped out from the blackness and wrapped itself around Odevan's waist. The demon screamed in agony and tore at it with his hands. Beshara and Barthelmy cried out together, but it was Beshara who dove forward to grab Odevan's arm. With her free hand she sent a gout of fire at the tentacle. The blackness continued to draw Odevan closer, and Beshara with him. She did not release her hold, even when the black thing overwhelmed them.

Kayl wanted to turn her head away, but she did not dare. Another tentacle flashed toward her; she slashed at it and deflected it enough to dodge the rest of the way out of its path. She heard Evla scream, and her heart contracted.

Glyndon was leaning heavily against the crystal, shaking his head as if to clear it. Kayl shouted at him to do something; they needed everyone, even a groggy Varnan wizard. Then a wave of mental agony struck her and she staggered, knowing that one of her star-sisters was dead. The blackness oozed closer, and Kayl slashed at it angrily, hopelessly, uselessly. . . .

"Mother? Mother, are you all right? Mother?"

Dara's voice, growing more and more frantic, brought Kayl back to herself. The crystal had rolled a little away from her hand and Glyndon's; looking at it, she shuddered. She forced herself to look up and meet Dara's worried gaze. "It's all right, Dara. I'm fine. I think."

"Are you sure? You looked . . ." Dara stopped, shaking her head for lack of any better description.

"There's no harm done," Kayl said. She glanced across at Glyndon, then turned back to Dara. "Would you and Mark go down and get a couple of mugs of wine from the inn-keeper? It will break the warding, but I don't think that matters much anymore, and Glyndon and I could use them."

Mark and Dara exchanged glances, and Dara nodded. They slipped out of the room. Kayl looked back at Glyndon as the door closed. "Are you all right? You look a little . . ." She made an ambiguous gesture.

"I'm fine," Glyndon said with an attempt at a smile. "I think that thing just brought back the worst effects of last night's ale."

"Maybe next time you won't drink so much of it, then," Kayl said, trying to match his tone. "And I thought you told me it was winter wine."

"It was." Glyndon shook his head experimentally. "At least the effects of the crystal don't last as long as the effects of the wine. What did it do to you?"

"Nothing like that, but then I wasn't drinking last night. This time I remembered a circular room at the top of the Twisted Tower, with a big cube of crystal."

Glyndon looked up quickly. "I saw the same thing. A vision . . ."

"That was no vision," Kayl said flatly. "It was a memory. An impossible memory. We never got past the door at the top of the stairs; the black thing was waiting for us."

Glyndon did not answer. Kayl stared at him, an unwelcome suspicion growing in her mind. "We never got past the top of the stairs," she repeated. "Did we?"

Glyndon looked miserable. "Kayl, please don't ask me."

"Then explain to me how I can remember something that never happened."

"I can't."

"Can't or won't? What did you do while I was fighting that black thing?"

"I don't know!" Glyndon all but shouted.

Kayl studied him, and the anguished self-doubt in his expression shook her to the core. "Tell me what you do know, then," she said in a quieter voice.

"I tried to use the Crystal," Glyndon said. "I thought the black thing was its guardian; that's why it appeared when Kevran knocked the chip off the corner of the Crystal. I thought if I could reach the black thing through the Crystal somehow . . . It didn't work."

"But you did do something."

"I don't know what or how. I don't remember anything about the Twisted Tower after I tried to reach into the Crystal, except for some vague images of fighting on the stairs."

"None of us seem to remember that fight very clearly," Kayl said in a grim tone. "But you've known about the Tower room and the Crystal all these years, haven't you? Why didn't you say anything?"

"And make you all certain I'd gone mad?" Glyndon said bitterly. "The visions were bad enough without claiming I remembered something nobody else did.''

Kayl stared at him. Had the trip back to Kith Alunel really been that bad for him? She tried to remember. She had not paid much attention to Glyndon and Kevran then; she had been too wrapped up in her own grief and Barthelmy's. Did he think she had been avoiding him out of fear that he had lost his wits? ''If that's the way you saw it, I'm sorry,'' she said at last. ''I wish . . . I wish I'd known.''

There was a moment's silence. Kayl turned and picked through her scattered belongings until she found a long wool sash. Bending forward, she covered the crystal with the end of the sash, then picked it up and knotted the sash tightly around it. She wrapped the sash around her waist and tucked the end in, hiding the knot.

''Now what?'' Glyndon asked cautiously.

''I'm going to think,'' Kayl replied. ''And then—I don't know. I'm going to have to tell the Sisterhood something.''

''Kayl, you can't!''

''I have to. Don't you see, this is what the Elder Mothers wanted to know this morning. They were right; things *didn't* happen the way Barthelmy and I said they did. And if they're right about that, they may be right about the Tower interfering with their magic.'' And she herself might have to rethink her determination not to return to the Twisted Tower, Kayl thought. She put the thought aside, for later consideration, and looked at Glyndon.

Glyndon looked away. ''I suppose so,'' he said at last. He sounded unhappy and very tired.

''It's also the only way I can think of to get the Elder Mothers to let us look at that scroll,'' Kayl said gently. Glyndon did not answer. A rap at the door announced Mark and Dara's return. Kayl looked at Glyndon's slumped shoulders a moment longer, then said, ''I'll talk to you again before I say anything to the Sisterhood.''

''All right.''

Kayl stared at him and tried to think of something else to say. There was another rap at the door; Mark was probably getting impatient. Shaking her head, Kayl rose to her feet to let them in.

CHAPTER

NINETEEN

Kayl slept poorly that night and she awoke before dawn the following morning. The bit of crystal was an unyielding lump inside her sash, demanding a decision. Should she give it to the Sisterhood with a full explanation, or keep it hidden? How would the Elder Mothers react if she told them the whole story? Part of Kayl wanted to dump the whole sorry tangle on the presumably wiser heads of the Elder Mothers; another part had grave doubts about the advisability of such a course.

The mental argument made her restless, and eventually drove her down the stairs to the serving room. She had no desire to wake Mark and Dara with her pacing. There were one or two other early risers below, but they were more interested in their breakfasts than in Kayl. She, in turn, ignored them as she prowled about the room.

She was on her fourth circuit when the door of the inn opened. Kayl turned, curious to see who would be arriving at such an early hour. To her surprise, the dark-cloaked figures were the Elder Mothers Mika and Javieri.

Kayl crossed to them and bowed, wishing they had waited until she knew what her own intentions were. "You're looking for me?"

"We are," Mika said. "Is there somewhere we can talk in private?"

"I'm afraid this is it," Kayl said, gesturing at the serving

169

room. "The children are still sleeping, and I won't have them waked."

Javieri raised her eyebrows in surprise. "Under the circumstances, it seems like a minor consideration," she said mildly.

"To you, perhaps," Kayl replied.

"Javieri has never had many dealings with children," Mika said. She looked up at her companion, and her eyes held amusement. "If you had, you'd understand. Wake them now, and they'll be grumpy as bears for the rest of the day."

"I defer to your superior knowledge," Javieri said, smiling. "The table by the hearth?"

Kayl nodded acceptance, and they crossed the room and seated themselves. Kayl looked at them expectantly.

"We have come on behalf of the Elder Mothers of all the Sisterhood to ask you to go once more to the Twisted Tower," Mika said. "And your friend Glyndon shal Morag as well."

"You want Glyndon, too?" Kayl said, surprised. "Why?"

"For the same reason we want you and Elder Sister Barthelmy," Javieri said, and hesitated.

"The three of you are the only ones they're certain can get past the spells on the Tower door," Mika said bluntly. "There was an expedition about five years ago—"

"Barthelmy told me," Kayl said. "But she said they didn't try to go inside."

"Oh, they tried. They gave up after the spells on the door killed the first two women who went through it."

"And you think we can do better?" Kayl said incredulously.

"You have already done so," Mika pointed out. "We think that Glyndon shal Morag and Elder Sister Barthelmy can, between them, duplicate the spells that got your Star Cluster safely inside the Tower fifteen years ago. No one else has succeeded in that."

"And you will know more about the Tower than either of the first two Star Clusters we sent," Javieri said.

"The Ri Astar Diary?" Kayl said, looking at them skeptically. "You place that much faith in it?"

"Not in the diary alone," Javieri said. "We hope to confirm its information elsewhere."

"You *hope* to? You've had it a year or more; why haven't you confirmed it already?"

Mika sighed and glanced reprovingly at her younger companion. "We have no certainty of our ability to do so, and perhaps we should not have mentioned it. But—the last group who sought the Tower heard rumors of a man, a scholar and wanderer who may know much of the Twisted Tower. He was in another part of the mountains then, and they would not delay their journey to seek him out. We intend that the next expedition shall do so."

"You must be very sure he knews something worth hearing," Kayl said, not bothering to conceal her skepticism. "I'd prefer to base a hope of success on something stronger."

"So would we," Javieri said soberly. "But we have reached the point where we must grasp at whatever hope is offered, though it break like winter grass in our hands."

Kayl could hear the desperation behind the level words, but she shook her head. "*If* you can find this person, and *if* he really knows something useful about the Twisted Tower, and *if* he is willing to tell you . . . Too many *if*s for me, Your Serenity."

"It is why I had not planned to mention it," Mika said.

"There seem to be a number of things you haven't mentioned," Kayl snapped. "Such as just what you expect this expedition to do when it reaches the Twisted Tower."

"I thought Barthelmy had told you that," Javieri said.

"Barthelmy's story seems to have missed a few things," Kayl said coldly. She was angry as much on Barthelmy's account as her own. Kayl was sure Barthelmy had told the truth as she knew it, which meant the Elder Mothers had been lying to her as well as to Kayl. "That business about trying to get inside, for instance, or why you are so sure the Tower is the cause of your . . . difficulties."

Javieri glanced quickly around, checking to make sure no one was within earshot. Mika gave Kayl a grim smile. "You are not making this easy, are you?"

"Why should I?" Kayl retorted. The discovery of the crystal chip had made her willing to listen, even willing to reconsider her determination to go to the Tower, but it had not made her willing to let the Elder Mothers know that she was thinking such things. "Ever since Corrana appeared at my inn you've been lying to me and manipulating me. Why should I help you?"

"To save the Sisterhood," Javieri said, so softly Kayl could hardly hear her.

"After all you've done, I'm not sure I want to."

"You have been one of us; you know the good the Sisterhood does," Mika said. Her expression was stern. "We make mistakes, but who does not? Do not demand greater goodness in us than you yourself possess."

Javieri leaned forward. "Even if you do not think the Sisterhood worth saving for its own sake, think what will happen if we fall. The Sisterhood of Stars has long been one of the supports of the Estarren Alliance. If the support collapses, what then? The Alliance is already dying, but slowly; would you see it end in your own lifetime?"

"You think a lot of yourselves," Kayl said. Javieri's argument had a certain appeal, but she was careful not to show it.

"Have you no unanswered questions of your own about the Twisted Tower?" Mika said quietly. "No doubts or suspicions about what happened there, even after what happened at the meeting yesterday?"

Kayl hesitated. "You have a good point," she acknowledged. Better than the Elder Mothers knew, but Kayl had promised Glyndon not to speak of the false memory without discussing it with him first. "But I doubt that your arguments will persuade Glyndon to help, even if you manage to convince me."

"But if there is a way to stop his visions?" Javieri said softly. "That would persuade him, I think."

Kayl stared, her thoughts in chaos. If it were possible to free Glyndon from his random fits of seeing, could she deny him that chance? She knew the answer as soon as the question phrased itself in her mind, and again she turned the conversation. "Barthelmy has agreed to go?"

"Yes. I believe she always intended to." Javieri gave Kayl a sidelong look. "I also will be going."

"We don't expect you to make a decision quickly, Kayl," Elder Mother Mika said. "For one thing, I expect you'll want a chance to look at this first." She nodded to Javieri.

Javieri reached into the folds of her cloak and pulled out a scroll, tied with a silver ribbon. She offered it to Kayl.

Reluctantly, Kayl took it. "The Ri Astar Diary?" she asked.

Mika nodded. "A copy only. You'll find a report at the end explaining the reasons for our conclusions, and giving details of the proposed expedition. We have another for your friend Glyndon.''

''I'll deliver it for you,'' Kayl said. ''Glyndon tends to sleep late.''

Javieri handed her a second scroll. Kayl stared down at the two rolls of parchment in her hands. She felt suddenly guilty for keeping her own knowledge secret; the crystal in her sash dug into her waist. She opened her mouth to tell them.

''No. Do not make this decision on impulse,'' Mika said. ''Wait until you have read the scrolls and thought about them, before you tell us yes or no.''

Kayl stared in momentary confusion, then realized that Mika had jumped to a mistaken conclusion about what she had been about to say. Her advice was still good, though; Kayl nodded.

''We'll send someone for your answer tomorrow,'' Mika went on. ''Or would you prefer to have more time?''

''Tomorrow will be fine.''

''Good. Then we'll be leaving; I expect you're eager to look at those.''

The Elder Mothers started to rise, but Kayl waved them back to their seats. ''There's something else you should know before you leave. Dara—my daughter—was stopped yesterday by a man in a green cloak who asked a lot of questions about the Star Hall.''

Mika's eyes narrowed. ''Tell us the whole story, if you please.''

Rapidly, Kayl summarized the incident and repeated the description Dara had given her. ''I may be overanxious,'' she finished, ''but I'd feel better if I knew who he was, what he wanted and why. And if I were sure he wasn't going to be a danger to my children.''

''I think you're right to worry,'' Javieri said. ''This isn't the only odd encounter someone's had recently. It's time they were investigated.'' Her eyes were challenging as she looked at Mika.

Mika sighed. ''I'm afraid you're right. It will take Sisters away from other urgent tasks, but it must be done. I'll see to it as soon as we get back.''

''Thank you,'' Kayl said. She walked to the door with them, then went back to the table and sat down. She did not immediately open the scroll Mika had given her. Instead she sat staring into the fire.

The proposed trip to the Twisted Tower would be long and hard, and Kayl knew all too well the dangers that lay at its end. The trip could also be a chance to return to the things Kayl had loved most about her years in the Sisterhood, and it was tempting to concentrate on that. Tempting; but foolish. This trip could never be like old times. Varevice and Evla were dead; the younger, brasher Kayl and Barthelmy had grown and changed. None of them could go back, not really. Kayl realized suddenly that she did not even want to try. She had followed an old dream to Kith Alunel, only to find she had outgrown it; she no longer belonged with the Sisterhood, any more than she belonged in Copeham. If she decided to go to the Twisted Tower now, it would be for Glyndon's sake, not for the Sisterhood.

Slowly, Kayl picked up one of the scrolls and slid it out of its ribbon. Unsmiling, she unrolled the top of the scroll and began to read.

The first part of the Ri Astar Diary was a long-winded description of Shandel ri Astar's escape from Sadortha just before the first of a series of attacks by the armies of the Shadow-born. Kayl skimmed until she found the first mention of the Twisted Tower, then backed up several inches and read more carefully.

Shandel ri Astar's grandfather, one Timlin ri Astar, had apparently visited the Twisted Tower as a young man. The list of his companions on that venture read like a Minstrel's roll of legends—Karinobra Dragonsdaughter, Philomel the Healer, Nevarra Treewoman and her cousin Taldor of Greykeep, the Minstrel Nerewind, Quain, Macarato Firesword . . . the list went on and on. Kayl wondered cynically whether Timlin had been exaggerating to impress his grandson or whether Shandel was exaggerating to impress his readers.

Timlin's other claims might be questionable, but he had clearly been to the Twisted Tower at some time. The description of the valley and the Tower were vivid enough to make Kayl shiver. He and his companions, whoever they were, had fought and defeated the wizard of the Tower, then divided his belongings among themselves. Among the wizard's possessions was a huge crystal cube called Gadeiron's Crystal.

Kayl stopped and reread the section carefully. Gadeiron's

Crystal fit the description of the cube her Star Cluster had found in the Tower. She fingered the lump in her sash absently as she waded slowly through the archaic phrasing. Suddenly she stopped. "And they sealed the Tower with the power of the Crystal itself," read the manuscript, "so that no evil might go out of the Tower and none might enter."

Sealed with the power of the Crystal? What would happen to that seal if the Crystal were broken or chipped? Kayl thought of the black thing in the Tower, and felt cold. It was with effort that she kept her hands away from the knot in her sash. She had to speak to Glyndon about this, soon.

Quickly she scanned the remainder of the diary, but found nothing else of interest in Shandel's account. She spent a little more time on the report at the end, noting that the explanation of the Elder Mothers had included an extremely detailed description of the proposed expedition. She was rerolling the scroll when she saw Glyndon coming down the stairs. She waved, and he came over to join her.

"Morning, Kayl. What have you got there?" he asked, nodding at the scrolls.

"A present from the Sisterhood," Kayl said. "Here, this one's yours. Take it up to your room and read it, right now."

"What about my breakfast?" Glyndon said plaintively.

"I'll bring it up to you," Kayl said, taking his arm and steering him back toward the stairs. "Go on, get busy."

"All right, all right. What is it, anyway?"

"The Ri Astar Diary."

Glyndon's eyes widened. He looked down at the scroll and swallowed hard. "I see. Don't be too long with that breakfast." He started up the stairs; by the time he reached the landing he was taking them two at a time. Kayl smiled and went to see about getting something to eat from the innkeeper.

Kayl had to knock twice at Glyndon's door before the Varnan wizard answered. Finally, the door opened. "Oh, good, breakfast," Glyndon said, and stepped aside to let her in.

"Have you found the part about the Tower and the Crystal yet?" Kayl asked as she entered. She set down the steaming bowl of porridge she was carrying and looked at Glyndon expectantly.

"Yes." He glanced at her, his expression ambiguous, then

started pacing along the side of the bed. "It wasn't as much help as I'd hoped."

"Sit down. You're making me nervous," Kayl said, and set a good example by dropping onto the wood footstool by the door.

Glyndon hesitated, then seated himself on the bed beside the half-unrolled scroll. "What did you have to promise them to get this?" he asked, fingering the edge of the parchment and carefully not looking in Kayl's direction.

"Nothing," Kayl said.

"Nothing?" Glyndon looked up in surprise. He gave her a searching look, then shook his head. "I don't believe it. The Sisterhood would never give away a bargaining counter."

"They're hoping it will persuade us to go back to the Tower."

"No," Glyndon said in the exasperated tone of one repeating the obvious for the fourth time. "I told you, if you go back to the Tower, that thing will get out."

"And if I don't go back?" Kayl said slowly, groping for an idea that hovered just out of reach.

"I assume it will stay safely inside, where it belongs."

"But do you *know* that?"

Glyndon looked up with an arrested expression. "What do you mean?"

"Did you read all the way to the end of the Tower section in the diary?"

"Not quite; I was studying the description of Gadeiron's Crystal."

Kayl rose and crossed to the other side of the bed. She leaned across and unrolled the scroll another handsbreadth, studied it for a moment, then pointed. "Look here."

Glyndon bent over the scroll, and a wisp of his brown hair grazed Kayl's arm. She moved away a little and stood looking down at the top of his head. At last he nodded and looked up. "Well?"

"According to the diary, they used the Crystal to seal the Tower."

"Well, we knew there was something odd about the spells on the door. But I don't see—" He broke off suddenly, his eyes widening.

Kayl said it anyway. "We took a chip out of that crystal.

What effect might that have on the spells that seal the Tower?''

"I don't know," Glyndon said slowly. "If it was important to the spell that the cube be absolutely perfect . . . I don't know."

"But it might weaken the sealing spell. And if that's what's holding the black thing inside the Tower, it may get out eventually whether I go back or not." And the main reason that remained for her reluctance to return to the Tower was her trust in Glyndon's vision of the black thing's escape.

"If it's the guardian of the Crystal—"

"We don't know that, either." Kayl shook her head, willing him to see. "The diary doesn't mention the black thing at all; it may have gotten trapped in the Tower later."

Glyndon stared at her for a long time without speaking. "You've decided to go," he said finally.

"I—" Kayl stopped, then nodded slowly. "I hadn't realized it, but you're right. I'm going."

Glyndon closed his eyes and took in a deep breath. "Damn them," he said softly. "Damn them and demons take their souls."

"Glyndon! This is my decision, and believe me, I'm not doing it for the Sisterhood."

"Why, then?"

Kayl hesitated. "I thought I just explained that."

"To save all Lyra from the monstrous thing that lurks in the Tower?" Glyndon said with savage mockery.

"I can at least try," Kayl replied, struggling to keep her temper. "We started something at the Twisted Tower; we ought to finish it."

"Finish it? Your death will finish it."

"You don't know that," Kayl said furiously, while part of her mind wondered at the bitterness in Glyndon's voice and the unexpected strength of her own reaction to it. "And even if you did, it would still be my choice whether or not to go."

Glyndon's mouth twisted. He stared silently down at the half-unrolled scroll on the bed in front of him. "I'm sorry, Kayl," he said finally, and his voice sounded tired. "I know better than to try and wrap you in fleece like that farmer in Copeham. So you're going back to the Twisted Tower. When do you leave Kith Alunel?"

"That depends." Kayl looked at him, wondering whether or not she had ruined her chances of persuading Glyndon to join the expedition. "Will you be coming with us?"

"I?" Glyndon snorted. "Kayl, you know the Sisterhood better than that. They'd never let a second-rate Varnan exile get involved with this, especially one half-crippled with false visions." He smiled ruefully. "If there were more truth in what I 'see' you might have a chance of persuading them."

Kayl stared at him. "Glyndon, weren't you listening? The Sisterhood wants all of us, not just Barthelmy and me. Why do you think they sent you a copy of that scroll? *They're* hoping to persuade *you*."

Suddenly Glyndon laughed, but without humor. "I seem to have misjudged your Sisterhood. Perhaps I ought to apologize."

"I think they'd rather have you come on the expedition."

"Do you? Then I suppose I'll make them happy."

Kayl made an exasperated noise. "Does that mean you'll come with us?"

"Yes," Glyndon said without looking at her.

"I haven't even told you what they have to offer you."

Glyndon shrugged and said nothing. Kayl stared at him for a moment, and his words of a moment before echoed in her mind ". . . like that farmer in Copeham." Very gently, she said, "They think they may find a way to control your visions."

"I don't think it's possible," Glyndon said without looking up. "But I'll try it."

"I'll tell them when I visit the Star Hall this afternoon." Kayl paused, studying him uncertainly. "Are you sure about this, Glyndon?"

He raised his head and gave her a crooked smile. "Someone has to be there to keep you out of trouble," he said with attempted lightness.

"Oh?" Kayl tried to match his tone. "And I thought you'd just promised not to try wrapping me in fleece."

"Did I say that?" He shook his head sadly. "And you're such a fragile, helpless sort. I must be slipping."

Kayl picked up the scroll and hit him with it.

CHAPTER

TWENTY

Elder Mother Mika was extremely pleased by the news that both Kayl and Glyndon were willing to undertake the expedition. Mark and Dara were pleased as well, until they discovered that Kayl intended to leave them behind. Mark sulked for nine days. Dara spent her time thinking up reasons why they ought to go with Kayl—they were seasoned travelers after the trip from Copeham; Kayl would need someone to help with day-to-day chores; they wanted Kayl to continue their lessons in swordcraft; they would pine away and die if they were left behind.

Kayl was not as firm about stopping the complaints as she might have been. For one thing, she had her own doubts about the wisdom of leaving the children in Kith Alunel. Elder Mother Mika promised to look after them, but the Sisterhood was not the place Kayl would have chosen for either Mark or Dara. Then, too, the incident of the green-cloaked man who had questioned Dara continued to make Kayl uneasy. Still, Kith Alunel would be safer for the children than a long, uncertain journey with the Twisted Tower and the black thing at the end of it.

The Star Hall's preparations were time-consuming. It was soon clear, to Kayl at least, that the expedition would not be out of Kith Alunel before the winter storms arrived. That would mean at least another month's delay; no one traveled during the storm season if it could be helped.

Kayl was not unhappy to be kept waiting, even though she was now committed to the project. She spent much of her time with her children, showing them the sights of Kith Alunel. And, as promised, she took them to the Frost Fair on the day it opened.

The weather was perfect for such an exhibition—cold and clear, with an icy blue winter sky hanging above the new snow. Tents and temporary booths filled the King's Park, their bright colors a vivid contrast to the snowy whiteness. A light breeze swept away the smoke that rose from the many braziers, and kept the banners and pennants fluttering above the tents.

Though they arrived early, the fair was already crowded. Kayl reminded the children to stay close to her or Glyndon, and Mark and Dara responded with the expected eye-rolling. Fortunately, the excitement of the fair quickly distracted them.

"Mother, look! Flame-jugglers!" Mark cried, pulling at Kayl's cloak as though he were several years younger than he was. "This way!"

"No, over there!" Dara said. "There's a conjurer's sign!"

"Take it easy, both of you," Kayl said, laughing in spite of herself. "We have all day. The conjurer first, I think."

The conjurer was quite good; he even had a trick or two that smelled of true magic, rather than depending entirely on sleight-of-hand. Dara was wide-eyed through the entire performance, and Mark was nearly as interested, though he tried not to show it.

The flame-jugglers turned out to be even more impressive. The whirling brands seemed to leave fiery trails in the air, weaving intricate patterns of light. Dara did not even try to look uninterested; she was as fascinated as Mark.

When the juggling was over, Kayl took the children to a nearby booth selling a mixture of snow and berry juices that had always been one of Kayl's favorite Frost Fair treats. The last time she had had one was the winter before the disastrous trip to the Twisted Tower. She and Barthelmy had dragged Evla to the Frost Fair for a belated celebration of Evla's birthday. . . .

"This is good!" Dara said.

"My teeth freeze when I try to chew it," Mark said.

"Try sort of scooping it up on your tongue and sucking," Kayl advised.

Glyndon was eyeing his cupful dubiously. "It looks like purple slush," he complained.

"I'll take it if you don't want it," Mark volunteered hopefully.

"I don't think your mother would approve," Glyndon said, glancing at Kayl.

"Go on, go on, try it," Kayl said, laughing at his expression. "It won't kill you."

"All right, but I wouldn't do this for anyone else." Cautiously, Glyndon licked at the purplish snow. The children watched him closely as he turned it over in his mouth. He frowned slightly and took a larger mouthful. "It's not bad," he said finally.

Kayl grinned. "Your tongue is purple."

They wandered through the fair for most of the day. Kayl found a leatherworker whose goods pleased her and spent some of the money the Star Hall had given her on a new belt and boots. Glyndon slipped away for a few hours near midday and returned with a heavier purse and a smug expression; Kayl assumed he'd found a dice game and cleaned it out. The children played ring-toss and tried to climb a swaying net of rope called a Kulseth Stairway. Periodically, they stopped to buy steaming buttered corn or crisp shreds of carrots fried in batter.

Finally, Kayl called a halt. "One last stop," she said. "Where will it be?"

"The Shanhar games!" Mark said at once. "You said we could see them, you promised!"

"The Shanhar will just be more fighting," Dara objected. "I want to see the horses."

"Just fighting!" Mark stared, appalled almost to speechlessness by the depth of Dara's ignorance. "The Shanhar are the greatest warriors in the Alliance! In the whole world, probably! And you want to look at *horses*?"

"Take it easy, both of you, or I'll take you straight back to the inn," Kayl said.

"But Mother!" the children chorused.

Kayl sighed and looked apologetically at Glyndon. "Would you mind taking Dara—"

"Not at all," Glyndon said. "Shall we catch up with you, or the other way around?"

"We'll find you, I think. Just don't stray too far from the horses."

"I'll do my best. Coming, Dara?"

Kayl watched them, marking the direction in her mind, then took Mark and headed for the Shanhar games. A large square of snow had been roped off, and three people dressed in pale brown stood inside. Two were women and the third was a man, but all had the same straight-cropped dark hair, the same black eyes, and the same slightly amused expression. Each wore both sword and dagger, and their belts bristled with more esoteric weapons.

Mark moved a little away from Kayl in order to see better. Kayl smiled, remembering how eager she had been the first time she had seen the Shanhar display their skills. Then the demonstration began, and she craned forward as avidly as Mark.

They began with throwing weapons—knives, axes, and the deadly little four-spiked clusters called raven's-feet. Kayl found the synchronization of their movements at least as impressive as their accuracy. When the targets were bristling with patterns of black spikes and dagger-hilts, the Shanhar turned to personal combat. Swordplay followed barehand, then went on to a unique ambidextrous style with both hands holding and occasionally exchanging weapons.

The crowd around her cheered and shouted encouragement to this or that combatant, but Kayl doubted that many of them really appreciated the elegance of the deadly dance they watched. She turned to see how Mark was enjoying it. He was gone.

Frowning, Kayl scanned the leading edge of the crowd. She did not see him. With a sigh she began working her way through the crowd, looking for her son's fair hair. She was growing seriously worried when she heard Mark's voice cry out.

Politeness forgotten, Kayl shouldered through the crowd in the direction of the cry. She broke free at last and looked hurriedly about her; then she saw Mark. He was struggling with a tall man in dark brown, half hidden by the shadows of a closed and shuttered booth.

Kayl ran forward, drawing her dagger as she ran. The tall man saw her coming and hesitated. Then Mark kicked backward. Kayl heard the man curse; his grip on Mark shifted and he threw the boy out of the shadows toward Kayl. Mark sprawled face down in the muddy snow. Kayl reached him an instant later and bent to make certain he was not seriously hurt. When she looked up, she was not surprised to see that the tall man had vanished.

Mark sat up, shivering half with cold and half with reaction. "M-mother! He was—he—"

"Sshhh, it's all right, we'll talk about it later." Kayl helped him up, then almost knocked him off his feet again by hugging him with all her strength. She was shaking almost as much as Mark was. She hadn't been this frightened since her first serious sword fight, when it had finally sunk in that this man was trying to *kill* her. With difficulty, she controlled her fear and sat back, keeping an arm around Mark's shoulders as much for her own comfort as for his.

They were beginning to attract curious stares. Kayl frowned, wondering whether she could possibly have been the only one who had seen what had happened. She glanced again at the shuttered booth and nodded to herself. The tall man had been clever as a demon. The shadowy gap between the booths would have hidden him from almost every angle, and the Shanhar exhibition was enough to hold the attention of most of the passers-by. Involuntarily, Kayl's arm tightened around Mark's shoulders.

"Mother?"

Kayl looked down at Mark's white face and forced herself to smile encouragingly.

"Mother, was I brave? I was trying, I really was."

"You were very brave, dear," Kayl said, trying to keep her voice from quivering. "I'm proud of you."

Mark stole a glance upward. "Even though I went off without telling you?"

"Even then. And I won't give you the scolding you deserve for it, either. This time."

Mark heaved a sigh of relief. "I'm glad."

Kayl felt him shiver against her arm. His cloak was wet through, and he was beginning to feel the effects of the shock he had just had. "Let's go find Glyndon and Dara," she said.

"You can tell me what happened while we walk, all right?"

Mark nodded, and they set off. Kayl had to prompt him once or twice to begin his tale, but once he got started the words poured out. The tall man had, apparently, struck up a conversation with Mark about the Shanhar, then offered to unlock the shuttered booth and let Mark see some of the ancient Sadorthan swords he claimed to have inside. In the shadows by the booth, he had grabbed Mark. Mark had managed to cry out once, but that was all. If Kayl had not heard him . . .

"There's Glyndon," Mark said. Kayl looked in the direction he was pointing and saw the Varnan wizard. There was no sign of Dara, and her heart contracted. Then Glyndon moved forward, and Kayl saw Dara on his other side, where she had been hidden by the bulk of his cloak. With a sigh of relief, Kayl hurried forward.

Glyndon saw them and stopped, looking first surprised, then concerned as Kayl drew close enough for him to see her expression clearly. Swiftly Kayl explained what had happened, and the four of them started back toward the inn. Kayl had Mark repeat his story for Glyndon's and Dara's benefit while they walked.

"What did this man look like?" Glyndon asked when Mark finished.

"He had dark hair," Mark said, frowning. "He was . . . I don't know."

"That's all?" Dara said. "I did better than that!"

"Well, my man didn't have a mustache," Mark said, stung. "Just a little cut on his face, by the corner of his mouth."

Kayl and Glyndon looked at each other. "Cut himself shaving it off?" Kayl suggested.

"Quite possibly," Glyndon said thoughtfully. "Did you notice anything else, Mark?"

"He had a ring," Mark offered after a moment.

"A ring?"

"I saw it when he was talking to me," Mark said. "Silver, with a little green stone in the middle and some squiggly decorations. The sides looked like wings."

Kayl stiffened. "Wings? Mark, are you sure?"

"I'm sure. I got a good look at it when I bit him." Mark said proudly.

"You bit him?" Dara said, clearly torn between pride in her brother and envy of his accomplishment. "Mark!"

Kayl let the children talk; she was busy considering the implications. The Magicseekers would not have risked sending one of their number to Kith Alunel just to keep track of a former member of the Sisterhood of Stars. Nor would they need to question Dara for details of the day-to-day routine of a Star Hall. And Magicseekers would have no reason to try to abduct Mark . . . unless they knew more than anyone had thought about Kayl's involvement with the Sisterhood's expedition to the Twisted Tower. And if that was the reason for the Magicseeker's interest in Kayl and her children, they would not give up until the matter of the Tower was done with.

The Sisterhood's expedition would, Kayl hoped, settle the business of the Tower. But Kith Alunel no longer seemed a safe place to leave Mark and Dara while Kayl traveled for eight months. Yet could she justify taking two children with her? The first part of the journey would be safe enough; they would be traveling through the heart of the Estarren Alliance. For the last month, however, they would be passing through the fringes of the Alliance, and for the final week they would be in the Windhome Mountains.

Kayl reviewed the route through the mountains in her mind, cudgeling her memory for every scrap of detail. The terrain was rough, but not impossibly so, she decided. And she could keep the children well away from the Tower itself. Kayl shook her head. Was she actually contemplating taking Mark and Dara with her? But to leave them in Kith Alunel to be the prey of Magicseekers . . .

She wrestled with the question all the way back to the inn. When they arrived, she sent the children directly to bed, despite their protests. Once they were settled, she went in search of Glyndon. "I'm going to the Star Hall," she said baldly as soon as she found him.

"You think the same as I do, then. Magicseekers?"

Kayl nodded. "And if I have my way, we'll be leaving Kith Alunel within three days. Preferably two."

Glyndon's eyebrows rose. "I'm surprised you'd consider leaving Mark and Dara so soon after . . ." He gestured ambiguously.

"I'm bringing them with us," Kayl said grimly.

"To the Twisted Tower?"

"I have to," Kayl snapped. "If I leave them here, I'd spend the whole trip wondering whether they were all right. The Magicseekers could claim they had either of them, and I'd have no way of knowing whether it was true."

"The protection of the Sisterhood—"

"Glyndon, the Circle of Silence is nasty and powerful and right now any one of their magicians can do more than the whole Sisterhood put together. Mark and Dara will be much safer traveling with you and Barthelmy. Why are you making so many objections?"

"I wanted to make sure you had the answers thought out before you descended on the Sisterhood," Glyndon said with a lopsided grin. "They're not going to like this, you know."

"I know. And the timing's bad, too; we'll be trying to travel at the height of the storm season. Still, I'd rather be snowed in in Thurl Wood than murdered in Kith Alunel."

"Do you really think you can get the Sisterhood to move that fast?"

Kayl smiled grimly. "If they don't, the four of us will leave without them, and they can forget about their precious expedition for good."

"I see." Glyndon studied her thoughtfully. "You're right; that'll convince them, if anything will."

Kayl chuckled, then sobered. "Glyndon—watch the children while I'm gone."

"I will."

"Thank you." Kayl touched his cheek lightly, then swung her cloak around her shoulders and went out.

Kayl spent half the night at the Star Hall, arguing with the Mothers and Elder Mothers who were in charge of organizing the expedition. When she left at last, she was tired and hoarse, but she had won. The expedition would leave Kith Alunel secretly, in two days.

By the following morning, Mark seemed almost his old self. He snapped at Dara when she tried to fuss over him, then tried to persuade Kayl that he needed extra honey on his porridge because of his scare the previous day. Kayl refused, pointing out that if he'd stayed by her as he'd been told, nothing would have happened. Secretly, she found his high spirits a decided relief.

The children were wildly delighted when they learned they would be going on the expedition after all, and they made extravagant promises of good behavior. Kayl took shameless advantage of the situation; it might, just possibly, make some of the trip to the Tower more bearable.

Two days later, the Sisterhood's expedition left Kith Alunel, disguised as part of a group of merchant folk heading south with their profits from the Frost Fair.

INTERLUDE:

Gadeiron's Crystal

From that battle, Timlin and his companions emerged victorious. They stayed a day and a night in the dry and lifeless valley, studying the works left by the wizard of the Tower, and they learned much. And Timlin ri Astar was of them all the most knowledgeable, wherefore in later years he was called Timlin the Wise.

Then they destroyed many of those things that were of use only for evil, and those they could not destroy they sealed within the Twisted Tower. But the remainder of the wizard's possessions they bore away with them. And when they were at a safe distance, they divided the spoils among themselves. Nerewind the Minstrel took three feathers of the Firebird, and Philomel the Healer a vial of evensrud, and others bore away things equally rare and valuable.

Timlin himself took the great cube of crystal, in which things past and present and yet to come could be seen. He made a solemn compact with his friends that they might use the Crystal whenever they had need, and so they all concurred. And the Crystal came to be called Gadeiron's Crystal, after the wizard who caused it to be made and then turned to evil in the Twisted Tower.

The appearance of Gadeiron's Crystal was this: It was a great cube, perfect in every respect, and each edge was twice the length of a tall man's forearm. It was made of the clearest and purest crystal, in which no haze or bubble or distortion

could be found. It required three strong men to move it, and if
struck with a silver hammer it rang with a pure sound that
could be heard for twelve miles in all directions.

And the nature of the Crystal was this: It commanded the
past, present and future. For whenever a man stared into one
of its surfaces for many minutes, the interior of the Crystal
would grow cloudy, and then he would see what scenes the
Crystal would show. More, if the watcher fixed his heart on
some one thing, past or present, that too he would see pictured
in the Crystal. And if one with power and the knowledge of
certain spells recited them over the Crystal, it would show
things possible in the future. But what other magic was used in
its presence, the Crystal took unto itself, to bind forever.

Time came when the heroes who had taken the Twisted
Tower separated and went their several ways. Timlin took
Gadeiron's Crystal into his home, and there he studied it. He
learned much of its working and its power, and by its aid he
was able to do much good. For the Crystal had greater power
than the mere showing of visions, but of that he would not
speak. From time to time one of his erstwhile companions
would seek the Crystal, and Timlin honored his bargain with
them. And so it was for many years.

Then a time of troubles came upon the land, and great
strife. Timlin sought Gadeiron's Crystal to discover the cause
behind the conflict, for it seemed to him that it ran deeper
than the petty quarrels that men claimed as reasons. And the
Crystal showed him that the Shadow-born were preparing to
make war upon the peoples of Lyra once more, as they had in
his youth, and the strife that lay upon the land was but the
beginning of their fell designs.

At this Timlin was sorely troubled, and again he sought
Gadeiron's Crystal, to learn what might be done. And the
Crystal showed him many things, both good and ill. But
Timlin saw that the Crystal itself would be the source of the
greatest evil, if the Shadow-born turned its power to their own
ends.

Timlin sought further to find a way of preventing such
misfortune. He saw but one: to place Gadeiron's Crystal once
more in the tower where he had found it, for there alone the
Shadow-born might not reach. He took counsel with those of
his friends who remained, and all agreed that they should not
chance the Crystal's falling into other hands. Therefore

Timlin took the great Crystal and returned it to the bent and blackened Tower, lest the Evil Ones discover it and make use of its power. And he sealed the Tower with the power of the Crystal itself, so that no evil might go out of the Tower, and none might enter.

All this is as my grandfather, Timlin ri Astar, told me before his death in battle with the Shadow-born. I record these things in warning, that they may not be forgotten utterly, leaving none to watch and guard Gadeiron's Crystal against the malice of the Shadow-born.

*—From the Diaries of Shandel
ri Astar, circa 200 B.W.B.*

PART III
The Twisted Tower

CHAPTER

TWENTY-ONE

Kayl sat in a corner of Riventon's only inn and tavern, cradling her almost empty mug of ale in both hands and watching her comrades morosely. Six members of the two Star Clusters occupied one end of a long table on the other side of the fire; they sat talking with a quiet companionability that excluded everyone else in the room. Kayl felt a twinge of tired envy whenever she looked at them. The three Elder Mothers, Javieri, Miracote, and Alessa, sat at the next table with two Mothers and three Elder Sisters. The Sisterhood of Stars seemed to think numbers alone would take the Twisted Tower.

"Here is your ale," Corrana said. She sat down on the opposite side of the table and pushed one of the mugs she had been carrying toward Kayl. "How you can drink it is more than I can understand."

"You haven't tasted the wine yet," Kayl replied, nodding at Corrana's drink. "It's worse."

Corrana raised an eyebrow. "Is that possible?"

"Try it and see."

The Elder Sister took a cautious sip and made a face. "You are right again. I should listen when you give your opinion of an inn's provisioning."

"Here you are!" said a pleased voice from the end of the table. "Mind if I join you?"

Kayl turned. The speaker was Risper Aschar, the slim, dark-

eyed healer for one of the two Star Clusters. She and Demma
Jol, one of the warriors, were the only Sisters besides Javieri
and Corrana who did not treat Kayl and Barthelmy with some
degree of suspicion and hostility. Demma was clearly reserving
judgment, but Risper's cautious curiosity had grown and
changed during the journey into real friendship.

"Go ahead and sit down," Kayl said, waving at the bench
beside Corrana. "What are you drinking? The ale's bad, but
the wine's worse."

Risper looked smug. "The water isn't. Where's Barthelmy?"

"Upstairs, with Mark and Dara," Kayl said, and took a
large swallow of ale. During the past three and a half months,
Barthelmy had gradually taken over the job of watching the
children. Kayl had been disconcerted at first; then she realized
that Barthelmy was using Mark and Dara as an excuse to stay
away from her fellow Sisters as much as possible. Kayl understood and sympathized—as the only remaining effective magician in the Sisterhood, Barthelmy's position was equivocal, at
best—but she could not keep from occasionally resenting
Barthelmy's actions.

"Glyndon is with them," Corrana said. Her voice still held
a touch of reserve when she spoke of him, but an undercurrent
of warmth seemed to be developing.

"Is he all right?" Risper asked.

"This evening? I think so," Kayl said. She did not bother to
add that she was worried anyway; both Corrana and Risper
knew that already.

"His visions have been coming closer together, haven't
they?" Risper persisted.

"Yes, but it isn't just that. This whole trip has been very
hard on him." Kayl took another gulp of ale. Glyndon had en-
dured the hostility of the Sisters with more patience than she
had thought he possessed, but new lines had appeared around
his eyes, and his smiles were increasingly rare. It hurt Kayl to
see what was happening to him. She glared across the fire at
the tables full of Sisters.

Risper's eyes followed Kayl's. "I could ask one of the Elder
Mothers to say something to them about the way they treat
him," she offered.

"I have already discussed it with Elder Mother Javieri,"

Corrana said, to Kayl's considerable surprise. "Unfortunately, there is little that can be done. They cannot be forced to like him."

"He shouldn't have come," Kayl said emphatically. "He's been traveling alone for fifteen years, and he's used to being able to *leave* when people don't like him. Now he's stuck with nearly twenty people, three-quarters of whom dislike and distrust him just because he's a Varnan. He should have stayed in Kith Alunel."

"He must want very badly to be free of those visions," Risper said soberly.

"That's not why he's here," Kayl said without thinking.

Corrana and Risper both looked at her. "No?" Corrana said, and her tone demanded an explanation.

Kayl sighed and set down her mug of ale. She'd had enough, if she was starting to make slips like that. "He came because of me," she said angrily, not really knowing whether she was angry with Corrana for making her say it, with Glyndon for doing it, or with herself for letting him. "I should have made him stay in Kith Alunel," she muttered.

"I doubt that you could have done so," Corrana said, and gave Kayl one of her small, secretive smiles. "From what I know of him, you are well matched in stubbornness."

"We only have another two weeks or so before we get to the Tower," Risper said. "That's not long."

"First we have to find that scholar the Elder Mothers think is so important," Kayl said. "We've been waiting here nearly a week already—"

"Four days," Risper corrected.

"—and who knows how much longer it'll take? And once we finish with the Tower, there will still be a four-month trip back to Kith Alunel."

"Glyndon doesn't have to go back to Kith Alunel with us when we're finished," Risper pointed out.

"No, he doesn't," Kayl agreed. But he will, she thought. If I stay with the Sisters, he'll stay, too. And I have to stay with them, at least for a while. What would I do with two children in the middle of the Windhome Mountains? We'll have to travel at least part of the way back to Kith Alunel with them, and if we fail at the Twisted Tower a second time the rest will take it out on Glyndon and Barthelmy.

"Here comes the innkeeper," Risper said. "Do either of you want anything more?"

"No," Corrana said, looking at the barely touched mug of wine in front of her. "One was enough."

"None here, either," Kayl said. She leaned forward to let the innkeeper pass, and a snatch of conversation at a nearby table caught her attention.

"—fur-faces," a surly young man was saying. "Six of 'em this time. And Barak's letting them camp next to the mill!"

"Barak lets anyone camp there," the innkeeper said as he turned to that table and set a cluster of mugs on it. "Ruin my business, he would, if more travelers knew of it."

"Blast your business!" the young man said. "What about the demon-bred fur-faces? We ought to run them off, the way Dinstown does."

"Why bother?" a lazy-looking youth asked. "They'll be gone in the morning."

"They should be gone now! Sneaking little—"

"Calm down, Joss," a gray-haired man said. "They're doing no harm."

"They're doing no good, either," Joss replied, frowning into his ale.

"Some might say the same about you," a brown-haired woman said. She was solidly built, with an air of competence about her. "What about that axle of Sish's?"

This was apparently an old joke; the entire table burst out laughing, and the conversation turned to various foolish or embarrassing things the drinkers remembered each other's having done.

"Kayl?" Risper said. "What is it? I've said your name three times."

"I just overheard something that bothers me." Kayl frowned at her mug for a moment, then stood. "I'm going for a walk; I'll be back in a few minutes."

Risper and Corrana nodded. "Do you want some company?" Risper asked.

"Thanks, but no," Kayl said with a smile. "You can stay here and finish my ale."

Risper looked at Kayl's mug with a dubious expression and shook her head. Kayl laughed; then, wrapping her cloak around herself, she slipped out of the tavern.

Outside she paused. They had crossed a creek on the way

into town, but she had not noticed a mill. It would be in the other direction, then, upstream and toward the east. She started forward at a brisk walk.

The night was clear and smelled of melting snow. Kayl could see down the road to the end of the village and the fields beyond. The dark silhouettes of the Windhome Mountains loomed behind them on the eastern horizon, blocking out great swaths of stars. Kayl shivered, glad that Elewyth had risen high enough to be well above the mountains. The silver-green moon was nearly full, and provided more than enough light for Kayl to see her way. Kaldarin, the smaller, reddish moon, had not yet cleared the peaks.

As she walked, Kayl kicked at dirt-covered chunks of snow, sending them whirling into the darkness or occasionally splattering them wetly in all directions. She had almost given away too much in the inn, talking about Glyndon as she had. Her suspicions about the nature of Glyndon's affection for her had hardened into certainty, and now she did not know what to do. It would be easier if Glyndon were like Jirod: someone she simply trusted and cared for as a friend. But her feelings for Glyndon were more than that; how much more she did not want even to think about yet, much less to discuss with Corrana and Risper.

The sound of the water pouring over the millwheel brought Kayl out of her reverie, and a few more minutes brought her within sight of the mill itself. It was a small, square building made of stone. Beside it the water wheel turned slowly and endlessly, gleaming in the moonlight. Kayl circled the mill warily, but the wet snow around it had been trampled into a muddy sea. She saw no sign of any camp. She was about to return to the tavern and forget the whim that had called her out into the darkness, when a voice behind her said, "Excuse me; are you looking for something?"

The voice had the characteristic piping timbre of a Wyrd's. Kayl turned without haste. A small figure stood a few paces away in the shelter of a small clump of trees, barely visible as a darker, more solid shadow among the shadows.

"I believe I have found what I was looking for," Kayl said. Other Wyrds would be watching from the bushes. She let her arms hang loosely at her sides, carefully empty of threat.

"So." The Wyrd's tone was courteous, but it held no warmth. "Why have you come looking for us?"

"I overheard some of the villagers talking in the tavern. They spoke of six Wyrds from the south, passing through this village. One man was in favor of driving you off as the people of Dinstown do."

"And you came to warn us of this plan?" The Wyrd's skepticism was evident.

Kayl shook her head. "It was mostly ale talking. Dinstown, however, is north and a little west of here; it would make a logical next stop for a group such as yours. I thought you might find it useful to know their attitude."

"Thank you for your warning," the Wyrd said with cool politeness. "But you will, I hope, pardon us if we remain wary. Who are you, that you would help Wyrds?"

"I am a traveler, like yourselves," Kayl said. "And I have a friend among your people in Mindaria. My name is—"

"Kayl! By the Tree, what are you doing here?"

"Bryn?" Kayl whirled, peering incredulously into the darkness.

"Over here."

Kayl saw a small figure approaching rapidly from the far corner of the mill. In another moment, she could make out the familiar features of Copeham's carpenter. "It really *is* you. What are you doing here, of all places?"

"I asked you first," Bryn said, grinning fiercely.

"She claims she is here to warn us of an unfriendly town ahead," said the Wyrd who had first addressed Kayl.

"Then that's why she came. Don't act like a Rathani bureaucrat, Shav," Bryn said. Shav subsided, muttering. Bryn looked at Kayl. "Anything else you want to tell him?"

"I've covered the main point," Kayl replied.

"Then let's go somewhere and talk."

"Not the camp," Shav said quickly.

"All right, if you insist," Bryn said, sounding irritated. "We'll be by the mill steps, if you want us for anything. This way, Kayl."

Kayl nodded a farewell to Shav and followed Bryn. The steps proved to be stone, still cold with winter frost, but Kayl said nothing as she seated herself. The alternatives were a Wyrd tent, with the suspicious Shav probably hovering in the background, or the village tavern, half-full of the Sisterhood. At least the air smelled faintly of the coming spring, despite its chill.

"How are Mark and Dara?" Bryn asked. "And what *does* bring you out here? Jirod said you were headed for Varna."

"I told him that in case the Magicseekers questioned him," Kayl said. "We went north instead, to Kith Alunel."

Bryn frowned and started to say something, then stopped and asked, "Why were you so sure the Magicseekers were interested in you?"

Kayl sighed. "Fifteen years ago, I belonged to the Sisterhood of Stars."

Bryn nodded, but she seemed unsurprised. Kayl peered at her, trying to read some expression through the darkness and the fur. "You knew?" she said finally.

"It was pretty clear that something odd was going on," Bryn said dryly. "First that black-haired woman turning out to be a Silver Sister, then you and your household bolting like that. And when Utrilo Levoil turned out to be a Magicseeker—"

"*What?*"

Bryn's pointed teeth gleamed in the moonlight as she grinned. "Utrilo Levoil was the leader of that group of Magicseekers who came through Copeham."

"I don't believe it! That fat, pompous windbag?"

"You didn't see him in armor, snapping orders."

"Prefect Islorran must have sent him along to guide the Magicseekers, that's all."

"And they just happened to have a spare set of scaled lorica and an eagle helmet with them, which just happened to fit Levoil as if they'd been made for him. And all of the Magicseekers were perfectly willing to take orders from Islorran's secretary. Including orders to march east, double-time, to catch up with you."

"I—" Kayl shook her head. She could not picture Utrilo Levoil, Islorran's oily secretary, as any kind of leader, much less a leader of Magicseekers. On the other hand, Bryn seemed very sure. And Glyndon had seen seven eagle-helms, not six. . . . "You stayed in Copeham for a while, then?"

"About another week. Alden was out looking for rocks, to carve something for Xaya, and he saw Utrilo and the rest of them coming back. He watched long enough to be sure you weren't with them, then slipped away to warn us. We left before they arrived in Copeham."

"I can hardly blame you," Kayl said with mock seriousness.

Bryn grinned again. "I would hope not. We've been on the road since then, with one batch of travelers or another. We met Shav and his sisters about three months ago. He said he knew of a settlement out in this direction, so we thought we'd try. I'm beginning to suspect he hasn't the slightest idea where he's going, though."

"I thought you were planning to head north."

"We're a lot farther north than we were when we started, aren't we? And two adults and a child can't just take off into the wilderness alone. So we keep following rumors, like this rabbit-chase of Shav's, hoping to hear word of somewhere really safe."

"I hope you find it," Kayl said. She hesitated. "How was Jirod? And the inn?"

Bryn was silent for a moment; then she said, "I'm afraid the Magicseekers burned your inn. I'm sorry; I know how much that place meant to you."

"It's all right." Kayl was surprised to find that her only reaction to the news was a distant sorrow; she had more than half expected the news. "I never really believed I'd be able to go back. What about Jirod?"

"He's . . . recovering."

Kayl felt as if someone had dealt her a blow in the stomach. "He is? Present tense?"

"We've had news since we left. The Magicseekers beat him senseless the first time they came through, after they found out you'd disappeared. When they came back, Zia hid him and told them he'd died. Levoil didn't think Zia was capable of lying to him, so he didn't even look for Jirod. He had his men burn the inn, and then they left."

"I see." Kayl was silent for a moment, then angrily struck her fist against her thigh. "I told Jirod he should come with us! Why wouldn't he listen?"

"If you're feeling guilty, just say so," Bryn advised calmly.

Kayl started to snap at Bryn, then caught herself. "You're right," she said finally. "I do feel guilty."

"How much of what happened with the Silver Sister and the Magicseekers and Levoil could you actually have done anything about?"

"I—" Kayl stopped and, reluctantly, smiled. "None of it, I suppose, not really. I still feel as if I should have tried, though."

Bryn muttered something under her breath that sounded suspiciously like "Humans!" then said, "It's too late now. Still, I certainly wouldn't mind if you explained what it was all about." She gave Kayl a sidelong look.

"I'll tell you what I can," Kayl said, "but some of it is still Sisterhood business."

Bryn nodded, and Kayl launched into an edited account of her travels and the reasons behind them. She did not mention the decline of the Sisterhood's magical abilities and she was deliberately vague about the Twisted Tower and the exact purpose of the current expedition.

Bryn listened closely, her nose twitching occasionally as it did when she was concentrating hard on something. "So you got caught in the middle of a fight between the Sisterhood and the Circle of Silence over something that happened fifteen years ago," Bryn said thoughtfully when Kayl finished.

"More or less," Kayl said. "There's no way Corrana and the Magicseekers could have shown up so close together by coincidence, and the Magicseekers didn't seem to be following her. Although if Utrilo Levoil was one of them . . ." Kayl frowned.

"Then he probably had suspicions about you even before Corrana arrived," Bryn said. "And whatever is going on is important enough to him to keep him tied to a small village, pretending to be a pompous idiot of a secretary, for nearly a month."

"I hadn't thought of it that way, but you're right," Kayl said slowly. "I'd assumed that they followed Corrana, but if Levoil was one of them, that's impossible."

Bryn gave Kayl a sober look. "They won't have given up, you know."

"I know. I just have to hope that they won't cross the borders of the Alliance, or at least that they'll be severely limited inside it." Kayl knew it was a forlorn hope; they were nearing the eastern boundary of the Estarren Alliance, and the authority of the Senate was already running thin. The Windhome Mountains, four days' journey away, were only nominally under the control of the Alliance. Kayl was sure that the Magicseekers would not think twice about defying the Senate's order of exile there. "You haven't seen any sign of them, or heard any rumors, have you?"

"Not exactly."

"What does that mean?"

"It means I'm not sure. We ran across some very odd merchants about a week ago—surly and standoffish, no wagons or packs of goods, and all of them with horses. We kept out of their way."

"A week ago," Kayl said, frowning. "Where was this?"

"A little south and west of here. Not quite a week's travel; we lost some time because of a broken wheel on one of the carts."

Less than a week away, and they had horses. Kayl's frown deepened. At least they hadn't actually crossed the expedition's trail; if they were Magicseekers, they might not know how close they were to their prey. "I'll have to tell the Elder Mothers about this. Would you be willing to talk to them?"

Bryn's ears twitched forward. "If they're willing to talk to me."

"The Sisterhood doesn't think Wyrds or Shee or Neira are automatically suspicious," Kayl said, stung by the injustice of the assumption.

"That's not what I meant. Your Sisterhood has a lot of information; I'd like to trade."

"They're not my Sisterhood," Kayl muttered.

Bryn ignored the comment. "I want to know if they've heard anything of a Wyrd settlement in the north."

"I think I can promise you they'll tell you if they know anything about it," Kayl said. "But what if they haven't?"

"Even that's information, of a sort. I'll meet you outside the tavern in an hour; will that be enough time for you to arrange things with these Elder Mothers?"

"It should be. Thanks, Bryn." Kayl rose and stamped her feet. Then, with a nod of farewell, she started back toward the tavern.

CHAPTER

TWENTY-TWO

When Kayl arrived, the tavern was in an uproar. Fifteen or twenty of the townspeople stood in angry clumps in front of the door, muttering among themselves and glaring toward the center of the room. Corrana's voice rose in icy anger from that direction, ordering someone back. Kayl tried to peer over or between the heads that blocked her view. She caught a glimpse of Elder Mother Alessa's shining hair, and the members of the Star Clusters, but she still could not tell what was going on. She pressed her lips together and began to shoulder her way forward.

"Demon-cursed Varnan," she heard someone say beside her. Kayl went cold. If something had happened to Glyndon. . . . It wasn't like Glyndon to be careless; how had these people guessed he was Varnan?

"Traveling with a whole harem, bold as anything," someone else said loudly. Kayl pushed herself between the last of the villagers and stopped.

The women of the two Star Clusters stood in a defensive half-circle, facing the villagers. None of them had drawn weapons, and all of them looked unhappy. Elder Mother Alessa was standing to Kayl's left, just behind Risper, talking to the Star Cluster in a voice too low for Kayl to hear. Elder Mother Miracote stood near the other end of the string of star-sisters, studying the townsfolk through narrowed eyes.

Behind the Star Clusters, the remainder of the Sisterhood's expedition stood or sat in three clumps. The first consisted of

Corrana and the two Mothers, talking in soothing tones to the indignant tavern-keeper. Kayl's opinion of the man, which had not been high to begin with, dropped sharply; he should be out here trying to talk the townsfolk out of starting a fight. Two Elder Sisters stood at the nearer end of one of the tables, watching the villagers. Glyndon sat at the other end of the table, white and shaking. Barthelmy and Elder Mother Javieri stood beside him, concern written across both their faces, while Mark and Dara hovered protectively a little way away. Kayl needed only the briefest glance to be certain that Glyndon had had another of his visions. She wanted to go to him, but dealing with the villagers could not wait. She hoped fleetingly that Mark and Dara would have time enough to run if things got ugly.

"You, there," she said to a burly man in her best drillmaster's voice. "What's troubling these people?" She waved at the glowering townsfolk.

"What?" The man looked confused, then suspicious. "Who's asking?"

"I am. Well?"

"That man's a Varnan," the man said accusingly. An angry murmur from the people behind him bolstered his courage, and he added, "And we're going to get him!"

"Really?" Kayl said. She pitched her voice with care, trying to achieve a tone of mild curiosity that would still carry to the rear of the room. "And I'd heard this was such a friendly town. What are you going to do with him when you have him?"

"Put him in the stocks," shouted someone.

"Tar and sawdust," yelled another.

"Hang him!"

There were uneasy murmurs among the crowd at that; evidently hanging was more than most of the villagers were ready to stomach. Kayl felt a touch of relief; they hadn't really gotten worked up yet. "Sounds like a lot of effort," Kayl commented. "What's he done? Turned the ale bad?"

A stocky, brown-haired woman laughed. "If he tried that with Penshar's ale, no one would notice!" she called.

Kayl recognized her as the same woman who had earlier sidetracked the angry young man's diatribe against Wyrds. "In that case, I'd hang the brewer, not the wizard," Kayl said.

She saw a few smiles among the crowd; their initial fear was beginning to fade.

"He's a Varnan," someone shouted from the back, but the voice was not as angry as the earlier ones had been.

"The brewer?" Kayl said.

There was a scattering of chuckles. "That's why the ale's so bad!" the stocky woman said.

"Don't you bad-talk my business, Thela!" the tavern-keeper shouted from across the room. "I serve good ale."

"Good for what?" said a skinny youth.

Kayl shot a quick glance at in the direction of the Sister-hood. The defensive stance of the Star Clusters had relaxed somewhat, but they were still standing. She caught Miracote's eye and made a small patting motion with her left hand. Miracote nodded fractionally; a moment later, two of the Sisters returned to their seats.

The mood of the crowd had shifted; they were baiting the tavern-keeper now. Kayl saw several of those in back slip quietly out the door. A tall, gray-haired man caught her eye; he was watching the crowd with a detached air. Something about him struck a familiar chord in Kayl's mind. She turned slightly so that she could keep an eye on him. Then she deliberately stretched and yawned. "Well, if there's not going to be any excitement, I'm going to bed," she announced. "I've had a long day."

"So have we all," the gray-haired man said. His voice was deep and gentle, and somehow the tone of it reminded Kayl that she really was nearly as tired as she had been pretending to be.

The man's voice had the same effect on the villagers. Several more of them drifted out the door, and Kayl could almost see the energy draining out of the rest. "What about that Varnan?" someone called halfheartedly.

"Leave him here with Penshar's ale," the stocky woman suggested. "That's punishment enough for anything!"

The remnant of the village crowd laughed and began break-ing up. Most of them left in ones and twos and small clumps. Kayl let out a small sigh of relief. She heard benches scrape on the floor as the rest of the Sisters resumed their seats. Kayl glanced over her shoulder and saw Mark and Dara, still stand-ing behind Glyndon. Mark's eyes were wide with excitement;

Dara looked relieved. Kayl turned back and saw the stocky woman coming toward her.

"Thanks for your help," Kayl said as the woman reached her.

The woman shrugged. "I don't like fights." She hesitated, then nodded toward the Sisters and went on, "You're with them, aren't you?"

"Yes," Kayl admitted. "But I could hardly announce it."

"I thought I'd seen you with some of them earlier." The woman paused again. "It might be wiser for your friend to be gone before morning."

"I'd already come to that conclusion," Kayl said. "But thanks for your advice."

The stocky woman nodded and left. Kayl looked around and discovered the tavern-keeper heading purposefully in her direction.

"What do you mean by chasing away all my business?" the man demanded with frightened belligerence.

"Would you rather have had those people work themselves up until they started breaking mugs and smashing benches?" Kayl snapped. "Have some sense!"

"I know these people!" the tavern-keeper said. "They wouldn't have—"

"They'd have tried," said a voice from behind Kayl. She turned and found that the gray-haired man had come over. "And you wouldn't be so frightened if you weren't sure of that, Penshar," the man went on.

"Well, but what am I supposed to do now?" Penshar demanded, then jumped as Corrana's calm, musical voice came over his shoulder.

"We shall, of course, pay extra to have privacy for the remainder of the night," Corrana said.

The tavern-keeper brightened perceptibly. "How much?"

"Shall we discuss it?" Corrana said, and they moved away, talking in low voices.

The gray-haired man turned to Kayl and said, "You did a remarkable job of calming those people down, young woman."

"I used to be an innkeeper," Kayl replied cautiously. The man still seemed familiar somehow, but the reason continued to elude her.

"Used to be?" The man raised an eyebrow, then smiled.

"Pardon me; inquisitiveness is my besetting fault. But is there anything I can help you with now?"

Kayl started to decline politely, then paused. The gray-haired man showed no sign of wishing to leave the tavern, and until he was gone, or Kayl was sure of his motives, she and the Sisters would not be able to talk freely. Kayl glanced around. Corrana and the tavern-keeper had finished their discussion. Corrana had rejoined the Mothers, and the tavern-keeper was staring with avid curiosity at Glyndon and the Elder Mothers who surrounded him. Kayl smiled, seeing a way to dispose of two difficulties at once.

"If you could keep him out of the way for a little while . . . ," she said, nodding in Penshar's direction.

The gray-haired man smiled. "Happy to oblige you." He gave her a shallow bow and strolled in the tavern-keeper's direction. After a brief conversation, the two men departed in the direction of the kitchen.

Kayl heaved a sigh of relief and at last headed for Glyndon. He appeared partially recovered; Dara had brought him a mug of something while Kayl was busy with the villagers and the tavern-keeper. Kayl hoped it wasn't the ale. She took a seat opposite Glyndon and asked bluntly, "What happened?"

"Your Varnan wizard had one of his fits," one of the nearby Sisters said sweetly. "Isn't it obvious?"

Glyndon raised his head. "I suppose this is your way of reminding me not to take the harem comment seriously," he remarked. He paused for an instant, then added reassuringly, "Don't worry; I wouldn't have."

The woman who had spoken turned and glared at him. Beside her, one of her companions said pettishly, "It's too bad Elder Sister Barthelmy couldn't keep him upstairs. If he hadn't come down babbling like that, none of this would have happened."

Kayl looked around the table. Several heads were nodding, and there was agreement on many faces. Kayl's temper gave way. "And if any of you had the good will you were born with, the situation would never have arisen. You all know what this expedition is trying to do, why Glyndon and Barthelmy and I are here, but all of you except Risper and Demma have done nothing but snipe at us since the day we left Kith Alunel. Do you think the people in this village didn't notice your suspicions?"

"Kayl—"

"Shut up, Glyndon! I've been wanting to say this for a long time and I'm going to finish. All of you know what Glyndon's visions are like; he's had enough of them on this trip. Any one of you could have said something to keep the villagers from ever getting worked up—you could have passed it off as the fit you called it a minute ago. You didn't even try, did you? You let Javieri and Corrana deal with Glyndon, and you sat watching like so many Frost Fair dolls."

"We were ready to defend him," said one of the warriors of the Star Clusters.

"So you were, Your Justice." Kayl gave a sarcastic twist to the formal address. "You had to. It's a pity that didn't occur to you earlier, when you could have done something to avoid the problem. Instead you almost got yourselves attacked by a mob of half-drunk, unarmed villagers."

"I don't have to listen to this," one of the sorceresses said, rising.

"Sit down, Holmi," Elder Mother Javieri said. Her voice was low, and colder than the northern ice fields. "Or do you claim you need not listen to me?"

The woman dropped back into her seat as if someone had kicked her knees from behind.

"Kayl is right in her complaints," Javieri went on, "and I am deeply disappointed in you."

Kayl saw Corrana sit back a little, as if in satisfaction. Glyndon was listening with an abstracted expression, as though the conversation had nothing to do with him. Barthelmy looked worried; Risper was having trouble not grinning.

"This is not the first time I have heard complaints about the treatment some of you give Glyndon shal Morag," Javieri went on. "Nor have all the complaints come from Kayl Larrinar. I have also watched and seen for myself. I should have spoken sooner, and perhaps this night's work would have been avoided."

"It wasn't even a tavern brawl," someone muttered.

Javieri's eyes flashed. "It did not have to be. Some of you seem to have forgotten that this is no pleasure trip. The future of the Sisterhood depends on us. Furthermore, there are Magicseekers looking for us, and you have just allowed a scene that none of these villagers will forget. In three days it will be the talk of the countryside. You have been so busy with your dislike of Glyndon, Barthelmy, and Kayl that you have not thought about what we are doing. Where is your training?"

"We have seen no sign of Magicseekers since we left Kith Alunel," Elder Mother Alessa pointed out.

"*They* aren't making spectacles of themselves," Kayl said, and paused. "Besides, there's a good chance that they're ahead of us already."

"What!" said several voices at once.

"I ran into an old friend of mine, a Wyrd who's heading north," Kayl said. "A week ago, she saw a very suspicious-looking group of men at a village just south of here. She thinks they might have been Magicseekers, and I agree with her. They had horses; add up the travel time yourselves."

There was a murmur of dismay from the Sisters. "Where is this friend of yours?" one of the Elder Sisters asked. "We should ask her a few questions."

"Ask away," said a voice from the direction of the doorway.

Heads turned. Bryn stood just inside the tavern, her dark-furred face unreadable. Beside her stood Alden and their eleven-year-old daughter, Xaya. There was a moment's silence; then Mark and Dara cried, "Xaya! Bryn!" and ran forward, babbling excitedly.

Bryn's eyes narrowed as she gazed indulgently at the three children, all of whom were talking at once. She waited a moment, until the first spate of excited chatter had passed, then said, "Xaya! Why don't you take Mark and Dara somewhere and show them the Kulseth knot trick you learned in Salfirn?"

"Try the back room," Kayl said. "I think it's empty."

The children left quickly, still chattering, and Alden and Bryn came forward. Kayl noticed that they had latched the door behind themselves.

"Bryn saMural and Alden toBrilan, these are my traveling companions," Kayl said, waving at the company. She suppressed a temptation to leave it at that, and ran quickly through the list of names instead. "I think you've met Elder Sister Corrana," she finished.

"I remember," Bryn said, and looked at Corrana. "You have a way of making an entrance."

"So have you," Corrana replied dryly, and Bryn grinned.

"Kayl tells us you have seen men who may be Magicseekers," Elder Mother Miracote said to Bryn. "Tell us of them."

Bryn glanced at Kayl and cocked an ear questioningly. Kayl shook her head. "I didn't have time to mention it. Things were a bit confused when I got here."

"What are you talking about?" Miracote demanded.

"I agreed to talk to you if I could get some information in return," Bryn said. "I want to know if you've heard of any Wyrd settlements near here."

"If we knew, be sure we would tell you," Javieri said. "I, for one, have not been told of any." She glanced around the faces of her fellow Sisters, but all of them shook their heads.

"And in the north?" Bryn asked.

Again, Javieri shook her head. "I am sorry."

Bryn shrugged. "You can't tell me what you don't know. It was worth trying, though."

"Then you will answer our questions?" Miracote asked. The Wyrd woman nodded, and Miracote went on, "Tell us your tale."

One of Bryn's ears twitched forward at Miracote's tone, and behind her Alden's eyes widened to amber discs. Then Bryn gave a half shrug and repeated the story she had told Kayl. When she finished, Alden told his own version, adding more details about the people he had seen. One of them fit the description of the man who had questioned Dara, but a great many men could be described as "sort of tall and plain, with a mustache."

"Not entirely convincing," Miracote said when the two Wyrds had finished.

"Must it be so?" Javieri said. "Kayl is right; we have taken too many chances with this mission already."

"Alden," Kayl said suddenly, "did any of those men wear rings?"

"No," the Wyrd replied. "Some had the habit of it, though. Fairly heavy rings, I'd say, on the left hand's middle finger."

"How many of the men?"

"At least three of them; the others I didn't see closely enough to notice."

"How can you know that?" Elder Mother Alessa asked curiously.

"I am a jewelsmith, lady," the Wyrd replied.

"Even if these men were Magicseekers indeed, what would you have us do?" Miracote said to Javieri. "It is too late to prevent them from getting ahead of us."

"We'll have to give up or try to slip by them," Kayl said promptly, before Javieri could answer. "There aren't any other choices, unless you're considering a full-fledged battle."

"We could stay here awhile," one of the Mothers said in a doubtful tone.

"After the fuss you let happen this evening?" Kayl said. "You can stay, if you like; I won't."

There was a brief silence. Then Javieri said with decision, "We cannot give up now, so we must try to avoid these men. Your suggestions, please."

The Sisters all started talking at once, reminding Kayl vividly of the behavior of Mark, Dara, and Xaya a few minutes earlier. Kayl did not bother to listen closely. She had done as much as she could, for now, in persuading the Sisters to discuss the problem at all. In the end, the Elder Mothers would make the decision themselves. Kayl looked across at Glyndon and saw that he had regained most of his color. She caught his eye and nodded slightly in the direction of the kitchen.

Glyndon smiled, rose, and left. The Sisters did not comment on his departure, but when Kayl rose a moment later they looked questioningly at her.

"I'm going to check on the children," she said to no one in particular. "Join me, Bryn?"

Bryn nodded. Only Kayl's long acquaintance with her allowed her to see the amusement in Bryn's inhuman eyes as the two Wyrds joined her in leaving the room.

CHAPTER
TWENTY-THREE

The tavern-keeper was not in the kitchen, for which Kayl was grateful. The gray-haired man was sitting on a bench near an open hearth, telling a story to the three fascinated children. Glyndon was watching the group with a bemused expression; when Kayl and the Wyrds came in, he looked up and came quickly over.

"Where did he come from?" Glyndon asked in a low voice as he joined Kayl. "He seems familiar somehow."

"He's a villager, I think," Kayl said dubiously. "Though he seems familiar to me, too."

"Listen to that story he's telling."

Kayl listened. It was something about a group of magicians and an island and a white bird or a woman. "It's the story of the founding of Varna," Glyndon said. "I didn't think anyone on the mainland knew it."

Kayl blinked and studied the gray-haired man more closely. He was clean-shaven, gray-eyed, tall and lean. His voice was deep and smooth, flowing like wine beneath the words of his story. He had no trace of the Varnan accent that still flavored Glyndon's speech, but then, Kevran had not had an accent either. The thought of Kevran lit a candle in Kayl's mind, and she said in a low, urgent voice, "Glyndon! Remember the man who told us how to find the Twisted Tower, the one Kevran talked to in that little town just outside the mountains? He had dark hair then, but his voice is the same."

"You're right," Glyndon said after a moment. "I wonder why he's here now?"

Before Kayl could reply, the storyteller turned his head, as though aware that he was under scrutiny. "If you're looking for Penshar, he's gone out," he called. "I told him I'd keep an eye on things for a few hours."

"Oh?" Kayl frowned, thinking of Magicseekers. "Where's he gone?"

"There's a woman he visits whenever he gets upset," the gray-haired man said with a smile. His voice held a wealth of amusement. "And he's had a rather upsetting evening."

Kayl's opinion of Penshar's innkeeping dropped another notch; after the confrontation between the villagers and the Sisters, she herself would not have left the main room unattended, much less the whole inn.

The man must have seen her expression change, for he added, "I've done this before. Is there anything I can get you?"

"All we need is a place to stand and talk awhile," Kayl said. "The main room is a little busy."

"Well, if you want something, just ask," the man said, and returned to his storytelling. The children did no more than nod at Kayl and Bryn before returning to their absorption.

"Whoever he is, I wish I knew his secret," Bryn commented. "I haven't seen Xaya so quiet since before we left Copeham."

Kayl turned back to Glyndon. "Glyndon, was there anything new in what you 'saw'?"

Glyndon shook his head. "Nothing. And there should have been."

"What do you mean?"

"The vision is always the same, but it still doesn't feel certain. Yet normally I would have 'seen' an alternative by now, if there were one."

"Perhaps it's the outcome of the vision that changes," Bryn suggested. "Or the significance it has."

"It's possible, I suppose," Glyndon said, frowning. "I don't think it's ever happened before."

"Have you ever had visions of the Tower before?" Kayl asked pointedly.

"I know, I know. It doesn't make me any happier about going there, though."

"You can still back out," Kayl said. "All the Sisterhood is offering you is a chance. You might not be losing anything."

"You'd still be going."

"Yes," Kayl said, meeting his eyes steadily.

Glyndon nodded. "Then there's nothing more to be said."

"This is fascinating," Bryn said. "Or I'm sure it would be, if I knew what you were talking about. But aren't you forgetting a little matter of some Magicseekers who may be ahead of you? What do you expect to do about them?"

"I don't know," Kayl said. She glanced toward the door and shook her head. "The Sisters in there will talk about it for hours; I only hope they come up with something good. It'll have to be, to get a group this size past Magicseekers without being noticed."

"Our woodcraft is at your disposal," Alden said, bowing.

"Such as it is," Bryn added.

"What?" Kayl said. "I thought you were going with Shav and his group."

"When Shav heard there might be Magicseekers about, he decided we should split up," Alden explained in a dry voice. "Bryn and I are of the opinion that we'd be safer joining you than traveling alone in this territory."

Kayl stared. "Are you mad? We're talking about going into the Windhome Mountains and trying to sneak past an unknown number of Magicseekers who are probably looking for us. Once we get past them, if we do, we have to get inside a tower with a death spell on the door and some kind of voracious black goo inside. And you think that'll be safer than traveling alone?"

"Probably—for Wyrds," Bryn said cheerfully.

"You *are* mad," Kayl said.

"Excuse me," said the deep voice of the gray-haired man, "but you come from the Sisterhood of Stars, do you not?"

Glyndon turned, frowning, and Kayl saw the gray-haired man behind him. Dara was standing beside the hearth, drawing a diagram on the stone with a half-burned twig to show Xaya where they had been; Mark was leaning over from the other side to correct any mistakes.

"Forgive me for startling you," the gray-haired man said, addressing Kayl and Glyndon. "I couldn't help overhearing some of your discussion, and then, of course, I recognized you."

"Did you." Kayl kept her voice flat. The man was too sure of himself; he made her uneasy.

"Yes. My name is Ferianek Trone. I doubt that you remember me, but we met some sixteen years ago in a village a little south of here."

"We remember you," Kayl said grimly.

"Really?" The man looked surprisingly pleased. "I'm so glad. It will make things much easier. You see, I've been looking for you."

"Looking for us?"

"*All* of us?" Bryn put in, twitching an ear.

"In a way," Ferianek replied calmly. "I need your help, and I think you may be glad of mine."

"Really." Kayl made herself smile at Ferianek. "And just what help do you need from the Silver Sisters?"

"There are twenty swordsmen from the Circle of Silence on the road to Glendura's Tomb," Ferianek said bluntly. "Alone, I can do little more than slow them down."

"Why would you wish to?"

"Tradition, a sense of honor, a wish to remedy my own mistakes . . ." Ferianek shrugged.

"Your own mistakes?" Glyndon said, pouncing on Ferianek's final words like a cat pouncing on the end of a dangling string. "What do you mean?"

"My family has watched over Glendura's Tomb since the Wars of Binding; in some sense it is my responsibility," Ferianek replied evasively.

"I'm afraid you go too fast for me," Kayl said. "I have never heard of a place called Glendura's Tomb."

"Forgive me; I forget, sometimes, that the name is obscure. You may know the place as Iralor's Sorrow, or Iralor's Bane, or perhaps Kalervon's Curse. And the folk around the mountains, those few who know of it, call it the Twisted Tower. It is a fearful place." Ferianek paused, studying Kayl. "Have I convinced you yet that I am what I claim to be?"

Kayl sighed. "I believe you . . . I think. Not that it matters; it's the Elder Mothers you'll need to convince." By now she was reasonably sure that Ferianek was the wandering scholar the Elder Mothers had been hoping to find; she wondered what they would make of him. "In the meantime, you might explain just what help you are offering us."

"I can show you how to avoid the Magicseekers," Ferianek

said promptly. "I know several ways of reaching Glendura's Tomb besides the one I told you of so many years ago. I doubt that anyone unfamiliar with the mountains would be aware of them."

"Which won't help at all if the Magicseekers have already reached the Tower, or if they come to the valley while we're still there," Glyndon said.

"I am afraid the Magicseekers will not find the path as easily as they had expected," Ferianek said solemnly, but Kayl could hear the currents of mischief buried in the depths of his voice. "I doubt that they will reach the valley before you, unless you travel very slowly indeed."

"I take it you have arranged to delay them," Kayl said.

Ferianek nodded. "Delay, yes. But it will not stop them."

"Then it seems we have little choice," Kayl said. Glyndon looked at her in surprise, and she shook her head. "If Ferianek has set traps along the main road to the Tower, we must find another way to reach it. You remember what those mountains are like, Glyndon; we could spend days or weeks looking for a passable route. We'll have to accept Ferianek's help."

"I suppose you're right," Glyndon muttered. He studied Ferianek for a moment, then asked abruptly, "Why do you call the valley Glendura's Tomb?"

"It is a personal preference only," Ferianek replied. "That name seems . . . less ominous, somehow, than the others. Perhaps it is because Glendura's story is the only one that comes from before the Tower was twisted and the valley died."

"Would you tell us some of these stories?"

"Of course," Ferianek said. His voice took on a richer tone that pulled his listeners into the story almost at once. "Glendura lived long before the Wars of Binding. She and her husband, Iralor, were magicians more powerful than any wizard living today, for they knew all of the arts which were lost in the Times of Darkness, and others besides which we no longer even remember. Their home was a tower of gold, built in a single night by virtue of their power. But all their magic was not sufficient to keep catastrophe from falling on their children. Glendura died trying to protect them; Iralor alone escaped.

"All of the legends agree on that much. What killed Glendura and her children varies from story to story. Several versions have them killed by the evil Shadow-born; in others, they die of a curse. One has them ambushed by Wyrds in the Kathkari Mountains." Ferianek broke off and looked apologetically at Bryn and Alden. "Iralor seems to have had a grudge against Wyrds, and I think someone wanted to account for it."

"We understand," Alden said. He sounded mildly amused. "Please continue."

Kayl felt a hand touch her arm. She looked down to find Dara standing beside her, with Mark and Xaya just beyond; apparently Ferianek's storytelling had attracted their attention. Kayl smiled. She took her daughter's hand and drew her a little to one side, so that Mark and Xaya could come nearer.

"It is not clear whether Iralor ran from whatever killed his family, or whether he fought his way free but was unable to save them as well," Ferianek went on. "He may not even have been present when Glendura and her children died. But whatever the reason, he *did* survive, and he brought their bodies back to the valley and buried them there. In his grief and guilt, he used his magic to twist and blacken the Tower. He lived there for years—centuries, some stories claim—bitter and angry and grieving for his wife. And so the valley is called Iralor's Sorrow, as well as Glendura's Tomb.

"There are even more stories about Iralor's death than about his life. Some legends say that his magic twisted him, even as it had twisted the Tower, and so he brought about his own death. Another version has it that he was killed by his brother, Iraman, when he turned to evil in his grief and bitterness. But all the tales agree that Iralor died in the valley, hence the name Iralor's Bane."

"You mentioned another name as well," Kayl said when Ferianek did not go on. "Kalervon's Curse. Where does that come from?"

Ferianek smiled and shook his head. "Another legend, even more confused and obscure than the stories about Iralor. Kalervon was another magician who fought against Iralor. He was defeated or destroyed—it is not clear which—and in dying he set loose, or perhaps became, a dreadful creature that either destroyed Iralor in turn or became his servant. The creature made its home in the valley, and both the valley and the creature were called Kalervon's Curse."

"I see why you said it was confused," Bryn murmured.

Kayl and Glyndon exchanged glances. "Do the tales give any description of the creature itself?" Kayl asked.

"Very little, which is unusual. 'A dark creature,' 'an evil power,' and 'a wave of shadow' are the extent of it. Most stories are much more graphic about the looks of their monsters."

"Why didn't you tell us any of these stories sixteen years ago?" Kayl said. "You must have suspected we would find them useful."

Ferianek looked uncomfortable. "No one asked, and I wasn't sure I ought to volunteer. Most people don't think of legends as a particularly reliable guide."

"Ignorance is a worse one," Glyndon said. "You can make up for your negligence now. Have you ever heard of a man named Gadeiron in connection with the Tower?"

"Oh, he was long after Iralor's death," Ferianek said. He seemed relieved to return to the subject of the Twisted Tower. "Gadeiron wasn't very interesting, really; just a fairly typical evil magician who was killed in the end by a band of heroes."

"I want to hear that one!" Mark said.

"You always want stories about heroes and magicians," Dara complained.

"Some other time, Mark," Kayl said. She wondered what Javieri would think of Ferianek and his stories.

"Perhaps we should return to the question of paths through the mountains," Ferianek suggested.

"An excellent idea," Glyndon said blandly. "You said you knew several routes to the Tower. Would all of them be passable this early in the spring, or would we have to wait a week or two?"

"Mother?" Mark spoke softly, so as not to interrupt Glyndon or Ferianek.

Kayl turned. "What is it, Mark?"

"Is Ferianek coming with us?"

"I don't know yet. It will depend on what Javieri and Miracote decide."

"I hope he does," Dara said wistfully. "He's nice."

"He certainly seems to be. Now, I think it's time for you two to get to bed."

"But Mother!" Mark protested. "It's still early!"

"And we haven't seen Xaya in *ages*," Dara added.

Kayl was pleased to note that, despite their dismay, both of the children kept their voices low. She was tempted to give in as a kind of reward, but she knew it would be unwise. "We're going to have to leave before sunrise," she said, trying to sound gentle as well as firm. "I don't want you half-asleep on the trip."

Before Mark and Dara could resume their pleading, Xaya said, "Mother?" Both Bryn and Alden turned, and Xaya said, "Kayl is sending Dara and Mark to bed, and I wondered whether you'd decided anything."

Bryn sighed and glanced at Kayl. "Not yet, dear. In the meantime—Kayl, would it be too much trouble to let mine spend the night with yours? It might turn out to be convenient."

"Oh, yes, Mother, please!" Dara said.

Kayl hesitated, then nodded. "But only if you go up to bed right now," she said.

"Oh, we will," the children chorused, and trooped out of the kitchen.

"They'll be awake half the night, talking," Kayl said, shaking her head.

"But they'll be determined not to show it in the morning," Alden pointed out.

They rejoined Glyndon and Ferianek, who had moved to the hearth and were using Dara's discarded twig to draw maps of their own on the gray stone. Halfway through Ferianek's explanation, Barthelmy walked into the kitchen, frustrated and fuming over the endless repetition of the Sisters' discussion. When Kayl gave her a summary of Ferianek's story, she insisted on summoning Javieri at once, and the whole thing had to be gone over again.

Javieri listened with a carefully neutral expression to the various suggestions, then nodded thoughtfully. "We seem to have little choice," she said, echoing Kayl's earlier observation. "Still, at least now we know how many Magicseekers we have ahead of us."

"Then you agree?" Barthelmy said.

"I do, but there are still the others to convince." Javieri glanced around the kitchen. "I think it would be best if I was the one to present this suggestion to them."

Kayl saw Glyndon's mouth twist in a wry smile as he joined the rest in nodding agreement. "Very good," Javieri said. She looked at Ferianek. "Will you come and tell us your stories, if

I send for you in a few minutes?"

"I would be glad to," Ferianek said.

As Javieri started to leave, Alden stopped her and said something in a low voice. Javieri nodded and went out. Alden came back to the little group by the hearth, looking smug.

Kayl studied him. "You aren't still seriously thinking about coming with us, are you?"

"If you're willing to have us, yes," Alden replied.

"Why?"

Bryn gave Alden a fierce grin. "I told you she would insist on knowing. We're taking a chance, Kayl. The last half-reliable rumor we heard put a city of Wyrds somewhere in the north end of the Windhome Mountains. We'll be heading in that direction in any case."

"The Magicseekers—"

"It's still safer for us to travel with humans, at least as long as we're in human-settled territory," Bryn said. "Believe me, we know."

Barthelmy looked surprised and angry. "But this is the Estarren Alliance!"

Alden shrugged. "Things are better here than in Mindaria, but that's not saying much."

"Why do you think we've spent so much time looking for a *Wyrd* settlement?" Bryn added. "There are still plenty of human cities that have a good-sized Wyrd section, but we've seen what happens when humans and Wyrds try to live together."

"Humans and Wyrds have lived together for over twelve hundred years," Barthelmy said. "It's only recently that there's been trouble."

"Things have been going wrong for a lot longer than you think," Alden said. "It's just that they've finally gone wrong enough for you to notice."

"True," Ferianek said. "But Her Virtue is right to say that it is not because humans and Wyrds live in the same place. The real problem is that the use of magic comes easily to only three of the Four Races: the Wyrds, the Shee, and the Neira. Therefore few humans understand magic, and they resent and envy those who do."

"Which is part of the reason Varnans are so unpopular," Glyndon put in. "You wouldn't believe the number of people

I've met in the past fifteen years who think anyone from Varna can dry up rivers, walk through mountains, and make gold from ashes and air."

Kayl saw Barthelmy nod reluctantly; she had good reason to know how ex-magicians, at least, reacted to one who still had power.

"Whatever the cause, we have to deal with the result," Bryn said. "So if any of you hear of a Wyrd city . . ."

"None of us are likely to, if we haven't already," Kayl said. "Unless Ferianek has another surprise under his cloak."

"Not exactly," Ferianek said slowly. "There's a Waywalker settlement in a valley a bit north of Glendura's Tomb that's mainly Shee and Wyrds, but I believe they're planning to leave soon."

"How do you know that?" Kayl said. She had heard of the Waywalkers; they were a small group, generally considered to be harmless eccentrics. They also had the reputation of being close-mouthed, particularly in regard to the locations of their permanent settlements.

"I'm a follower of the Way of the Third Moon myself," Ferianek said apologetically.

"Why are they leaving?" Alden asked.

"And where are they going?" Bryn added.

"There's an island just south of the Melyranne Sea that the Waywalkers bought from the Empire of Rathane a few years ago. We've started a colony there. The settlement in the mountains is a gathering place for people who plan to move to the island permanently."

"Moving or not, they'd be worth talking to," Bryn said. She looked at Alden, who twitched an ear at her. Bryn nodded decisively. "It's settled, then. Now all we need to know is whether your Elder Mothers will agree to take us."

"They aren't *my* Elder Mothers anymore, and I still think you're mad," Kayl said.

"If it were that bad, you wouldn't be taking the children," Bryn said flatly.

Kayl was silenced. She could not say that she had begun to have nightmares of Mark dissolving into a black pool and Dara hacked to pieces by grinning, eagle-helmeted Magicseekers. Glyndon was watching her with a grave expression; somehow he always seemed to know Kayl's private worries.

Or was she reading more into his face than was really there? Kayl gave herself a mental shake and came back to the conversation.

"I don't think they'll object," Barthelmy was saying. "But you'll have to talk—"

The door opened and Risper came in. "Ferianek Trone? Would you and the Wyrds come in now? You, too," she added, nodding at Barthelmy and Kayl. "You really ought to listen to the discussion."

"All right," Barthelmy said. "Coming, Kayl?"

"I suppose so. But what about Glyndon?"

Risper looked dubious. "He has every right to be there," she said apologetically, "but it's bound to start another argument. Some of them are just looking for an excuse."

"I see. Tomorrow may be even more interesting than I'd expected," Glyndon said thoughtfully. "Never mind; I think I'll join the children in an early bedtime."

"You're sure?" Kayl said doubtfully, though there was nothing in Glyndon's tone or expression to make her think that he resented exclusion from the discussion.

"I don't want to spend three or four hours arguing about who ought to go where, with whom, and why," Glyndon said. "I'll leave that to you and Barthelmy. If anything important happens, you can tell me about it in the morning."

Kayl hesitated. Then a trick of the firelight sent shadows flickering across Glyndon's face, and she saw the tiredness he was trying to hide. Glyndon was frequently exhausted after one of his visions; she should have remembered that. She wished fervently that she could take some of his fatigue on herself, or that she could at least keep his nightmares at bay long enough for him to recover a little. But she could not say anything; Glyndon would not thank her for fussing.

"Sleep well, then," she said as lightly as she could. "But don't think you're getting out of anything. I'll make you sit through a stroke-by-stroke description tomorrow."

"I'll be sure to brace myself for it," Glyndon said with a flicker of amusement.

"Come on, Kayl, they're waiting," Risper said, and Kayl went to join her.

CHAPTER
TWENTY-FOUR

The discussion lasted well into the night, but in the end the Sisters agreed that they had no more reasonable alternative than to take one of Ferianek's suggested routes to the Tower. They left at sunrise next morning. Both Ferianek and the Wyrds came with them, much to the delight of Mark and Dara.

Ferianek made a marvelous traveling companion—endlessly interested in everything he saw or heard, always willing to listen, yet with an uncanny ability to sense what subjects to avoid and when to be silent. His storytelling ability was unequaled in Kayl's experience, and his supply of tales never seemed to dry up. The children would have monopolized him completely, had they had their own way, but Ferianek's duties made that impossible. He acted as both guide and scholar for the party, and the Elder Mothers spent hours questioning him about the Tower and the valley, hoping to discover some clue to the power that had taken their magic from them.

The expanded party took six days to reach the foothills of the Windhome Mountains. The road was nearly level, which made walking easy, and the weather remained clear and sunny. On the third day after leaving the village Kayl saw the first quick shoots of a snowdrop poking up beside a rapidly dwindling mound of snow. The children kept each other amused, for the most part, and their occasional quarrels blew over quickly. In many ways, Kayl found it the most enjoyable part of the journey thus far.

Under Ferianek's guidance, they turned north for half a day when they reached the foothills, then resumed their easterly direction. Tensions among the adult members of the group began to increase. Barthelmy and Glyndon started spending much of their spare time discussing various magical alternatives with Corrana, Javieri, and the other Sisters who would be directly involved in the attempt to penetrate the Twisted Tower. Bryn and Alden joined Risper and Demma as advance scouts, searching for any sign of the Magicseekers, for none of the Elder Mothers was prepared to trust blindly Ferianek's assurances.

All this activity left Kayl with little to do but think. The Elder Mothers seemed uninterested in making use of Kayl's strategic skills; the attack on the Tower would, after all, be almost solely magical in nature, and they had Ferianek to provide details of the terrain around the valley. Kayl began to wonder why they had wanted her along at all. She started volunteering for the late watches, so that she could at least feel she was contributing something. The technique was only moderately successful; she continued to feel restless and uncertain. Late one night, after making the rounds of the camp, Kayl settled herself in front of the fire and forced herself to begin putting her thoughts in order.

She began with the Sisterhood of Stars. In Kith Alunel she had discovered that she could not return to her life with the Sisterhood, but she had never thought that she might come to an active distaste for them and all they stood for. She had enjoyed traveling from Copeham to Kith Alunel with Corrana in spite of the irritations; the current journey was another story entirely. She was no longer sure the Sisterhood of Stars was worth saving, but a lingering sense of duty and honor held her to her promise. She would see this enterprise through to its finish.

That thought led, inevitably, to the well-worn reconsideration of her reasons for joining the expedition in the first place. Taken singly, they seemed too trivial a justification for such a dangerous commitment. There was the hope, however frail, that Glyndon might be cured of his visions; there were the threats to Mark and Dara; there was the obligation to try to mend something she might have had a hand in breaking; there was a continued affection for what the Sisterhood of Stars had once meant to her; there was a stubborn and senseless urge to be present for the end of the adventure she had begun sixteen years before. And, buried so deeply she was almost unaware of it, there was the desire to see some part of her past finished and its ghosts laid to rest, so that she could go on ...

Go on to what? Kayl realized suddenly that she had not thought past reaching the Twisted Tower. She scowled and shifted uneasily, staring into the fire. She was letting herself drift again, as she had in Copeham after Kevran's death, as she had on the journey to Kith Alunel. She was a better strategist than that, or she had been, once. When had she taken to reacting to things as they happened, instead of thinking ahead and preparing for them?

Kayl's frown deepened as she realized that again she was looking backward. Deliberately, she set herself the problem: what were she and her children going to do once the Sisterhood was finished with the Twisted Tower? The easiest path would be to return to Kith Alunel with the expedition, but what then? She would not rejoin the Sisterhood, and she had known for a long time that a widow with two children to raise could not make her living as a mercenary soldier or guard. She might be able to find work in an inn, but she found that the idea had little appeal for her now.

And if she did not return to Kith Alunel? She could, she supposed, take the children to Varna, as she had told Jirod so long ago. But she did not know how the Varnans would react to Kevran's northern-born, Sisterhood-trained wife and his half-Varnan children, nor did she think she would be comfortable for long in such a strange and rigid culture.

Then there was Glyndon. Kayl could no longer deny the strength of her feelings for him, any more than she could fool herself into thinking his love for her did not exist. She found herself wishing she were twenty again, serenely confident that love was all that mattered. But she was not twenty, and she knew better. She had the children to think of, and even if she had not, she did not know what sort of life she would lead with Glyndon, or if either of them would be happy in it. So she continued to avoid admitting aloud what she knew they would both have to face sooner or later.

The real difficulty was, and had always been, that she had no clear idea of what she wanted to do with the rest of her life.

She knew a great deal about what she did not want, but she could not plan her future on the basis of avoiding this place or that group. A branch broke in the fire, sending up a swirl of tiny sparks, and Kayl blinked. It was later than she had realized; her watch was over. She rose and stretched, then went to wake up her replacement, the unanswered questions still milling aimlessly about in her mind.

Kayl awoke early the next morning and decided to get her sword practice in before breakfast. She dressed as quietly as she could, to avoid awakening the children, then took her sword and went looking for a level spot to exercise.

Just outside the tent, she met Risper, who had drawn the early morning watch. "Where away?" said the healer. "And why so early?"

"Practice," Kayl said, touching the hilt of her sword. "I couldn't sleep. Do you know if there's a reasonably flat area anywhere close?"

"There's a spot over by the birches that Demma and Forrin were using last night," Risper said, and pointed. "It's just around that hill there."

"Thanks. If Mark or Dara wake up worried, would you let them know where I am?"

Risper nodded, and Kayl started off in the direction the healer had indicated. She found the place easily, a grassy patch of land between two hills, and soon she was lost in the familiar rhythm of the exercises.

She was in the middle of a particularly complicated series of figures when she heard someone coming toward her from the direction of the camp. She finished the sequence just as Glyndon came into sight. "Good morning," he called.

"Good morning," Kayl said, straightening. She sheathed her sword and walked toward him. "You're up early."

"I wanted to talk to you."

Kayl waited, but Glyndon did not continue. "Well, what is it?" she asked finally.

"Have you still got that crystal chip we found in Kevran's rod?" Glyndon said.

"Of course I have it," Kayl said. The question of that demon-cursed bit of glass had been pricking at her since before the expedition had left Kith Alunel. She let some of her annoyance and worry show as she went on. "Does this mean you're finally going to let me speak to Javieri about it?"

"I'd still rather you didn't." Glyndon's tone was absently apologetic, as if he had more important things to concern him.

"Why not? We're only three or four days from the valley; we have to tell them now, while Javieri still has time to allow for it in her plans. It's going to be hard enough to explain why we didn't mention it months ago."

"No," Glyndon said, and looked away from Kayl. "Not yet."

Kayl pressed her lips together for an instant, then voiced the suspicion that had been growing in her mind for the last week. "You don't intend to tell the Elder Mothers about the chip at all. Why? Glyndon, what are you hiding?"

"Must I be hiding something? Kayl, if I thought that knowing about the crystal would help the Sisterhood get us safely into the Twisted Tower, I would have told them of it myself, long ago. But it won't. They'll only try to keep us outside the Tower, and perhaps destroy the crystal chip as well. And that would be disastrous."

"Javieri has more sense than that."

"Perhaps. But it will take more than good sense to solve the problem of the Tower. And even with all her magic intact, I do not think Javieri capable of understanding the magic of the crystal."

"And you can?"

"As much as anyone." Glyndon's eyes were haunted. "Please, trust me."

"I should never have promised not to speak of that crystal without your consent," Kayl muttered.

"But you did promise. I'm sorry, Kayl, but I don't want to take the chance."

Kayl looked at him, wondering how far to press him. "Then what do we do?"

Glyndon hesitated. Then, fixing his eyes on the mountains that loomed above them, he said, "I was going to ask you to give it to me."

For a long moment Kayl could not collect her thoughts. "Is that what you came out here to ask me about?" she said at last.

"Yes."

"No explanation?" Kayl felt her temper slipping. "You can

do better than that, Glyndon.''

Glyndon lowered his eyes to hers. He did not seem reassured by what he found there, but he said with single-minded stubbornness, ''Will you give me the crystal?''

''Why do you want it?''

Again Glyndon hesitated. ''I think—I hope—it may help me understand what I 'see', or at least make the visions clearer.''

''There's more to it than that,'' Kayl said with certainty. ''I want the whole story, Glyndon. Now.''

''Kayl . . .''

''Is it the visions again?'' Kayl asked more gently, ''or is it something else this time?''

Glyndon muttered something under his breath, then said with difficulty, ''It's the same thing. My visions are linked to the big crystal somehow, but they're also tied to that chip you have, and it's still part of the Crystal in the Twisted Tower. . . .''

''How do you know?''

''I don't know how I know! But I'm right. I can feel those cursed crystals even in my sleep, and the closer we get to the Tower, the worse it gets. If I had the chip, I could work out what's happening.''

''All by yourself?'' Kayl said skeptically.

Glyndon raised his head. ''I am still a Varnan wizard.''

''Is that the real reason you don't want to tell the Elder Mothers about the crystal? Because they aren't Varnans? You're as bad as they are!''

''No! You don't understand. That's a separate thing; it has nothing to do with my wanting to study the crystal.''

''Maybe it should,'' Kayl said grimly. Her immediate impulse was to drag Glyndon back to camp at once and find Javieri, but she forced herself to stop and think first. The Elder Mothers would certainly react badly to the long concealment of the crystal chip; Glyndon was right to fear that they might bar him and Kayl from entering the Twisted Tower. On the other hand, the crystal seemed to be at the center of the mystery of the Tower; letting the Sisters try to enter without knowing as much as possible about it went against all Kayl's training as a strategist and tactician. . . . ''There has to be some way of telling the Elder Mothers,'' Kayl muttered.

''No!'' Glyndon said sharply. Then he bit his lip and turned aside, as if he thought he had given away too much.

Kayl waited. When at last Glyndon turned back to face her, she asked, "What are you afraid of, Glyndon?"

"I—" Glyndon stared at her for a moment; then his shoulders slumped. "It's my fault," he said in a low voice.

"What is?"

"The Tower. I was afraid to come back, and now it's been too long and it's all out of hand."

"What are you talking about?" Kayl demanded when Glyndon did not go on. "Even if you thought you could do something, you'd have been a fool to come back alone."

"You don't understand. I wouldn't have had to come back alone. I avoided being asked."

"Your visions," Kayl said, suddenly understanding. "You kept away from the Sisterhood the same way you kept away from the Magicseekers."

"Not exactly; the Sisterhood wasn't actively looking for me until recently. But I avoided a number of chance encounters that would eventually have led me back to the Tower. I never went near Kith Alunel, for instance. I got very good at it, until . . ."

"Until I got involved," Kayl said softly.

Glyndon looked away. There was a long pause. Kayl could feel the chill sweat from her practicing as it dried on her back. "Yes," Glyndon said at last.

"I see." It was Kayl's turn to hesitate. "The way you feel about me isn't new, then," she said finally.

"I've loved you for nearly sixteen years," Glyndon said. He stiffened like a man about to face the King's justice and met her eyes. "How long have you known?"

"I think I've known since Kith Alunel, when you decided to come with the expedition without waiting to hear what the Sisterhood had to offer. It took me a long time to admit it to myself, though." Kayl smiled slightly and shook her head at her own stubbornness.

Glyndon was silent for a moment, studying her. "What happens now?"

"Nothing, for a while," Kayl said. Then, seeing the look on his face, she added quickly, "It isn't that I don't care for you, Glyndon—"

"But you just can't see me as a lover," Glyndon finished. "I know that; why do you think I've never said anything?"

"You're being an idiot," Kayl said, half annoyed, half sorry for him. "The problem isn't how I feel about you. If I were twenty and didn't have the children to worry about, I'd have seduced you weeks ago. Possibly months."

"You don't mean that."

Kayl gave an exasperated snort. She stepped forward and, before Glyndon could object, put both her hands behind his head and pulled his mouth down to hers.

"You meant it," Glyndon said in a dazed voice several minutes later.

"Of course I meant it," Kayl said. She felt more than a little dazed herself.

"Then why are you . . ."

"Hesitating?" Kayl sighed and, reluctantly, moved away from him. "Because it isn't a simple decision. What kind of a life would we have, Glyndon? Do I take the children wandering along with you, or do you settle down to innkeeping with me? It isn't an easy thing to do, giving up your way of life for somebody else; Kevran and I found that out. And what happens at the Twisted Tower could change everything. . . . I can't decide now, it's just too soon."

Glyndon studied her gravely. "I think I understand," he said at last. "But you can't keep running away from your future, Kayl."

"This from the man who spent years running away from the mere possibility of returning to the Twisted Tower," Kayl said, smiling.

Reluctantly, Glyndon returned the smile. "Yes. We're that much alike. We may run from different things, but we both run."

Kayl nodded slowly. Glyndon was only voicing her own thoughts of the night before in different words. "Maybe we can help each other face things," she said.

"Maybe." Glyndon paused, considering. Then he sighed. "All right; I'll start. Let's go talk to the Elder Mothers about that crystal chip."

CHAPTER

TWENTY-FIVE

They found Javieri talking quietly with Corrana, while all around the other Sisters broke camp. Kayl drew them well out of the way of the hum of activity. The story of the crystal would, of necessity, be told to every member of the expedition before they reached the Twisted Tower, but Kayl felt that Javieri should hear the news first, in as much privacy as possible.

Javieri listened with increasing coldness to Kayl's awkward explanation, but Corrana's expression did not change. "And just touching this chip made you remember the truth?" she said when Kayl finished.

"It was more than remembering," Kayl said with an involuntary shudder. "I felt as if I were living through it again."

"Interesting," Corrana said thoughtfully. "I would like to see this chip."

"We should have been informed of this crystal earlier," Javieri said, and there was a frigid undercurrent to her tone.

"Why?" Glyndon demanded. "What would you have done differently?"

"Had we known of the crystal, we would have had time to study it, and perhaps learn what manner of power it holds," Javieri replied.

"You would have learned nothing," Glyndon said flatly. "Without magic—"

"More can be done without spells than you may think, Varnan," Javieri said. "So much, at least, we have been forced to learn. Nor are we completely magicless."

"We acted as we thought best, Your Serenity," Kayl said with as much courtesy as she could muster.

"And we have little time for more disagreements and recriminations," Corrana murmured. Her eyes stayed firmly on Glyndon's face as she spoke.

Javieri looked suspiciously from Kayl to Corrana; then she nodded. "You are right, Elder Sister," she said. "Ask Alessa and Miracote to join us, please, and Elder Sister Barthelmy. They must be told of this, so that we may consider it while we travel."

Corrana bowed and left. Javieri turned to Kayl. "May I see this chip of crystal?"

Kayl glanced at Glyndon. "She'll have to, sooner or later," Glyndon said with a shrug.

"I'll get it, then," Kayl said, and left.

The tent Kayl shared with the children had not yet been taken down; inside, Kayl found Dara, just finishing the packing. "Thank you, dear," Kayl said. "I'd been wondering when I was going to find time for that. Where did you put your father's rod?" Kevran's hiding place had seemed the best spot to leave the crystal; certainly Kayl preferred not to carry it around unprotected.

Dara looked startled, then injured. "In your pack. I wouldn't take it when you said I couldn't."

"That's not what I meant," Kayl said quickly. "I want to show it to Elder Mother Javieri, and I didn't want to disarrange all your bundles looking for it."

"Oh." Dara dug for a minute in one of the packs, then pulled out the oilcloth-wrapped rod. "Here it is. Why does Her Serenity want to see it? Can I come, too?"

Kayl hesitated, then nodded. The time for concealment was clearly past. She waited until Dara had resettled the pack, and they left the tent together.

Barthelmy and the Elder Mothers were waiting with Glyndon when Kayl and Dara arrived. Javieri gave Kayl a warning glance, then launched into a brief summary of what Kayl had told her. Kayl noticed that she did not include details of the memory-visions the crystal had brought to Kayl and Glyndon.

Elder Mother Miracote scowled at Kayl and Glyndon when Javieri finished, and even Barthelmy looked somewhat shocked. Javieri raised a hand, and the resentful murmurings ceased. The Elder Mother looked at Kayl and said, "Have you brought it?"

Kayl nodded without speaking and untied the knots that held the wrappings around Kevran's rod. Javieri frowned as the rod came into view. She opened her mouth as if to speak, then appeared to think better of it. Kayl smiled grimly, and devoted her attention to manipulating the rod through the heavy oilcloth. Carefully, she twisted the ends of the rod.

The rod separated in the middle, and with even greater caution, Kayl tilted the hollow section and shook the chip of crystal onto the center of the oilcloth. She let the pieces of the rod slide out of her grasp and, still keeping the cloth between her fingers and the chip, held the crystal out for Javieri and the Elder Mothers to look at. The three Elders leaned forward, and after a moment Alessa reached out.

"I don't think you should touch it," Kayl said softly, but she did not pull her hands away.

Alessa frowned and glanced at Javieri. "Later, I think," Javieri said. She looked at Kayl. "I would prefer to begin by discovering whether this crystal affects Elder Sister Barthelmy in the same way you say it did the two of you."

Javieri's tone was formal, but it seemed to Kayl that the Elder Mother was requesting, rather than commanding. Kayl nodded. It was only sensible to find out whether the crystal chip had the same effect on all three of those who had been part of the original expedition to the Twisted Tower.

Barthelmy stepped forward, her eyes wary. "It's not bad," Kayl said in a low voice. "Just a bit of a shock." She held out the crystal, and the sunlight made it glitter coldly against the brownish cloth.

Barthelmy forced a smile and touched the tip of her finger to the crystal in Kayl's protected hands. She stiffened and went pale, then sucked in her breath in a small, involuntary gasp. A second gasp echoed Barthelmy's, but this one came from beside and just behind Kayl.

Automatically, Kayl lowered her hands and whirled, in time to see a white-faced Dara sway and stumble. Kayl clenched her left hand around the crystal chip and flipped the oilcloth over and around it with her other hand as she stepped forward to catch her daughter in her arms.

Dara clung to her as she had when she was a small child

afraid of the Night Men. Kayl murmured soothing words and stroked her hair, while behind them a babble of questions broke out.

"Enough." Javieri's voice cut through the hubbub, and the Elder Mothers quieted. "Barthelmy, what happened?"

Dara's shivering had stopped, so Kayl half turned to hear the answer, keeping a reassuring arm around her daughter's shoulders. Barthelmy was still pale, and she looked worried, or perhaps frightened. "I . . . saw the Twisted Tower," she said slowly. "The interior, when we were there fifteen years ago. But it did not happen as I have remembered it."

"Ah." Javieri glanced at Kayl. "How did it happen?"

"We got to the room at the top of the Tower," Barthelmy said, her expression changing to bewilderment. "There was a huge crystal; Kevran knocked a chip from the corner, and—"

"And the black stuff came!" Dara said, and buried her head in Kayl's shoulder. "And it calls and *calls*," she mumbled against the rough linen of Kayl's over-tunic.

"What?" Javieri said sharply.

"Let her alone," Kayl said, her tone a match for the Elder Mother's. "Can't you see she's had a shock?"

"I can see it," Javieri said dryly. "And I am wondering why. The child was not the one who touched the crystal." She looked pointedly at Barthelmy.

Barthelmy swallowed, then raised her chin. "It may be the link between teacher and student that is the cause of Dara's reaction. I have been instructing her in the basics of magic for several weeks."

"What?" The cry tore from Kayl's throat, and it was a moment before she realized that Javieri's voice had joined hers.

"I asked her to, Mother," Dara said, raising her head.

"Exactly what is it that you have done?" Javieri asked Barthelmy. Her voice was as cold as it had been when she told Kayl that the Sisterhood should have been informed of the crystal's existence much earlier than it had been.

"I have taught Dara what any foundling child may learn in the Star Halls before her fourteenth birthday," Barthelmy said, meeting Javieri's gaze steadily. "The shaping of spells, the words and rituals that mold all magic, and the beginnings of focusing power. Should I have denied her request?"

"I wish you had told us of it," Javieri said, gesturing to include the other Elder Mothers. She turned toward Kayl and

Dara, and her face softened. "Tell us, child, what you felt and saw when Barthelmy touched the chip your mother holds."

Dara glanced doubtfully at Kayl, then, when Kayl nodded, she said, "It was like I was in a big room made of glass, and I could see people outside through the walls. Then there was a noise like a bell, and the glass cracked, and—and the black stuff came. It was outside, but I could feel it calling through the glass." Kayl felt her shudder. "I can *still* feel it. I wish it would stop!"

"Calling?" Javieri said, looking at Barthelmy. "Do you know what she means?"

"I may," Glyndon broke in, and his tone was grim. As he came forward, Kayl felt an irrational gladness in simply knowing he was present.

"If you know something, tell us," Javieri said.

Glyndon's eyes were fixed on Barthelmy. "When you taught Dara the beginnings of focusing her power, did you teach her the Sisterhood's method of using a name as the channel?" he asked. His voice was hard and shook slightly; he was clearly struggling to contain his anger and only just succeeding.

"Yes, of course I did," Barthelmy said, sounding puzzled. "And Dara is an apt pupil, the best I have ever had. She—"

"Of course she's an apt pupil for that kind of magic!" Glyndon said furiously. "She has demon blood!"

Javieri and the other Sisters stared at Kayl and Dara in shocked surprise. Kayl pulled Dara closer and glared back at them, wondering what Glyndon was getting at. Barthelmy went white. "Demon blood . . . And *sklathran'sy* are vulnerable through their names! But I didn't know!"

"You knew," Glyndon contradicted her flatly. "Or you would have known if you'd bothered to stop and think."

"No!" Barthelmy insisted. "Dara—"

"Dara is Kevran's daughter. I was there when Kevran told you about his grandmother; I remember how shocked you were by the whole idea of a Varnan having a child by a demon. But you didn't want to remember that, did you? And now you've put Dara in a position—"

"Glyndon." Kayl reached up and touched his arm, and Glyndon stopped.

"I'm sorry, Kayl," Barthelmy whispered. "I didn't . . . . If I'd had the slightest suspicion . . ."

"I know." It was difficult to say, but Kayl forced herself to do it, because it was the truth. "I didn't remember it myself until just now."

"You think the calling the child spoke of has something to do with this . . . sensitivity of hers?" Miracote asked Glyndon.

"It must," Glyndon said. He glanced at Barthelmy again and added bitterly, "Though I doubt that it would have happened at all if it hadn't been for her."

"Mother, what does he mean?" Dara whispered. "Am I a demon?"

"No, of course not," Kayl said. "Your great-grandmother was, but that's a long time ago. Don't worry; it will be all right." She wondered whether her reassurances were doing any good. She didn't feel reassuring; she was angry and frightened and very, very worried. A thought struck her, and she looked at Barthelmy. "What about Mark?" she asked in a voice she hardly recognized as her own.

"Mark wasn't interested in learning magic," Barthelmy said hastily.

"He's been having sword lessons with Demma instead," Dara said eagerly. Then her face fell and she said in a forlorn voice, "We wanted to surprise you."

Kayl summoned up a laugh. "Well, you've certainly managed it." She was relieved to know that Mark, at least, was not likely to have felt whatever had touched Dara. She knew, however, that if demon blood were a source of danger, Mark was as much at risk as Dara.

"Not *that* way," Dara said indignantly.

Kayl laughed again, glad that Dara seemed to be recovering. "I should hope not."

"Kayl." Glyndon had finished whatever he had been saying to the Elder Mothers; now he was looking at Dara again. "Do you think Dara could answer a few more questions now?"

"Dara?" Kayl said.

"All right, Mother," Dara said.

"You don't have to, if you'd rather not," Kayl said, feeling her daughter stiffen slightly.

Dara's chin came up. "Mark answered questions, when that man in Kith Alunel tried to take him away, and I'm older than he is. I'll be all *right*, Mother."

Glyndon chuckled. "Good," he said. "Can you tell us anything more about this thing that was calling you?"

"It isn't calling *me*," Dara corrected him. "It's just calling. I think it's been calling for a long time, only I couldn't hear it before."

"And now you can?"

Dara nodded. "I don't like it. It sounds just as nasty and awful as it looked."

"Do you mean you can still hear it?" Kayl interrupted. Dara nodded again, and Kayl turned to Javieri. "That settles it," she said. "Dara can't go on to the Twisted Tower, and Mark probably shouldn't either."

"We cannot leave her behind alone," Javieri said. "And there is no one to stay with her."

"I—" Kayl stopped, knowing that she could not turn back now. She was sure that whatever Dara was feeling came from the black thing in the Twisted Tower, and that it would be dangerous to take Dara any closer. But she was equally certain that leaving the mystery of the Tower unsolved would be even more dangerous, to Dara and everyone else. Kayl could not desert the expedition, but— "I'll ask Bryn and Alden if they'll wait here with the children. No one is likely to come by, and they have no need to go to the Tower with the rest of us."

"No," Glyndon said. Javieri and Kayl both looked at him in surprise, and he went on, "Dara needs to know as many of the protective spells as she can learn. I can teach her, if she comes with us."

"We'll be at the valley in two days," Kayl objected. "Three at most. How much can you teach her in that time?"

"Quite a bit, I hope," Glyndon said.

"I learn very quickly," Dara put in hopefully.

"And what if it isn't enough?" Kayl retorted. "What if that black thing gets to her somehow?"

"For all we know, that could happen here as easily as in the valley," Glyndon said. "At least if Dara comes with us I can try to do something about it."

Javieri nodded approval. "And the protection of the Sisterhood—"

"The Sisterhood got us into this in the first place," Glyndon interrupted. "I wouldn't put too much emphasis on it now, if I were you."

Kayl stood still, staring around the circle of faces. She saw sympathy on some, but no support, and she felt her temper rising. Dara was *her* daughter, *her* responsibility; how dare these people try to say what she must do? Yet . . . Glyndon was right. Miles were no protection against magic, but the companionship of wizards might be. Kayl scowled. Barthelmy's companionship so far could hardly have been called a protection. Kayl knew she would have a hard time forgiving her old friend for what had happened, however harmless the original reasons for the magic lessons had been. But that was past; Kayl could not deny the validity of the argument just because circumstances had worked against it in a single instance.

Still feeling angry and worried, and feeling, as well, as if she were being pushed and bullied into agreeing against her better judgment, Kayl nodded. "All right," she said. "Mark and Dara stay with the expedition."

CHAPTER

TWENTY-SIX

The news of the finding of the crystal chip, and of Barthelmy's and Dara's reaction to it, had spread quickly through the expedition. Kayl could almost feel the curious gazes of the Sisters as they traveled. She did her best to ignore them, and walked in silence beside Dara and Glyndon. She had no real reason to stay close to them while they traveled; Glyndon was concentrating on remembering every bit of demon-lore and every protective spell he had ever heard, and Dara was completely absorbed in what Glyndon was telling her. Kayl had very quickly lost track of the conversation, but it made her feel better to be close at hand.

Mark walked with her during the early part of the day, clearly torn between worry about Dara and irritation with her for spoiling their planned surprise. Kayl heard him mutter, "I *told* her magic was stupid" as they started up a steep incline.

"And why do you think magic is stupid?" Kayl said.

Mark looked up, startled; he had evidently not expected to be overheard. "Nobody *does* anything with it," he said, waving toward the Sisters ahead.

"They can't, Mark," Kayl reminded him. "That's why we're here."

"Glyndon never does anything either," Mark said. "Except see things, and he doesn't do that on purpose." Kayl

"Mark!" Xaya came down the incline, half running, half sliding past the amused Sisters. "Mark, Father says there's a stream up ahead that's got the kind of rocks with fish in them, and Mother says we can hunt for some if we want to. If it's all right with you," she added, looking at Kayl.

"Rocks don't have fish in them!" Mark said scornfully.

"They do too!" Xaya retorted. "Sometimes, anyway. Father showed me one once, that the old Prefect was having him make into a scroll-weight. They're inside, and you have to smash the rocks open to find them."

On Kayl's other side, Dara stopped talking to Glyndon to listen to Xaya. "Is that true, Mother?" she asked.

"Yes, it is. I've seen the kind of thing Xaya means. They aren't common, but if Alden says the stream ahead may have some, it probably does."

"Live fish?" Mark said, still skeptical but willing to be convinced.

"No, silly," Xaya said. "Bones and things. Like somebody made a clay cast of a fish, only in rock."

"That's weird," Mark said.

"Why would a wizard want to wrap a rock around a fish?" Dara asked Glyndon.

"What makes you think a wizard did it?" Glyndon said.

"Well, how else could it happen? But it doesn't sound as if it would be any use."

"Wizards are always doing things that aren't any use," Mark said before Glyndon could answer. "When they do anything at all."

"Why don't you see if you can find a couple of these rocks?" Kayl said quickly. "Maybe you can figure it out for yourselves."

"Can I go too, Mother?" Dara asked.

Kayl looked at Glyndon, who nodded. She gave her permission, and the three children scrambled up the hill almost as fast as Xaya had come down it. Kayl watched them go, then turned to Glyndon with an inquiring look.

"She'll be able to absorb things more quickly if she gets a break now and then," he said. Then he smiled. "And so will I."

"What do you mean by that?"

"I have to find out how much Dara knows, how she's been taught," Glyndon said. "The Sisterhood's approach to magic is . . . very unusual."

"Why don't you talk to Barthelmy about it?"

Glyndon blinked. "Because I hadn't thought of it," he confessed. "Excuse me." He scanned the string of Sisters above them in search of Barthelmy, then began to climb more rapidly.

Kayl did not try to follow him. She finished the climb alone, feeling glad he had not stayed and yet wishing he had. She wanted someone to snap at or quarrel with in order to relieve the mounting pressure of her worries about Dara, about the crystal, about the Sisterhood, about the Tower. The realization made her feel ashamed, but it did not lessen her irritability. She set her teeth and tried to empty her mind of everything but climbing.

The technique was only partially successful; the incline was not really steep enough to demand such concentration, and she had nearly reached the top. The descent on the other side was just as frustrating. It required enough attention that she could not ponder her troubles deeply enough to resolve them, but it did not occupy her mind fully enough to allow her a respite from worry. When they stopped for lunch beside the stream at the foot of the mountain, Kayl felt like a bear just out of hibernation—hungry, cross, and ready to tear the arms off anyone who got in her way.

Her first act was to check on the children, whom she found happily smashing fist-sized rocks against larger rocks by the side of the stream. She withdrew without interrupting them and went to collect her ration of cheese and journey-bread. She saw Glyndon and Barthelmy, deep in conversation, and waved at them but did not stop. After a brief search, she found a place a little apart from the rest of the expedition and sat down to eat.

The day was relatively warm, though Kayl could still see snowcaps on the tops of the mountains around them. The sun was high enough for its rays to reach even to the bottom of the canyons between the mountains; the stream sparkled like a flow of diamonds. Kayl stretched her legs out into a patch of sunlight and let her cloak fall open to enjoy the warmth.

"May I join you?" The deep voice was unmistakable.

Kayl turned and found Ferianek Trone standing behind her, looking unusually grave. "If you wish," she said.

"Thank you." Ferianek seated himself. Kayl began eating her lunch, wondering what the scholar wanted. After a time, Ferianek said, "I heard about your girl and the crystal."

"I'm not surprised," Kayl said, struggling to keep the sarcasm out of her voice. "I think everyone knows the story by now."

"Probably." Ferianek's head turned toward the stream, where the sounds of shouting and laughter were still occasionally punctuated by the sharp cracking noise of one rock hitting another. "I think I owe you an apology," he said.

"For what?" Kayl said. "Don't tell me you've been teaching Dara as well!"

"No," Ferianek said, smiling. The smile faded and he said seriously, "In a way, that's the problem."

"I don't suppose you could be a little clearer?"

Ferianek sighed. "I feel responsible for what has happened to your daughter, and to your friends as well."

"You mean Glyndon?"

"And those who died at Glendura's Tomb, yes." Ferianek sighed again, and held up a hand to forestall Kayl's objection. "I know. I know. I wasn't there. That's the whole point."

Kayl stared at him. "Ferianek, if you—"

"No, listen to me. My family have been Watchers of the valley for over a thousand years; there's a binding between us and the place you call the Twisted Tower that keeps us here, in these mountains, close to the valley. It serves little purpose, now, for most of the spells we once knew have been lost or forgotten. But the binding goes on." His voice deepened further, and the bitterness in it was evident. "I am tied to the Windhome Mountains. For more than thirty years I have been searching for a way to break that tie.

"I knew of the Sisterhood's search for the Tower, so I came to you sixteen years ago and told you how to find it. I hoped that you would destroy it, or at least change somehow the spells that hold me. But I did not tell you all that I could have; I did not speak of the sealed doors or the crystal that powers the Tower's spells. I could not ask you to harm the Tower, nor help you do so, but I could hope. Unwarned of what lay within, you might have smashed the crystal or abolished the spells on the Tower or taken its power to use for yourselves."

"You were willing to wager all our lives on the *hope* that we would accidentally set you free?" Kayl said incredulously.

"I was desperate. And I did not know there was danger in the Tower beyond the spells that guarded it. I did not know the black creature was there, and alive! I thought all you had to fear was magic, and the Sisterhood has a good reputation for that. So I let you and your friends find a way inside, without telling you what you might find. And from that error, the rest has followed."

"And the second expedition the Sisterhood sent?" Kayl asked. "Did you know about it, too?"

Ferianek nodded. "I knew, and again I did nothing. I shirked my duty as Watcher of the Tomb and let them come; I betrayed my oath as a follower of the Way of the Third Moon and let them die. And all because I wanted to be free of the obligations that hold me here."

"And now you are trying to redeem yourself by helping us?"

"I wish I could say yes," Ferianek said, speaking with more bitterness than Kayl had ever heard in his voice before. "But this time there are Magicseekers on the road to the Tower. Their reputation is as bad as the Sisterhood's is good; I have no choice but to try to find some way of stopping them. So, again, I use you for my own purposes."

"I see." Kayl was surprised to find that she did see. Ferianek was a scholar at heart, not a man of action. His desire to leave the duties he had never wanted was easy to understand; so was the desperation that had led him to clutch at the unlikely possibility that the Sisterhood's first venture to the Tower might, somehow, free him. His guilt over the consequences of his inaction was almost too familiar. But how much would really have happened differently if they had heard Ferianek's tales before they entered the Tower that first time? Kevran would not have broken the crystal, true, but they would surely have tried to take it with them. And if Glyndon was right, and the black thing was guarding the crystal, the results might well have been the same.

"It's easy to blame yourself for might-haves and might-not-haves," Kayl said at last. "It's easy, and it's human. It's also stupid."

Ferianek looked at her in surprise, then laughed. "You sound like Adept who taught me the Way of the Third Moon."

"He must have had children."

"She did," Ferianek said, smiling.

They ate in silence for a moment, then Kayl asked, "What would you do if you could leave the Windhome Mountains?"

"I'd go to Kith Alunel," Ferianek said promptly. His eyes lit with longing for a dream long denied, and his voice was eager. "There are scrolls in the Queen's Library. . . . I could spend years there."

"You'd spend the rest of your life in a library?"

Ferianek laughed sheepishly. "Not all of it, I hope. I'd like to visit the Waywalker settlement on the Island of the Moon, too."

"Is that the colony you told Bryn and Alden about?"

Ferianek nodded. "I would like to have a hand in building it. From here, I can only send others to help." He smiled. "My daughter and my eldest son are already there."

Kayl realized with a slight shock that this was the first time, in over two weeks of traveling together, that she had heard Ferianek speak of anything personal. She was about to question him further, when a shout echoed through the trees.

Ferianek looked up. "Time to go."

Kayl pushed herself to her feet with a groan. "I thought I'd gotten back into shape after ten months of traveling."

"Climbing mountains uses different muscles from ordinary walking," Ferianek pointed out. "The tops of the thighs, for instance."

"I know, I know," Kayl said. "But knowing doesn't make them any less sore."

Ferianek laughed and went off to collect his pack. Kayl shook the crumbs out of her cloak and started down the hill toward the stream.

The three children accosted her excitedly as soon as she came in sight, and proudly displayed their finds. Mark had found a smallish rock which, when broken open, revealed a star-shaped skeleton. He also had two larger rocks, one containing the impression of a twisted leaf, the other showing the skeleton of a fish's tail. Dara had found the pattern of a delicate, fernlike leaf, and Xaya had a large rock which had split perfectly in half, showing a complete fish on either side.

"Very impressive," Kayl said. "Have you eaten? Good; leave the rocks and go get your packs. It's time to go now."

"Leave them!" Mark said indignantly. "I'm not going to leave them."

Kayl studied him for a moment. "All right, if you want to walk around with a pack full of rocks, you can. But if you take them, you'll have to carry them until we camp tonight, and I don't want to hear any complaints about how heavy they are, either."

"I won't," Mark promised, and immediately began gathering up his three pieces. Dara looked thoughtfully at her own find, as though wishing it were smaller, but finally she picked it up. Xaya had already fitted both halves of her fish-rock back together and was cradling them protectively in her arms.

Kayl went with Mark and Dara to help them find room for the rocks in the bundles they carried. She was reasonably sure that the rocks, however interesting, would not be carried past the first rest stop, so she made sure that they were easily accessible. By the time they finished, Ferianek had started out along the bank of the stream, with the first of the Sisters just behind him, and Kayl had to hurry to catch up.

The afternoon's march provided Kayl with even more time to think than had the morning's journey. She had more than enough to think about; her conversation with Ferianek had shaken her. She could not help seeing parallels between his situation and her own, but it was the differences that disturbed her most. She had been trapped by circumstances into coming on this expedition, and she resented it fiercely. But Ferianek, who was bound to this task far more surely than she, and with less consent, did not seem to feel resentment or anger toward anyone. Kayl had been laying her troubles at the door of the Sisterhood, blaming them for their interference in her life. Ferianek blamed no one but himself.

Kayl was quiet and thoughtful for the rest of the day and into the evening, but she came to no conclusions and found no way around her worries. Finally she forced herself to let her tired body sleep, but even her dreams were troubled. Next morning she felt almost as tired as she had when she lay down. She tried to suppress her irritability during the day's travel, with only partial success.

So absorbed was Kayl in her thoughts that she did not at first realize that the late-afternoon rest halt had become the end of the day's journey. When the various activities of setting up camp finally registered on her mind, she went looking for Javieri.

"Ferianek says that we are less than an hour's walk from the valley," Javieri said in response to Kayl's question. "I am sending the scouts to make certain the Magicseekers have not reached it ahead of us. Besides, after what you and Barthelmy have told us, I have no desire to spend a night in that place. We will go on in the morning."

Kayl looked up at the mountains and shivered.

CHAPTER
TWENTY-SEVEN

Demma Jol, Bryn and Alden returned to the camp before dark with word that the valley around the Twisted Tower was deserted. Javieri nodded and summoned those most immediately involved to her tent for a final conference. Kayl followed Glyndon in. Barthelmy and Corrana were already present; so, to Kayl's surprise, were Ferianek Trone and the Wyrds. Kayl sat down on the ground just inside the door of the tent. Glyndon followed suit, and Javieri began.

"Tomorrow we will reach the Twisted Tower," the Elder Mother said. "I have decided that the entire expedition will accompany us to the valley."

Barthelmy made a surprised noise. "All of us? I thought—"

"According to Ferianek, there are twenty Magicseekers somewhere between the edge of the Windhome Mountains and the valley of the Twisted Tower," Javieri said patiently. "We know they have not yet reached the valley; we have no guarantee that they will not arrive while we are there. If they do, we will need every sword we have. And every spell, no matter how feeble."

"If it really is the Tower that is interfering with your magic, do you think it wise to use even weak spells so close to it?" Glyndon asked.

"Perhaps not," Corrana put in dryly. "But I, for one, think it better than being killed by Magicseekers."

"The scouts will, of course, check once again to be sure that

the Magicseekers have not arrived before we enter the valley,"
Javieri said. "Bryn and Alden have proven matchless at finding traces in the woods. They will cover the forest on the
slopes around the valley. Demma Jol and Forrin will—"

"No," said Kayl.

Javieri looked at her with narrowed eyes. "What?"

"She means you should have asked us before you made all
these plans," Bryn said. "We aren't members of your Sisterhood, remember?"

"I beg your pardon." Javieri had the grace to look uncomfortable. "You have been so helpful I had forgotten."

"Flattery will do nothing for you," Bryn said. "After what
we've heard about that Tower, this is as close as we want to
come to it."

"Besides," Alden added, "I don't think you wish to leave
any of your swords behind to watch the children."

"And I'm not letting Dara and Mark get any closer to the
Tower than this," Kayl finished. "I know Bryn and Alden feel
the same way about Xaya. They've already agreed to watch
my two so I can go to the Tower with you; we discussed it
yesterday."

"You seem to have arranged everything," Javieri said in a
tightly controlled voice. "But what if the Magicseekers come
upon this camp while we are away?"

"That's unlikely," Glyndon said, and flashed Kayl a brief
smile. "We're coming at the valley from almost due north; if
they followed the path we took the first time, the Magicseekers
will be coming from the southwest."

"Kayl," Barthelmy said in a low voice, "are you sure Mark
and Dara wouldn't really be safer in the valley, with more of
us around to protect them?"

"It is not only Magicseekers that Dara Kaylar has to fear,"
Corrana said in a cool voice before Kayl could answer. "You
are forgetting her link to the Crystal. Since we do not understand the nature of that link, it seems unwise to expose the girl
more than is necessary."

Barthelmy stiffened and glared. Javieri gave Corrana a look
of angry dislike. Corrana gazed back at them with the same
unruffled, enigmatic expression that had so frequently irritated Kayl. "I agree," Kayl said quickly. "But even if Dara
had never had a link with the Crystal, I wouldn't want her any
nearer to the Tower. If the Magicseekers do get through

Ferianek's traps, they'll be at the valley, not here. And if they don't . . . well, the Tower isn't a safe place for anyone, much less a child."

"You have an answer for everything," Javieri said. "Everything but the Twisted Tower itself."

"The Twisted Tower is my affair," Kayl said. "Mine and Glyndon's and the Sisterhood's. It's not my children's concern, and not Bryn's or Alden's either."

"Very well," Javieri said. She looked at the Wyrds. "You are determined?"

"We aren't going any closer to the Tower, if that's what you mean," Alden said.

"Then there is no reason for your further presence here," Javieri said. "You may go."

Kayl found Javieri's tone annoying, but the Wyrds seemed simply amused by their lordly dismissal. They rose and picked their way around people to the door of the tent. Bryn paused and said with a fierce smile, "The luck of the Tree to you, Sisters." Then they were gone.

"If your Wyrd friends will no longer help us, Demma and Forrin will have to scout the forest as well as the valley." Javieri gave Kayl a cold look, as she resumed her speech. Then she looked at Corrana and her eyes narrowed. "I think enough of your skills remain that you should assist the scouts, Elder Sister. Magic may find what others miss."

Corrana inclined her head. "I am honored by Your Serenity's trust," she said, and Kayl heard the smooth irony in her voice.

"When we are sure there are no Magicseekers near, the rest of us will join the scouts at the base of the Twisted Tower," Javieri went on after a final sharp glance at Corrana. "Elder Sister Barthelmy and Glyndon shal Morag will remove the spells that seal the Tower, as they have done before; the magicians among us will give them what aid we can."

"Remove the spells?" Ferianek said, frowning. "Is that wise? If the creature of the Tower is still present, as you say—"

"If we do what we did last time, we won't be removing any spells," Glyndon said. "It's more like making a door-sized hole in them, and the hole closes again as soon as we stop holding it open."

"But that means whoever goes inside the Tower won't be

able to get out again!'' Ferianek said, startled.

"Neither will the black thing," Barthelmy said. "And we can open the hole again quickly, once it's been made."

"Furthermore, I intend that Glyndon and Elder Sister Barthelmy remain outside the Tower," Javieri said.

"What?" Glyndon sat up, startled and angry.

"You can re-open the Tower door as easily from outside as from inside, can you not?" Javieri asked.

"Yes, but—"

"Then you will do so. You are the keys that let us into and out of the Twisted Tower; if one or both of you should be killed inside the Tower, those of us inside would indeed be trapped. We will all be safer if you are outside."

And you still don't trust either of them, Kayl thought. Even after what's happened on this trip, you don't trust them.

"Who will be going inside the Tower, then?" Barthelmy asked.

"Myself, Elder Mother Miracote, and Mother Siran," Javieri replied. Then she looked at Ferianek and said carefully, "We would be pleased to have your company as well."

Ferianek shifted uncomfortably. "I am not sure that is possible," he said, and looked down.

"Not possible?" Javieri said, raising both eyebrows. "What do you mean?"

"I am bound in certain ways, particularly regarding the Twisted Tower. I do not know whether entering the Tower is one of the things I am forbidden; the opportunity has never arisen before." Ferianek looked up. "I will try, but that is all I can promise."

"We can ask no more," Javieri said. She paused. "The final member of the first group to go inside the Tower will be Kayl Larrinar, for we shall need a guide who has been there before."

"So that's why—" Kayl began.

"No," Glyndon said loudly.

"And what is your objection?" Javieri said with barely concealed exasperation.

"If Kayl is going inside the Tower, I am going with her," Glyndon said firmly.

"But you have to stay outside, Glyndon!" Barthelmy said. She put a hand on Glyndon's arm, and Kayl felt an unreasonable surge of anger. "I can't open the seals alone."

"Yes, you can," Glyndon said. "Once the spell is set, either of us can use it. Kevran did it last time, remember?"

"I remember," Barthelmy said. "But I don't know anymore whether I can trust my memories of the Tower. Or have you found some way of separating the true memories from the false?"

Glyndon paled slightly. "I—no."

"Leave him alone," Kayl said angrily. "He's had more trouble because of that Tower than any of the rest of us."

"Then he should prefer to remain outside it," Javieri said.

"No." Glyndon's voice was firm, but he still looked whiter than he should have. "If Kayl goes inside, I go too. That, or you'll have to find some other way of getting in."

"I can take care of myself, Glyndon," Kayl said irritably.

"I know. That's not the point."

"Oh?"

"I believe Glyndon's point is the same one you made a moment ago regarding the Wyrds," Corrana put in. "He was not consulted when these plans were made."

Javieri cut off Kayl's reply. "Are you all determined to see this venture fail?" she said in a tone of cold fury. "If I did not need your skills—"

"But you do need us," Kayl said. She was angry herself now: angry at Barthelmy, angry at Javieri, and, most of all, angry at the Sisterhood that had taught them to act in such a highhanded manner. "You could have asked us weeks ago whether we agreed with these plans of yours."

"It seemed wiser to me to wait," Javieri said stiffly.

"Why? Were you hoping that if you sprang this on us at the last minute, we wouldn't have time to object? Or did you think that we'd have to do it your way for lack of any alternative?"

"I—"

"I thought you were put in charge of this expedition because you understood," Kayl said. "I thought that was why you backed me up in Riventon two weeks ago. But that wasn't it, was it? You just wanted to make sure nothing endangered the expedition. And it didn't occur to you that the Sisters' attitude toward Glyndon and me might do that until that scene at the tavern. *That's* why you didn't say anything earlier. You're just like the rest of them; you don't trust us."

"Have you given me reason to trust you?" Javieri demanded, so fiercely that Kayl was startled. "The help you give has been reluctantly offered, you make it clear that you refuse the authority of the Sisterhood, and you have hidden the crystal chip from us for months. Do you expect me to confide in you?"

"I expected you to remember that some of us don't *have* to take your orders without asking questions," Kayl said stiffly, unwilling to admit the justice of Javieri's complaint.

"Kayl." Corrana's voice was quiet, and so unexpected that Kayl stopped short almost without thinking. "Whatever your opinions, we must face the Twisted Tower tomorrow, or chance the Magicseekers' arrival. Is this the time for such recriminations?"

"I may not get another chance," Kayl muttered, but she made herself sit back and look at Javieri with a semblance of control. "So. Glyndon and I will be your guides inside the Twisted Tower. What's next?"

Javieri gave her a dark look, but said, "We will go directly to the room where Gadeiron's Crystal is kept. Once there, you will keep watch for the black creature while the rest of us study the Crystal. If the stars will it, we will find the threads that bind our power and loose them; once that is done, we must make sure that the Crystal cannot be used against us again."

"You will not destroy it," Glyndon said, and his tone was a command.

Ferianek looked at him, startled, as though it had never occurred to him that the Sisters might contemplate such a thing. Javieri's eyes locked on Glyndon's. "We have never considered it," she said, and Kayl knew she was lying.

"The black thing appeared when Kevran chipped the Crystal," Kayl pointed out. "I'd rather not think about what might happen if someone shattered it."

Javieri gestured impatiently. "The Crystal must be guarded so that it can never steal the Sisterhood's magic again, and the Tower sealed so that the Magicseekers can never enter it. Until we reach the Crystal room, we cannot know how this may be done."

Kayl nodded, but she was not satisfied and she could see that Javieri knew it. "And if the thing comes?"

"Then we will fight it." Javieri looked over at Barthelmy. "If we do not return in two hours, or signal from the Tower's top, you will let Elder Mother Alessa, Mother Lonava, and

Elder Sister Corrana into the Tower to try their fortunes, and
after two more hours a third group. If no one returns, you will
seal the Tower as completely as possible and return to Kith
Alunel with the news. Do you understand?''

"What about the Magicseekers?" Barthelmy said.

"Alone, there is little you can do against them, and if we
fail inside the Tower your fellow Sisters will have few spells to
aid you. We will have to trust the spells that seal the Tower to
defeat the Magicseekers, as they defeated us five years ago.''

"I understand."

"And if we succeed?" Kayl said.

"Then we will withdraw to the slopes above the valley and
keep watch on the Tower until the Magicseekers come,"
Javieri said. "With the full strength of our magic returned to
us, we should have no difficulty in destroying them if they
should breach the Tower."

Kayl doubted that it would be that easy, but she said nothing. She had had enough of arguing with Javieri this evening,
and in any case the problem would not be hers. Once the expedition was finished with the interior of the Twisted Tower, she
would consider her commitment fulfilled. She let Javieri, Corrana, Barthelmy, and Ferianek discuss the details of the proposed ambush, and rose with alacrity when they finished. "If
there's nothing else, may I go?" she said to Javieri. "I'd like
to get a good night's sleep."

"So would we all," Javieri said, but she nodded dismissal.
Glyndon started to rise and join her, but Kayl shook her head.
He hesitated. Kayl forced herself to smile, and Glyndon sank
back to his place, reassured.

Kayl went out into the cool night air. The trees around the
tent were old and tall; Kayl had to move a little way up the
hillside before she found a place where she could catch a
glimpse of the stars. She stood staring at them for a long time,
but the twinkling points of light offered no answers, and no
reassurance.

CHAPTER

TWENTY-EIGHT

Early next morning the expedition started for the valley of the Twisted Tower. Mark and Dara watched in glum silence as Kayl buckled on her sword and carefully slipped the crystal chip into a pocket in her belt. The two children were obviously far from pleased with her decision to leave them behind. Kayl stayed with them as long as she could, then gave them each a hug and left quickly.

Glyndon was waiting for her at the edge of the camp. The last of the Sisters had already gone; they had to hurry to catch up. A light mist veiled the mountains, making everything seem far away and ghostly. No one spoke much.

They reached the top of the saddle between two mountains and stopped. On the farther side, the mist thickened into a woolly fog, hiding the floor of the valley from sight. Kayl frowned. If the Magicseekers had found their way to the Twisted Tower, the scouts would have a hard time discovering it in this soup. She resigned herself to a long wait.

A figure broke away from the clump of Sisters just ahead and came toward Kayl and Glyndon; Kayl did not realize that it was Corrana until she was almost upon them. "Glyndon, Elder Mother Javieri would speak with you," Corrana said in a low voice as she reached them.

Glyndon nodded and moved off into the fog. Kayl looked at Corrana and raised an eyebrow inquiringly.

Corrana gave her a small smile. "The Elder Mother wants the fog removed," she explained. "Glyndon and Barthelmy are the only ones who might be able to do so, and Javieri is afraid that the Magicseekers will notice if Barthelmy tries. They are more used to looking for our sort of spells than for Varnan wizardry."

"If the Magicseekers are that close, they'll notice when the fog disappears no matter who does it."

"A good point, but a little late in coming," Corrana said. "Look."

Kayl turned. Glyndon had stepped away from the group of Sisters and raised his staff. He stood motionless for a long moment, then gestured with his free hand. The staff began to glow a bright gold. Glyndon stretched it forward and said something that rumbled out into the fog like thunder.

The fog began to thin, slowly at first, then more and more rapidly. Glyndon lowered his staff and the glow died. Kayl stepped forward, frowning at the tired droop of his shoulders. Glyndon straightened as she drew nearer. "Are you all right?" she asked.

"More or less. It's been awhile," he said apologetically.

"You should have told Javieri to do it herself," Kayl said. "You shouldn't be exhausting yourself now, not with the Twisted Tower still to come."

"Now who's trying to wrap whom in fleece?" Glyndon said. "I have time enough to recover; we have to wait for the scouts, remember."

"Then sit down and rest," Kayl said crossly. "You're as bad as Mark."

"Oh?" Glyndon looked at her with a quizzical expression.

"Always showing off."

Glyndon grinned suddenly. "I doubt that Mark would appreciate that assessment."

"Stop chattering and sit down before you fall over!"

"Small chance of that," Glyndon said, but he lowered himself onto a nearby rock. He sat half leaning on his staff, staring out over the valley.

The fog had cleared from the valley floor, leaving only a few stray shreds hovering ghostlike above the rocky ground. The forested slopes of the mountains, however, were still barely visible. The forest ended abruptly at the base of the mountains; the valley itself was barren, black, and dead. Kayl could see the Tower below, only a little way from the foot of the slope on which they stood.

The Twisted Tower was nearly as black as the floor of the

valley, and warped and bent as if some giant had wrung it like a dishcloth. Kayl had seen trees twisted by whirlwinds that were straight by comparison. Deep, irregular grooves spiraled around the Tower, and here and there a streak of dull gold broke up the mass of blackness. Partway around, Kayl could just make out the iron door that was the only entrance to the Tower.

Someone moved behind Kayl, and she turned. Barthelmy had come over to join them. Her eyes, too, were fixed on the Twisted Tower. "It hasn't changed," she said. "I thought it would have, somehow."

"We're the ones who have changed," Kayl said.

"Have we?" Barthelmy's gaze did not waver from the Tower door. "We're different, the expedition is different, but have we really changed?"

"What do you mean?" Kayl said, but Barthelmy did not answer. Kayl did not press her, and they continued their wait in silence.

Finally the scouts returned and Javieri gave the signal to descend. The Tower was closer than it looked; in a matter of minutes the entire group stood in a rough semicircle before the iron door. Kayl found a place just inside the ring, near the others who would make up the first group to enter the Tower.

Glyndon and Barthelmy stepped forward, each grasping one end of Glyndon's staff. Together, they began to chant, repeating the same phrases over and over. After four repetitions, their voices diverged; first rhythm of the words changed, then the words themselves, until each of them was speaking a different chant. The door of the Twisted Tower began to flicker as if seen through a haze of heat.

Kayl watched in silence, fingering the lump that the crystal chip made in her belt. She wished this were over. She felt as if she had been waiting for days, for months, for years; waiting for the Sisterhood to find her, waiting for the Twisted Tower to come back into her life, waiting for everything and nothing to happen at once. She was very tired of waiting.

The chanting stopped. Kayl blinked and stared at the door. If her memories were correct, it should be ajar now that the spell was finished, but it had not moved. Beside her, Javieri started forward, but Glyndon held out an arm to bar her way. "It didn't work," he said.

Javieri stared at him, then shook herself. "Why not?"

"I don't know," Glyndon replied. "But something in the

spell has changed. Perhaps your last expedition did it accidentally. In any case, we won't be able to open the door until we
find out what it is."

"I see." Javieri pressed her lips together for a moment, then
gave a sharp nod. "Keep trying."

Barthelmy and Glyndon held a low-voiced conference; a
few minutes later, they resumed their positions and began
chanting once again. This time the flickering at the door was
more pronounced, but when the two magicians finished, the
door was still closed.

"This is ridiculous," Glyndon said, running a hand distractedly through his hair.

Barthelmy grimaced. "Why don't we try—"

"Mother!"

The shout echoed around the silent valley. Kayl jerked and
spun, staring back at the slope that led toward the camp. A
small figure stood dangerously near the edge of a projecting
rock, waving both arms. "Mark!" Kayl shouted. She pushed
her way to the outer edge of the Sisters clustered around the
Tower door. "Mark, you get down from there!"

The figure waved and stepped back out of sight. A moment
later, Kayl saw movement among the trees that covered the
slope. "It seems your son has ideas of his own about staying
behind," Corrana murmured from immediately behind Kayl.

"It isn't just Mark," Kayl said grimly. She could see at least
three figures moving through the trees, and she had to force
herself not to speculate about the reasons why they had come.
It seemed an eternity before Mark burst out of the forest at the
bottom of the slope. After a brief pause, Bryn and Dara
followed at a somewhat slower pace.

"I thought I told you stay in camp," Kayl said as Mark
came panting up. "What happened?"

"It was the bees," Mark said. He puffed, and added, "And
Dara. She's coming."

"*Bees?*" Javieri said incredulously. "You came shouting
through the mountains and interrupted a vital spell-casting
because of bees?"

"Excuse me, Your Serenity." Kayl kept her voice frigidly
polite. "Mark did not interrupt; Barthelmy and Glyndon had
just finished. And I would appreciate it if you would remember that Mark is *my son*, not one of the Sisters you command."

"Then find out what he means, so we can get on with our work!" Javieri said.

"He means that we left the camp rather hurriedly because he injudiciously stirred up a hive of bees," Bryn said. She had come up to the half-ring of Sisters during Kayl and Javieri's verbal skirmish. She had one arm around Dara, who was looking at the Twisted Tower with a dazed expression.

"Explain," Javieri commanded.

Bryn gave her a long look, then turned to Kayl. "The bees were just beginning to get active after the winter, so nobody got too badly stung, but we didn't want to stay nearby. So the five of us came about halfway up the saddle, figuring we'd meet you there on your way back. Then Dara started . . . behaving oddly."

"What do you mean, behaving oddly?" Kayl snapped anxiously.

"She was staring up the mountain as if she saw something there, and she complained that someone was shoving her," Bryn replied. "Then she went stiff and wouldn't talk at all. After the fuss about the way she reacted to the crystal and the magic lessons, I thought I'd better bring her here."

"She looked like a wood puppet," Mark put in.

Bryn threw him a sidelong glance. "*He* was supposed to stay with Alden and Xaya on the other side of the mountain."

"I couldn't. Dara's my sister," Mark said, as if that excused everything.

"I think you were wise to bring Dara to us," Javieri said to Bryn.

Kayl glared at her, then turned back to Dara. The girl still looked dazed, as though she had just awakened from a heavy sleep, but she was frowning at the Twisted Tower the way she always did when she was studying something. Kayl found that reassuring. "Dara?" she said softly.

"What?" Dara turned her frowning gaze to Kayl.

"Are you all right? What happened?"

"Nothing happened. That's the Twisted Tower, isn't it? It's uglier than I thought."

"You don't remember coming here?" Kayl asked.

Dara shrugged. "We walked. It didn't take long." Her eyes kept straying back to the Tower.

Kayl looked at Bryn. "Don't ask me to explain it," the Wyrd said. "She seemed pretty foggy to me most of the way here. She came out of it for a little while, then had a relapse. The second spell ended just as we got to the top of the saddle."

Behind her, Kayl heard Glyndon mutter, "Oh, lord. If that's the problem . . ."

"If what's the problem?" Kayl demanded, turning.

"With opening the Tower," Glyndon said, Beside him, Barthelmy's eyes widened, and she stared at Dara.

Kayl stepped protectively between the two wizards and her daughter. "What are you talking about?"

"Both of them have taught Dara," Corrana said coolly from a little to one side. "Your daughter also appears to have a link with the Crystal that seals the Tower. She has two periods of 'behaving oddly' which seem to coincide with the two unsuccessful attempts to breach the spells on the Tower. The conclusion would seem obvious."

"No," Kayl said without conviction.

"It's all right, Kayl," Barthelmy said. "I mean, it will be all right, now that we know."

"It isn't all right," Glyndon said. "But we need Dara, and she's safer here, where we can see what's going on and do something about it if we need to."

"I—" Kayl shook her head. She felt trapped, and for a moment she hated them both. Then Dara tugged at her arm, and she turned.

"They're right, Mother," she said.

"Dara, you don't have to—"

"Yes, I do." Dara's voice sounded amazingly adult. She was still looking past Kayl to the Twisted Tower. "Please, Mother; I don't think we should waste any time."

Kayl stared at the suddenly unfamiliar child-woman she had borne and raised and cherished. Slowly, she nodded. "All right, Dara, if you're sure you want to do this."

"I'm sure." Dara stepped forward, toward Barthelmy and Glyndon. Glyndon flashed an uncertain look at Kayl, then bent to talk to Dara. A moment later, he and Barthelmy each took one of the girl's hands.

"Don't try to do anything yourself," Barthelmy cautioned. "Just cooperate with us."

Dara nodded. Glyndon raised his staff one-handed, and Barthelmy caught the other end. For the third time they began to chant. The heat-haze flickered into existence in front of the iron door. It intensified swiftly into pulsing waves of distortion that made Kayl's eyes ache to look at. Dara stood straight as a willow rod between the two magicians, her hands clenched around their fingers and her eyes wide and sightless.

Finally the chanting stopped. Kayl blinked and realized that the Tower door was ajar. "We did it!" Glyndon shouted. He dropped his staff to scoop Dara up and swing her, laughing, in a wide circle. "We did it!" Barthelmy grinned with relief and tossed her head, sending her black hair flying in all directions. Javieri relaxed slightly, like a laborer resting between two parts of a difficult task when the harder work was yet to come. Even Corrana smiled.

"You certainly did," said an unpleasant voice from outside the half-ring of Sisters.

Kayl's sword was in her hand almost without thought. She turned, shoving Mark behind her, and saw a score or more of grinning, eagle-helmeted men and women arrayed in a neat line between the Sisterhood and the edges of the valley. In front of the newcomers was a short, solidly built man with bright, cold eyes. Kayl stared in disbelief. "Utrilo Levoil!"

Utrilo inclined his head. "Mistress Kayl. You would be surprised to know how glad I am to see you."

"Your timing is remarkable, Magicseeker," Javieri said. She made a small gesture with her right hand, and the defensive ring of Sisters shifted slightly, closing the gap between it and the Tower.

"Is it indeed, Your Serenity," Utrilo replied affably. He rocked back onto his heels as he spoke, a gesture both like and unlike the pompous mannerisms Kayl remembered from Copeham. "Then perhaps you will not be surprised to learn that we have been watching you since you arrived."

Javieri threw a withering glance at Corrana. "On the contrary."

"Oh, don't blame your scouts," Utrilo said. "They did what little they were capable of." He favored Corrana with a broad, toothy smile. "We are simply better than you."

Kayl studied Utrilo as he spoke. She could hear traces of Islorran's secretary in the way he spoke, and occasionally the tilt of Utrilo's head or a fleeting expression brought the man she remembered from Copeham vividly to mind, but that was all. Utrilo was a consummate actor, Kayl realized; he had played the part of an unctuous servant for an entire month without slipping once. But how could she have missed seeing the muscle beneath his paunch, or recognizing that there was a purpose behind his questions?

"You'd have done better not to waste your time on those quaint little traps you set in our path," Utrilo went on. "I fear they delayed you more than us."

Ferianek flushed. Kayl raised a mental eyebrow at Utrilo's phrasing. So the Magicseekers did not know that the booby-traps were Ferianek's work!

"Have done with this game," Javieri said. "What is it you want?"

"Why, the same thing you want, Your Serenity," Utrilo said. "The key to this Tower."

"Mother!" Dara's voice was soft but insistent; she had come up behind Kayl to stand beside Mark.

Kayl tilted her head back, not taking her eyes from the Magicseekers. "Quietly Dara. What is it?"

"They're who the thing in the Tower is calling," Dara whispered. "I can feel it."

"Tell Glyndon and Ferianek, if you can." Both men were well within the protective ring. "But try not to attract attention." Kayl felt Dara nod and move slowly away. She returned most of her attention to the conversation between Javieri and Utrilo, wondering how soon the Magicseekers would attack and why they had not yet done so.

"Then how did you succeed in opening the door?" Utrilo was saying. "If magic alone were enough, we would have done it ourselves yesterday, and there would be no need for this farce."

"Perhaps we are simply better than you," Javieri suggested.

Utrilo's eyes narrowed to slits. "Give us the key."

"No," said Javieri.

Utrilo gestured. A tall, hawk-faced man stepped forward to stand beside him. He called three words in a strange language and pointed. Fire lanced out from his finger—and spattered harmlessly against an invisible barricade a few feet in front of the foremost Sisters. Kayl turned her head and saw Barthelmy, white-faced, staring with great concentration at the smear of flame.

The Magicseekers hesitated, then two more came forward to join Utrilo and the hawk-faced wizard. The rest drew their swords and started toward the ring of Sisters. Kayl glanced back quickly to make sure that both of the children were safely behind her, then took a firmer grip on her sword.

The first wave of attackers arrived, and the neat lines dissolved in a chaos of individual fights. One of the Magicseekers broke through beside Kayl. He swung a saw-toothed bronze blade at Kayl's head. She parried, and her sword caught in the toothed edge of her attacker's sword. He twisted it in an attempt to disarm her. Kayl wrenched her sword free in time to parry as a second Magicseeker struck at her arm. She was in trouble now, she thought with the clearheaded calm of battle. She couldn't handle two of them for long without moving too far to protect the children.

Kayl parried another stroke by her first opponent, but barely managed to duck under the second's swing. As she rose, she saw an opening and sent her sword toward it. Then, an instant too late, she realized that the move would leave her open to a counterattack from the Magicseeker's partner. As her sword sank home, she twisted, hoping to avoid most of the blow she expected.

The Magicseeker crumpled. Kayl pulled her sword free and whirled, wondering in the back of her mind why she wasn't dead. Then she saw that the second Magicseeker was bleeding from a slanting scratch on his right arm, just below the bronze scales of the armor that protected his shoulder. Whoever had tried to disable him had failed, but the attempt had apparently thrown his stroke off far enough to save Kayl's life.

Kayl attacked with a ferocity that surprised even herself, and the Magicseeker was driven backward. Kayl let the crowd of combatants swallow him; she dared not risk getting too far away from the children. She edged backward, watching for a renewed attack. "Mark? Dara?" she called. "Are you all right?"

"They are fine," Corrana's voice said in her ear. "Inside, and join them."

"What? No!" Kayl's cry was half denial, half horror as she realized what Corrana had to mean.

"Inside!" Corrana grabbed Kayl's arm and swung her around. Kayl's sword came up automatically, but Corrana ducked under it and shoved her from behind. Kayl took two steps forward and fell sprawling through the doorway of the Twisted Tower.

CHAPTER

TWENTY-NINE

"I thought I'm the one who's supposed to make awkward entrances," Glyndon's voice said from somewhere in front of Kayl.

Kayl shook herself and looked around. "Glyndon? What are you doing in here? Barthelmy can't handle three Magicseekers alone!"

"She doesn't have to," Corrana said, coming past Kayl into the Tower. "Seal the door, Glyndon."

"Mother, are you all right?" Mark asked urgently.

"Glyndon, don't!" Kayl said, ignoring Mark. "The Magicseekers—"

"The Magicseekers are currently facing the full strength and power of three Elder Mothers and two full Stars of the Sisterhood," Corrana said with maddening calm. "I'm surprised you didn't notice."

"Notice what?"

"Ferianek has managed to temporarily lift the influence of the Tower on our magic," the sorceress replied. The star-shaped emblem of the Sisterhood glittered on her shoulder, as though emphasizing her words. "Unfortunately, there is no way of knowing how long Ferianek's spell will last, so the three of us must complete his work."

"Mother, are you all right?" Mark insisted.

"I'm fine, Mark," Kayl said, still staring at Corrana. "Why did you bring the children in here?"

"I did that," Glyndon said. Kayl was too stunned to reply at once, and he went on. "The Magicseekers would have figured out fairly quickly that Dara is the 'key' they're looking for. This is the only place where they can't get at her, and she's as safe here as out there."

"Safe? Are you out of your wits? The creature—"

"The thing that calls is back that way," Dara broke in. She pointed at a narrow wooden doorway beside the stone stairs. "It's waiting."

Kayl shook her head. Too much was happening too quickly; it was more than she could take in. "What?"

"The thing that calls is waiting for something," Dara repeated. "I can feel it. It doesn't know we're inside. So it's all right for us to stay here for a while."

"No, it is not," Corrana said. "We do not have much time, and we have wasted enough of it already. We must find Gadeiron's Crystal, and quickly."

"I doubt that it's moved," Glyndon said.

"Lead us, then."

Glyndon looked at Kayl. Kayl made herself nod.

"Warn us if you feel the thing that calls coming closer," Glyndon said to Dara. He lifted his staff and started up the stone staircase.

Corrana followed at once. Mark and Dara looked hesitantly at Kayl. She had a lingering impulse to leave them there or send them back outside, but she suppressed it. There was no sense in pretending that either place was any safer than accompanying Glyndon would be. She motioned the children to go ahead of her, then followed with her sword ready.

The climb seemed to take much longer than she remembered. Halfway up, Mark peered out a slender window and announced, "They're still fighting outside."

"Good," Kayl said. "Then we still have a little time."

Mark leaned forward. "There's Ferianek! He doesn't look too good."

"That's enough, Mark!" Kayl said, hauling him back. "Do you want to get an arrow through your throat?"

"Aw, nobody could hit me way up here!"

"They certainly could. Why do you think these windows were made so small? It's so archers inside the Tower could fire without giving enemy archers much of a target to shoot back at."

"Really?" Mark craned his neck, studying the narrow window with new interest.

Kayl gave her son a push. "Climb, Mark."

They reached the top of the stairs at last and paused before the wooden door. Glyndon looked at Dara. "Anything happening?"

"It's still waiting," Dara reported.

Glyndon nodded and pushed the door open. Kayl blinked at the brightness of the light that poured into the gloomy stairwell, then followed the others into the circular room beyond. The arched windows, the tapestry-covered walls, and the high dome were unchanged. The knee-high pedestal and the enormous crystal cube that stood on it were not even dusty. Kayl was surprised to realize how familiar it all felt, despite the fact that she had hardly thought of it in the months since she had remembered its existence.

"I don't like this place," Mark said softly. "It feels like somebody died."

"More than one," Kayl said. She looked at Mark uneasily; she had felt the same way, the first time she had entered this room. "Stay away from the walls and as close to the Crystal as you can without getting in anyone's way," she told him. "And don't touch anything!"

Mark and Dara exchanged disgusted glances, but moved obediently forward. Glyndon and Corrana were already standing beside the Crystal. Glyndon looked a little pale; Kayl tried to convince herself that it was because of the brightness of the light reflecting off the surface of the Crystal. Then he leaned forward and brushed the tip of a finger across one edge of the cube.

Nothing happened. Glyndon's shoulders relaxed somewhat. He looked at Dara, who shook her head, and more of the tension drained visibly away. He leaned against his staff and turned to Corrana.

"Call up as much of your magic as you dare, then touch the Crystal," he told her. "But keep it brief."

Corrana raised an eyebrow. "I thought we were going to try to repair it."

"First I intend to make sure I'm not running my head into a noose," Glyndon said. "For all I know, using any magic in connection with this crystal may summon the black thing. If that happens we're all dead."

"Must we waste time this way? You used spells on it before," Corrana said, but she raised her hand above the Crystal.

"The Crystal wasn't broken last time I was here. Who knows what that's done to it? And if we're going to speak of wasting time . . ."

Corrana's hand came down in a smooth, graceful motion; Kayl almost missed the moment when the fingers brushed the cube. Again, nothing happened. Glyndon breathed a sigh of rlelief. "Good. Now, if you'll link your magic with mine . . ."

The conversation became technical. Kayl walked to the window at the front of the Tower and looked down on the fighting. A half-dome of silver light rose protectively over the little group of Sisters that stood before the door of the Twisted Tower. Kayl smiled. The star-shield was a powerful protection indeed; the Magicseekers had already fallen back, and their wizards were consulting with Utrilo.

Then Kayl studied the group inside the dome more closely, and her smile faded. The body of a Magicseeker lay just inside the dome of light; beside it, one of the healers was tending a crumpled figure in the robes of the Sisterhood. A second casualty had been moved nearer to the Tower, where she would be out of the way of further fighting. The rest of the Sisters were drawn up in two lines, guarding the Elder Mothers and the Tower door. Barthelmy stood just in front of the Tower door, with Ferianek crouched beside her. Kayl frowned. Until Glyndon and Corrana managed to remove the spell that was blocking the Sisters' magic, Ferianek remained the key to holding off the Magicseekers. And it did not look as if Ferianek would last much longer. The Sisters might be forced to take refuge in the Twisted Tower. She did not find the thought comforting.

Kayl turned back to the Crystal to find Corrana and Glyndon staring into it as if entranced. Each of them rested one hand on the top face of the cube. Kayl hesitated, wondering whether she ought to be concerned. She was about to knock Glyndon's hand away from the Crystal, when he sighed, shifted, and blinked. An instant later, Corrana followed suit. The two wizards took their hands from the Crystal and stared at each other.

"Nothing," Corrana said in tones of deep frustration. "All that effort, and we're no further than we were when we began.

This thing might as well be a lump of granite for all we can find out about it!''

"I expected as much," Glyndon said. "The first time we were here, none of us could get so much as an echo of power from any spell we tried on it."

"If you expected this, why did you insist that we try?" Corrana demanded. "We haven't time to repeat the mistakes you made sixteen years ago!''

"That isn't fair, Corrana," Kayl broke in. "Glyndon is doing all he can.''

Corrana turned. "Is he?" Her tone held a cool curiosity that was somehow far worse than anger or sarcasm.

"Can you think of another way to discover what blocks your magic besides repeating the things we did and see which one affects you?" Glyndon demanded. "If we knew what we were doing, it would be a different matter.''

"I think such efforts would mean more if the Crystal were repaired first," Corrana replied sweetly.

Kayl's hand went automatically to the belt-pocket where she had put the crystal chip that morning. She stopped in mid-reach, angry at the way Corrana was baiting Glyndon and afraid of the possible consequences of repairing the Crystal. The nagging feeling that Corrana was right only made Kayl more irritable. "Whatever the two of you are going to do, stop arguing and do it," she said at last in the tone she used to tell Mark and Dara to stop squabbling. "You're both wasting time.''

"All right," Glyndon said. His eyes met hers, and she saw her own fears reflected in them. Then Glyndon held out his hand. "Give me the chip."

Kayl fumbled at her belt. The chip sprang free unexpectedly, and fell. Instinctively, Kayl caught it; then she sucked in her breath as she realized what she had done. But no uncomfortable memories washed over her, and she looked up, her face stiff with astonishment.

"Kayl—" Glyndon started, his voice full of concern.

"It's all right, Glyndon; it doesn't seem to do anything now," Kayl cut in. "Here, see for yourself."

She held out the chip of crystal and, after a momentary hesitation, Glyndon took it. His eyes widened; then he shook his head. "I don't know why I'm surprised. The main cube didn't force memories on me, but it never occurred to me that this might behave the same way, in here."

"Can we get on with our task?" Corrana said pointedly.

Glyndon nodded with an absent air; he was still looking at the crystal chip. Then he shook himself. He stepped to the broken corner of the cube and fitted the chip against it. Corrana laid her hand over his and they both began murmuring once more. It seemed to Kayl as if the spell went on forever. At last the wizards finished, and Glyndon sagged against his staff.

Corrana lifted her hand; after a moment, Glyndon did likewise. For an instant, the cube appeared whole and perfect; then the crystal chip slid to the floor with a pure, ringing note. Glyndon jerked upright and closed his eyes. "It didn't work."

"Then we must try something else," Corrana said sharply. She bent and picked up the crystal chip. "Perhaps it could be melted into place."

"How?" Glyndon shook his head. "No, we're going at this all wrong."

"Indeed. Well, then, just what would you suggest?"

"We should have stayed to examine the way Ferianek lifted the spell that blocks your magic. Watching it might have given us a useful approach to this," Glyndon said, waving at the cube. His face was a study in frustrated irritation.

"You would not have learned much," said Utrilo Levoil from the doorway. "Your friend's efforts simply did not last long enough."

Kayl swung around and took two long steps forward as she reached for her sword, placing herself between Mark and Dara. She checked herself before her hand touched the hilt. Three Magicseekers stood beside Utrilo, and one of them held a dagger at Javieri's throat. The Elder Mother looked completely stunned; it was obvious to Kayl that, though she had spoken of it, Javieri had never really believed in the possibility of defeat.

"Very sensible of you," Utrilo said approvingly as Glyndon and Corrana also let their hands fall away from their weapons. "We brought her along merely as a token of our intentions; the rest of your people are also hostage to your good behavior."

"That's impossible!" Kayl said. Corrana would surely have known if Ferianek's spell had been broken, for her own magic would have failed with it. Kayl did not point this out to Utrilo;

instead, she gestured toward the window behind her. "I just saw—"

"You saw what Sessever and his associates arranged for you to see," Utrilo said in a smug voice. "He's quite good with illusions, though his real strengths lie in other areas."

"I'm surprised Barthelmy let you in," Glyndon commented. He raised his left hand and dropped it casually onto the top of the crystal cube.

"With the proper inducement, anyone can be made to see reason," Utrilo replied. The Magicseeker holding Javieri twisted her arm for emphasis; Javieri flinched. "Throw your weapons against that wall," Utrilo went on in the same casual tone. "Or we kill your friends, starting with her. And you, get away from that cube."

Quickly, Corrana stripped off her dagger, sheath and all, and tossed it lightly in the indicated direction. Glyndon hesitated, then stepped away from the Crystal and did likewise. "The staff and the star, too," Utrilo said. "And your sword as well, Mistress Kayl."

Kayl knew better than to argue; it wouldn't take much imagination for Utrilo to think of threatening Mark and Dara. She unbuckled her swordbelt and followed Utrilo's order. Corrana moved more slowly, her fingers lingering on the symbol of her magic and her ties to the Sisterhood. Glyndon studied Javieri and the Magicseekers for a moment, then looked at Kayl. She nodded, and Glyndon reluctantly slid his staff across the floor to join the rest of the weapons.

"So." Utrilo looked speculatively from Kayl to Glyndon. "I'd been wondering how you fit into this, wizard. I think now I know."

Glyndon inclined his head ironically, and Kayl had to force herself not to scream at him. He must know how much Magicseekers hated Varnans; he shouldn't bait them, particularly if there was a chance Utrilo had not realized that Glyndon was Varnan.

"Does that change whatever you want from us now?" Corrana asked. Her face was expressionless and her voice gave away nothing of her thoughts.

"Naturally not." Utrilo gave her another of his patronizing, toothy smiles. "But before we move on to our main task, I wish to see what it is that you are trying so hard to conceal there in your hand."

Corrana did not move. Utrilo gestured one of his companions forward. The woman obeyed, drawing her dagger as she came across the floor. She stopped in front of Corrana and held out her right hand, the dagger ready in her left. Corrana shrugged and dropped the crystal chip into the Magicseeker's palm.

"Mother!" Dara whispered. "Mother, I think that the calling thing is coming."

Kayl looked down. Her daughter's face was white and frightened. "Utrilo!" Kayl said urgently.

The leader of the Magicseekers continued to study the crystal chip. "Take it down to Sessever," he told the woman holding it. "He may be able to make something of it."

The woman bowed and left. Utrilo turned calmly to Kayl. "Now, I believe you wanted something?" he said with mocking politeness.

"We have to get out of here at once," Kayl said. "There's a . . . a creature coming that will kill us all if we stay."

"Oh, I doubt that," Utrilo said, rocking back on his heels. "I do doubt that."

"It doesn't matter, Kayl," Glyndon said. "As soon as I saw them, I used the cube to re-seal the Tower. We'd have to start from the beginning to open it again. Even if we had the time, I couldn't do it alone."

"Then we're trapped?" Kayl said numbly. "Trapped, with the black thing coming? Glyndon, why?"

"It's better than letting the Magicseekers control the Crystal," Glyndon said. "I'm sorry, Kayl."

Utrilo laughed. "Such a futile gesture! I don't want to control the Crystal, wizard. I intend to destroy it." His eyes glittered as he spoke.

"You can't!" Glyndon cried. "The crystal is what holds the black creature prisoner here!"

"Exactly." Utrilo stepped forward, drawing his sword.

The wall behind Utrilo began to ooze blackness. Corrana took an involuntary step backward. Dara whimpered, and Kayl pushed her closer to the Crystal, remembering vaguely that the blackness had seemed to avoid that area until the very last. The Magicseekers near the doorway shifted uneasily and moved farther into the room, away from the wall and the open doorway. Utrilo did not appear to notice; his eyes were fixed on the Crystal. Glyndon glanced at the blackness, his face rigid, then stepped in front of the Crystal, forcing Utrilo to look at him.

"Are you mad, wanting to loose that thing on the world?" Glyndon demanded. "Look at it!"

"But it won't be loose," Utrilo said softly. He bared his teeth in a grimace that might have been intended as a smile. "When I destroy the Crystal that masters it, I will become its Master. That's why it called me here, to bring it out of the Tower and guide it."

"You cannot control that," Corrana said quietly. "You are a fool indeed to think of trying."

A scream of agony came echoing up the stairs, then abruptly cut off. "I think your messenger has discovered the spell that seals the Tower door," Glyndon said to Utrilo.

Dara shuddered and her eyes went wide. "It's free," she said. "The thing is free."

"No!" Utrilo howled. "I have to be the one to free it!" He lunged for Gadeiron's Crystal, sword raised.

CHAPTER

THIRTY

Glyndon jumped sideways and caught the Magicseeker's sword arm. Kayl cried out and leaped to help Glyndon. One of Utrilo's men thrust himself into Kayl's path, blocking her from reaching Glyndon. Corrana, who had also moved toward the struggle, stopped as well, her eyes flickering from Glyndon and Utrilo to the man still holding his dagger against a limp, dazed Javieri.

Kayl stared down the length of the sword that the Magicseeker held warningly in front of her. "Don't be a fool!" she said desperately. "We'll all die if we don't work together now."

"She is right," Corrana said. "Will you throw your life away in the service of a madman? Look!" She gestured toward the doorway.

The wall was now a mass of shivering blackness that completely blocked the exit. It crept forward with excruciating slowness, inching along the walls and occasionally surging forward to occupy another handsbreadth of floor. Kayl could hear cries of terror drifting faintly through the window of the Tower. The black creature must be spreading outside as well; perhaps that was why it seemed to be taking so long to surround the Tower room.

The Magicseeker hesitated visibly, and for a moment Kayl hoped. His companion shifted uneasily and turned his head, trying to get a better look at the threat behind him. As he did,

Javieri came suddenly alive. She twisted, then threw all her weight against the man who held her. The Magicseeker staggered backward, closer to the doorway and the darkness. Corrana sprang to Javieri's assistance, and the man in front of Kayl moved sideways to stop her.

Kayl took a half-step backward and planted her left foot. Then she brought her right leg around in a powerful kick that connected perfectly with the Magicseeker's wrist. His sword flew across the room, hit the floor with a clang, and slid into the curtain of living darkness. Before he could recover himself, Kayl stepped forward and struck him solidly on the jaw with her left hand. He shook his head and swung at her, groping for his dagger with his other hand. Kayl ducked and kicked at him again.

The blow knocked the Magicseeker's feet from under him, and he went down. Kayl leaped over him toward Glyndon and Utrilo. At the same moment Utrilo snarled and twisted, wrenching his arm from Glyndon's grasp at last. Still snarling, Utrilo brought his sword around in a vicious cut that caught Glyndon's left arm just below the shoulder and knocked him backward.

Glyndon fell heavily, blood pouring from the deep wound. Kayl ran to him, knowing that the blood loss had to be stopped until a healer could see to him. Her hands went automatically to her waist, seeking something to tie around his arm, but she had removed her sword-belt earlier at Utrilo's command.

"No!" Glyndon gasped as she reached him. "The Crystal!"

Simultaneously, a pure, ringing sound echoed through the Tower room. Utrilo had struck the crystal, but it had not broken. Kayl thought she saw the blackness flinch away from the sound, but she had no time to consider what that might mean. She forced herself to turn away from Glyndon, and saw that Utrilo had raised his sword for a second blow. She threw herself forward, knowing as she did that she could not reach him in time.

Suddenly Utrilo cried out and staggered. His sword came down in a crooked, glancing blow that sent another chime ringing through the room but did no harm to the crystal cube. Utrilo clutched at his thigh and glared at a small, blond figure that had darted at him from around the pedestal on which the Crystal rested.

"Little demon-spawn!" Utrilo spat. "I'll kill you for that."

Mark said nothing. He stood in a fighter's crouch, watching Utrilo warily. His face was pale and there was blood on the small bronze-bladed dagger he held. He backed toward the doorway. Utrilo lunged forward, evading Kayl almost by accident. Kayl scrambled to change direction, hoping she could reach Utrilo before he reached Mark or Mark backed into the black thing that covered the wall. She heard Javieri scream from behind her, and the hoarse cries of the Magicseekers, but she did not turn to look. Then she saw a lump the size of a baby's head bulge out of the darkness behind Mark, and she cried a warning.

Mark danced aside as a thick, black tentacle lashed out from the bulge, narrowly missing him. Utrilo started to move to his left to cut off the boy's retreat. Kayl lowered her shoulder, took three fast steps forward, and hit Utrilo Levoil in the small of his back, throwing him toward the groping tentacle.

As Utrilo stumbled forward, trying desperately to regain his balance, the black tentacle whipped sideways. Utrilo gave a scream of terror as it wrapped itself around his legs; Kayl could see his armor smoking where the black thing touched it. The tentacle began to retract, pulling Utrilo off his feet and toward the wall of blackness. He slashed uselessly at the tentacle, then dropped his sword and clawed at the floor, trying to halt his slow progress toward the wall.

Kayl grabbed Mark's arm and pulled him back toward the center of the room and relative safety. Utrilo screamed again, this time in agony; the black thing had eaten through his armor. Kayl plucked Mark's knife out of his hand, hefted it briefly to test the balance, then threw it at Utrilo's agonized face.

The knife struck cleanly through Utrilo's right eye into the brain. Utrilo's body convulsed once, then went limp. An instant later the black thing surged forward over the remains of the Magicseeker leader.

Mark shuddered and hid his face in Kayl's side. Kayl drew him farther back from the advancing creature and glanced quickly around to see how her companions were faring. Dara was kneeling beside Glyndon, doing her best to stop the bleeding from his wounded shoulder. Corrana was staring, white-faced, at an area of the black creature near the doorway. One of the Magicseekers had a one-handed grip on her arm. His other hand held his sword ready, but the weapon faced the black thing, not Corrana. The Magicseeker's sword blade was dark and pitted; he had obviously tried attacking the blackness with it at least once. Kayl saw no sign of Javieri or the other Magicseeker.

"Get back!" Kayl called sharply to all of them. "Back beside the cube. It'll be safe there for a little while yet."

She pulled Mark with her as she followed her own advice. "Stay there," she said firmly, positioning him beside the Crystal. Then she turned to Corrana and the Magicseeker. "Help me move Glyndon."

"What is that thing?" the Magicseeker demanded. He let go of Corrana's arm, but his eyes remained fixed on the slowly spreading darkness.

"If we knew, maybe we could stop it," Kayl said. "Come on." She knelt by Glyndon, who was groggy but not yet quite unconscious, and gently slid her arms beneath his head and his good shoulder.

The Magicseeker did not move. "Maybe we could jump out the windows."

"If the fall didn't kill you, the creature would," Corrana said. "It is no longer limited to the Tower."

The blackness was oozing dangerously near to Glyndon. "I can't move him alone," Kayl snapped at Corrana, hiding her fear behind anger. "Or do you want to let that thing have him?"

"What's the use?" the Magicseeker said. He started to sheath his sword, then looked at the blackened, pitted blade and flung it away with a curse.

Corrana gave him a long look, then turned and joined Kayl. She knelt and worked her arms carefully under Glyndon's legs. Then, without looking up, she said in a low voice, "I couldn't keep that thing from taking Javieri. I'll do what I must to keep it from getting Glyndon as well."

"Don't blame yourself," Kayl said. "Nothing seems to do any good against that stuff. Now lift, easy."

Together, they slid Glyndon a little closer to the crystal cube, away from the encroaching blackness. "Again," Kayl said. "I want him right at the foot of the pedestal."

As they shifted into better positions for the next effort, the Magicseeker crouched beside Corrana and added his strength to theirs. With his help, they reached the base of the pedestal in one try. "Thank you," Kayl said.

The Magicseeker stood up and turned away with a shrug. "It's halfway around the room now," he said, and his voice was unsteady. "What happens next?"

Kayl smoothed wisps of hair back from Glyndon's forehead and rose. Mark and Dara moved closer to her, and she automatically put an arm around each of them. "I don't know," she told the Magicseeker. "It isn't behaving the same way it did last time I was here."

"How much time do we have?" Corrana said quietly.

"I can't—" Kayl started, then stopped short as Glyndon's hoarse voice broke in.

"Time," said Glyndon in a pain-filled whisper. "The Crystal. You'll have to use the Crystal."

"What does he mean?" the Magicseeker demanded.

Corrana bent over Glyndon. "How?" she said urgently. "What did you do to use it before? Tell me, and I'll try!"

"I don't know," Glyndon said. "I'm sorry, Kayl."

"It's all right," Kayl said. She leaned closer, wanting to tell him while there was still time how much she cared for him, how much she had always cared for him. "I love you" seemed inadequate, too short a phrase to convey all the things she felt. "I love you," she said.

Glyndon smiled. "I love you, too," he said, and for a moment his voice sounded stronger. "Use the Crystal, Kayl. It's the only way left." Then his eyes closed and his head rolled sideways.

"Unconscious," Corrana said before Kayl had time for more than a brief stab of fear. The Elder Sister looked at Kayl. "Well?"

"I'm not a magician."

"At the moment, neither am I. But we have no choice but to try." She gestured at the room, which was slowly darkening as the blackness covered one window after another.

"Mother."

Kayl turned and saw Dara standing calmly with one hand resting on the Crystal. "Dara, get away from—"

"I'm all right, Mother, but I can't do it myself. You have to help."

Kayl hesitated, fighting her instinctive desire to pull Dara away from the Crystal, then stepped forward to join her daughter. She saw Mark standing beside Dara, his face blank and rigid with the effort not to disgrace himself by crying. Kayl felt Corrana beside her, and saw the remaining Magic-seeker take up a position on the opposite side of the Crystal. Then her hand touched the cool, smooth surface of the cube.

For a moment, nothing seemed to happen. Then, with a suddenness that left her dizzy, she was part of the crystal cube. She tried to shake herself, to dispel the vertigo, but she had lost all sensation from her body. Dara and Mark were with her, linked to Kayl by blood and to the Crystal by talent and heritage. Kayl could sense Corrana and the Magicseeker as well, but not as clearly. They, too, had become part of the Crystal, but Kayl could tell that they were not as closely linked to it as she and the children were.

Wondering what to do now, Kayl tried to look about her. The effort set off something in the magic of the cube. Pictures began flashing before her, visions of strange people and stranger places. A tall woman with the hard hands of an artisan and golden skin knelt on a slender bridge made of crystal, hammering a band of silver into place along its edge. A blond man in a ragged tunic cut and stabbed at a huge, gray-green creature that snapped at him with foot-long fangs. A green-haired Neira boy swam cautiously through drifts of seaweed toward a delicate structure of coral and mother-of-pearl. A demon, dark-haired and human-looking, fought desperately against a faceless man in a dark cape, while behind him a muscular youth sent ravens into the battle. A human girl with the slanted green eyes of a Shee rode out of a snowstorm into a cave and collapsed. A black-furred Wyrd grinned fiercely and lifted a silver goblet in a toast to a Shee woman dressed in red silk. A slender woman with dark, fine hair raised a sword of fire in a triumphant gesture. A band of Thar raiders trudged across a wilderness of ice; a ship with blue sails ran before a storm; armies battled around the foot of a sinister black mountain; a strange, silver-hued moon cracked and broke apart. . . .

Kayl recoiled from the flood of images. They stopped as suddenly as they had begun, and once again she was a disembodied part of the cube. Kayl shook herself, remembering the description of the cube in the Ri Astar Diary. "Whenever a man stared into it . . . he would see what the Crystal would show." The writer of the diary had understated the effect.

Kayl had not simply seen pictures; it was as if she had actually been present at each of the places she had been shown. She wondered whether she could control the phenomenon if she tried.

From somewhere outside herself, the knowledge floated up that Kayl could, indeed, control the visions. She was startled at first; then another phrase from the diary drifted through her mind: ". . . if the watcher fixed his heart on some one thing, past or present, that too he would see pictured. . . ." Again, the diarist had apparently understated. The Crystal was not limited to visions; it could provide information as well. Kayl considered briefly, then filled her mind with the desire to know how Glyndon had used the Crystal to save the remnant of the first expedition, sixteen years before, and how she might repeat it.

Pictures began unrolling before her once more, painfully familiar yet oddly skewed. Kayl realized after a moment that she was seeing her first visit to the Tower, but from a viewpoint inside the crystal cube. She watched Kevran, Beshara, Varevice and Glyndon arguing over the purpose of the cube; saw Kevran knock a corner from the cube with the hilt of his dagger; saw the black creature swallow Beshara and her demon; watched her younger self hacking uselessly at the oozing darkness. . . .

A soundless, twisting explosion rocked the room, and for an instant time stopped. In that moment, Kayl knew what Glyndon had done, and saw as well the price they had all paid as a result. For Gadeiron's Crystal was far more than a simple scrying tool; in the hands of a wizard, it could actually manipulate the past. Glyndon had not been powerful enough to reach very far back in time, but he had been able to change things so that they had never reached the Crystal room. Enough so that some of them had survived.

But the Crystal could not alter what had happened to itself. Kevran had kept the corner he had chipped from it, without realizing any longer what it was. All of the survivors of the expedition had kept two sets of memories, though one was buried deep in their minds. And Glyndon . . . Glyndon had remained unknowingly joined to the Crystal, unable either to use its power consciously or to sever the link. Kayl felt a pang of pity for him as she wondered why the Crystal had shown her all this. She was no wizard; she could take visions from the

Crystal, and knowledge, but she could never use it as Glyndon
had.

A mental nudge brought Kayl back to the present. Corrana
was beside her, wordlessly demanding to know whether Kayl
had found a solution to their problem. With a sense of surprise, Kayl realized that Corrana had seen and felt nothing of
the vision Kayl had just had. She explained what she had
learned, and its futility, and felt Corrana's denial.

"Alone, you could not use the power of the Crystal," Corrana said. "But with your daughter beside you, you can save
us all. Hurry, before it is too late!"

Kayl started to protest, but the knowledge of the Crystal
confirmed Corrana's words. Dara was close beside her, and
she could feel the power surging around them. All she had to
do was reach out. Still, Kayl hesitated. If she repeated Glyndon's spell with the Crystal, was she not repeating his mistakes
as well? And she could not help feeling that trying to change
the past, to go back to what should be memory, was a mistake.
If she had learned anything in the last year, it was that. There
must be some other way to get out of the Tower, some other
way to destroy the black thing. . . .

Knowledge poured into her mind. With a violent pull, Kayl
wrenched herself and the others free of the Crystal. She stood
panting for a moment, watching the confusion on their faces
give way to surprise. "What are you doing?" Corrana cried.

"Getting rid of that thing for good," Kayl said, nodding at
the wall of blackness. It had moved closer while they were entranced by the Crystal; on one side it was little more than two
paces from the base of the pedestal that supported Gadeiron's
Crystal. Kayl set her shoulder to the cube and pushed.

The Crystal did not move; it was heavier than she had
thought. "Don't stand there; push!" Kayl panted, shoving at
the cube again.

The children shook themselves out of their immobility and
joined her. The Magicseeker hesitated, glanced at the blackness, and added his efforts to theirs. Corrana stared at them.
"Stop! You'll destroy the Crystal!"

"Would you rather that creature destroyed us?" Kayl said.
"Together now; heave!"

The Crystal slid a finger's width, and the pedestal rocked.
"Again!" Kayl said. Together, they shoved at the Crystal.
The pedestal teetered. Then, with a kind of majestic slowness,

it toppled over. An instant later the crystal cube disappeared into the curtain of blackness.

The surface of the blackness twitched, then froze. Kayl held her breath, expecting something dramatic to follow. Nothing happened. Cautiously, she stepped forward. The black creature did not move; no tentacles lashed out to drag her into it. Kayl took another step and peered at the black wall. It looked as if it were made of smooth black stone.

Kayl heaved a sigh of relief and turned to her companions. "I think it's—"

The rest of her sentence was lost in a noise like thunder. The floor swayed beneath Kayl's feet. As she struggled to keep her balance, she saw the blackness crack. Shards began falling from the walls; great sheets split away from the windows that the blackness had covered. Kayl heard Corrana shouting, but the noise from the crumbling creature was too great for her to make out the words.

The floor itself began to break apart. Kayl jumped frantically back toward the children, but the stones beneath her feet fell even as she leaped. Then something caught her and lowered her slowly, knocking aside the wickedly pointed shards of blackness that filled the air, while the Twisted Tower came apart around her. When the air cleared, Kayl found herself standing atop a pile of rubble, blinking in the sunlight. Mark and Dara were a little way away with the Magicseeker and Corrana; Glyndon lay sprawled at their feet, still unconscious.

Corrana's face was split by the first broad smile Kayl had ever seen her wear. "I am a sorceress again!" she cried triumphantly.

CHAPTER

THIRTY-ONE

Kayl blinked at Corrana for a moment, unable to absorb the meaning of her words. "Oh," she said at last. "Then it was your spell that let us down, there at the end."

"Of course." Corrana was the cool sorceress of the Sisterhood once more, but beneath the calm façade Kayl sensed an undercurrent of disappointment at her reaction.

"I am glad for you," Kayl said quickly, "but I just can't . . ." Her voice trailed off as her eyes were drawn irresistably to Glyndon's recumbent form.

"You are right," Corrana said. "We must find the others. Risper will be able to help him."

If she is still alive, Kayl thought, but she did not voice her doubts. She started across the shifting rubble, toward Glyndon and the children. As she reached them, Mark, who was facing away from her, shouted and began waving his arms. "Hey! We're up here!"

Kayl put her hand on his shoulder in time to keep him from trying to jump up and down on such unsteady footing. She looked past him and saw a small group of figures near the foot of the pile of rubble.

"Barthelmy's down there," Dara said positively. Kayl nodded, surprised to find that she felt none of the relief she would have expected even a few days before. That reaction, more than anything else, told Kayl that she was finished with the Sisterhood at last. The final tie had been broken when the crystal cube disappeared into the black thing; now she was free of her past. It didn't seem to matter as much as she had thought it would. She shrugged mentally and started carefully down the hill of rubble, hoping that one of the healers was among the survivors. Mark and Dara came sliding after her.

The first face Kayl made out as she neared the foot of the hill was Risper's, and a wave of relief swept her. "Risper! We need you. Glyndon's badly hurt."

Risper started up the treacherous heap of stones. She looked tired and drawn, and there were shadows in her eyes that made Kayl wonder whether she had lost one of the Sisters of her Star Cluster. "If it was another one of his visions, I can't do much," Risper said as she reached Kayl.

"It's a sword wound in his left arm, just below the shoulder," Kayl replied. "I'm not certain, but I think it hit the bone. He's unconscious."

Risper began climbing more rapidly. "Blood loss or shock. Was anyone able to do anything for him?"

Kayl turned and joined Risper's climb. "Dara tried."

"Did she stop the bleeding?"

"I think so," Dara volunteered. She looked worriedly at Risper. "He's going to be all right, isn't he?"

"I won't know that until I look at him." Risper caught at the hand Corrana was reaching down to her, and scrambled the last few feet to the top of the pile of rubble. She hesitated briefly when she saw the Magicseeker, then glanced at Corrana. Corrana made an ambiguous gesture. Risper shrugged and squatted beside her patient.

"He'll live," she said after a quick examination. "But we have to get him down from here. If you two," she waved at Corrana and Kayl, "will help me lift him—"

Kayl and Corrana bent to assist Risper. To Kayl's surprise, the Magicseeker joined them. Risper gave him one penetrating look, then went on with her instructions.

"Shouldn't you be off to join your friends?" Kayl whispered to the Magicseeker.

"When we're finished here," the man said. "I believe in paying my debts whenever possible."

They carried Glyndon carefully down the heap of shards and tumbled stone that was all that remained of the Twisted Tower. Elder Mother Miracote and three of the Sisters met them at the bottom. Miracote waited until Risper had established Glyndon in a sheltered spot, then drew Kayl and her companions a little way away. "What happened?" the Elder Mother demanded unceremoniously.

"We found the crystal room, and Utrilo found us. He wounded Glyndon; the black creature killed Javieri, Utrilo, and one of Utrilo's men. The Crystal and the creature . . . destroyed each other." Kayl paused. "The details and the guesswork can wait until later. What's happened here?"

Miracote frowned, but answered. "I assume Corrana told you of Ferianek's attempt to lift the spell that bound us? It failed quickly, and the Magicseekers overwhelmed us. Their leader took three of his followers and Javieri into the Tower; shortly after, a . . . a blackness swept out of it. The Magicseekers tried to fight it, but . . ." Miracote shrugged.

"What about Bryn? And Ferianek?"

"They are both alive, but we lost two Sisters and Mother Siran in the fighting with the Magicseekers, and four others to that creature. Fortunately, the black thing seemed to find Magicseekers more to its taste."

The man beside Kayl made a choking noise, and Miracote looked at him closely for the first time. "And what are we to do with him?" she asked Kayl disapprovingly.

"Need we do anything?" Corrana said. "There is nothing left here for us to fight over."

"True." Miracote turned and addressed the Magicseeker directly. "And what is your opinion?"

"Of you, or of your plans, star-witch?" the Magicseeker said with evident dislike.

Kayl broke in quickly, before Miracote could answer. "If we let you leave, will you give us your word not to attack us?"

The Magicseeker shrugged, but his tone was less hostile as he said, "I see no reason not to."

"Can you speak for your companions as well?" Miracote demanded.

"They're reasonable people," the Magicseeker said, in a tone that implied Miracote wasn't. "And as your friend said a minute ago, there's nothing left here for us to fight over."

"Go, then," Corrana said.

Miracote's eyes narrowed at Corrana's assumption of authority, but she was too shrewd to correct the Elder Sister in front of a stranger and enemy. The Magicseeker gave Corrana and Kayl each a brief nod of farewell, looked at Miracote with dislike, and strode off toward the forest that bordered the valley. "He'll find few of his companions to persuade," Miracote said with some satisfaction as she watched him go. "The creature killed most of them."

"Without his help in the Tower, we would all have died," Kayl said coldly.

Miracote looked at her. "He's a Magicseeker. Don't ask me to feel sorry for him."

Kayl suppressed a wave of irritation and said, "I won't. What can we help with here?"

Miracote put them to work helping Risper with the wounded. The second healer had been among the fatalities, so Risper was forced to tend all of the most severely injured herself. She had little time or energy for anyone else. Kayl cleaned and bandaged flesh wounds, cuts and scrapes for close to two hours. Then she joined the more able-bodied in burying the dead.

Alden and Xaya arrived shortly after the Tower's fall, drawn by the noise of the collapse. They were relieved to find Bryn only slightly injured, and volunteered almost at once to be part of a group heading back to the camp for supplies. By noon they had returned with Risper's bags of medicine, two tents to shelter the wounded, and enough flatbread and yellow cheese to provide lunch for everyone. They also brought several brimming waterskins, for which everyone was grateful. A brackish trickle at the far end of the valley was the only source of water near the Twisted Tower, and Risper, after one look at a sample, had refused to allow anyone to drink from it.

Several more trips were made back to the camp on the other side of the hills, for it quickly became evident that they would have to spend the night in the valley. Risper refused to allow certain of the wounded to be moved, Glyndon among them, and there no longer seemed to be a good reason to avoid camping in the valley. Kayl did not argue with the decision. As she set up the tent for herself and the children, however, she made sure that every particle of black stone had been removed from the ground beneath the tent. Most of the Sisters copied her precaution.

By evening, the camp had been moved to the valley. Things began to look more normal, though the atmosphere remained subdued. Neither grief nor victory had had time to penetrate the minds of the survivors; that, Kayl knew from experience, would come with the morrow.

Over dinner, Kayl and Corrana told their story to the remnant of the expedition, omitting only the exact details of their brief experience with the magic of the Crystal. When they finished, Elder Mother Alessa stirred. "So the crystal cube is gone," she said.

"It's such a waste," Ferianek said in a mournful tone. "A thing that could actually show the past! We could have learned so much from it."

Alessa gave him a sharp look. "Indeed we could."

"We had no other choice," Kayl said firmly. "Not really."

"No?" Alessa said skeptically. "You could not have used it as the Varnan did, instead of destroying it?"

Corrana's eyes met Kayl's briefly, and a message of understanding passed between them. "No," said Corrana. "We could not have used the Crystal."

"What we did was the only possible way to kill that black thing," Kayl added. "And it had to be killed. You had a brief taste of it; imagine what it would have done if we hadn't stopped it here!"

"But how did it get out of the Twisted Tower?" one of the sorceresses asked. "It shouldn't have been able to get out. The door was sealed; it shouldn't have come out."

Kayl recognized the woman and felt a deep pang of sympathy. Of the four members of her Star Cluster, two had been killed by the black creature. Kayl knew all too well what that was like.

"I cannot say for certain what set the creature free," Corrana said. "I can, however, speculate. I believe the chip of crystal broke the seals that held the creature inside the Tower."

"I don't understand," the woman said.

"When Kayl brought the chip into the Twisted Tower, Glyndon and Barthelmy had weakened the sealing spells. If they had not, the spells would have killed anyone who tried to enter. But when Glyndon realized that Magicseekers had also come into the Tower, he used the power of the crystal cube to renew the spells that sealed the doors. Thus, when Utrilo's swordswoman tried to carry the chip out of the Tower, it passed through the full strength of the spell. I think the spell could not hold against even a small piece of the Crystal which powered it, and so the sealing was broken."

"What of the chip itself?" Miracote said, leaning forward.

Corrana shrugged delicately. "I looked for it, but all I found was the body of the Magicseeker who carried it. Perhaps passing through the seal was too great a strain for it to bear, and it crumbled like the Tower."

"Ah." Miracote sat back not bothering to hide her disappointment. "Then we have nothing to show for all our efforts."

"We have our magic again," Corrana said gently. "I think that is enough." Her eyes flickered across Kayl's as she spoke.

Kayl nodded, acknowledging Corrana's unspoken message in a way that the others would take as agreement. She was careful to keep her hands in her lap, away from the small, hard lump under her belt. She was sure now that Corrana suspected Kayl of having the chip; this was Corrana's way of showing that she would not mention her suspicions to anyone else. Kayl was glad. She had been the first to find the body of the Magicseeker, and she had spotted the chip of crystal at once, lying in the dust less than a hand's breadth from the outstretched fingers. She had taken it and gone on, leaving the body for someone else to discover.

What she would do with the chip, Kayl did not know. Touching it no longer brought her visions of her past, and she was not magician enough to discover and use whatever other powers it possessed. She only knew that she could not give it to the Sisterhood, and she did not want to spend any more of her time in fruitless arguments with them. She was grateful to Corrana for sparing her that.

"We still do not know what took our magic from us, or how it was returned," Alessa pointed out. She gave Barthelmy a sidelong glance as she spoke.

"Your spells came back with the destruction of the Twisted Tower," Kayl contradicted sharply. "Do you have to know for certain whether it was the creature, the Crystal, or the Tower itself that took them?"

"Yes." Alessa's voice was sharp, and there were nods of agreement among the Sisters. "We must be sure it cannot happen again."

"It cannot," Corrana said quietly.

Alessa's attention snapped from Kayl to Corrana. "You do not know that."

"My knowledge comes from Gadeiron's Crystal," Corrana said, lifting her eyebrows fractionally. "I doubt that it is false."

Kayl looked at her, startled. So Corrana, too, had been able to draw information from the Crystal! Somehow it had not occurred to Kayl that the sorceress might have done so.

"Explain, then," Miracote commanded.

"Our difficulty stemmed from the nature of our magic," Corrana said. "Our founders chose to tie our powers to our names, as the magic of the *sklathran'sy* is bound to theirs. In a way I do not completely understand, the black creature was an ancient enemy of the *sklathran'sy*, and its attacks on them came most often through their magic. Through their names.

"When our Sisters," Corrana nodded toward Kayl and Barthelmy, "breached the Tower sixteen years ago, and Gadeiron's Crystal was broken, the spells that held the creature were weakened enough to let it wake, but it was still bound within the Tower. When it found no physical way out, it sought a magical means of escape.

"It must have learned our ways when it killed Varevice and Evla, and since our magic is similar to that of the *sklathran'sy*, the creature attacked us as it would have attacked a group of demons. But there are no demons in the Sisterhood, and it could not control us through our magic as it could have controlled *sklathran'sy*. All it could do was to feed on our power. But its feeding disrupted our spells, and we felt its evil, and so we all but ceased to work magic. And when we did not call on our power, the creature could not reach it without great effort. That is why it took so long to grow strong enough to call someone to the Tower who would be more . . . amenable to its desires."

"Utrilo Levoil," Kayl said.

Corrana nodded. "I think the creature was not able to convey very much, but it was enough to make the Magicseekers look more closely at what they knew of the Sisterhood's two expeditions to the Tower. When they realized that one of those who had accompanied the first group had left the Sisterhood, they began searching for you." Corrana smiled suddenly. "I do not think they quite believed that a common innkeeper could possibly be the woman they sought. It is why they watched you for so long, instead of taking you at once. A mistake would have been embarrassing.''

"Then when the black creature—we really must find some other way to name it—was destroyed, it ceased feeding on our magic and we could use our power freely again,'' Alessa said. "A tidy tale. But why was Elder Sister Barthelmy not affected?''

Barthelmy stiffened, but Corrana only smiled again. "Barthelmy is a demon-friend, trained to teach *sklathran'sy* to protect themselves from vulnerability through their names. I think the creature reached for her during the fight in the Tower, and she unconsciously used her skills to protect herself. Any of our demon-friends could have done as much, had they actually faced the creature. The creature learned quickly; its attack on the Sisterhood was subtle enough not to cause the same response in anyone else.''

Elder Mother Miracote snorted in disgust. "If we had known, we could have stopped that thing before it ever started.''

"Perhaps." Corrana's tone was thoughtful. "But I think it would have found some other way.''

"We still don't know enough!'' Barthelmy said in frustration. "What *was* that black thing, really? And why did touching the cube freeze it? And—''

"There is little point in worrying over answers we shall probably never get,'' Corrana interrupted.

"And I, for one, have had a very long day,'' Kayl said. "I want some rest.''

There were smiles among the Sisters, and Miracote said, "So do we all. Enough, for now; we will talk again later.''

They spent nearly two weeks camping in the valley, while the wounded recovered and the Elder Mothers studied the ruins of the Twisted Tower. Four days after the Tower's fall, when most of the injured were well enough to attend, they held a memorial for their dead. The day after, they moved the camp to the forested slopes above the valley. They saw the remnant of the Magicseekers only once, when they came to the valley to bury their comrades. The two groups stayed well apart from each other, and there was no trouble.

Kayl divided her time almost equally between her children and Glyndon. She made sure that Mark and Dara both knew how proud she was of them, but she could see that, though they appreciated her words, they did not have the same need to hear them that they used to. They knew they had done well. There was a new confidence in both children; Kayl could see it in their eyes and in the way they carried themselves, even when they ran shrieking up and down the hills with Xaya. It made her prouder than ever, though a little sad. Mark and Dara were rapidly growing up.

The Wyrds expressed a firm determination to stay with the camp until the Sisters were ready to depart for Kith Alunel. Kayl did not bother trying to fathom their reasons; she was simply glad of their presence. Bryn's skills as a handywoman were much in demand, and Alden made himself useful to the group studying the ruins of the Tower. Kayl found him there late one afternoon, sifting shards of night-black stone through his fingers.

"Ho, Alden!" she greeted him. "Bryn says to tell you that if you're late to dinner again, she and Xaya are going to eat your share."

"It can't be that late already," Alden said absently. "Have you looked at these?" He waved at the stones in front of him. "There are two distinct types. Three, if you include the blocks the Tower itself was made of, but they seem to be ordinary granite."

"What are the other two?" Kayl asked, more out of friendship than curiosity.

"One's a hard, jet-black rock; that's all over. The other is a kind of brittle crystalline stuff—"

"You mean you've found pieces of the cube?" Kayl broke in.

"I don't think so," Alden said, undisturbed by her interruption. "You described it as clear, didn't you? Well, look at this."

He held up a slender piece of stone. Kayl thought at first that it was the same as the rest of the black debris; then she looked more closely and saw that it was partially transparent. "It looks like smoked crystal," she said. "But I've never seen any so dark."

"It does, doesn't it?" Alden lowered the stone and studied it again. "It would cut well, I think; so would the other."

"Cut well?" Kayl said, puzzled.

"I mean they'd be easy to shape."

"Shape? You mean for jewelry?" Kayl shuddered, thinking of the black creature. "I wouldn't recommend it."

Alden looked up and grinned. "You're quite right. I'm afraid I get carried away at times." He tossed the smoky crystal back onto a pile of rubble, then rose and accompanied Kayl back to camp.

Ferianek Trone also remained with the camp, helping as best he could. Kayl considered it the least he could do after the way he had used them all, but she found it hard to be angry at the tall, deep-voiced scholar. The ties that held him to the Windhome Mountains had been broken at last, and he had already approached the Elder Mothers about accompanying them back to Kith Alunel.

The work at the Tower ruins uncovered little, and the Sisters began preparing to leave. Kayl watched them thoughtfully, then went off to the woods to hunt and think. When she returned, she sought out Elder Mother Miracote and spoke briefly with her. An hour later, Barthelmy came to find her.

Kayl looked up from the branch she was whittling a point on to replace a broken tent-stake. "What is it, Barthelmy?"

"Elder Mother Miracote says you're not coming back to Kith Alunel with us," Barthelmy said. "Is that true?"

"Yes."

Barthelmy was silent for a moment. Then she said, "Why?"

"I thought it would be better. There's nothing waiting for me in Kith Alunel; there's no point in going back."

"It isn't because of me, is it?" Barthelmy asked, and looked away as if she was afraid to know the answer.

"No," Kayl said gently. "It's because of me. I'm not one of you anymore, Barthelmy, not even in my dreams. My sword and star-gem are buried out there under a mountain of rubble, if the black creature didn't destroy them completely, and I'm not sorry."

"The attitude of the other Sisters has changed since Corrana explained what really happened to their magic," Barthelmy offered.

"I've noticed." Most of the suspicion and resentment the Sisters felt toward Kayl and Barthelmy had died with the black creature. When the shock and grief that followed the battle had worn off, a few of the Sisters had made tentative, apologetic overtures toward Kayl. She had acknowledged them politely, but they had not brought her the satisfaction they once would have. "I just don't belong in the Sisterhood anymore."

"It's Glyndon, then, isn't it?"

"Barthelmy!" Kayl let her irritation show. "Glyndon doesn't know about this yet, and I don't want him told. I've given you my reasons for leaving the expedition; stop trying to find other excuses."

"You mean it, don't you?" Barthelmy said. Kayl nodded emphatically. Barthelmy's shoulders moved unhappily. "I think I always knew you wouldn't come back, but I didn't want to believe it. I wanted things to be the way they used to be. The Sisterhood meant so much to both of us. . . . To me, it still does."

"I know. But you can't live in the past, Barthelmy, and you can't make the present into a reflection of it. It doesn't work."

"No." Barthelmy was quiet for a moment. "What will you do now?"

Kayl grinned, feeling suddenly like a mischievous fifteen-year-old. "I don't know. I'll write when I find out, all right?"

"You'd better." Barthelmy said, returning the grin. "You'd just better."

Glyndon was recovering slowly. He had spent four days in bed, and only slowly begun moving around the camp. He had not had one of his visions since the Tower fell. His left arm was still in a sling; Risper had said in Kayl's hearing that he would have to wear it for five or six more weeks, at least. Kayl had done more than her share of the shifts of caring for him while he was bedridden, and visited him frequently once he was able to move about, but their conversations during that time had been carefully casual. Kayl had been half expecting, half hoping that he would seek her out before the expedition left. Finally, the day before the Sisters were to break camp, Glyndon did.

"Walk with me a bit, Kayl?" he said.

Kayl nodded, and together they left the camp. They headed up the mountain in companionable silence. "How's the arm?" Kayl said after a little.

"Sore," Glyndon said, and winced. "Risper says I'll just have to wait; she's hurried things along as much as she can."

He hesitated, then went on, "She thinks I'll regain most of the use of the hand, but she says there won't be much strength in it and there's not much she can do about the shoulder. She showed me some exercises for it."

"I'm sorry," Kayl said quietly. She could not pretend to be surprised; though Risper had not told her the details, she had seen enough serious wounds to have some idea what to expect.

"It's a good thing I'm a wizard and not a swordsman," Glyndon went on. "There aren't many spells that really *require* two hands."

"And the visions?" Kayl asked. "Do you think they're—"

"They're gone," Glyndon said with certainty. He glanced down at his sling, then looked at Kayl and smiled. "The trade was worth it."

"What will you do now?"

"I don't know. Go home, maybe." He hesitated, then said carefully, "And you?"

"In the long run? I'm not sure. I'm not going back to being an innkeeper, that's sure. Maybe I'll try to find a way of helping the Wyrds and Shee who're leaving the southern countries. They might be able to use a good strategist." Kayl smiled down at a tiny patch of unfamiliar blue flowers beside a boulder. "You know, I used to think I had to know things like that, that once I made a decision I had to stick to it. I think that's why I spend so much of my time mulling over the past."

"What?" Glyndon looked puzzled, but interested.

"I was trying to prove that the decisions I'd made were the right ones," Kayl explained. She shrugged. "Now . . . Well, I have another twenty or thirty years left; I don't have to decide today exactly what they're going to be like. I never really knew that before."

"Um." Glyndon tilted his head backward to stare at the branches of the trees above them. "I hadn't really expected to talk philosophy with you today."

"Oh?"

"Kayl, you know that I love you, and I want to stay with you. But I don't think I can face a four-month trip back to Kith Alunel with the Silver Sisters."

"Neither could I. So I'm not going with them."

"What?" Glyndon stared at her. "I thought . . ."

Kayl smiled and shook her head. "You and Barthelmy. I

don't *belong* in the Sisterhood anymore, Glyndon. I've known that for months. It just took me awhile to stop wishing I did, that's all."

"But if you aren't going to Kith Alunel, then what?"

"I talked to Bryn and Alden last night. When the camp breaks up, they're going on to that Waywalker settlement Ferianek told them about. The children and I are going with them. The whole group will be leaving for the coast soon, to hire a ship to take them to the island once the spring storms are over. I don't think it will be too hard to persuade them to stop and let us off somewhere on Varna."

"Varna? Kayl, are you sure?"

"Well, if they won't, we can find a ship that's headed there," Kayl said practically. "It shouldn't be hard, at this time of year."

Glyndon laughed. "Why didn't you tell me?"

"You didn't ask. Glyndon! Be careful; your shoulder!"

"Demons take my shoulder," Glyndon said. He pulled her to him with his good arm and fastened his lips over hers. "Does this mean you'll marry me?" he asked a few minutes later.

"Do you want me to?" Kayl laid a hand on his mouth to stop his immediate protest, and went on, "I'm not going to spend the rest of my life on Varna, you know. And I meant it about trying to help the Wyrds."

"We'll do it together," Glyndon promised. "After fifteen years of wandering, I don't think I could settle permanently on Varna even if I wanted to. It'll be nice to go home, though. Now, answer the question: Will you marry me?"

"If I don't want to set a bad example for the children, I'm going to have to." Kayl tried to make her tone serious, but she could not keep a straight face. Her mouth insisted in stretching out into what felt like a remarkably foolish grin.

Glyndon laughed and started to kiss her again. He was interrupted by a muffled cheer from a nearby clump of bushes. Startled, he and Kayl looked at each other; then Kayl shook her head and stepped away from him. "We heard that," she called in the sternest voice she could manage. "So come out here, right now."

With a series of rustling noises, punctuated by crashes, the eavesdroppers made their appearance: first Mark, then Dara, then Xaya. Mark looked somewhat downcast but pleased;

Dara and Xaya were trying hard to appear properly repentant in spite of their excitement. "I thought I'd taught you better than to listen to other people's conversations," Kayl said, but she was too happy to put her heart into the scolding.

"Well, but it was important to us, too," Dara said. "And oh, Mother, I'm glad!"

"So am I," Glyndon confided.

"Don't encourage them, Glyndon," Kayl warned. He gave her a smile that made her head swim, and she forced herself to look back at the children. "Whose idea was this, anyway?"

"Mine," three voices said promptly.

Kayl rolled her eyes. "All right, then, back to camp with the three of you. I'll figure out what to do with you later. Go on!"

The children went. As they disappeared among the trees, a breath of wind brought Dara's satisfied voice back to Kayl and Glyndon: "I *told* you she was going to marry him. She just takes a long time to *say* so, that's all."

"Huh," was Mark's comment, and the children were gone.

Glyndon looked at Kayl, his eyes dancing. "I can see that being a stepfather is going to be an enlightening experience. I wonder if I ought to ask Dara what you really think, the next time I'm not sure?"

"You do and I'll put salt in your ale for a week," Kayl threatened.

"Your wish is my command," Glyndon replied. He reached for her with his good arm. "Now, where were we?"

CAPTIVATING TALES OF FANTASY WORLDS BY TODAY'S BRIGHTEST YOUNG AUTHORS

PATRICIA McKILLIP

____	0-425-09452-9	The Forgotten Beasts of Eld	$2.95
____	0-425-09206-2	The Moon and the Face	$2.95
____	0-425-08457-4	Moon-Flash	$2.75

ROBIN McKINLEY

____	0-425-08840-5	The Blue Sword	$2.95
____	0-425-08907-x	The Hero and The Crown	$2.95

PATRICIA C. WREDE

____	0-441-13897-2	Daughter of Witches	$2.95
____	0-441-31759-6	The Harp of Imach Thyssel	$2.95
____	0-441-75976-9	The Seven Towers	$2.95
____	0-441-76014-7	Shadow Magic	$2.95
____	0-441-79591-9	Talking to Dragons	$2.25

JANE YOLEN

____	0-441-09167-9	Cards of Grief	$2.75
____	0-441-16622-9	Dragonfield and Other Stories	$2.95
____	0-441-51563-0	The Magic Three of Solatia	$2.75
____	0-441-52552-0	Merlin's Booke	$2.95

Available at your local bookstore or return this form to:

BERKLEY
THE BERKLEY PUBLISHING GROUP, Dept. B
390 Murray Hill Parkway, East Rutherford, NJ 07073

Please send me the titles checked above. I enclose _____. Include $1.00 for postage and handling if one book is ordered; add 25¢ per book for two or more not to exceed $1.75. CA, IL, NJ, NY, PA, and TN residents please add sales tax. Prices subject to change without notice and may be higher in Canada. Do not send cash.

NAME_____

ADDRESS_____

CITY_____STATE/ZIP_____

(Allow six weeks for delivery.)   496

Stories

✠ of ✠

Swords and Sorcery

⚜⚜⚜⚜⚜⚜⚜⚜⚜⚜⚜⚜⚜⚜⚜⚜⚜⚜⚜⚜⚜⚜

☐ 76600-5	**SILVERGLASS** J.F. Rivkin	$2.95
☐ 38553-2	**JHEREG,** Steven Brust	$2.95
☐ 11452-0	**CONAN,** Robert E. Howard	$2.95
☐ 81653-3	**TOMOE GOZEN** Jessica Amanda Salmonson	$2.75
☐ 13897-7	**DAUGHTER OF WITCHES** Patricia C. Wrede	$2.95
☐ 10264-6	**CHANGELING,** Roger Zelazny	$2.95
☐ 79197-2	**SWORDS AND DEVILTRY** Fritz Leiber	$2.75
☐ 81466-2	**TO DEMONS BOUND** **(Swords of Raemllyn #1)** Robert E. Vardeman and Geo. W. Proctor	$2.95
☐ 04913-3	**BARD,** Keith Taylor	$2.95
☐ 89644-8	**WITCH BLOOD,** Will Shetterly	$2.95

⚜⚜⚜⚜⚜⚜⚜⚜⚜⚜⚜⚜⚜⚜⚜⚜⚜⚜⚜⚜⚜⚜

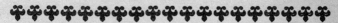

Available at your local bookstore or return this form to:

ACE
THE BERKLEY PUBLISHING GROUP, Dept. B
390 Murray Hill Parkway, East Rutherford, NJ 07073

Please send me the titles checked above. I enclose _____. Include $1.00 for postage and handling if one book is ordered; add 25¢ per book for two or more not to exceed $1.75. CA, IL, NJ, NY, PA, and TN residents please add sales tax. Prices subject to change without notice and may be higher in Canada.

NAME_____

ADDRESS_____

CITY_____ STATE/ZIP_____

(Allow six weeks for delivery.)